"You have to ge[t]

"Nope. It's May." Tra[vis'] hands were free to p[ick up his] shake the cell phone out of it.

"It's May? What kind of answer is that? Do you fast in May or do a colon cleanse or something?"

He looked up at her joke, but his grin died before it started. Judging by the look on her face, she wasn't joking. "The River Mack rounds up in May."

She looked at him, waiting. He realized a woman from Hollywood probably had no idea what that meant.

"We're busy. We're branding. We have to keep an eye on the late calving, the bulls—"

Sophia flapped one hand toward the kitchen behind her. "I have nothing to eat. You have to help me."

He stomped into his second boot. "Not unless you're a pregnant or nursing cow."

At her gasp, he did laugh. "Or a horse. Or a dog. You could be a chicken, and I would have to help you. I keep every beast on this ranch fed, but you, ma'am, are not a beast. You're a movie star, a woman who can take care of herself, and you're not my problem."

HOME ON THE RANCH:
TROUBLE IN TEXAS

————————— ⚓ —————————

USA TODAY Bestselling Author
CARO CARSON

CATHY GILLEN THACKER

Previously published as *A Cowboy's Wish Upon a Star*
and *A Texas Cowboy's Christmas*

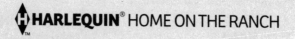 **HARLEQUIN**® HOME ON THE RANCH

ISBN-13: 978-1-335-44564-3

Home on the Ranch: Trouble in Texas

Copyright © 2019 by Harlequin Books S.A.

A Cowboy's Wish Upon a Star
First published in 2016. This edition published in 2019.
Copyright © 2016 by Caro Carson

A Texas Cowboy's Christmas
First published in 2016. This edition published in 2019.
Copyright © 2016 by Cathy Gillen Thacker

Recycling programs
for this product may
not exist in your area.

Printed in U.S.A.

HARLEQUIN®
www.Harlequin.com

CONTENTS

Despite a no-nonsense background as a West Point graduate, army officer and Fortune 100 sales executive, Caro Carson has always treasured the happily-ever-after of a good romance novel. As a RITA® Award–winning Harlequin author, Caro is delighted to be living her own happily-ever-after with her husband and two children in Florida, a location that has saved the coaster-loving theme-park fanatic a fortune on plane tickets.

Books by Caro Carson

Harlequin Special Edition

American Heroes

The Lieutenants' Online Love
The Captains' Vegas Vows
The Majors' Holiday Hideaway

Texas Rescue

Not Just a Cowboy
A Texas Rescue Christmas
Following Doctor's Orders
Her Texas Rescue Doctor
A Cowboy's Wish Upon a Star
How to Train a Cowboy

Montana Mavericks: What Happened at the Wedding?

The Maverick's Holiday Masquerade

The Doctors MacDowell

Doctor, Soldier, Daddy
The Doctor's Former Fiancée
The Bachelor Doctor's Bride

Visit the Author Profile page at Harlequin.com for more titles.

A COWBOY'S WISH UPON A STAR

CARO CARSON

This book is dedicated to You,
the reader who
spent time to meet me at the book signing, or
spent time to send me the note to say
you love the love stories that I
spent time to write.
Thank you.

Chapter 1

It was the end of the world.

Sophia Jackson strained to see something, anything that looked like civilization, but the desolate landscape was no more than brown dirt and scrubby bits of green plants that stretched all the way to the horizon.

She might have been in one of her own movies.

The one that had garnered an Academy Award nomination for her role as a dying frontier woman had been filmed in Mexico, but this part of Texas looked close enough. The one that had made her an overnight success as a Golden Globe winner for her portrayal of a doomed woman in a faraway galaxy had been filmed in Italy, but again, this landscape was eerily similar.

Doomed. Dying. Isolated.

She'd channeled those emotions before. This time, however, no one was going to yell *cut*. No one was going to hand her a gold statue.

"Are we there yet?" She sounded demanding, just like the junior officer thrust into a leadership role on a space colony.

Well, not really. She had the ear of an actor; she could catch nuance in tone and delivery, even in—or especially in—her own voice. She didn't sound like a commander. She sounded like a diva.

I have the right to be a diva. I've got the gold statue to prove it.

She tossed her hair back with a jingle of her chandelier earrings, queen of the backseat of the car.

In the front bucket seats, her sister's fiancé continued to drive down the endless road in silence, but Sophia caught the quick glance he shared with her sister. The two of them didn't think she was a young military officer. They didn't even think of her as a diva.

She was an annoying, spoiled brat who was going to be dropped off in the middle of abso-freaking-lutely nowhere.

Her sister, Grace, reached back between the seats to pat her on the knee. "I haven't been here before, either, but it can't be too much farther. Isn't it perfect, though? The paparazzi will never find you out here. This is just what we were hoping for."

Sophia looked at Grace's hand as it patted the black leather which covered her knee. Grace's engagement ring was impossible to miss. Her sister had been her rock, her constant companion, until very recently. Now, wearing a different kind of rock on her left hand, Grace was giddy at the prospect of marrying the man who'd encouraged her to dump her own sister.

Sophia mentally stuck out her tongue at the back of the man's head. Her future brother-in-law was a stupid doctor named Alex, and he'd never once been impressed with Sophia Jackson, movie star. Since the day Sophia and Grace had arrived in Texas, he'd only paid attention to Grace.

Grace's hand moved from Sophia's knee to Alex's shoulder. Then to the back of his neck. The diamond played peek-a-boo as her sister slid her hand through her fiancé's dark hair.

Sophia looked away, out the side window to the desolate horizon. The nausea was rising, so she chomped on her chewing gum. Loudly. With no class. No elegance. None of the grace that the world had once expected of the talented Sophia Jackson.

Pun intended. I have no Grace, not anymore.

Grace didn't correct her gum-smacking. Grace no longer cared enough to correct her.

Sophia was on her own. She'd have to survive the rest of her nine-month sentence all by herself, hiding from the world. In the end, all she'd have to show for it would be a flabby stomach and stretch marks. Like a teenager in the last century, she was pregnant and ashamed, terrified of being exposed. She had to be sent to the country to hide until she could have the baby, give it up for adoption, and then return to the world and spend the rest of her life pretending nothing had ever happened.

If she had a world to return to. That was a very big *if*.

No one in Hollywood would work with her. It had nothing to do with the pregnancy. No one knew about that, and she wasn't far enough along to even begin to show. No, the world of movie stardom was boxing her out solely because of her reputation.

A box office giant, an actor whom Sophia had always dreamed of working with, had recently informed a major studio he would not do the picture if she were cast opposite him. Her reputation had sunk that low. They said there was no such thing as bad publicity, but the publicity she'd been generating had hurt her. Her publicist and her agent had each informed her that she was unmarketable as is.

Ex-publicist. Ex-agent. They both left me.

Panic crawled up the back of her throat. They were all leaving her. Publicist, agent, that louse of a slimy boyfriend she'd been stupid enough to run away with. And worst of all, within the next few minutes, her sister. She was losing the best personal assistant in the world, right when she needed a personal assistant the most.

There was no such thing as loyalty in Hollywood. Not even her closest blood relative was standing by her side. Nausea turned to knots.

"Oh, my goodness," her sister laughed. The tone was one of happy, happy surprise.

Alex's laugh was masculine, amused. "Just in case you needed a reminder that you're in the middle of a genuine Texas cattle ranch…"

He brought their car to a stop—as if he had a choice. The view through the windshield was now the bulky brown back of a giant steer. A thousand pounds of animal blocked their way, just standing there on the road they needed to use, the road that would lead them to an empty ranch house where Sophia would be abandoned, alone, left behind.

Knots turned to panic. She needed to get this over with. Her world was going to end, and she couldn't drag this out one second longer.

Let's rip this bandage off.

"Move, you stupid cow!" she hollered from the backseat.

"Sophia, that's not going to help."

But Sophia had already half vaulted over Alex's shoulder and slammed her palm on the car horn. "Get out of the road."

The cow stared at her through the glass, unmoving. God above, she was tired of being stared at. Everyone was always waiting for her to do something, to be crazy or brilliant, to act out every emotion while they watched passively. Grace was staring at her now, shaking her head.

"Move!" Sophia laid on the horn again.

"Stop it." Alex firmly took her arm and pushed her toward the backseat. His stare was more of a glare.

He and Grace both turned back toward the front. Sophia had spoiled their little delight at a cow in the road, at this unexpected interlude in their sweet, shared day.

I can't stand it, I can't stand myself, I can't stand this one more minute.

She yanked on the door handle and shoved the door open.

"Sophia! Stay in the car." Grace sounded equal parts exasperated and fearful.

Sophia was beyond fear. Panic, nausea, knots—a terrible need to get this over with. Once the ax fell, once she was cut off from the last remnants of her life, she could fall apart. She wanted nothing more than to fall apart, and this stupid cow was preventing it.

She slammed the car door and waved her arms over her head, advancing on the cow. Or maybe it was a bull. It had short horns. Whatever it was, it flinched.

Emboldened—or just plain crazy, like they all said— Sophia waved her arms over her head some more and advanced toward the stupid, stationary cow. The May weather was warm on the bare skin of her midriff as her crop top rose higher with each wave of her arms. On her second step, she nearly went down as her ankle twisted, the spike heel of her over-the-knee boot threatening to sink into the brown Texas dirt.

"Move, do you hear me? Move." She gestured wide to the vast land all around them. "Anywhere. Anywhere but right here."

The cow snorted at her. Chewed something. Didn't care about her, didn't care about her at all.

Tears were spilling over her cheeks, Sophia realized suddenly. Her ankle hurt, her heart hurt, her stomach hurt. The cow looked away, not interested in the least. Being ignored was worse than being stared at. The beast was massive, far stockier than the horses she'd worked with on the set as a dying frontier woman. She shoved at the beast's shoulder anyway.

"Just *move*!" Its hide was coarse and dusty. She shoved harder, accomplishing nothing, feeling her own insignificance. She might as well not exist. No career, no sister, no friends, no life.

She collapsed on the thick, warm neck of the uncaring cow, and let the tears flow.

Someone on the ranch was in trouble.

Travis Chalmers tossed his pliers into the leather saddlebag and gave the barb wire one last tug. Fixed.

He scooped up his horse's trailing reins in one hand, smashed his cowboy hat more firmly over his brow, and swung into the saddle. That car horn meant something else needed fixing, and now. He only hoped one of his men hadn't been injured.

The car horn sounded again. Travis kicked the horse into a gallop, heading in the direction of the sound. It didn't sound like one of the ranch trucks' horns. A visitor, then, who could be lost, out of gas, stranded by a flat tire—simple fixes.

He kept his seat easily and let the horse have her head. Whatever the situation was, he'd handle it. He was young for a foreman, just past thirty, but he'd been ranching since the day he was born, seemed like. Nothing that happened on a cattle operation came as a surprise to him.

He rode up the low rise toward the road, and the cause of the commotion came into view. A heifer was standing in the road, blocking the path of a sports car that clearly wouldn't be able to handle any off-road terrain, so it couldn't go around the animal. That the animal was on the road wasn't a surprise; Travis had just repaired a gap in the barb wire fence. But leaning on the heifer, her back to him, was a woman.

What a woman, with long hair flowing perfectly down her back, her body lean and toned, her backside curvy— all easy to see because any skin that wasn't bared to the sun and sky was encased in tight black clothing. But it was her long legs in thigh-high boots that made him slow his horse in a moment of stunned confusion.

She had to be a mirage. No woman actually wore thigh-high leather boots with heels that high. Those boots sent sexual signals that triggered every adolescent memory of a comic book heroine. Half-naked, high-heeled—a character drawn to appeal to the most primal part of a man's mind.

Not much on a cattle ranch could surprise him, except seeing *that* in the middle of the road.

The horse continued toward the heifer, its focus absolute. So was Travis's. He couldn't take his eyes off the woman as he rode toward her.

She lifted her head and turned his way. With a dash of her cheek against her black-clad shoulder, she turned all the way around and leaned against the animal, stretching her arms along its back like it was her sofa. As the wind blew her hair back from her face, silver and gold shining in the sun, she held her pose and watched him come for her.

Boots, bare skin, black leather—they messed with his brain, until the car door opened and the driver began to get out, a man. Then the passenger door opened, too, and the heifer swung her head, catching the smell of horse and humans on the wind. The rancher in him pushed aside the adolescent male, and he returned his horse to a quicker lope with a *tch* and a press of his thigh.

That heifer wasn't harmless. Let her get nervous, and a half ton of beef on the hoof could do real harm to the humans crowding her, including the sex goddess in boots.

"Afternoon, folks." Travis took in the other two at a glance. Worried woman, irritated man. He didn't look at the goddess as he stopped near the strange little grouping. His heart had kicked into a higher gear at the sight of her, something the sound of the horn and the short gallop had not done. It was damned disconcerting. Everything about her was disconcerting. "Stay behind those doors, if you don't mind."

"Sophia, it's time to get back in the car now," the man said, exaggeratedly patient and concerned, as if he were talking a jumper off a ledge.

"No."

"Oh, Sophie." The woman gave the smallest shake of her head, her eyes sad. Apparently, this Sophie had disappointed her before.

Sophie. Sophia. He looked at her again. Sophia Jackson, of course. Unmistakable. A movie star on his ranch, resting against his heifer, a scenario so bizarre his brain had to work to believe his eyes.

She hadn't taken her blue eyes off him, but she'd raised her chin in challenge. The *no* was meant for him, was it?

"Walk away," he said mildly, keeping his voice even for the heifer's benefit—and hers. "I'll get this heifer on her way so you can get on yours."

"No. She likes me." Sophia's long, elegant fingers stroked the roan hide of the cattle.

"Is that right?" He reached back to grab his lasso and held the loops in one hand.

"My cow doesn't want to leave me. She's loyal and true."

It was an absurd thing to say. Travis didn't have time for absurd.

"Watch your toes." He rode forward, crowding the heifer, crowding Sophia Jackson, and slapped the heifer on the hindquarters with the coiled rope. She briskly left the road.

Sophia Jackson looked a little smaller and a lot sillier, standing in the road by herself. He looked down at her famous face as she watched the heifer leave. She actually looked sad, like she didn't want the heifer to go, which was as absurd as everything else about the situation.

Travis wheeled his horse away from Sophia in order to talk to the driver.

"Where are you heading?"

"Thanks for moving that animal. I'm Alex Gregory. This is my fiancée, Grace."

Travis waited, but the man didn't introduce the

woman in boots. He guessed he was supposed to recognize her. He did. Still, it seemed rude to leave her out.

"Travis Chalmers." He touched the brim of his hat and nodded at the worried woman, then twisted halfway around in his saddle to touch his hat and nod again at the movie star in their midst.

"Chalmers, the foreman?" asked the man, Alex. "Good to meet you. The MacDowells told me they'd explained the situation to you."

Not exactly.

Travis hooked his lasso onto the saddle horn. "You're the one who's gonna live in Marion MacDowell's house for a few months?"

"No, not us. Her. Sophia is my fiancée's sister. She needs a place to hide."

He raised a brow at the word. "Hide from what?"

"Paparazzi," Grace answered. "It's been a real issue after the whole debacle with the—well, it's always an issue. But Sophie needs some time to…to…" She smiled with kindness and pity at her sister. "She needs some time."

Sophie stalked around the car on spiked heels, looking like a warrior queen who could kick some serious butt, but instead she got in the backseat and slammed the door.

"Time and privacy," Alex added. "The MacDowells assured us your discretion wouldn't be an issue."

His mare shifted under him and blew an impatient breath through her nose.

"Should we go to the house and have this discussion there?" Grace asked.

Travis kept an eye on the heifer that was ambling away. "I'm gonna have to round up that heifer and put her back on the right side of the fence. Got to check on the branding after that, but I'll be back at sundown. I go past the main house on the way to my place. I'll stop in."

"We weren't planning to stay all day." The woman threw a look of dismay to her fiancé.

They couldn't expect him to quit working in the middle of the day and go sit in a house to chat. He ran the River Mack ranch, and that meant he worked even longer hours than he expected from his ranch hands.

Heifers that wandered through broken fences couldn't be put off until tomorrow. May was one of the busiest months of the year, between the last of the calving and the bulk of the branding. Travis hadn't planned on spending any time whatsoever talking to whomever the Mac-Dowells were loaning their house, but obviously, there was more to the situation than the average houseguest.

"All right, then. Let's talk." He swung himself off the horse, a concession to let them know they had his time and attention. Besides, if he stayed on horseback, he couldn't see Sophia in the car. It felt like he needed to keep an eye on her, the same as he needed to do with the wandering heifer.

On the ground, he still couldn't see much through the windshield. He caught a glimpse of black leather, her hands resting on her knees. Her hands were clenched into fists.

Travis shook his head. She was a woman on edge.

"Sophia just needs to be left alone," her sister said.

"I can do that." He had no intention of staying in the vicinity of someone as disturbing to his peace of mind as that woman.

"If men with cameras start snooping around, please, tell them nothing. Don't even deny she's here."

"Ma'am, if men with cameras come snooping around this ranch, I will be escorting them off the property."

"Oh, really? You can do that?" She seemed relieved—amazed and relieved.

What did these people expect? He took his hat off and ran his hand through his hair before shoving the hat right back on again. His hair was getting too long, but no cowboy had time in May to go into town and see a barber.

"We don't tolerate trespassers," he explained to the people who clearly lived in town. "I'm not in the business of distinguishing between cameramen and cattle thieves. If you don't belong here, you will be escorted off the land."

"The paparazzi will offer you money, though. Thousands."

Before Travis could set her straight on this insinuation that he could be bribed to betray a guest of the MacDowells, Alex cut in. "That's only if they find her. We've gone to great lengths to arrange this location. We took away her cell phone so that she wouldn't accidentally store a photo in the cloud with a location stamp. Hackers get paid to look for things like that. That's how extreme the hunting for her can be."

"She's got a burner phone for emergencies," Grace said. "But if you could check on her…?"

Travis was aware that the front doors to the car were wide open, man and woman each standing beside one. Surely, the subject of this conversation could hear every word. It seemed rude to talk about her as if she weren't there.

"If she wants me to check on her, I will. If she wants me to leave her alone, I will."

He looked through the windshield again. The fists had disappeared. One leather-clad knee was being bounced, jittery, impatient.

"How many other people work on this ranch?" the man asked.

"Will they leave my sister alone?" the woman asked.

Travis was feeling impatient himself. This whole conversation was moving as far from his realm of normal as the woman hiding in the car was.

That was what she was doing in there. Rather than being part of a conversation about herself, she was hiding. This was all a lot of nonsense in the middle of branding season, but from long habit developed by working with animals, Travis forced himself to stand calmly, keep the reins loose in his hands, and not show his irritation. These people were strangers in the middle of the road, and Travis owed them nothing.

"I'm not in the habit of discussing the ranch's staffing requirements with strangers."

The man nodded once. He got it. The woman bit her lip, and Travis understood she was worried about more than herself.

"But since this is your sister, I'll tell you the amount of ranch hands living in the bunkhouse varies depending on the season. None of us are in the habit of going to the main house to introduce ourselves to Mrs. Mac-Dowell's houseguests." Travis spoke clearly, to be sure the woman in the car heard him. "If your sister doesn't want to be seen, then I suggest she stop standing in the middle of an open pasture and hugging my livestock."

The black boot stopped bouncing.

Grace dipped her chin to hide her smile, looking

as pretty as her movie star sister—minus the blatant sexuality.

"Now if you folks would like to head on to the house, I've got to be going."

"Thank you," Grace said, but the worry returned to her expression. "If you could check on her, though, yourself? She's more fragile than she looks. She's got a lot of decisions weighing her down. This is a very delicate situa—"

The car horn ripped through the air. Travis nearly lost the reins as his mare instinctively made to bolt without him. *Goddammit.*

No sooner had he gotten his horse's head under control than the horn blasted again. He whipped his own head around toward the car, glaring at the two adults who were still standing there. For God's sake, did they have to be told to shut her up?

"Tell her to stop."

"Like that'll do any good." But the man bent to look into the car. "Enough, Sophie."

"Sophie, please…"

One more short honk. Thank God his horse trusted him, because the mare barely flinched this time, but it was the last straw for Travis. Reins in hand, he stalked past the man and yanked open the rear door.

Since she'd been leaning forward to reach the car horn, Sophia's black-clad backside was the first thing he saw, but she quickly turned toward him, keeping her arm stretched toward the steering wheel.

"Don't do that again."

"Quit standing around talking about me. This is a waste of time. I want to get to the house. Now." She honked the horn again, staring right at him as she did it.

"What the hell is wrong with you? I just said don't do that."

"Or else what?"

She glared at him like a warrior, but she had the attitude of a kindergartner.

"Every time you honk that horn, another cowboy on this ranch drops what he's doing to come and see if you need help. It's not a game. It's a call for help."

She blinked. Clearly, she hadn't thought of that, but then she narrowed her eyes and reached once more for the steering wheel.

"You honk that horn again, and you will very shortly find the road blocked by men on horses, and we will not move until you turn the car around and take yourself right back to wherever it is you came from."

Her hand hovered over the steering wheel.

"Do it," he said. "Frighten my horse one more time. You will never set foot on this ranch again."

Her hand hovered. He stared her down, waiting, almost willing her to test him. He would welcome a chance to remove her from the ranch, and he wasn't a man to make empty threats.

"I don't want to be here, anyway," she said.

He jerked his head toward the steering wheel. "You know how to drive, don't you? Turn the car around then, instead of honking that damned horn."

The silence stretched between them.

Her sister had leaned into the car, so she spoke very softly. "Sophie, you've got nowhere else to go. You cannot live with me and Alex."

Travis saw it then. Saw the way the light in Sophia's eyes died a little, saw the way her breath left her lips. He saw her pain, and he was sorry for it.

She sagged back into her seat, burying her backside along with the rest of her body in the corner. She crossed her arms over her middle, not looking at her sister, not looking at him. "Well, God forbid I should piss off a horse."

Travis stood and shut the door. He scanned the pasture, spotted the heifer twice as far away as she'd been a minute ago. Those young ones had a sixth sense about getting rounded up, sometimes. If they didn't want to be penned in, they were twice as hard to catch.

Didn't matter. Travis hadn't met one yet that could outsmart or outrun him.

He had a heifer to catch, branding to oversee, a ranch to run. By the time the sun went down, he'd want nothing more than a hot shower and a flat surface to sleep on.

But tonight, he'd stop by the main house and check on a movie star—a sad, angry movie star who had nowhere else to go, no other family to take her in. Nowhere except his ranch.

With a nod at the sister and her fiancé, Travis swung himself back into the saddle. The heifer had given up all pretense at grazing and was determinedly trotting toward the horizon, putting distance between herself and the humans.

Travis would have sighed, if cowboys sighed. Instead, he spoke to his horse under his breath. "You ready for this?"

He pointed the mare toward the heifer and sent her into motion with a squeeze of his thigh. They had a long, hard ride ahead.

Chapter 2

She was alone.

She was alone, and she was going to die, because Grace and Alex had left her, and even though Alex had flipped a bunch of fuses and turned on the electricity, and even though Grace had carried in two bags of groceries from the car and set them on the blue-tiled kitchen counter, Sophia's only family had abandoned her before anyone realized the refrigerator was broken, and now the food was going to spoil and they wouldn't be back to check on her for a week and by then she'd be dead from starvation, her body on the kitchen floor, her eyes staring sightlessly at the wallpaper border with its white geese repeated ad nauseam on a dull blue background.

Last year, she'd worn Givenchy as she made her acceptance speech.

I hate my life.

Sophia sat at the kitchen table in a hard chair and cried. No one yelled *cut*, so she continued the scene, putting her elbows on the table and dropping her head in her hands.

I hate myself for letting this become my life.

Was that what Grace and Alex wanted her to come to grips with? That she'd messed up her own life?

Well, duh, I'm not a moron. I know exactly why my career is circling the drain in a slow death spiral.

Because no one wanted to work with her. And no one wanted to work with her because no one liked her ex, DJ Deezee Kalm.

Kalm was something of an ironic name for the jerk. Deezee had brought nothing but chaos into her life since she'd met him…wow, only five months ago?

Five months ago, Sophia Jackson had been the Next Big Thing. No longer had she needed to beg for a chance to audition for secondary characters. Scripts from the biggest and the best were being delivered to her door by courier, with affectionate little notes suggesting the main character would fit her perfectly.

Sophia and her sister—her loyal, faithful assistant—had deserved a chance to celebrate. After ten long years of hard work, Sophia's dreams were coming true, but if she was being honest with herself—*and isn't that what this time alone is supposed to be about? Being honest with myself?*—well, to be honest, she might have acted elated, but she'd been exhausted.

A week in Telluride, a tiny mining town that was now a millionaires' playground in the Rocky Mountains, had seemed like a great escape. For one little week, she wouldn't worry about the future impact of her every decision. Sophia would be seen, but maybe she wouldn't be stared at among the rich and famous.

But DJ Deezee Kalm had noticed her. Sophia had been a sucker for his lies, and now she couldn't be seen by anyone at all for the next nine months. Here she was, alone with her thoughts and some rapidly thawing organic frozen meals, the kind decorated with chia seeds and labeled with exotic names from India.

There you go. I fell for a jerk, and now I hate my life. Reflection complete.

She couldn't dwell on Deezee, not without wanting to throw something. If she chucked the goose-shaped salt shaker against the wall, she'd probably never be able to replace the 1980s ceramic. That was the last thing she needed: the guilt of destroying some widow's hideous salt shaker.

She stood with the vague idea that she ought to do something about the paper bags lined up on the counter, but her painful ankle made fresh tears sting her eyes. She'd twisted it pretty hard in the dirt road when she'd confronted that cow, although she'd told Alex the Stupid Doctor that she hadn't. She sat down again and began unzipping the boots to free her toes from their spike-heeled torture.

That cow in the road…she hoped it had given that cowboy a run for his money. She hoped it was still outrunning him right this second, Mr. Don't-Honk-That-Horn-or-Else. Now that she thought about it, he'd had perfect control of his horse as he'd galloped away from them like friggin' Indiana Jones in a Spielberg film, so he'd lied to her about the horn upsetting his horse. Liar, liar. Typical man.

Don't trust men. Lesson learned. Can I go back to LA now?

But no. She couldn't. She was stuck here in Texas, where Grace had dragged her to make an appearance on behalf of the Texas Rescue and Relief organization. Her sister had hoped charity work and good deeds could repair the damage Sophia had done to her reputation. Instead, in the middle of just such a big charity event, Deezee had shown up and publicly begged Sophia to take him back. Sophia had been a sucker again. With cameras dogging their every move, she'd run away to a Caribbean island with him, an elopement that had turned out to be a big joke.

Ha, ha, ha.

Here's something funny, Deezee. When I peed on a plastic stick, a little plus sign showed up.

Sophia had returned from St. Barth to find her sister engaged to a doctor with Texas Rescue, a man who, unlike Deezee, seemed to take that engagement seriously. Now her sister never wanted to go back to LA with her, because Alex had her totally believing in fairy tale love. Grace believed Texas would be good for Sophia, too. Living here would give her a chance to rest and *relax*.

Right. Because of that little plus sign, Grace thought Sophia needed some stress-free *alone time* to decide what she wanted to do with her future, as if Sophia had done anything except worry about both of their futures for the past ten years. Didn't Grace know Sophia was sick of worrying about the future?

Barefooted, Sophia went to the paper bags and pulled out all the cold and wet items and stuck them in the sink. They'd already started sweating on the tiled countertop. She dried her cheek on her shoulder and faced the fridge.

It had been deliberately turned off by the owner, a woman who didn't want to stay in Texas and *relax* in her own home now that her kids were grown and married. Before abandoning her house to spend a year volunteering for a medical mission in Africa, Mrs. MacDowell had inserted little plastic wedges to keep the doors open so the refrigerator wouldn't get moldy and funky while it was unused.

Sophia was going to be moldy and funky by the time they found her starved body next week. She had a phone for emergencies; she used it.

"Grace? It's me. Alex didn't turn the refrigerator on." Sophia felt betrayed. Her voice only sounded bitchy.

"Sophie, sweetie, that's not an emergency." Grace spoke gently, like someone chiding a child and trying to encourage her at the same time. "You can handle that. You know how to flip a switch in a fuse box."

"I don't even know where the fuse box is."

Grace sighed, and Sophia heard her exchange a few words with Alex. "It's in the hall closet. I've gotta run now. Bye."

"Wait! Just hang on the line with me while I find the fuse box. What if the fuse doesn't fix it?"

"I don't know. Then you'll have to call a repairman, I guess."

"Call a repairman?" Sophia was aghast. "Where would I even find a repairman?"

"There's a phone on the wall in the kitchen. Mrs. MacDowell has a phone book sitting on the little stand underneath it."

Sophia looked around the 1980s time capsule of a

kitchen. Sure enough, mounted on the wall was a phone, one with a handset and a curly cord hanging down. It was not decorated with a goose, but it was white, to fit in the decor.

"Ohmigod, that's an antique."

"I made sure it works. It's a lot harder for paparazzi to tap an actual phone line than it would be for them to use a scanner to listen in to this phone call. You can call a repairman."

Sophia clenched her jaw against that lecturing tone. From the day her little sister had graduated from high school, Sophia had paid her to take care of details like this, treating her like a star's personal assistant long before Sophia had been a star. Now Grace had decided to dump her.

"And how am I supposed to pay for a repairman?"

"You have a credit card. We put it in my name, but it's yours." Grace sounded almost sad. Pitying her, actually, with just a touch of impatience in her tone.

Sophia felt her sister slipping away. "I can say my name is Grace, but I can't change my face. How am I supposed to stay anonymous if a repairman shows up at the door?"

"I don't know, Sophie. Throw a dish towel over your head or something."

"You don't care about me anymore." Her voice should have broken in the middle of that sentence, because her heart was breaking, but the actor inside knew the line had been delivered in a continuous whine.

"I love you, Sophie. You'll figure something out. You're super smart. You took care of me for years. This will be a piece of cake for you."

A piece of cake. That tone of voice…

Oh, God, her sister sounded just like their mother. Ten years ago, Mom and Dad had been yanked away from them forever, killed in a pointless car accident. At nineteen, Sophia had become the legal guardian of Grace, who'd still had two years of high school left to go.

Nothing had been a piece of cake. Sophia had quit college and moved back home so that Grace could finish high school in their hometown. Sophia had needed to make the life insurance last, paying the mortgage with it during Grace's junior and senior years. She'd tried to supplement it with modeling jobs, but anything local only paid a pittance. For fifty dollars, she'd spent six hours gesturing toward a mattress with a smile on her face.

It had really been her first acting job, because during the entire photo shoot, she'd had to act like she wasn't mourning the theater scholarship at UCLA that she'd sacrificed. With a little sister to raise, making a mattress look desirable was as close as Sophia could come to show business.

That first modeling job had been a success, eventually used nationwide, but Sophia hadn't been paid one penny more. Her flat fifty-dollar fee had been spent on gas and groceries that same day. Grace had to be driven to school. Grace had to eat lunch in the cafeteria.

Now Grace was embarking on her own happy life and leaving Sophia behind. It just seemed extra cruel that Grace would sound like Mom at this point.

"I have to run," her mother's voice said. "I love you, Sophie. You can do this. Bye."

Don't leave me. Don't ever leave me. I miss you.

The phone was silent.

This afternoon, Sophia had only wanted to hide away and fall apart in private. Now, she was terrified to. If she started crying again, she would never, ever stop.

She nearly ran to the hall closet and pushed aside the old coats and jackets to find the fuse box. They were all on, a neat row of black switches all pointing to the left. She flicked a few to the right, then left again. Then a few more. If she reset every one, then she would have to hit the one that worked the refrigerator.

It made no difference. The refrigerator was still dead when she returned to the kitchen. The food was still thawing in the sink. Her life still sucked, only worse now, because now she missed her mother all over again. Grace sounded like Mom, and she'd left her like Mom. At least when Mom had died, she'd left the refrigerator running.

What a terrible thing to think. Dear God, she hated herself.

Then she laughed at the incredible low her self-pity could reach.

Then she cried.

Just as she'd known it would, once the crying started, it did not stop.

I'm pregnant and I'm scared and I want my mother.

Sophia sank to the kitchen floor, hugged her knees to her chest, and gave up.

Would he or wouldn't he?

Travis rode slowly, letting his mare cool down on her way to the barn while he debated with himself whether or not he'd told the sister he would check on the movie star tonight, specifically, or just check on her in general. He was bone-tired and hungry, but he had almost another mile to go before he could rest. Half a mile to the barn, quarter of a mile past that to his house. A movie star with an attitude was the last thing he wanted to deal with. Tomorrow would be soon enough to be neighborly and ask how she was settling in.

The MacDowell house, or just *the house*, as everyone on a ranch traditionally called the owner's residence, was closer to the barn than his own. As the mare walked on, the house's white porch pillars came into view, always a pretty sight. The sunset tinted the sky pink and orange behind it. Mesquite trees were spaced evenly around it. The lights were on; Sophia Jackson was home.

Then the lights went out.

On again.

What the hell?

Lights started turning off and on, in an orderly manner, left to right across the building. Travis had been in the house often enough that he knew which window was the living room. Off, on. The dining room. The foyer.

The mare chomped at her bit impatiently, picking up on his change in mood.

"Yeah, girl. Go on." He let the horse pick up her pace. Normally, he'd never let a horse hurry back to the barn; that was just sure to start a bad habit. But everything on the River Mack was his responsibility, including the house with its blinking lights, and its new resident.

The lights came on and stayed on as he rode steadily toward the movie star that he was going to check on tonight, after all.

Chapter 3

Travis couldn't ride his horse up to the front door and leave her on the porch. There was a hitching post on the side that faced the barn, so he rode around the house toward the back. The kitchen door was the one everyone used, anyway.

The first year he'd landed a job here as a ranch hand, he'd learned real quick to leave the barn through the door that faced the house. Mrs. MacDowell was as likely as not to open her kitchen door and call over passing ranch hands to see if they'd help her finish off something she'd baked. She was forever baking Bundt cakes and what not, then insisting she couldn't eat them before they went stale. Since her sons had all gone off to medical school to become doctors, Travis suspected she just didn't know how to stop feeding young men. As a twenty-five-year-old living in the bunkhouse on

canned pork-n-beans, he'd been happy to help her not
let anything get stale.

Travis grinned at the memory. From the vantage point
of his horse's back, he looked down into the kitchen as
he passed its window and saw another woman there.
Blond hair, black clothes...curled up on the floor. Weeping.

"Whoa," he said softly, and the mare stopped.

He could tell in a glance Sophia Jackson wasn't hurt,
the same way he could tell in a glance if a cowboy
who'd been thrown from a horse was hurt. She could
obviously breathe if she could cry. She was hugging
her knees to her chest in a way that proved she didn't
have any broken bones. As he watched, she shook that
silver and gold hair back and got to her feet, her back
to him. She could move just fine. There was nothing
he needed to fix.

She was emotional, but Travis couldn't fix that.
There wasn't a lot of weeping on a cattle ranch. If a
youngster got homesick out on a roundup or a heartbro-
ken cowboy shed a tear over a Dear John letter after a
mail call, Travis generally kept an eye on them from a
distance. Once they'd regained their composure, he'd
find some reason to check in with them, asking about
their saddle or if they'd noticed the creek was low. If
they cared to talk, they were welcome to bring it up.
Some did. Most didn't.

He'd give Sophia Jackson her space, then. Whatever
was making her sad, it was hers to cry over. Tomorrow night would be soon enough to check in with her.

Just as he nudged his horse back into a walk, he
caught a movement out of the corner of his eye, Sophia
dashing her cheek on her shoulder. He tried to put it

out of his mind once he was in the barn, but it nagged at him as he haltered his mare and washed off her bit. Sophia had touched her cheek to her shoulder just like that when he'd first approached her on the road this afternoon. Had she been crying when she'd hung on to that heifer?

He rubbed his jaw. In the car, she'd been all clenched fists and anxiously bouncing knee. A woman on the edge, that was what he'd thought. Looked like she'd gone over that edge this evening.

People did. Not his problem. There were limits to what a foreman was expected to handle, damn it.

But the way she'd been turning the lights off and on was odd. What did that have to do with being sad?

His mare nudged him in the shoulder, unhappy with the way he was standing still.

"I know, I know. I have to go check on her." He turned the mare into the paddock so she could enjoy the last of the twilight without a saddle on her back, then turned himself toward the house. It was only about a hundred yards from barn to kitchen door, an easy walk over hard-packed earth to a wide flagstone patio that held a couple of wooden picnic tables. The kitchen door was protected by its original small back porch and an awning.

A hundred yards was far enough to give Travis time to think about how long he'd been in the saddle today, how long he'd be in the saddle tomorrow, and how he was hungry enough to eat his hat.

He took his hat off and knocked at the back door.

No answer.

He knocked again. His stomach growled.

"Go away." The movie star didn't sound particularly sad.

He leaned his hand on the door jamb. "You got the lights fixed in there, ma'am?"

"Yes. Go away."

Fine by him. Just hearing her voice made his heart speed up a tick, and he didn't like it. He'd turned away and put his hat back on when he heard the door open.

"Wait. Do you know anything about refrigerators?"

He glanced back and did a double take. She was standing there with a dish towel on her head, its blue and white cotton covering her face. "What in the Sam Hill are you—"

"I don't want you to see me. Can you fix a refrigerator?"

"Probably." He took his hat off as he stepped back under the awning, but she didn't back up to let him in. "Can you see through that thing?"

She held up a hand to stop him, but her palm wasn't quite directed his way. "Wait. Do you have a camera?"

"No."

"How about a cell phone?"

"Of course."

"Set it on the ground, right here." She pointed at her feet. "No pictures."

He fought for patience. This woman was out of her mind with her dish towel and her demands. He had a horse to stable for the night and eight more to feed before he could go home and scarf down something himself. "Do you want me to look at your fridge or not?"

"No one sets foot in this house with a cell phone. No one gets photos of me for free. If you don't like it, too bad. You'll just have to leave."

Travis put his hat back on his head and left. He didn't take to being told what to do with his personal property. He'd crossed the flagstone and stepped onto the hard-packed dirt path to the barn when she called after him.

"That's it? You're really leaving?"

He took his time turning around. She'd come out to the edge of the porch, and was holding up the towel just far enough to peek out from under it. He clenched his jaw against the sight of her bare stomach framed by that tight black clothing. She hadn't gotten that outfit at any Western-wear-and-feed store. The thigh-high boots were gone. Instead, she was all legs. Long, bare legs.

Damn it. He was already hungry for food. He didn't need to be hungry for anything else.

"That's it," he said, and turned back to the barn.

"Wait. Okay, I'll make an exception, but just this one time. You have to keep your phone in your pocket when you're around me."

He kept walking.

"Don't leave me. Just…don't leave. Please."

He shouldn't have looked back, but he did. There was something a little bit lost about her stance, something just unsure enough in the way she lifted that towel off one eye that made him pause. The way she was tracking him reminded him of a fox that had gotten tangled in a fence and wasn't sure if she should bite him or let him free her.

Cursing himself every step of the way, he returned to the porch and slammed the heel of his boot in the cast iron boot jack that had a permanent place by the door.

"What are you doing?" Her head was bowed under the towel as she watched him step out of one boot, then the other.

"You're worried about the wrong thing. The cell phone isn't a problem. A man coming from a barn into your house with his boots on? That could be a problem. Mrs. MacDowell wouldn't allow it." And then, because he remembered the sister's distress over the extremes to which the paparazzi had apparently gone in the past, he dropped his cell phone in one boot. "There. Now take that towel off your head."

He brushed past her and walked into the kitchen, hanging his hat on one of the hooks by the door. He opened the fridge, but the appliance clearly was dead. "You already checked the fuse, I take it."

"Yes."

Of course she had. That had been why the lights had gone on and off.

She walked up to him with her hands full of plastic triangles. "These wedges were in the doors. I took them out because I thought maybe you had to shut the door all the way to make it run. I don't see any kind of on-off switch."

The towel was gone. She was, quite simply, the most beautiful woman he'd ever seen. Her hair was messed up from the towel and her famously blue eyes were puffy from crying, but by God, she was absolutely beautiful. His heart must have stopped for a moment, because he felt the hard thud in his chest when it kick-started back to life.

She suddenly threw the plastic onto the tile floor, making a great clatter. "Don't stare at me. So, I've been crying. Big deal. Tell all your friends. 'Hey, you should see Sophia Jackson when she cries. She looks like hell.' Go get your phone and take a picture. I swear, I don't care. All I want is for that refrigerator to work. If you're just going to stand there and stare at me, then get the hell out of my house."

If Travis had learned anything from a lifetime around animals, it was that only one creature at a time had better be riled up. If his horse got spooked, he had to be calm. If a cow got protective of her calf, then it was up to him not to give her a reason to lower her head and charge. He figured if a movie star was freaked out about her appearance, then he had to not give a damn about it.

He didn't, not really. She looked like what she looked like, which was beautiful, red nose and tear stains and all. There were a lot of beautiful things in his world, like horses. Sunsets. He appreciated Sophia's beauty, but he hadn't intended to make a fuss over it. If he'd been staring at her, it had been no different than taking an extra moment to look at the sky on a particularly colorful evening.

He crossed his arms over his chest and leaned against the counter. "Is the fridge plugged into the wall?"

She'd clearly expected him to say something else. It took her a beat to snap her mouth shut. "I thought of that, but I can't see behind it, and the stupid thing is too big for me to move. I'm stuck. I've just been stuck here all day, watching all my food melt." Her upper lip quivered a little, vulnerable.

He thought about kissing just her upper lip, one precise placement of his lips on hers, to steady her. He pushed the thought away. "Did you try to move it?"

"What?"

"Did you try to move it? Or did you just look at it and decide you couldn't?" He nodded his head toward the fridge, a mammoth side-by-side for a family that had consisted almost entirely of hungry men. "Give it a shot."

"Is this how you get your jollies? You want to see if I'm stupid enough to try to move something that's ten times heavier than I am? Blondes are dumb, right? This is your test to see if I'm a real blonde. Men always want to know if I'm a real blonde. Well, guess what? I am." She grabbed the handles of the open doors and gave them a dramatic yank, heaving all her weight backward in the effort.

The fridge rolled toward her at least a foot, making her yelp in surprise. The shock on her face was priceless. Travis rubbed his jaw to keep from laughing.

She pressed her lips together and lifted her chin, and Travis had the distinct impression she was trying to keep herself from not going over the edge again.

That sobered him up. He recrossed his arms. "You can't see them, but a fridge this size has to have built-in casters. No one could move it otherwise. Not you. Not me. Not both of us together."

"I didn't know."

"Now you do."

She seemed rooted to her spot, facing the fridge. With her puffy eyes and tear-streaked face, she had definitely had a bad day. Her problems might seem trivial to him—who cared if someone snapped a photo of a famous person?—but they weighed on her.

He shoved himself to his tired feet. "Come on, I'll help you plug it in."

"No, I'll do it." She started tugging, and once she'd pulled the behemoth out another foot, she boosted herself onto the counter, gracefully athletic. Kneeling on Mrs. MacDowell's blue-tiled counter, she bent down to reach behind the fridge and grope for the cord. Travis knew he shouldn't stare, but hell, her head was behind the fridge. The dip of her lower back and the curve of her thigh didn't know they were being fully appreciated.

When she got the fridge plugged in, it obediently and immediately hummed to life. She jumped down from the countertop, landing silently, as sure of her balance as a cat. He caught a flash of her determination along with a flash of her bare skin.

Hunger ate at him, made him impatient. He picked his hat up from its hook by the door. "Good night, then."

"Where are you going?"

"Back to work." He shut the door behind himself. Stomped into the first boot, but his own balance felt off. He had to hop a bit to catch himself. He needed to get some food and some sleep, then he'd be fine.

The door swung open, but he caught it before it knocked him over. "What now?"

"I need groceries."

There was a beat of silence. Did she expect him to magically produce groceries?

"Everything melted." She looked mournfully over her shoulder at the sink, then back at him, and just… waited.

It amazed him how city folk sometimes needed to be told how the world ran. "Guess you'll be headed into town tomorrow, then."

"Me? I can't go to a grocery store."

"You need a truck? The white pickup is for general use. The keys are in the barn, on the hook by the tack room. Help yourself."

"To a truck?" She literally recoiled a half step back into the house.

"I don't know how else you intend to get to the grocery store. Just head toward Austin. Closest store is about twenty miles in, on your right."

"You have to get the groceries for me."

"Nope. It's May." He stuck his hat on, so his hands were free to pick up his second boot and shake the cell phone out of it.

"It's May? What kind of answer is that? Do you fast in May or do a colon cleanse or something?"

He looked up at her joke, but his grin died before it started. Judging by the look on her face, she wasn't joking. "The River Mack rounds up in May."

She looked at him, waiting. He realized a woman from Hollywood probably had no idea what that meant.

"We're busy. We're branding. We have to keep an eye on the late calving, the bulls—"

He stopped himself. He wasn't going to explain the rest. Managing a herd was a constant, complex operation. Bulls had to be separated from cows. The cow-calf pairs had to be moved to the richest pastures so the mamas could keep their weight up while they nursed their calves. Cows who had failed to get pregnant were culled from the herd and replaced with better, more fertile cattle.

Sophia flapped one hand toward the kitchen behind her. "I have nothing to eat. You have to help me."

He stomped into his second boot. "Not unless you're a pregnant cow."

At her gasp, he did chuckle. "Or a horse. Or a dog. You could be a chicken, and I would have to help you. I keep every beast on this ranch fed, but you, ma'am, are not a beast. You're a grown woman who can take care of herself, and you're not my problem."

She looked absolutely stricken. Had he been so harsh?

"Listen, if I'm going toward town, I don't mind picking you up a gallon of milk. That's just common courtesy. I expect you to do the same for me."

"But I can't leave the ranch."

"Neither can I." He touched the brim of his hat in farewell. "Now if you'll excuse me, I've got horses to feed before I can feed myself."

Chapter 4

A pregnant cow.

It was fair to say women pretty much spent their lives trying not to look like pregnant cows. Yet if Sophia Jackson, Golden Globe winner and Academy Award nominee, wanted help on this ranch, she needed to look like that cow she'd hugged in the middle of the road.

She didn't look like that. She looked like a movie star, and that meant she would get no help. No sympathy.

That was nothing new. Movie stars were expected to be rolling in dough and to have an easy life. Everyone assumed movie stars were millionaires, but she was more of a hundred-thousandaire. Certainly comfortable and a far cry from her days pointing at mattresses with a smile, but the money went out at an alarming rate between jobs. Even when she was not being paid, Sophia paid everyone else: publicists, managers, agents, fitness trainers, fashion stylists…and her personal assistant, Grace.

Sophia had to pay them to do their jobs, so that she could land another job and get another burst of money. An actor only felt secure if the next job got lined up before the current job stopped paying. Then, of course, the next job after that needed to be won, a contract signed, and more money dished out.

There would be no new jobs, not for nine months. Sophia slid her palm over her perfectly flat, perfectly toned abs. The whole pregnancy concept didn't seem real. It was a plus sign on a plastic stick and nothing more. She didn't feel different. She didn't look different.

Alex the Stupid Doctor had explained that she was only weeks along, and that for a first-time mother, especially one who stayed in the kind of physical shape the world expected Sophia to be in, the pregnancy might not show until the fourth or fifth month. Maybe longer.

She could have filmed another movie in that time…

But nobody in Hollywood wanted to work with her…

Because she'd fallen for a loser who'd killed her hardworking reputation.

Round and round we go.

Always the same thoughts, always turning in that same vicious cycle.

If only she hadn't met DJ Deezee, that jerk…

She picked up the goose salt shaker and clenched it tightly in her fist. For the next nine months, instead of paying her entourage's salaries, Sophia would be paying rent on this house. The rent was cheaper than the stable of people it took to sustain fame, which was fortunate, because the money coming in was going to slow considerably. Her only income would be residuals from DVD sales of movies that had already sold most of what they would ever sell—and her old manager and her old agent would still take their cut from that, even though they'd abandoned her.

She was going to hide on this ranch and watch her money dwindle as she sank into obscurity. Then she'd have to start over, scrambling for any scrap Hollywood would throw to her, auditioning for any female role. Her life would be an endless circle of checking in with grouchy temps, setting her head shot on their rickety card tables, taking her place in line with the other actors, praying this audition would be the one. She wasn't sure she could withstand years of rejection for a second time.

She shouldn't have to. She'd paid her dues.

The ceramic goose in her hand should have crumbled from the force of her grip, the way it would have if she'd been in a movie. But no—for that to happen, a prop master had to construct the shaker out of glazed sugar, something a real person could actually break. Movies had to be faked.

This was all too real. She couldn't crush porcelain. She could throw it, though. Deezee regularly trashed hotel rooms, and she had to admit that it had felt therapeutic for a moment when he'd dared her to throw a vase in a presidential suite. Afterward, though…the broken shards had stayed stuck in the carpet while management tallied up the bill.

She stared for a moment longer at the goose in her hand, its blank stare unchanging as it awaited its fate. "There's nothing we can do about any of this, is there?"

The kitchen was suddenly too small, too close. Sophia walked quickly into the living room. It was bigger, more modern. Wood floors, nice upholstery, a flat-screen TV. A vase. The ceilings were high, white with dark beams. She felt suddenly small, standing in this great room in a house built to hold a big family. She was one little person dwarfed by thousands of square feet of ranch house.

She heard her sister's voice. Her mother's voice. *You've got nowhere else to go. You cannot live with me.*

She couldn't, could she? Her sister was in love, planning a wedding, giddy about living with her new husband. There was no room for a third wheel that would spin notoriety and paparazzi into their normal lives.

And her mother... Sophia could not move back home to live with her. Never again. Not in this life. Other twenty-nine-year-olds might have their parents as a safety net, but Sophia's safety net had been cut away on a highway ten years ago.

The ceilings were too high. The nausea was rising to fill the empty space, and it had nothing to do with pregnancy, nothing at all. Sophia squeezed her eyes shut and buried her face in her clenched fists. The little beak of the salt shaker goose pressed into her forehead, into her hard skull.

The house was too big. She got out, jerking open the front door and escaping onto the wide front porch. In the daylight, the white columns had framed unending stretch of brown and green earth. At night, the blackness was overwhelming, like being on a spaceship, surrounded by nothing but night sky. There were too many stars. No city lights drowned them out. She was too far from Hollywood, the only place she needed to be. *All alone, all alone...*

This was not what she wanted, not what she'd ever wanted. She'd worked so hard, but it was all coming to nothing. Life as she'd known it would end here, on a porch in the middle of nowhere, a slow, nine-month death. Already, she'd ceased to exist.

She hurled the salt shaker into the night, aiming at the stars, the too-plentiful stars.

The salt shaker disappeared in the dark. Sophia's gesture of defiance had no effect on the world at all.

I do exist. I'm Sophia Jackson, damn it.

If she didn't want to be on this ranch, then she didn't have to be.

You know how to drive, don't you? Turn the car around, then, instead of blowing that damned horn.

There was a truck, the cowboy had said. A white truck. Keys in the barn. She ran down the steps, but they ended on a gravel path, and her feet were bare. She was forced off the path, forced to slow down as she skirted the house, crossing dirt and grass toward the barn.

I don't want to slow down. If I get off the roller coaster of Hollywood, I'll never be able to speed back up again. I refuse to slow down.

She stepped on a rock and hissed at the pain, but she would not be denied. Instead of being more careful, she broke into a sprint—and stepped on an even sharper rock. She gasped, she hopped on one foot, she cursed.

I'm being a drama queen.

She was. Oh, God, she really was a drama queen— and it was going to get her nowhere. The truck would be sitting there whether she got to the barn in five seconds or five minutes. And then what? She'd drive the truck barefoot into Austin and do what, exactly?

I'm so stupid.

No one had witnessed her stupidity, but that hardly eased her sense of embarrassment as she made her way more carefully toward the barn. It was hard to shake that feeling of being watched after years of conditioning. Ten years, to be precise, beginning with her little sister watching her with big eyes once it was only the two of them, alone in their dead parents' house. *But Sophie, do you know how to make Mom's recipe?*

Don't you worry. It will be a piece of cake.

Sophia knew Grace had been counting on her last remaining family member not to crack under the pressure of becoming a single parent to her younger sister. Later, managers and directors had counted on Sophia, too, judging whether or not she would crack before offering her money for her next role. She'd had them all convinced she was a safe bet, but for the past five months, the paparazzi had been watching her with Deezee, counting on her to crack into a million pieces before their cameras, so they could sell the photos.

The paparazzi had guessed right. She'd finally cracked. The photos were all over the internet. Now no one was counting on her. Grace didn't need her anymore. Alex had stuck Sophia in this ranch house, supposedly so she'd have a place where no one would watch her. Out of habit, though, she looked over her shoulder as she reached the barn, keeping her chin up and looking unconcerned in the flattering light of the last rays of sunset. There was no one around, only the white pickup parked to the side. The cowboy must have gone to get his dinner.

Well, that made one of them. Sophia realized the nausea had subsided and hunger pangs had taken its place. Maybe inside the barn there would be some pregnant-cow food she could eat. She slid open the barn door and walked inside.

Not cows. Horses.

Sophia paused at the end of the long center aisle. One by one, horses hung their heads over their stall doors and stared at her.

"You can quit staring at me," she said, but the horses took their time checking her out with their big brown eyes, twitching their ears here and there. The palette of their warm colors as they hung their heads over their iron and wood stalls would have made a lovely setting for a rustic movie.

There were no cameras here, no press, no producers. Sophia stopped holding her breath and let herself sag against the stall to her right. Her shoulders slumped under the full weight of her fatigue.

The horse swung its head a little closer to her, and gave her slumped shoulder a nudge.

"Oh, hello." Sophia had only known one horse in her life, the one that the stunt team had assigned her to sit upon during a few scenes before her pioneer character's dramatic death. She'd liked that horse, though, and had enjoyed its company more than that of the insulting, unstable director.

"Aren't you pretty?" Sophia tentatively ran the backs of her knuckles over the horse's neck, feeling the strength of its awesome muscles under the soft coat. She walked to the next stall, grateful for the cool concrete on the battered soles of her feet.

The next horse didn't back away from her, either. Sophia petted it carefully, then more confidently when the horse didn't seem to mind. She smoothed her hand over the massive cheek. "Yes, you're very pretty. You really are."

She worked her way down the aisle, petting each one, brown and spotted, black and white. They were all so peaceful, interested in her and yet not excited by her. Except, perhaps, the last one with the dark brown face and jet-black mane. That horse was excited to snuffle her soft nose right into Sophia's hair, making Sophia smile at the tickle.

"It's my shampoo. Ridiculously expensive, but Jean Paul gives it to me for free as long as I tell everyone that I use it. So if he asks, do a girl a favor and tell him you heard I use his shampoo."

How was that going to work, now that she was out of the public eye? She rested her forehead against the horse's solid neck. "At least, he used to give it to me for free."

The horse chuffed into her hair.

"I'd share it with you, but I might not get any more, actually. Sorry about that, pretty girl. Before this is all over, I may have to borrow your shampoo. I hear horse shampoo can be great for people's hair. Would you mind?"

"Did you need something else?"

Sophia whirled around. Mr. Don't-or-Else stood there, all denim and boots and loose stance, but his brown eyes were narrowed on her like she was some kind of rattlesnake who'd slithered in to his domain.

"I thought you were gone," she said. She adjusted her posture. She was being watched after all. She should have known better than to drop her guard.

"You are not allowed in the barn without boots on."

The horse snuffled some more of her hair, clearly

approving of her even if her owner didn't. "What's this horse's name?"

"No bare feet in the barn." The cowboy indicated the door with a jerk of his strong chin—his very strong chin, which fit his square jaw. A lighting director couldn't ask for better angles to illuminate. The camera would love him.

Travis Chalmers. He'd tipped his hat to her this afternoon as he'd sat on his horse. Her heart had tripped a little then. It tripped a little now.

She'd already brought her ankles together and bent one knee, so very casually, she set one hand on her hip. It made her body look its best. The public always checked out her body, her clothing, her makeup, her hair. God forbid anything failed to meet their movie star expectations. They'd rip her apart on every social media platform.

Travis had already seen her looking her worst, but if he hoped she'd crack into more pieces, he was in for a disappointment.

Sophia shook her hair back, knowing it would shine even in the low light of the barn. "What's the horse's name? She and I have the same taste in shampoo."

"He's a gelding, not a girl. You can't come into the barn without boots or shoes. It's not safe. Is that clear?"

Sophia rolled her eyes in a playful way, as if she were lighthearted tonight. "If it's a boy horse, then what's *his* name? He likes me."

The cowboy scoffed at that. "You seem to think all of my stock like you."

"They do. All of them except you."

Travis's expression didn't change, not one bit, even though she'd tossed off her line with the perfect combination of sassy confidence and pretty pout. He simply wasn't impressed.

It hurt. He was the only person out here, her only possible defense against being swallowed by the loneliness, and yet he was the one person on earth who didn't seem thrilled to meet a celebrity.

Supposedly. He was still watching her.

The audition wasn't over. She could still win him over.

The anxiety to do so was familiar. Survival in Hollywood depended on winning people over. She'd had to win over every casting director who'd judged her, who'd watched her as impassively as this cowboy did while she tried to be enchanting. Indifference had to be overcome, or she wouldn't get the job and she couldn't pay the bills.

With the anxiety came the adrenaline that had helped her survive. She needed to win over Travis Chalmers, or she'd have no one to talk to at all. Ever.

So she smiled, and she took a step closer.

His eyes narrowed a fraction as his gaze dropped down her bare legs. She felt another little thrill of adrenaline. This would be easy.

"You're bleeding," he said.

"I'm—" She tilted her head but kept her smile in place. "What?"

But he was impatient, walking past her to glare at the floor behind her. "What did you cut yourself on?"

She turned around to see little round, red smears where she'd stopped to greet each horse. "It must have been a rock outside. I stepped on a couple of rocks pretty hard."

"Good."

"Good?"

He glanced at her and had the grace to look the tiniest bit embarrassed. "Good that it wasn't anything sharp in the barn. If it had been a nail or something that had cut you, then it could cut a horse, too."

"Thanks for your concern." She said it with a smile and a little shake of her chandelier earrings. "Nice to know the horses are more valuable than I am."

"Like I said earlier, it's my job to take care of every beast on this ranch. You're not a beast. You should know to wear shoes."

She wasn't sure how to answer that. She couldn't exactly insist she *was* a valuable beast that needed taken care of, and she certainly wasn't going to admit she'd run outside in a panic. Actors who panicked didn't get hired.

"Come on. I'll get you something for the bleeding."

He walked away. Just turned his back on her and walked away. Again.

After a moment, she followed, but she hadn't taken two steps when he told her to stop. "Don't keep bleeding on the floor."

"What do you want me to do?" She put both hands on her hips and faced him squarely. Who cared if it didn't show off her figure? She'd lost this audition already.

"Can't you hop on one foot?"

This had to be a test, another trick to see if she was a dumb blonde. But Travis turned into a side room that was the size of another stall, one fitted out with a deep utility sink and kitchen-style cabinets.

He wasn't watching her to see what she'd do, so maybe it wasn't a joke. After a moment of indecision, she started hopping on her good foot. The cut one hurt, anyway, and it was only a few hops to reach the sink.

Travis opened one of the cabinets. It looked like a pharmacy inside, stocked with extra-large pill bottles. He got out a box of bandages, the adhesive kind that came in individual paper wrappers. The kind her mother had put on her scrapes and cuts when she was little.

I am not going to cry in front of this man. Not ever again.

He tapped the counter by the sink. "Hop up. Wash your foot off in the sink."

"Why don't you come here and give me a little boost?"

He stilled, with good reason. She'd said it with a purr, an unmistakably sexual invitation for him to put his hands on her.

She hadn't meant to. It had just popped out that way, her way to distance herself from the nostalgia. Maybe a way to gain some control over him. He was giving her commands, but she could get him to obey a sexual command of her own if she really turned on the charm.

Whatever had made her say that, she had to brave it out now. Sultry was better than sad. Anything was better than sad.

She tossed her hair back, her earrings jingling like a belly dancer's costume. She turned so that she was slightly sideways to him, her bustline a curvy contrast to her flat stomach.

"The counter's too high for me. Give me a hand… or two."

Come and touch me. Her invitation sounded welcoming. She realized it was. He was nothing like the sleek actors or the crazy DJs she'd known, but apparently, *rugged outdoorsman* appealed to her in a big way. *You've got a big green light here, Mr. Cowboy.*

"Too high for you," he repeated, without a flicker of sexual awareness in his voice. Instead, he sounded impatient as he cut through her helpless-damsel act. "I already watched you hop up on Mrs. MacDowell's counter tonight."

Of course the counter height had been a flimsy excuse; it had been an invitation. She refused to blush at having it rejected. Instead, she backed up to the counter and braced her hands behind herself, letting her crop top ride high. With the kind of slow control that would have made her personal yoga instructor beam with approval, she used biceps and triceps and abs, and lifted herself slowly onto the counter with a smooth flex of her toned body. People would pay money to see a certain junior officer do that in a faraway galaxy.

Travis Chalmers made a lousy audience. He only turned on the water and handed her a bar of soap.

She worked the bar into a lather as she pouted. Even Deezee wouldn't have passed up the chance to touch her. Actually, that was all Deezee had ever wanted to do: touch her. If it wasn't going to end in sex, he wasn't into it. She'd texted him ten times more often than he'd texted her between dates. His idea of a date had meant they'd go somewhere to party in the public eye or drink among VIPs for a couple of hours before they went to bed together. There'd been no hanging out for the sake of spending time together.

Sophia held her foot still as the water rinsed off the suds. She'd mistaken sex for friendship, hadn't she?

"It's not a deep cut. You should heal pretty quickly." Travis dabbed the sole of her foot dry with a wad of clean paper towels, which he then handed to her. Before she could ask what she was supposed to do with damp paper towels, he'd torn the paper wrapper off a bandage and placed it over the cut. He pressed the adhesive firmly into her skin with his thumb. There was nothing sexual in his touch, but it wasn't unkind. It was almost…paternal.

"Do you have kids?" she asked.

For once, he paused at something she'd said. "No."

You ought to. There was something about his unruffled, unhurried manner…

Dear God, she wasn't going to start missing her father, too. She couldn't think about parents and sister any longer. Not tonight.

She snatched her foot away and jumped lightly off the counter, landing on the foot that hadn't been cut. She held up the wad of damp towels. "Where's the trash?"

"You need those paper towels to wipe up the blood on your way out. I'll get you something to wear on your feet."

On her way out. She was dismissed, and she had to go back to the empty house in the middle of nowhere. She didn't want Travis to fetch her boots; she wanted him to carry her. He was a man who rode horseback all day. A cowboy who stood tall, with broad shoulders and strong hands. He could carry her weight, and God knew Sophia was tired of carrying everything herself.

She wanted his arms around her.

But she'd failed this audition. He wasn't interested in her when she was either bossy or cute. He wasn't fazed by her sultry tone, and he didn't care about her hard-earned, perfect body. He wasn't impressed with her in any way.

She gingerly stepped into the center aisle to see where he'd gone. Across from the medical room was another stall-sized space where it seemed saddles got parked on wooden sawhorses. The next room was enclosed with proper walls and a door, with a big glass window in the wall that looked into the rest of the barn. She could see a desk and bookcase and all the usual stuff for an office inside. She felt so dumb; she hadn't known barns had offices and medical clinics inside.

Travis came in from the door at the far end of the aisle from the door she'd used. He dropped a pair of utilitarian rubber rain boots at her feet. "These will get you back to the house. Return them tomorrow, before sundown."

"So specific. Bossy much?" She could hear the snotty teenager in her voice. Whatever. She hated feeling dumb.

"Whoever brings the horses in tomorrow might want to wear them when they hose down a horse, so have them back by then."

It was a patient explanation, but she hated that he could tell she didn't know squat about how a ranch was run. "Someone else is coming? You're not going to be here tomorrow night?"

"We take turns during roundup. One of the other hands will have a chance to come in and shower and sleep in a bed. Someone's usually here before sundown."

"But I can't let anyone else see me."

He shrugged. "Then don't come into the barn at sundown."

Then turn the car around. Then go to the grocery store. As if life were that simple.

"If you do come into the barn, wear boots. Dish towels are optional. Good night." He walked back into the medical stall, closing cabinet doors and shutting off the light.

Dish towels are optional. The man thought she was a big joke. With as much dignity as she'd once been forced to muster each time a casting director had said *Don't call us, we'll call you*, Sophia stepped into the galoshes and headed for the door, bending over to wipe up little red circles as she went.

Travis returned to the center aisle in time to watch the most beautiful woman in the world stomp out of his barn like a goddess in galoshes. She slid the barn door closed behind herself with what he was certain was a deliberate bang.

Samson, his favorite gelding and apparent lover of women's shampoo, kept his head toward the door, ears pointed toward the spot where the woman had disappeared. Travis realized he and the horse were both motionless for a moment too long.

"You can stop staring at the door. She's not coming back."

The horse shifted, stamping his foot.

"All right, damn it, you're right. Her hair smelled amazing. Don't get used to it. We've got work tomorrow. It'd take more than a pretty woman to change our ways."

Chapter 5

Three days, he stayed away.

The days were easy, filled with dirt and lassos as the animals were rounded up, counted, doctored. Calves bawled for their mamas until the cowboys released them and let them run back to the waiting herd. Travis had to change his mount every few hours to give the horses a rest, so the additional challenge of controlling different mounts with their unique personalities kept his attention focused where it ought to be.

But for three nights…

He'd stretch out on his bedroll and stare at the stars while thinking of one in particular, the star that had fallen onto his ranch. Insomnia wasn't a problem after a day of physical work, but when his tired body forced his mind to shut down, he continued thinking about Sophia Jackson in his sleep. Sophia got flirty, she got angry, she was strong and she was weak, but she was always, always tempting in every dream version of her that his brain could concoct. For three nights, he dreamed of nothing else.

It was damned annoying.

In the afternoon of the fourth day, he rode in with Clay Cooper, the hand who was next up for a night off. As foreman, Travis had to get to his office to keep up with the never-ending paperwork that went with running any business. That was reason enough for him to leave camp for the night. Not one cowboy was surprised when he left with Clay and the string of horses that were due for a day's rest and extra oats in the barn.

But Travis knew the real reason he was going in was to check on the famous Sophia Jackson. He was tired of fighting that nagging feeling that he needed to keep an eye on her, a feeling that hadn't gone away since the moment he'd met her in the road.

The house came into view. Travis's horse perked up. Travis had worked with horses too long for him not to understand what drove their behavior. The horse had perked up with anticipation because the rider had perked up with anticipation.

Travis rolled his shoulders. Took off his hat and smacked the dust off his thigh. Relaxed into the saddle.

There was nothing to anticipate. He was going to see Sophia Jackson soon. No big deal. Sophia was a movie star, but he wasn't starstruck.

The horse walked on while Travis turned that thought over once or twice. It felt true. Sure, he'd seen her in *Space Maze*. It would be hard to find someone who hadn't seen that movie. But from the tantrum she'd thrown about being stared at, and from her sister's fear

of the paparazzi, he didn't think the Hollywood lifestyle was very attractive. It would have been better if
she hadn't been a movie star.

Better for what?

Just easier all around. He put his hat on his head
and turned back to check the string of horses following Clay. All was well.

As the foreman, he was riding in to check on the
new person renting the MacDowells' house, same as
he'd check on any new cowboy who came to the ranch.
Hell, he'd check on any new filly or fence post. Once he
was sure the MacDowells' guest had gotten her groceries and her fridge was still running, he'd mentally cross
her off his to-do list and move on to the next item: he
needed to order more barb wire before they got down
to the last spool.

He and Clay rode past the house. Travis had planned
to help Clay put up the horses first at the bunkhouse's
stable before checking on Sophia, but he noticed that
Clay didn't even toss a glance toward the house. It hit
Travis that none of the hands who'd come and gone
from camp seemed to be aware anyone was living in
Mrs. MacDowell's house. Travis would've told them
there was a guest staying there. No big deal. But no
one had mentioned seeing any signs of life for the past
three nights.

There were no signs of life now. No lights on. No
curtains open to take in the evening sunset. No rock-
ing chair on the porch out of place. Sophia was keeping
herself hidden pretty well, then. Or...

Or Sophia Jackson had left the River Mack ranch.

I don't want to be here, anyway, she'd said, hand
poised over the car's steering wheel.

It was the most likely explanation. He'd wanted her to leave when he'd first met her, so he ought to be relieved. Instead, that nagging need to see her intensified. He had to know if she was still on his land or not.

"I'll see you tomorrow," he said to Clay. He let his horse feel his hurry to reach Mrs. MacDowell's kitchen door until he stopped her at the edge of the flagstone patio. There, stretched out on one of the wooden picnic tables, was Sophia. She was laid out like she was the meal, her clothing white like a tablecloth, her body delectable, but her eyes were closed and her hand was open and relaxed as she slept.

He dismounted and looped the horse's reins loosely around the old hitching post. His horse tossed her head with a jangle of tack and the heels of Travis's boots made a hard noise with each step as he crossed the flagstone, but Sophia remained fast asleep.

He ought to be thinking of Sleeping Beauty, he supposed. Sophia was as beautiful as a princess in her innocent white clothing, if a princess wore shorts and a shirt.

Instead, he couldn't get the idea of a feast out of his head. Here was a woman who'd be a banquet for the senses. Old college memories came back, Humanities 101 and its dry textbook descriptions of Roman emperors who'd held feasts where the sex was part of the meal. The image of a fairy tale princess battled briefly with the Roman feast, but Travis's body clearly clamored for Rome.

He stopped at her side. Looked down at her, but didn't touch. "Sophia."

She didn't stir. He said her name again and waited, wondering how a shirt and shorts could look so sexy. Finally, he shook her arm. "Sophia, wake up. It's Travis."

She jerked awake, then jerked away from him, like an animal instinctively afraid of attack.

Fanciful notions from college studies evaporated in an instant. "Whoa. It's just me."

She rolled off the table, off the far side, so that she stood with the table between them. It was a seriously skittish move.

"What are you doing here?" she asked.

"This is my ranch."

"Ha. You don't spend a lot of time on it." She pushed her hair back with both hands, pausing to squeeze her temples with her palms as she looked around the horizon. "Crap. Is it already sunset?"

"Clay's already taken the horses to the stable."

She looked toward the barn, alarmed. "Did this Clay guy see me?"

Travis didn't envy her Hollywood life at all. She seemed to be on edge all the time.

She wasn't wearing a shirt and shorts, after all. It was all one piece, almost like a child's pajamas. Maybe she was embarrassed to be caught outside in her pajamas. "Don't worry. You're looking at the barn, not what we call the stables around here. The stables are on the far side of the horse pasture. You can't see it from the house."

He paused. He didn't have a reason to tell her more, except that it might buy her some time to ease into being awake. "The stables are close to the bunkhouse. Cowboys living there keep their horses in the stables."

But judging by the way she rubbed the sleep from her eyes, she'd tuned him out after *Clay can't see you.* "I have to go inside. It's sunset."

"No one else is due in tonight." His words fell on deaf

ears. Sophia stepped up on the little porch and disappeared into the house.

Travis caught himself staring at the closed door like Samson had the other night. He cursed under his breath and went to untie his horse. He had his answer: Sophia Jackson was still here. She looked fine, better than fine. She looked healthy as all get-out. It was time to move on and order that barb wire.

He led his horse to the barn. Caring for the mare was a familiar routine, one that should have let him unwind, but he had to work to ignore a lingering uneasiness. He unsaddled the mare, stored the tack, then took her outside to rinse the sweat marks from her coat with a garden hose.

The galoshes were sitting neatly by the hose, pushing his thoughts right back to Sophia.

Her presence in the barn that night had been unsettling in general. So had been one of her questions in particular: *Do you have kids?*

For just for a second, he'd thought he'd like to be able to answer *yes*. He was thirty-one and settled. He'd stood there with Sophia Jackson's perfectly arched foot in his hand and pictured himself married with a couple of little ones that he'd have to keep out of trouble. *It would be good to be a dad*, he'd thought for that flash of a second.

In reality, he didn't see himself getting married, and in his world, having children meant being married. He had nothing against the institution; he could understand why men did marry. Many a rancher's wife provided dinner every evening and clothes mended with love. They baked cakes and grew tomatoes in the garden, like Mrs. MacDowell.

Or there were wives who were partners in handling

cattle. Travis hired the same husband and wife team every fall when it came time to move the cattle to auction. The two of them seemed happy roping and riding together, and they worked smoothly in sync.

But Travis was fine as a bachelor. He liked his own cooking well enough. Working alone never bothered him. He was where he wanted to be, doing what he wanted to do. In order to even consider upending a perfectly good life, he'd have to meet a woman who was damned near irresistible.

Like Sophia Jackson.

Not anything like her. He'd need to find a woman who was irresistible but not crazy enough to wear a dish towel on her head and spike-heeled boots on a dirt road.

Unless that's what makes her irresistible.

He turned the hose back on and stuck his head in the stream of water.

Listen to yourself. A rancher's wife and a movie star are two different creatures. Too different.

This woman slept on top of a picnic table in the middle of the day. Crazy. A man did not marry *crazy*. A man didn't want *crazy* to be the mother of his children. Irresistible had nothing to do with it.

He shook the water out of his too-long hair as he unbuttoned his sweat-soaked plaid shirt and peeled it off. He had to lean over pretty far to keep the water off his jeans and boots, but the hose was good for taking off the first layer of trail dirt from his arms and chest.

Feeling a hundred times more clearheaded, he shut off the water and turned the mare loose in the paddock. His office was inside the barn. He kept a stack of clean T-shirts there. While he was at his desk, he'd order a dozen spools of quality barb wire, so he wouldn't have to give it a second thought for the rest of the year. Barb wire would be ordered—check. The MacDowells' houseguest was doing fine—check. He'd move on to the next item on his list.

He shoved the galoshes aside with the edge of his boot and left the darkening sky before the stars could come out and taunt his resolve.

It was useless. As he strode into the barn, he heard a distinctively feminine gasp. In the twilight of the barn's interior, Sophia practically glowed, all silver-blond hair and short, white pajamas. A star, right here in his barn. There was no list; there was nothing else to think about.

She dropped her gaze first.

Slowly.

She took him in deliberately, her gaze roaming over his wet skin, from his left shoulder to his right. To his bare chest. Lower.

I'm not the only one around here who's hungry, then.

The knowledge blinded him for a moment. To hell with the kind of woman he ought to want. Sophia was the woman he *did* want. Full stop. And he wanted her badly.

She came a step closer.

As water drops rolled down his skin, blood pounded through his veins, his desire for her ferocious in a way that was unfamiliar, as if he'd never really wanted a woman before.

She was about to say something, but as her lips parted, her gaze flicked from his chest back up to his eyes. Whatever she saw in his expression made her own eyes open wider. Whatever she'd been about to say turned into a little whoosh of "oh."

He couldn't remember feeling this power before, not

for any of the women who'd been so likely to be right for him. After dating for weeks or months or, once, a whole year, none had turned out to be right after all. Yet Sophia had only to exhale an *oh*, and the years of friends and lovers blurred into nothing. This woman was the one he'd been starving for.

Hunger caused problems on a ranch. Stallions kicked out stalls. Bulls destroyed fences.

"Why are you here?" he demanded. *Why you? Why now?*

She took a step closer, and a part of him—too much of him—didn't give a damn about the answers to his own questions. He just wanted her to keep coming.

She hesitated.

Then she took that next step closer, but it was too late. Her split-second pause, the widening of her eyes by a fraction of an inch, had betrayed the tiniest little bit of…fear? Perhaps fear of this power between them. Perhaps fear of him, personally. He was the bigger one, the stronger one, the one with an admittedly fresh surge of testosterone coursing through his body.

But he was no animal, no common beast, just as he'd told her she wasn't. He knew what was in his heart and mind and soul, and she didn't need to fear him.

She couldn't know that yet, not for certain. They barely knew one another. Travis didn't have any kind of minimum time limit in mind for how long he ought to know a woman before taking her to bed, but he did know this: she had to be one-hundred-percent certain of what she wanted. Sophia Jackson did not know what she wanted.

Travis stepped back.

Her frown of confusion was fleeting, replaced by a

new look of determination. She sauntered up to him, nice and close. Then she looked down his body again, her feminine eyelashes shading her blue eyes, turning him on as she ran one fingertip over his damp forearm.

"I came out here because it's lonely in that house. Very lonely."

God, that purr of hers...

It was an act. She was a good actress, but he'd seen that moment of fear or uncertainty or whatever it had been. Hunger couldn't be ignored forever, but it wouldn't kill a man to wait. Travis didn't intend to act on it or even talk about it in his barn just because he'd been caught out half-naked by a woman in skimpy pajamas.

He balled up his plaid shirt and used it to wipe the water off one arm, then the other. He pitched it through his open office door to land on his chair. *No feast today, Princess.*

"Did you need something before I go home?" he asked.

Her sexy act flipped to a more authentic anger pretty quickly. Apparently, she didn't take rejection well. "I don't need anything from you. I didn't even want you to be here. I came to see the horses."

"Is that so? In your pajamas and bare feet?" He turned his back on her and went into his office. He grabbed a T-shirt off the stack he kept on a bookcase. When he turned back, he nearly plowed her over; she'd followed him into his office, all indignation.

"I'm wearing sandals, and these aren't pajamas. You wish you could see me in my pajamas. You wish."

Her attempt at a set down was so childish, it sounded almost cute. Travis had to hide his smile by pulling his

T-shirt over his head. No harm in letting her think she'd scored a point against him.

"This is a *romper*," she huffed. "Straight from the runway. By a designer in Milan whom I wouldn't expect you to know. My stylist snatched it right out from under Kim K's nose. She probably died when I wore it first."

He stood with his hands on his hips, looking down at her, wondering what a guy like him was supposed to do with a girl like her. "I don't know Kim, but it looks real nice on you."

"Yeah. Sure." Apparently, she didn't believe his compliment. She turned her back on him and left the office, her designer clothes all in a white flutter.

Travis scrubbed his face with both hands. Then he shut off the lights and left the office, closing the door firmly. The barb wire could wait until tomorrow.

Sophia was nuzzling the spotted nose of a nice Appaloosa Travis had borrowed from the neighboring ranch for roundup. Travis watched her for a minute. The horse was loving the attention. *You're getting more action than I am, buddy.*

Still, Travis had to appreciate a person who had a natural affinity for horses. Her talent had to be natural and not learned, because he didn't think Sophia had ever set foot in a barn in her life before this week. She was wearing flip-flops, for crying out loud.

"Where's my horse?" she asked, keeping her eyes on the Appaloosa.

"Your horse?" He didn't like her wording. She had no idea what it meant to own a horse. To train, to groom, to feed, to care for without fail, to rely on when there was nobody for miles around.

"The boy horse whose name you won't tell me. You

left, and you took him with you. You took all of them. I came out here to say hello to the horses, and they were gone. Every single one."

Damn if she didn't sound like she was going to burst into tears.

"They aren't pets. They work."

"I returned the galoshes, just like you wanted, but you took the horses away. Without those horses, I've got no one to talk to. You're not interested in talking to me…or doing anything else with me."

Travis was good at picking up on animal behavior, not a woman's, but he could read her well enough. She felt betrayed. Lonely. Hell, she'd curled up into a ball and cried on a kitchen floor just days ago.

He'd have no peace of mind until he figured her out.

"Okay. You want to talk? Let's talk."

Chapter 6

The cowboy wanted to talk.

Sophia wasn't sure if he was kidding. She combed her fingers through the spotted horse's mane and peeked at big, bad Travis Chalmers. He looked pretty serious. Then again, that was his default expression. He grinned a little now and then, but otherwise, he was a serious guy.

Not a guy. A man.

A serious man who walked around here like he ran the place. Which she supposed he did, but still…

Travis took some kind of rope-and-leather thing that was hanging over an empty stall door and coiled it up. Tied it off. Tossed it into the room where the saddles were. It landed in a crate. It seemed that being in charge meant keeping everything in order.

Deezee would have dumped the crate out, flipped

it upside down, and stood on it like it was his stage, whooping and hollering and making sure no one else could talk while he was around.

Travis glanced down the row of stalls to the neat stack of perfectly square hay bales, then leaned back against a support post and gave her his full attention. Apparently nothing else was out of place—except her. "What did you want to talk about?"

She wasn't about to unburden herself to this man. She could pour out her regrets to the horses tomorrow morning. She didn't want Travis to know what an idiot she'd been. What an idiot she'd thrown away her career for.

Yet she'd just complained that she didn't have anyone to talk to, and Travis had called her on it. She had to come up with something to say. "What's this horse's name?"

Travis dipped his chin toward the horse, as matter-of-fact as if her question wasn't childish. "That's Arizona. He was named for the state. Texas isn't really known for Appaloosas. He was bought in Arizona as a wedding gift."

Oh, no. Please don't be married.

Dumb reaction. The man looked hot when he was shirtless. So what? That didn't mean she wanted to have a relationship with him. It didn't matter if he was married or not. Still…

"Not a gift for your wedding?" She tried to sound unconcerned.

"Trey Waterson's wedding. His brother gave him the horse. They own the ranch just west of us."

But Travis had that little bit of a grin about his mouth; he knew exactly why she'd asked. Her acting skills must be getting rusty already. She wished she hadn't run her finger down that muscled forearm, chasing a water droplet. She wished she hadn't made that stupid comment about being lonely.

She wished he hadn't rejected her.

"I'm not married," he said, making things perfectly clear. "Never been."

The horse, Arizona, shook his mane like Sophia wanted to. *That's right, horse. We don't care, do we?*

"So you don't own these horses, then. You're just the babysitter." She sneered the word *babysitter*.

She wished it back as soon as she said it. It was so rude. When had she started responding to everything as if she needed to insult someone before they could insult her?

But the answer was easy: when she'd spent too much time with Deezee and his buddies. Their ribbing and one-upmanship had been constant. At first, it had been a novelty to be treated like one of the guys instead of a flawless movie star, but she'd soon figured out that if she gave them an inch, they took a mile.

So maybe I've thrown up a few walls to protect myself. That's normal.

"Some horses are mine. Some are the ranch's." Travis patted Arizona's spotted neck. "Some I borrow."

His voice was so even. He couldn't care less about her nasty little dig. Did nothing irritate him? Or did he just not show it?

Judging by Travis Chalmers, it seemed the great actors in the movie industry, legends like Clint Eastwood and John Wayne, had acted their cowboy roles with more accuracy than Sophia had realized. They delivered their dialogue in an almost monotone way—never too excited, never shouting. Like Travis. Nothing like Deezee.

It was hard to imagine Travis jumping from a church pew to a communion railing and yelling *Yo, where's the ho?*

Deezee had meant her. Sophia had been standing in the vestibule of the Caribbean chapel, trying not to sweat through her white dress, waiting for the church music to start so she could walk down the center aisle to promise her life to him. He'd meant it as a joke, just another outrageous zinger for his posse's amusement. He hadn't bothered to change into a clean T-shirt. It was just a spontaneous elopement. No need to go to any trouble.

No crying in front of the cowboy.

"What's my horse's name?" she demanded. "And where is he?"

"Samson. He's still at camp. And he's my horse, not yours."

"Why did you ride that other horse today, then, if Samson belongs to you?"

"Because that other horse is mine, too. I own four right now, but you could say I babysit the rest."

Thank goodness the man's only facial expressions were somber and barely-a-grin. She'd insinuated that he owned nothing. If he laughed at her for how far she'd missed the mark, she might go all crazy diva on him. She couldn't stand to be laughed at.

"Four? For one man?" But her sarcasm was stupid, and she knew it.

"You can't ride just one horse all day, every day during roundup. That's why Arizona comes to work with me during roundup, see? So I have more horses to rotate. But Samson, he's a real special cow horse. I save him for when I'm actually cutting cattle out of the herd. It's a waste of talent to use him just to ride in from camp."

"You sound like a coach with a sports team."

"I hadn't thought of it that way. It's like setting up your batting order in baseball, now that you mention it. Samson's my star player. Don't tell Arizona that, though. He's been doing a great job pinch-hitting all week." Travis winked at Sophia, and he smiled. Not a grin, but a real smile that reached all the way to his eyes, a smile like she was in on the joke and part of his team.

Good Lord. The man was beautiful. She'd thought he looked hot the moment she'd spotted him riding toward her that first day on the road. Kind of stern and remote, but so masculine on horseback that he'd cut through her haze of misery. Today, shirtless and dripping wet, he'd looked like an athlete, a man in his prime, serious and strong. But when he smiled—oh, why would the women of Texas keep a man like this out here in the middle of nowhere?

For once in her life, she was the one doing the staring.

"B-baseball?" she repeated. Then, because she'd stuttered, she sneered a little, just to let him know she didn't care. "What would a cowboy know about baseball? There aren't enough humans around here to get a game going."

She caught the slightest shake of his head as he crossed his arms over his chest—a move that did lovely things to stretch that T-shirt tight around his biceps. His smile lingered. He found her amusing. Damn him.

"True enough. This cowboy played shortstop in college. Was there anything else you wanted to talk about besides horse names and baseball?"

She wondered how much of her thoughts he could guess. Could he see how much she wished she hadn't ruined her chances with a guy like him by making a huge mistake with a guy like Deezee?

You're an actor, Sophia. Don't let him see anything.

It was easier just to alienate people so they'd leave her alone. Her bridges were already burned. To hell with it.

"College? For a cowboy? What do they teach you, not to step in horse manure?"

Finally, *finally*, she'd pricked through his infuriatingly calm exterior. His eyes narrowed as she held his gaze defiantly.

That's right, I am a rattlesnake. You don't want to mess with me. She didn't want any man to mess with her, ever again.

His voice remained even. "My degree is in animal sciences from Texas A&M. They expect students to be smart enough to avoid horse manure before they enroll." He looked at her flip-flops, pointedly, and she fought the urge to curl her toes out of sight. "But I guess some people never do figure out what boots are for."

"Are you going to kick me out of your barn again?"

Please. Put me out of my misery. I'm screwing everything up here. Send me back to that awful, empty house and let me fall apart.

"I'm not your babysitter. You do what you want. If you don't have the common sense to stay out of trouble, well, some folks have to learn the hard way."

"I think I can avoid cow patties, thank you very much. I have eyes."

Travis pushed away from the post. "Then you might want to get going. It's getting dark real quick. It'll be harder to see those cow patties, and critters that like to bite toes will start coming out, too. Those flip-flops aren't going to protect you from a snake or a rat."

A rat. She glanced around the aisle. This place was too neat and organized for rats.

"We keep a barn cat," Travis said, reading the skepticism she hadn't bothered to hide. "She's a good mouser, but she does earn her keep."

He wasn't going to kick her out. She was going to have to force herself back to the lonely house. She acted like it didn't freak her out. "I'm leaving, anyway."

"I'll walk you to the door."

She jerked her arm out of his reach and stepped sideways, the side of her foot hitting a square hay bale. It felt like hitting a porcupine, except for her toes. Her toes made contact with something furry.

"A rat!" She nearly knocked Travis over, jumping away from the hay bale.

He caught her with a hand on her arm, but he was already frowning at the floor, bending down and reaching—

"Don't touch it." She tried to yank him away from the rat. He stood up with something brown in his hand and she let go of his arm. "Ew."

"It's not 'ew.' It's a kitten."

It wasn't moving. For the first time since Travis had woken Sophia from her nap, she felt the nausea rising. "Did I—do you think I... I didn't hurt it, did I?"

She felt him looking at her, but she had eyes only for the kitten, the tiniest one she'd ever seen. Travis pressed its baby paws with his thumb, wiggling each limb as he did. "Nothing seems to be broken or bent. You didn't hurt it."

Thank goodness. She sank weakly onto the hay bale, then leaped up as the hay poked her rear right through her designer romper from Milan.

Travis didn't seem to notice. His attention was on the kitten. He pulled at the collar of his T-shirt and tucked the brown fluff in, keeping it in place with one hand.

"Shouldn't we put it back so the mother cat will be able to find it?"

"He's cold. The mother cat must have abandoned him a while ago. If I can get him warmed up, we might be able to slip him back in with his brothers, but this is the second time the mother has moved him out of her nest."

"Why would she do that?"

Travis shrugged, the kitten completely hidden by his hand. "She might sense that there's something wrong with it."

"But you said it's not hurt."

"As far as I can see. The mother might know something I don't. Or the mother might have decided two kittens are all she can handle, so the third one gets abandoned."

"She leaves it out to die? That's awful. Can't you do something about that?" Anxiety tinged her voice, but she didn't care. Her anxiety to *not* see a kitten die felt pretty intense.

"I am doing something about that," he said drily. "I've got a kitten stuck down my shirt."

"You're going to keep it?" That sounded good. Really good.

He sat on the hay bale, the heavy denim of his jeans so much more practical than her white silk. "This kitten is really young. His eyes aren't open yet. His best bet for survival is with his mother."

Her anxiety spiked right back up. "But he has a terrible mother. She left him, just left the pitiful thing all alone. He's better off without her."

"No, he isn't." Travis spoke firmly, but he was looking at her with…concern. It took her a moment to recognize concern on a man's face. For the past ten years, the only person who'd ever looked at her with concern had been Grace. Her sister was the only one who'd ever cared.

Nausea tried to get her attention, but Sophia pushed it away. She didn't want to acknowledge it or what it might mean.

"You've never had a cat before, have you?" Travis asked.

"Ages ago, but she was neutered. You should neuter your cats. You have to neuter this one's mother right away. She's a bad mother. She doesn't deserve to have any more babies." Sophia pressed the back of her hand against her mouth abruptly to conquer the nausea.

But it was too late. The thing she didn't want to think about was now at the forefront of her mind: the little plus sign on that stick. Motherhood. Babies.

The word *pregnant* might not seem real to her, but Grace and Alex had been so deadly serious about it. They'd sat her down at Alex's kitchen table to talk through the options.

Sophia had immediately pounced on giving the baby up for adoption. It sounded simple. There'd be this baby that she would never even have to see, really, and the adoption agency would find the perfect couple. The couple would be happy. The baby would be happy. No harm all around.

That pregnancy test had probably been wrong, anyway, but adoption was a simple solution for a simple equation: one unwanted baby plus one couple who wanted a baby equaled success. Sophia would be doing a good deed. End of family meeting.

"Sophia." There was a definite note of concern in Travis's voice now, to match the way he was looking at her. "She might not be a bad mother. Sometimes Mother Nature knows more than we do. But for what it's worth, I agree with you about having cats neutered. This kitten's mother found us a couple of weeks ago. She moved herself in and was already pregnant. Accidents happen."

Oh god, oh god, oh god...

Tonight, faced with a few ounces of fluff she'd almost stepped on, Sophia suddenly realized what she'd left out of the equation: herself. Doing a good deed? She was the failure in the equation, not the hero. She was giving the baby away because she knew, deep down, she would be a terrible mother. She'd tried so hard with Grace, but she'd failed. Grace didn't even want to live with her anymore.

Travis had said the cat might have decided she couldn't handle that baby. Sophia knew she couldn't handle a baby, either. So what did that make Sophia? A terrible, horrible, selfish cat.

Travis tucked his chin into his collar and spread his fingers out, trying to see the kitten. "He's moving around. That's a good sign."

Sophia backed away from him, scared of the little bit of brown fluff and all that it represented.

"I'm going to go now." Her voice sounded thin, too high. "Good luck with the kitten."

She turned tail and ran. And ran. As fast as she could in the stupid flip-flops, she ran so that she was out of breath when she got back to the house.

It helped. It was only a sprint, maybe the length of a football field, nothing like the miles she'd had to put in to prepare for battling monsters in *Space Maze*, but she felt a little more normal. She felt her lungs and ribs expanding, contracting, taking in extra air. Muscles she hadn't used in weeks were suddenly awake, alive. She smoothed her hand over her stomach. The nausea was gone, and she felt hungry.

What she didn't feel was pregnant. Not one bit.

The pregnancy test's instructions had cautioned over and over that the results were not always accurate. Really, all that had happened was that Sophia had skipped a period, which was an easy thing to do. She probably wasn't even pregnant.

She was here to hide from the paparazzi, that was all. Her sister and Alex had both told Travis that. Sophia would lie low here for a few more weeks and let the media turn its attention elsewhere. Once they began a feeding frenzy on some other celebrity couple, Sophia would fly back to LA and start hunting for a new agent.

And you should make an appointment to get your tubes tied, because now you know you wouldn't be happy if you really were pregnant, and you'd be a lousy mother who couldn't take care of a baby, anyway.

She glanced out the kitchen window toward the barn, where some knocked-up stray cat was apparently her spirit animal. If the kitten-killing cat had been sent to show Sophia how much she was lacking, she'd done her job tonight. It was a good thing Sophia was planning on letting someone adopt the baby, because she wouldn't be a good mother. It was a crushing revelation.

The only light on in the whole house was the little one over the stove. That was plenty. The boxes of nonperishable food were still lined up on the kitchen counter, and Sophia had spent the week working her way through them, left to right. She didn't need a lot of light to pour herself another bowl of organic raisins and bran flakes.

She sat at the table and poked at the dry cereal with her spoon for a while. The organic milk substitute had gotten warm that first day, so she'd dumped it down the drain. Without a housekeeper, a personal shopper, or a sister, it hadn't been replenished yet.

Sophia didn't care. She just wanted to sleep, even after the nap she hadn't meant to take outside today. That had been a stupid slip up. It would have blown her cover if anyone except Travis had come by.

She couldn't get her act together enough to do a simple thing like hide. She'd dared to go outside because the house felt too empty. The sun had felt good on her skin after four days indoors, so she'd stretched out and fallen asleep.

No surprise there. She'd been tired for years. She'd been looking for a break when she'd taken Grace for that vacation in Telluride, but five months of Deezee hadn't been very refreshing. She was more tired than ever now.

Except when she talked to Travis. She'd felt alive and awake when Travis had walked into that barn with no shirt on. Nothing like a half-naked, incredibly buff man to snap a girl out of a fog.

The expression in his eyes had taken her breath away.

Boy meets girl. Boy wants girl. Or rather, man wants woman. Woman had wanted him right back, with an intensity that she couldn't handle.

No surprise there, either. She couldn't handle anything in her life. But she'd felt like she was really alive for the first time in ages, so she'd been determined to see how far he would go.

Not very far. One touch with her finger, and he'd literally stepped back from her and put on a shirt. So much for her bankable box office sex appeal. She'd lost her career, her sister—and her ability to attract a man. She sucked. Her life sucked.

On that note, she left her bowl on the table, stumbled into the living room, and did a face plant on the sofa. She never wanted to wake up again.

Chapter 7

"Sophia, wake up."

She jerked awake, heart pounding.

"It's just me. Travis. Are you okay?"

She sat up on the couch and dropped her face in her hands, willing her heart to slow down. She hated to be startled awake, because her first instinct was to flail about in case Deezee and his crew were in the middle of pulling some prank, like drawing on her face with a Sharpie just before she was expected to make an appearance. *It's funny, baby, whatchu getting upset for?*

She'd had to cancel that appearance, disappointing fans and angering her manager.

"I'm not okay. You just scared me to death, shaking my arm like that."

"Sorry. Nothing else was waking you up."

She was waking up now, fully aware of where she

was and who was standing over her. "What are you doing here?"

"Checking on you."

"What are you doing in my house? Did you just open the door and walk in?"

"Yes."

"What are you, some kind of stalker?"

"No."

His implacable, even tone set her teeth on edge. "But you just walked into someone else's house. You don't see anything wrong with that, do you?"

"I knocked first." His cell phone was in his hand, but he slipped it into his back pocket.

She stood up, furious. "I deserve privacy. I rented this house. I get that you're all Mr. I-Run-This-Place, but the house is mine for the duration. You can't just walk in any time you please. Have you been spying on me while I was sleeping? Standing over my bed without me knowing it every night?"

"Of course not. Quit spooking yourself."

"Spooking myself? What does that mean? That's not even a thing."

"You're letting your imagination run away with you. I walked in just now because we don't tend to stand on ceremony out here in the country. We can't. If someone's in trouble, you have to help. You can call nine-one-one, but it can take a long time for help to arrive. We take care of each other."

The man sounded like he actually believed what he was saying. He was oblivious to the invasion of her privacy. Living in the country couldn't be that different than living in the city.

"You had no reason to think I was in trouble."

"I thought I'd come and tell you some good news, but it looked like nobody was home."

"So?"

"If you hadn't come back to the house, then where were you? You ran out of the barn like a bat out of hell, so I figured you'd made it back to your place in a couple of minutes, but it didn't look like you were here. You'd run somewhere else. It's full dark out there. You aren't wearing much, and a person can start to lose body heat pretty quick once the sun goes down. You only had on flip-flops. If you'd gotten hurt—"

"I was right here on my own couch, minding my own business."

"Good. Now I don't have to saddle up Arizona and go out to look for you."

You would have done that for me? But the calm way he was looking at her, the steadiness of his voice told the truth. Just the fact that it had even occurred to him to go looking for someone who might be missing was…

It made her feel kind of protected. A nice feeling.

Crap. It was hard to stay mad at a man who'd honestly been worried about her. Not just worried, either. He actually would have done something about it.

She crossed her arms over her chest, but she couldn't force any real sting into her voice. "Well, we need to have an understanding that you won't sneak into my house again. Where I'm from, that's called breaking and entering. It creeps me out. Even the paparazzi don't dare to walk in my door. Don't do it, okay?"

He took his time thinking about his answer. "All right."

"I mean it." She didn't need any man mounting horseback search parties for her sake. She didn't.

"This wasn't sneaking in," he said. "You have my word I never will. But if I think you're in trouble, I'm going to do whatever it takes to help you, whether you like it or not."

Sophia blinked. *Why, you bossy son of a—* But then she realized she was looking at his back because he'd left the living room to go into the kitchen. She hurried after him.

He had already turned on the lights in the kitchen. He picked up her dry bowl of cereal. "Is this all you ate today?"

She stopped cold. There was only one reason a man would ask about that. Only one reason. "The paparazzi got to you already, didn't they?"

His gaze narrowed again.

I'm not the rattlesnake, dude. You are.

"I want to see your cell phone." She was seething. "How long have you been in here, photographing Sophia Jackson's hideout? Documenting Sophia Jackson's Hollywood diet secrets? Did you take pictures of me sleeping? Did you?"

"You're spooking yourself again."

"How much did they pay you? The kid at the deli by my condo got two thousand dollars for writing down my sandwich orders for a week. He took a photo of my sister picking up a bag with subs in it. When I didn't order a sandwich the next day, he lied and took a photo of someone else's sandwich. He got the cash. You know what I got?"

Travis set the bowl down with a soft curse.

He didn't want to hear her story? Too bad. He needed to know exactly what he was doing by giving the paparazzi supposedly harmless details of her life.

"I got reamed by America for setting a bad example for the youth of today. The youth of today! Because one of those youths took a picture of some insanely greasy concoction and claimed it was mine. Then everyone said the only way I could eat like that and keep my figure would be if I abused laxatives or stuck my fingers down my throat after every meal. The fact that they photographed me going in and out of a gym every single frigging day was irrelevant when it came to how I might be keeping my figure, but that's beside the point. I was suddenly personally responsible for every poor teenager with an eating disorder. I know how this game works, Travis. You'll get cash, and I'll get punished."

She nearly choked on his name. Travis—the betrayal shouldn't have hurt this badly. She didn't really know him any better than the deli counter kid.

"I'm not talking to any damned paparazzi. I don't think I've ever said that word out loud in my life. Paparazzi."

"I'm not stupid," she said, feeling very stupid for having let down her guard for an instant. "Since when does a big, tough cowboy suddenly take an interest in what kind of cereal a woman eats?"

"Since the big, tough cowboy got scared. Bad." He started walking toward her, two steps that covered most of the big kitchen. "I didn't just knock. I called the phone, too. You didn't move when I turned on the lights. I had my phone in my hand because I was going to call nine-one-one if I couldn't wake you. My grandpa had diabetes. I've seen what happens when a person's blood sugar gets too low. You scared me. That's all."

He took another step closer. She didn't back up, but she crossed her arms defensively. He was a lot of man, looming over her. A lot of man with a lot of honesty in his voice, and concern in his expression, and really beautiful brown eyes.

He ran his rough-warm palm over her arm, from her shoulder to her elbow, and kept his hand there, firm. "I'm very sorry I scared you in return."

Sophia felt her world turning. Pieces of her mind tumbled and landed in a new order. A better order. If she lived her life a different way…if she didn't always assume the worst…if she could believe someone wanted to help her instead of use her…

She could have a friend.

It was what she'd hoped for with Deezee. Things with him had started out with this kind of instant attraction, this desire to trust a man she barely knew.

Hope hurt.

Sophia took a step back.

Travis bowed his head, a quick nod to himself. When he looked up, he was the remote, stern foreman once more. "Do you always sleep so hard?"

He meant, *Is there something I should know about, because I'm responsible for all the horses and pregnant cows and cats around here?* She could hear it in his voice.

The truth would guarantee that he'd think of her as some kind of crazy diva: *No, I'm just sad. When I'm really sad, I deal with it by checking out of the world and going into hibernation.*

She couldn't tell him that.

"I'm just making up for a lack of sleep. A few years' worth of sleep."

"And do you always eat such a spartan diet? You never went to the grocery store, did you?"

"Don't start with that." This was why she didn't have friends. No one walked a mile in her shoes. No one understood.

She imitated his unruffled, even tone. "'If you need groceries, then go to the grocery store.' Everything is so easy for you, isn't it? You get to come and go as you please on any horse that strikes your fancy. You know what to do if you find a half-dead kitten, so you don't freak out. Of course you can decide whether or not you'll head to the store for more groceries."

She was afraid she might cry, but only because she wanted him to understand.

"Do you know why I have to wait for my sister to bring me groceries? It's not because I'm a diva. It's because I'll get hurt if I go out by myself. It's happened before." She held out the arm he'd stroked. "See these little half moons? That's how much my fans love me. If I walk down a street, I'll let them take their selfies and then I'll try to say goodbye, and they'll dig their fingernails into me. 'No, wait. You have to wait until my friend shows up.'

"I have to smile. I can't pitch a fit or else I'm a bitch or a diva or a monster. I've been held hostage, forced to wait on a sidewalk for a stranger's friend while people start penning me in from every direction. The police will stop to see what the crowd is about and they'll smile and wave at me. So I just sign autographs until it's the policeman's turn, and then I have to smile while I ask them to keep people from hurting me. 'Gee, Officer, could you possibly escort me back to my hotel?'"

Oh, hell, her eyes were tearing up, but she didn't care. Deezee had gotten off on these stories. He'd wanted them to happen to him. But Travis was frowning, and she didn't know if it was because he believed her or if it was because he thought she was *spooking* herself again.

But she had more proof, a secret that only a few hairstylists knew about. She turned her back to him and started pawing through her hair, piling her hair up until her fingertips found it, that dime-sized bit of her scalp where no hair grew. "This is how much they love me. Right after *Space Maze* came out, I was spotted at a grocery store. Honest to God, I had no idea how much people loved that movie. They pulled the hair out of my head as a souvenir. That's love. Right there."

She jabbed at the spot, such a small scar left after so much blood and pain, but Travis's hand stopped hers. He smoothed his thumb over the scar. She closed her eyes, remembering his thumb on the sole of her foot, smoothing an adhesive bandage into place, making everything better.

"I'm sorry," he said.

She dropped her hands, and her hair fell back into place with a shake of her head, just like Jean Paul had designed it to do. It was such a great perk of fame, those great haircuts and free shampoo. What a lucky girl she was.

"I'm sorry," Travis repeated, gruff words that whispered over her hair.

She felt all the fight go out of her. She couldn't remember what was supposed to take its place. Before Deezee, before the breakthrough roles, before her parents' deaths...what had life been like when she hadn't fought for everything?

She opened the door so Travis could leave, facing him with what she hoped was a neutral expression and not a desolate one. "You don't have to worry if you don't see me around. I think any normal person in my position would stay out of sight. It's just that my future brother-in-law told me that the MacDowells said I could trust the foreman, so I… I showed myself to you. Everyone else will just have to think there's a vampire living in the house or something."

Travis nodded and picked his hat up from the table. He must have tossed it there instead of using the hook by the door. It was the sort of thing someone might do in a rush.

He walked out the door. Sophia realized he already had his boots on. He'd come in without stopping at the boot jack, breaking his own rule about boots in the house. He'd really been worried about her.

A little rush of gratitude filled some of the empty space inside her.

"Travis?"

He turned back to her, his expression serious, illuminated by the light from the kitchen. Beyond him, the night was black, the night he would have ridden in, looking for her.

"I'm not a crazy recluse. I'm just a recluse, okay?"

"I get it."

She'd been holding her breath. Now she could breathe.

He tapped his hat against his thigh. "I never told you the reason I came looking for you in the first place. That kitten got more lively when he warmed up, so I found the mother cat's new hiding spot. She didn't object when I slipped him in with his brothers."

"Oh." She took a deeper breath. The night air felt fresh. "Oh, that's great news. She's not a terrible mother after all."

"I never said she was. She had her reasons. We just

don't know what they were. I put out some extra food, in case she was worried about having enough to eat. The other barn cat will probably get to it first, but it's worth a try. When I left, she was pretty relaxed and letting all three kittens nurse."

Maybe Sophia was crazy after all, because it felt like Travis had just given her the best gift. "Thank you. Thank you so much."

"I wouldn't want you to get too hopeful. That kitten's had a rough time of it so far."

"But now he'll be okay."

"We've given him a chance, at least. I'll see you when I get back in a few days. Good night." He touched the brim of his hat, and walked into the dark.

A few days?

She shut herself in the house.

Chapter 8

She didn't wake up until noon.

What was the point? Everyone was gone again. Everyone meaning Travis and the horses.

Sophia was willing to bet that Travis had been saddling up those horses before dawn, true to the cowboy stereotype. She looked out the window toward the empty barn and tried not to feel resentful that the horses had been taken away. They had to work.

She wished she had to work. Resentment for her ex bubbled up, a toxic brew that made her stomach turn.

Thanks, Deezee.

Actually, Deezee was probably working, too. The more he partied, the more people wanted to pay him to appear at their parties. The more outrageous he got, the more bookings he got. Busting into that Texas Rescue ball and making a scene had been a smart thing for him to do. During their week in Saint Barth, his cell phone had blown up with offers.

Not hers.

A movie studio didn't make job offers to actors who skipped town without notice. A production couldn't build a PR campaign if their star said outrageous, unpredictable things. What helped Deezee's career killed hers.

Looking back, she doubted Deezee had realized how much he was hurting her. She doubted he would have cared if he had.

But she should have known better. She should have cared.

Deezee had lied to her. He'd cheated on her with other women. But he hadn't forced her to party like a rock star. That was her fault.

Thanks, Sophia.

She couldn't spend all day at the kitchen window, waiting to see which cowboy would come in at sundown. It wouldn't be Travis; that was all that mattered. She couldn't be seen by anyone else. She couldn't make another stupid mistake like she had yesterday, falling asleep on the picnic table. Alex and Grace wouldn't be able to pull another great hiding spot out of thin air. This was it. This was her only place to sleep, eat, hide and sleep some more.

But today, she didn't have the desire to go right back to sleep. She felt at least a little bit rested for a change. She'd slept in a real bed instead of crashing on the couch with the television on.

All week, she'd been avoiding the master bedroom. It was too spacious and too obviously someone else's room, with its family photos of little boys and a handsome father from decades past. She knew Mrs. Mac-Dowell was a widow. She didn't like to look at photos of the dead father. She had her own.

But last night, after Travis had left, she'd wandered into one of the smaller bedrooms, one that looked like it was intended for guests. It had a queen-sized bed instead of a king. It had paintings of Texas bluebonnets on the walls instead of family photos. She'd been able to sleep there.

Great. So now she wasn't sleepy, but she still couldn't leave the house. Her one little foray to the picnic table yesterday had almost resulted in blowing her cover, because she'd lacked enough common sense to come back inside when sitting in the sun made her drowsy. She had no common sense. No self-discipline. She was in a prison of her own making, because she couldn't handle her own life.

Round and round her thoughts started to go. She hated them, because they always led to the same conclusion: she was a failure. She hated herself, and she was stuck.

But a new voice broke through the old soundtrack.

If you want to go outside, then open the door and walk outside.

Travis.

If he saw her standing here, if he could hear what she was saying to herself in her head, he would cut through all the nonsense with one of those infuriatingly simple solutions.

You're a grown woman, he'd say. A grown woman who was standing here, wishing she could go outside for a breath of fresh air but afraid that would be some catastrophic mistake. She'd fall asleep on a picnic table again, and let down Alex and Grace, and be laughed at in the press for being found on a cattle ranch, of all places. If she went outside, it would start a chain of disasters. It made sense to her.

Or it had, before last night. Before she'd spent some time with Travis and realized that all the puzzle pieces didn't have to go together in the complicated order she'd been putting them.

If you don't want to be in here, then open the door and go out there.

She opened the kitchen door, and stepped on a pile of zucchini.

She cursed as the zucchini scattered. She spewed every variation of the F-bomb that Deezee had ever shouted while playing a combat video game. She'd hated the way he'd lost control when he killed animated, imaginary enemies, yet she sounded just like him.

She shut up. It was zucchini, not the end of the world. Heck, her own *Space* character had managed to save an entire civilization without resorting to so much drama.

The zucchini rolled to a stop. A note was wedged into what remained of the pyramid by the door.

Sophia—
     When I got to my house, I saw that Clay had left a bunch of zucchini in my sink. His mother had a bumper crop, and she stopped by the bunkhouse when no one was there and left a ton in their kitchen. I don't think it's breaking and entering if someone's mother does it. The real crime here is that nobody can eat as much zucchini as Clay's mother grew. I'm passing off some of it onto you. It might make a nice change from cereal.
—Travis

P.S. I left you some milk in case you don't actually
like your cereal dry. It's in the barn fridge. Please
wear boots or shoes. You have enough scars. I
don't want you to get any more.

Sophia stared at the letter. The man had been doing
just fine, dropping little smart-aleck comments, but then
he'd had to finish it up with that line about the scars.
She must be crazy after all, because she felt all choked
up by a hastily written P.S.

Sophia picked up the zucchini one by one, cradling
them in her arm like a bouquet, and carried them into
the kitchen. She put the zucchini in the sink. The letter she spread out on the counter. She read it again and
smoothed out the crease. Read it again.

Then she went into the master bedroom, where Alex
had left her suitcases. She hadn't unpacked them yet.
Just reaching in and wearing the first thing she touched
had taken all the energy she had, but now she lifted out
the neat piles of clothes and carried them down the hall
to the bluebonnet bedroom.

Trip after trip, she emptied the suitcases her sister
had filled for her. As Sophia's personal assistant, Grace
had been packing her bags ever since they'd moved to
LA. Maybe Sophia hadn't wanted to unpack these final
suitcases. Alex was going to be the person Grace took
trips with from now on. These were the last shirts her
sister would ever fold for her with care and love.

"This is depressing as hell." Sophia spoke the words
loudly, but her voice didn't have to reach lofty rafters
in here. The carpet and quilts of the guest bedroom absorbed the sound. The words weren't as scary out loud
as they were when they echoed in her head.

Whether or not it was depressing, whether or not it was some kind of symbolic final vestige of her life with her sister, the suitcases had to be unpacked now, because Sophia needed her shoes. The only boots she had were the thigh-highs with the killer heels, but she knew that Grace would have packed workout clothes and a selection of running shoes for Sophia to choose from, depending on her mood and her clothes' color scheme.

She found the sneakers. Sophia left the empty suitcase on the king-sized master bed. In her bedroom, she changed into a shirt that had sleeves and a pair of shorts that barely covered her rear but were made of denim. She laced up her most sturdy pair of cross-trainers and once more opened the kitchen door.

She wasn't going to fall asleep or get caught by a stranger or ruin her career. She was going to get some milk that Travis had left for her in the barn.

Nothing bad was going to happen.

The fresh air cleared the last bit of fog from Sophia's head as she walked the hundred yards or so to the barn.

The heat of the day was building. Her yoga instructor would say every molecule of hot air shimmered with energy that she could welcome into her lungs with intentional breaths. Sophia could practice here, doing yoga outside on the flagstone, holding poses that took all her concentration in the May heat. If she set an alarm clock tomorrow, she could get up a little earlier and go for a run before it got too hot.

If she really wanted more work in Hollywood, that would be the smart thing to do. Having a great body was an essential part of winning roles. If she let herself go too long without exercise, she'd pay a price. She really didn't want to keep paying for stupid decisions. *If you want to keep your fitness level, then work out.*

She'd have to be careful who saw her. But if only she and Travis were around, and he should happen to catch her in the middle of a workout in her painted-on exercise clothing…her muscles working, her skin glistening…

The possibilities sent a sizzle of sexual energy through her.

She slid open the barn door, using chest muscles that still felt strong despite weeks of laziness. Every LA personal trainer emphasized pectoral tone to keep the breasts high. Having good breasts was part of her job.

She'd only had to reveal them once in her career, during a love scene in a serious crime drama. Her male costar's bare buttocks had been in the frame as well. As makeup artists had dabbed foundation on his butt cheeks and brushed shadow into her cleavage, the two of them had attempted awkward jokes until the director had called for quiet on the set. For hours, her costar kept popping some kind of bubblegum-flavored mints that smelled grossly sweeter with each take. There had been nothing sexy about filming that scene, but the director had known what he was doing, and the final cut had looked scorching hot on the big screen.

The movie had only gotten modest box office distribution, but Travis might have seen it. Had he found it arousing? He must have. One couldn't be human and not find the finished scene arousing.

She shut the door behind herself. The interior of the barn was dim after the blinding sun. She took a moment to let her eyes adjust, leaning against the same post Travis had leaned against last night. He'd given her his time and attention, willing to talk. Only to talk.

Not willing to be seduced. Not even by a movie star.

That sizzle died. When she'd reached out to touch him, he'd pulled on a shirt and left her standing in his office. Unemployed or not, she still looked like a movie star. What had she done that had made it so easy for him to resist her?

She walked slowly down the aisle, evaluating her posture and carriage, working on it as an actor. If she saw herself on film now, what kind of character traits would she be relaying to the audience?

She hadn't been very convincing in the role of seductress last night. She didn't believe she was still a movie star, so she wasn't acting like a movie star. That had to be the problem. Deezee's infidelity had shaken her confidence. The publicity had been humiliating, so now Sophia must be giving off some kind of insecure ex-girlfriend vibe.

Guys hated that. If she could turn back time to the person she'd been before Deezee, she would have Travis eating out of the palm of her hand. He'd be grateful if she chased a water droplet over his skin with the tip of her finger, because the sexy and smart Sophia Jackson would be the one doing the chasing, not the depressed and lonely creature she'd turned into. Travis couldn't resist a movie star.

Could he?

He already had. When they'd met on the road, she'd seen the precise moment on his face when he'd first realized who she was, but he hadn't exactly fallen all over himself to get her autograph. He'd told her to get behind the wheel and drive herself off his ranch, actually.

Don't call us; we'll call you.

She paused at his office window. There was nothing

in that functional space that implied he was enchanted by Hollywood or its stars. For the first time in her life, it occurred to her that being a celebrity could be a disadvantage.

She'd just have to make him want her, anyway.

Men had wanted her long before she was famous. Really, that was why she'd become famous. People of both sexes had always noticed her. *Charisma*, Grace called it. An aura. Whatever it was, it was the reason Sophia had been put in films. The public might think movie stars were noticeable because they were already famous, but that wasn't how it worked. The charisma came first. They were noticed first. Stardom came second.

Where did Travis fit in?

The refrigerator was in the medical room. She headed for it while fretting over sex appeal and stardom, wondering if she could stand rejection from a cowboy any better than from a producer, and nearly stepped on the proof that everything she worried about, all of it, was insignificant.

At her feet, curled into a little ball in front of the fridge, was the kitten.

Sophia picked him up gingerly. It was humbling to hold a complete living being in her hand. He was still alive for now, but he couldn't survive on his own. The weight of his impending mortality should have been heavy. It seemed wrong that he was little more than a fluffy feather in her palm.

Travis had said the kitten was weak to start with, and Sophia knew next to nothing about kittens. She was going to lose this battle. It was a pattern she knew too well. Losing her sister, losing her lover, losing her career, failing auditions, failing to keep her scholarship…

Failing. She hated to fail.

She studied the newborn's face. "I'm not a very good mother, either, but I'm going to try, okay?"

Then she slipped the kitten inside her shirt.

Chapter 9

Travis was not obsessed with Sophia Jackson.

He just couldn't stop thinking about her.

He'd left the milk in the fridge this morning with no intention of returning for the rest of the week, but as the morning had turned into afternoon, he'd already started convincing himself that he should head back to his office this evening. There were too many things on his to-do list that he hadn't touched last night.

He'd touched Sophia's scars instead.

Why had she let him into her personal life like that? *I'm not a crazy recluse.*

She wanted to be understood, that much was clear to him. He just didn't know how much to read into the fact that she wanted *him* to understand her.

A pickup truck pulled up to the fencing they'd built for this year's roundup. Travis recognized the pickup as belonging to one of the MacDowell brothers who was coming to work these last few days of branding and doctoring. Travis was grateful for the distraction. He left the calf pen to greet Braden.

Braden MacDowell, like his brothers, was a physician in Austin. He'd taken over the reins at the hospital his father had founded, but he valued his family's ranching legacy as well, so it wasn't unusual to see him here. At least one MacDowell was sure to lend a hand during the busy months, if not all three brothers.

Travis respected the MacDowells. They visited their mama. They knew how to rope and ride. And they'd been wise enough to hire him.

Not to get too full of himself, but it said a lot that they'd asked him to keep the River Mack thriving as a cow-calf operation. They could've just rented the land out to a corporate operation that maintained its headquarters in another state. Travis wouldn't have stayed on the River Mack in that case. He preferred to work with a family that knew how to keep their saddles oiled and their guns greased, as the saying went.

"I just got away from the office," Braden said as Travis walked up to him and shook hands. "I trust there's still plenty of fun to be had?"

"Talk to me tomorrow about how fun it feels. You leave your necktie and briefcase at home?"

The ribbing was good-natured. Braden was in shape, but there was still a big difference between bench-pressing weights in a gym and hauling around a hundred-pound calf who didn't appreciate being picked up.

"I've got aspirin in the glove box." Braden dropped the tailgate and thumped an oversized cooler. "I brought supplies."

Travis helped him carry the cooler full of sports drinks closer to the working crew and then helped himself to one. He drank while Patch, one of the best cow dogs in Texas, greeted Braden.

They kept sports drinks in the barn fridge, too. When Sophia got the milk, she'd see them. Travis hoped she knew she was welcome to take whatever she needed. He should have told her that in the note, maybe, and damn it all to hell, he was thinking about her again. Would he go five minutes without thinking of her today?

"All right, back to work with you," Braden said to the dog, but to Travis's surprise, Braden didn't head for the work area himself. "How's Sophia Jackson treating my house?"

Travis forced himself to swallow his drink around the surprise of hearing her name spoken. She was a big secret he'd been keeping from everyone, but it made sense that Braden knew. Of course he knew; he must have signed the lease.

"The house looks the same as always. You can't tell there's anyone's living there."

"No sounds of breaking glass coming from inside? She hasn't set the couch on fire or gone rockstar and destroyed it yet?"

Travis frowned at the expectation that she might. The closest thing he'd seen to any wild behavior had been when Sophia had dropped the plastic wedges on the kitchen floor. No harm there. "I'm not one to spy on your houseguests, but there's been nothing like that."

She cries a lot. She sleeps a lot. Those insights were his. He didn't care to share them. It felt like it would be betraying Sophia. She didn't want to be stared at. She didn't want to be talked about. Fair enough.

"She's not my houseguest," Braden said, his tone tight. "She's my tenant."

Travis turned to look over the milling herd and the distant horizon, waiting.

Braden studied the horizon, too. "I was against renting the house to her, but one of the ER docs, Alex Gregory, is engaged to her sister. Alex seems to think she's salvageable. He offered to cosign the lease. If she destroys the place, he's good for it, but if my mother comes back from her year in Africa and finds her grandmother's antiques destroyed, money won't make it right."

Travis kept a sharp eye on the calm herd. There was no reason to believe they would suddenly stampede— but they could. "You got a reason for assuming she'd bust furniture?"

"You don't keep up with celebrity news," Braden said.

"I'm surprised you do." That was putting it mildly.

"Only when it affects me. Twice, Texas Rescue invited her to make an appearance to help raise awareness of their work. Twice, she blew their event. My wife and I were going to one of them. I was expecting this elegant actress. My wife was excited to meet her. Instead, this banshee ruined the ball before it even got started. I should have read the gossip earlier. She'd been trashing hotel rooms and blowing off events for months. Now she's living in my home. I don't like it."

It was incredible that MacDowell thought Sophia would destroy someone's family heirlooms, but Travis had known the MacDowells for the past six years. He'd known Sophia six days.

Travis killed the rest of his bottle in long, slow gulps. It took only twenty ounces for him to decide to trust his gut. Sophia didn't mean anyone any harm. He'd seen the physical evidence of the harm others had done to her, and he'd seen her crying her heart out when she thought she was alone. She was a woman who'd been pushed to the edge, but she wasn't going to destroy someone else's lifetime of memories. She just wouldn't.

"She's serious about hiding," Travis repeated. "She's not going to do anything to attract attention to herself. Your stuff is safe."

Braden was silent for a moment. "She's beautiful, isn't she?"

Travis turned his head slowly, very slowly, and met the man's stare. "We weren't discussing Sophia's looks. If you think my judgment is so easily clouded, we'd best come to an understanding on that."

He and Braden gauged one another for a long moment, until, inexplicably, Braden started to grin. "I trust you on horses and I trust you on cattle. I've known you to have a sixth sense about the weather. Maybe you don't find women any harder to read than that, but as a married man, I'm not going to put any money down on that bet. It puts my mind at ease a bit to hear that you don't think Miss Jackson is going to fly off the handle, but I'm still going to stop by and pick up a few breakables before I go."

Travis saw his opportunity and took it. "She won't answer the door if she doesn't know you. I'll go in with you. I've got work at my desk I can knock out while you're gathering up your breakables. If we take the truck, we can be done and back here inside two hours."

"I'm locked out of my own house, technically." Braden sounded disgusted. "Landlords can't just walk into the property once it's been rented out."

Travis paced away from the kitchen door and Braden's legalities. The zucchini was gone. Sophia had gotten up and gone out, then. He wasn't going to jump to any crazy conclusions. She wasn't dead or dying, languishing somewhere, needing his help.

Where was she?

There were no horses in the barn, or else that would have been the logical place to assume she was.

"Let's hit the barn," Braden suggested. "Maybe she'll show up while you're taking care of your paperwork."

Travis had barely slid open the barn door when he heard Sophia calling out.

"Hello? Is someone there? Can you help me?" The distress in her voice was obvious as she emerged from his office. He'd already started for her before her next words. "Travis! It's you. Thank God, it's you."

She started down the aisle toward him at a half run, clutching her heart with two hands.

They met halfway. He stopped her from crashing into him by catching her shoulders in his hands. At a glance, she didn't seem to be hurt. Her expression was panicked, but her color was normal and she seemed to be moving fine. "What's wrong?"

She peeled her hands away from her chest to show him. "It's the kitten. It's dying."

"It's the—" Her words sank in. Travis let go of her shoulders and turned away for a moment to control his reaction, a harsh mixture of relief and anger. He'd thought she was having a heart attack.

"Do you hear that?" she cried.

He turned to look, and yes, she was really crying. She dashed her cheek on her shoulder.

"His cries are just so pitiful. He's been pleading for

help like that for six hours. I can't stand it. He cries until he's exhausted, and then he wakes up and cries again. I don't know what to do for him."

Her distress was real. She was just too softhearted for the hard reality that not every animal could be saved. Travis took off his hat and gestured with it toward the office. "Come on, I'll take a look. Did you say six hours?"

"I came in to get the milk from the fridge, and he was on the floor, just lying out there. I warmed him up like you did, but then I couldn't find the mother cat for the longest time. The kitten started crying while I went over every square inch of this place. It took me an hour to find her, but when I put the baby in with the others, the mother just up and left, like, 'Here, have three babies.'"

Travis pulled out his desk chair. "Have a seat."

"I've been in this chair all day. I couldn't look anything up on the internet about what to feed a kitten, because your computer is password protected."

"That it is."

She sat in the chair he offered, but she glared at him like he'd invented the concept of computer passwords just to annoy her. "You've got all these books on animals in here, but do you know what they contain? Info on how many calories are in a frigging *acre* of alfalfa to calculate how many calves it'll feed. Chart after chart on alfalfa and Bahia grass. What to feed a cow, how much to feed a cow, how much to *grow* to feed a cow. Who needs to know crap like that?"

"That would be me." Travis didn't dare smile when she was working through a mixture of tears and indignation. He let her vent.

"Do you know what those books don't contain? *What*

to feed a newborn kitten. Not one word. I couldn't call you for help. You're out on a horse all day."

"I'll give you my cell phone number, but there's no reception out on the range. If you leave a message, it'll ping me if I happen to catch a signal."

Braden strolled into the office with a dish in his hand. "Looks like you tried to give it a saucer of milk. On my mother's fine china."

Sophia jerked back in the chair, clutching the kitten to her chest.

Travis had seen that skittish reaction too many times. This time, he put his hand on her shoulder, a little weight to keep her from jumping out of her own skin.

"It's okay. This is Braden MacDowell, one of the ranch owners. He already knew you were here. Your name's already on his lease."

She sniffed and looked at Braden resentfully. "I remember you from that stupid ball. You're the CEO of the hospital."

"Guilty."

"You shouldn't sneak up like that. I thought I was alone with Travis. Usually only one person comes in at sundown."

The implication hit Travis squarely. "What if it hadn't been me tonight? You would've blown your cover. I told you it wouldn't be me tonight. You came out of that office without knowing who was here."

"Trust me, I had hours to think about that while this kitten cried his heart out. I knew whoever came in was going to get a big surprise, and then he was going to get rich. I'd have to pay him hush money to keep my secret. It's like being blackmailed, only you go ahead and get it over with and offer to pay them up front." She rested her head back on the chair and sighed. "It's only money. That's the way it goes."

Travis was stunned.

She frowned at him. "What did you expect me to do? I couldn't just let a kitten die because the paparazzi might find me."

"No, of course not." But of course, she could have done exactly that. She could have left the kitten where a ranch hand might find it and then run away to hide in safety. But she'd stayed to comfort a struggling animal instead of leaving it to cry alone.

"Sorry I startled you," Braden said. "I'm surprised you remember me. We'd barely been introduced at the fund-raiser when you…left."

"I remember everything about that night."

With that cryptic statement, she resumed her tale of frustration, how the kitten hadn't known what to do with the milk, and how she'd tried warming it and holding the kitten's mouth near the surface. Her story was full of mistakes, but it wasn't comical; she'd tried hard to succeed at something foreign to her.

He noticed something else as well. Now that Braden was present, her manner was slightly different. She sat a little straighter and told her story in a more measured way. The contrast was clear to Travis. When she'd thought it was just the two of them, she'd been more emotional. Raw. Real.

Sophia didn't keep her guard up around him. There was a trust between them, an intimacy that she didn't extend to everyone. He wondered if she was aware of it.

"I tried leaving the three kittens together. I snuck away and stayed away for at least half an hour. I wanted to give the mother a chance to come back for them, in case she was just scared of me, you know? But when I came back, they were all crying. All of them. The mother cat didn't come back until I took this kitten away again." Her blue eyes filled with tears, and she quickly turned away from Braden. She spoke softly to Travis. "For a while there, I thought I'd doomed them all."

"You were doing your best. You were being as kind as a person could be." And if he turned his back to Braden to shut him out of their private conversation, well, there was no crime in that.

The kitten began another round of plaintive, hungry mewing.

"The road to hell is paved with good intentions," she murmured. "Listening to this kitten cry has been hell."

"I imagine it has."

She looked up at him, tired and trusting. "I'm so glad you're here."

The words stretched between them, an imaginary line connecting just the two of them for one moment. Then it snapped. Her sleepy-lidded eyes flew open as she realized what she'd said. "To help, I mean. I'm so glad you're here to help."

She was still scared, then. Still unsure of this power between them. It made her nervous enough that she put up her guard, which for a movie star meant shaking back some incredible blond hair and flipping her tired expression to one filled with a devil-may-care bravado. "Besides, you just saved me a fortune in hush money."

Braden chuckled, the expected response, but Travis saw through the act. This wasn't a one-sided attraction on his part, but she wasn't ready to admit it. Now was not the time or place to do anything with the knowledge. He was a patient man. It was enough to know that she wanted to see him as much as he wanted to see her.

She still held the kitten in two hands against her chest, so Travis gave her a boost out of the chair by placing his hand under her elbow. "Come on. Abandoned kittens need a specific kitten milk replacer. Let's see if I have any around here. If I don't, Braden will go to the feed store and get you some."

Chapter 10

The pickup rocked over the rolling terrain, sending the headlight beams bouncing off fence posts and mesquite trees. Although Braden drove with all the speed one could manage on rough roads, they were getting back to camp far later than Travis had expected. Travis was returning with a hell of a lot more baggage than he'd expected, too, and all of it was in his head.

Maybe in his heart.

Definitely in his body.

Damn it. Every time he thought checking on Sophia would set everything to rest, he got more than he bargained for.

They'd found some powdered milk replacer in the bunkhouse kitchen. There'd been just a few scoops left-over from some other cowboy's past attempt to help out another cat, so they'd taken it back to the barn. While

Braden had made the run to the feed store, Travis had taught Sophia how to mix the replacer, how to slip an eyedropper into the kitten's mouth, how to hold the kitten a little counterintuitively while feeding it.

There'd been physical contact between the two of them, and a lot of it. Shoulders and hips had brushed as they huddled over the kitten. Hands guided hands to find just the right angle or apply just the right amount of pressure. He'd cuffed up his sleeves, and the sensation of Sophia's soft skin on his exposed wrist or forearm ignited awareness everywhere. By the time the kitten had been settled into a small box with a bit of an old horse blanket, that incidental contact had become so addicting, neither of them had moved away.

Sophia had been nearly as relieved as the kitten when it fell asleep from a full belly instead of from exhaustion. It would have been the most natural move for Travis to drop a kiss on Sophia's lips. Not one of passion, but one of camaraderie, the kind between couples who'd been together through thick and thin.

He'd almost kissed her. *You did well.*

She'd almost kissed him. *Thank you.*

But in the end, Braden had returned with enough milk replacer for ten cats, and Sophia had drifted closer to the light over the barn sink in order to read the instructions on the can. They said a kitten this young was going to wake up and cry for a feeding every two hours.

Travis was used to long nights caring for young or sick animals. Braden was a doctor who thought nothing of overnight shifts, but Sophia…

It turned out that movie production schedules pushed actors to work without sleep as well. Sophia didn't flinch at the schedule.

With his head, his heart, his body, Travis felt himself falling for her too deep, too fast.

Too reckless.

The pickup truck bounced out of the rut in the dirt road, and Travis cracked his head against the side window.

He cursed at an unapologetic Braden. "Your breakables would've been safer in the house. They probably just flew out of the truck bed."

Braden kept his eyes on the road. "I didn't take anything out of the house."

"You're not worried she's going to break everything?" Travis knew the past few hours had shown Braden a different Sophia Jackson than he'd been expecting to see, but Travis wanted to hear him say it. Anyone who maligned Sophia should have to eat his words.

"I've been thinking about that."

Not good enough. Travis managed a noncommittal grunt to keep him talking.

"I did see some pretty incriminating photos, but she was never alone while she was flipping birds and screaming at those photographers."

"Paparazzi," Travis corrected him. But hell, were there photos out there of beautiful Sophia being so ugly?

"That jerk of a boyfriend of hers is behind her in every one, or sometimes in front. Looked like he was shoving her out of his way in one. After seeing the way he crashed that ball, he probably was."

It was the last thing Travis wanted to hear. Not after all that warmth, all that soft skin, all those tears for a kitten. He couldn't let go of that. He couldn't let go of the Sophia he knew. He couldn't accept that she had a boyfriend.

"You got any more details than that?"

"It was a black-tie event. Thousand-dollar donation per ticket. Red carpet to give the guests a thrill for their money. You know how it is."

"Not really." *Get to the boyfriend.*

"Everyone's all pretty and on their best behavior. Every camera in the house is pointed at Sophia. That's what she's there for, to give everyone a little taste of glamor. People pay an outrageous price to eat dinner in the same room as the celebrities."

Had Sophia once enjoyed that?

Don't stare at me. Quit talking about me.

"Next thing I know, some jackass in basketball shoes and a ball cap is jumping on the table. Walking on the silverware, kicking the centerpiece, making a lot of noise. Alex pulled Sophia behind his back. That was the first thing I noticed, Alex keeping Sophia behind himself, so I knew this jerk had come to cause trouble for her."

There was nothing Travis could do about it but listen. His hand was clenched in a fist on his knee.

"My brothers and I were ready to take him out. He was standing on my wife's salad, goddammit, but once every camera in the place was focused on him, he dropped to one knee and started apologizing to Sophia. As apologies went, it was crap. Maybe a sentence. Alex was pissed. Her sister was stunned."

"And Sophia?"

Braden hesitated for only a moment. "She ditched her commitment to Texas Rescue and left with him. She looked pretty happy about it, so no one tried to stop her."

Travis couldn't speak. A knife in the chest would do that to a man. The thought of Sophia choosing to be with an ass who'd destroy the happiness of everyone around him was like a knife in the chest.

"But you see how that turned out. She's here alone. After getting to know her a little bit today, it's obvious the two of them aren't as alike as the photos make it look. My guess is that she's hiding from him as much as the rest of the world."

They hit another pothole, which gave Travis the perfect excuse to curse again. "I should have been told. Alex said she was hiding from cameras."

"If the boyfriend turns up again, things will break. More than my grandma's antiques. That kind of hyped-up guy dances too close to the line."

"Got a name?"

"DJ something. Something inane."

"*Paparazzi* is an inane word, too. I'll let the men know we're keeping everyone off the River Mack ranch whose name we don't already know."

"We would've been here sooner, but the gate at the main road was closed," Grace said.

Sophia nodded at her sister as if that made sense.

"All the gates were closed this time. I had to get out three times to open them. I saw a guy on a horse at the last one, the foreman we met last time. We waved at each other and he rode away."

Grace was talking to her through the open window of Alex's pickup. She'd started talking the moment they'd pulled up, not waiting for Alex to shut off the engine.

"We didn't see any cows, though. Not this time." Grace hopped out of the truck and gave the door a pat after closing it. "But we brought the truck, just in case. We can drive off the road if we have to go around a cow again."

Sophia nodded some more, so full of emotion at seeing her sister that she wasn't really listening to what she was saying. It was just so good to see her face. She'd missed her so much.

Sophia hesitated at the edge of the flagstone. Her sister had been so adamant that Sophia should only call for an emergency, and Grace hadn't called her once, not one single time in the past week to ask how she was doing. Was this how their relationship was supposed to be now? Polite and friendly visits once a week?

Sophia wanted to run to her sister and give her a bear hug. Instead, she twisted her fingers together as she kept nodding and smiling.

Alex got out of his side of the truck and spoke to Grace. "Sophia looks like she missed you almost as much as you missed her. Is one of you going to hug the other, or what?"

"You missed me?" Sophia asked, but Grace couldn't answer because she'd already run up to the patio and thrown her arms around her.

"I've been so worried about you," Grace said, hugging her hard.

Sophia took a split second to think before blurting out something snarky. *Yeah, I could tell by the way you totally ignored me.*

She pulled back from the hug just far enough to smooth Grace's dark gold hair into place, a gesture that went back to their tween years, when they'd first started playing with curling irons and hair spray. "When you're worried about me, you could give me a call. I'd love to hear from you."

"But—but I have called you. A lot."

"The phone hasn't rung once. I just assumed you were busy with your new job and with…" She gestured toward Alex, who was standing beside the truck. Then Sophia realized she'd made it sound like Grace was busy getting busy with Alex, which wasn't a great thing to think about her sister, even if it was probably true.

Sophia almost blushed. "I mean, with your wedding planning. I thought you were busy planning your wedding." *Without me.*

"I called, but you never picked up, so I figured you didn't want to talk. Or maybe I was calling you too late at night."

"I'm up all night long. I'm taking care of a kitten. It needs fed every two hours. It's pretty exhausting, but I volunteered for it, so…"

"You did?" Grace's amazement was genuine. She wasn't an actor.

Sophia was. She pretended not to be hurt that her sister was amazed she would volunteer to sacrifice her sleep for something besides herself. For years, Sophia had cared for Grace, but the freshest memory was obviously of Sophia blowing off everyone and everything for wild parties.

"It's just for a few days," Sophia said, a brilliant performance of perfect cheerfulness. She didn't sound offended at all, not hurt one bit. "The vet is scheduled to come out then, and Travis is sure he'll know a mother cat somewhere that just had a litter and can take another kitten. This one is so young, its eyes aren't even open yet, so it really needs a cat mother, not me."

"Wow. I'm so impressed. I had no idea you knew so much about cats." Grace gave her arm an extra squeeze. "But I'm not surprised. You've always been able to do anything you set your mind to."

Sophia didn't know what to say to that. It sounded like her sister still admired her. Considering the front-row seat she'd had to Sophia's self-destructing spiral, that was something of a miracle.

Sophia didn't want to start bawling and ruin a perfectly lovely conversation. She blinked away the threatening tears and focused on the barn. "I got a crash course on cats from Travis. The foreman you waved at."

"He promised me he'd check on you. He has, hasn't he?"

Sophia nodded some more and wished he was here to check on her now. It would be nice for him to see that her sister didn't hate her. He'd only seen them together that first day, snapping at each other over a cow on the road.

Well, Sophia had been doing most of the snapping. Travis must think Sophia was the world's worst sister.

Alex was standing back, giving them some personal space. He really was a pretty decent guy. Handsome, too, in a doctor-like, Clark Kent kind of way.

He turned toward the barn. "Speaking of Travis, is he around? Where is everyone?"

"It's May." Sophia said it the way Travis would.

"What does that mean?"

She shrugged. "I have no earthly idea, but it's the answer to everything around here. Apparently, cowboys are scarce on a ranch in May."

"Or else they're out working on the range," Alex said.

"I think its calving season. We get a few injuries in the ER every year at this time from roundups."

"I'm dying to see this kitten." Grace sounded as carefree as Sophia could remember her sounding since the day their parents had died. Alex must be more than just a decent guy, because Sophia knew she hadn't taken any burdens from Grace's shoulders, not lately. Alex must have lightened that load.

He picked up some grocery bags from the bed of the pickup. "Let's get these inside and check the ringer on that phone. I don't want you two to miss any more calls."

Sophia reached for one of the bags, but Alex shook his head. "It's okay. I've got it."

"Thank you." She meant for more than the groceries. Could he tell?

He winked at her, his eyes blue like her own. Like a brother might have had, if she'd ever had a brother. "She's happier when you're part of her life. I want Grace to be happy, you know."

"I know."

"Let's go fix that dinosaur of a phone."

Grace opened her cab door and reached for a basket. "I almost forgot. Our neighbor grows vegetables, and you wouldn't believe how much zucchini he had. I brought you some. You don't see this in LA. Isn't it great?"

"Oh, zucchini. Yes. Great."

If she could point at a mattress and smile for fifty bucks, she could certainly beam at a basket of zucchini that her sister thought would make her happy. Apparently, the gift of love in Texas during the month of May was zucchini, whether it was from a mother to a ranch hand, from Travis to her, from Grace to—

From Travis to her?

It would be crazy to think he loved her, just because he'd left her a batch of zucchini.

With a note that said he didn't want her to get any more scars.

As she held the door open for her family with one hand and balanced an overflowing basket of zucchini with the other, she couldn't help but look at the empty barn one more time.

A gift of love? She was being too dramatic again—but something felt different now. The zucchini had marked some kind of turning point. Before, Travis would have expected her to do something simple yet impossible: *if you need milk replacer, go to the feed store.* Instead, he'd sent Braden to get it.

It was almost June. May had been full of loneliness and failure and zucchini. But June might be different. A new month. A new vegetable? A new chance to spend time with Travis.

She could hardly wait for June.

Chapter 11

Tomatoes.

June was only half over, but if Sophia saw another to-mato, she might scream. Or barf.

It turned out the potted plants lining one side of the flagstone patio were Mrs. MacDowell's absurdly fertile tomatoes. There were so many, they ripened and fell off the vines, bounced out of their pots and split open on the patio, where they proceeded to cook on the hot stone in the June sun. Every deep yoga breath Sophia took brought in shimmering molecules of hot energy that smelled vaguely like lasagna.

The smell made her stomach turn.

She'd had such high hopes for June. She'd imagined basking in the sun, breathing deeply, feeling the health and strength of every muscle in her body as she went through all the yoga routines she could remember. Travis wouldn't be able to resist spying on her. Drooling over her silver-screen-worthy body, he would spend lots of time with her, and she wouldn't be lonely in the least.

Instead, she was the one who drooled over Travis, spying on him from the kitchen window. June had brought him back from wherever he'd been disappearing to, but although he spent part of every day in the barn, he was never alone. The ranch must be too big for just one person, because there were always other cowboys around. Usually, they left in pairs on horseback, off to do whatever the heck kept ranchers busy in the month of June.

Her eye was always drawn to Travis. She knew the way he sat a horse now, the set of his shoulders, the way a coil of rope always rested on the back of his saddle when he rode away, the way the rope was looped on the saddle horn and resting on top of his right thigh when he returned.

Not today. She heard what sounded like a motorcycle.

She ran to the window in time to catch Travis roaring away on an ATV. He was in jeans and a plaid shirt, as usual, but he wore no hat to keep the wind out of his hair. He drove the four-wheeler the way he galloped a horse, almost standing up, leaning over the handlebars into the wind. He looked so strong and young and free, something in her yearned to be with him.

"Wait for me." But saying the words out loud didn't make them seem any less pitiful than when they echoed in her head.

She put her hand on the glass, well and truly isolated. If only a director would yell *cut*. If only the prop team would help her out of a mock space capsule. If only Grace were waiting to bring her out of her self-induced sorrow, to remind her that it was only a movie, and the real Sophia could have a bowl of ice cream and paint her fingernails and never, ever have to wonder if she'd make it back to Earth.

Normalcy. It had always been such a relief to return to the normal world after experiencing a character's intense emotions. Now her real life was the unrealistic one, and her old, normal life was the fantasy.

As Travis rode away, Sophia kept her greedy eyes on him and indulged her favorite fantasy, the one where she wasn't famous yet and had no reason to hide. If she and Travis had met when she was nineteen instead of twenty-nine, she would have flirted outrageously with him. As a young cowboy, he wouldn't have been able to resist letting her hitch a ride to the barn on the running board of his ATV. She would've been the best part of his day, his pretty blond girlfriend holding on to him so she wouldn't fall off while he drove. He would've saved up his money to take her to the movies.

"Cut," she whispered to herself.

In real life, she was the one in the movies, a Hollywood star who couldn't hide forever. There was no stopping the fame now. She couldn't make people forget her face.

"No, really. Cut, before you drive yourself crazy."

She pushed hard with her hand, forcing herself away from the window. She was dressed for a morning yoga workout, but she hadn't kept track of where the ranch hands were. There were five different guys who showed up at least a few days each week. Who had shown up for work with Travis today? Was anyone still in the barn?

She couldn't go out to the patio if someone else might still be around. A few minutes of inattention while she'd wallowed in self-pity had cost her. Now she was stuck inside for the day. She'd already watched all of Mrs. MacDowell's DVDs and had browsed through some of her bookshelves. There were a lot of Hardy Boy volumes. The cover of a pregnancy handbook was so laughably 80s, Sophia had quickly shoved it back onto the shelf. There were a lot of cookbooks. She could give the air conditioner a workout by heating up the kitchen as she tried every single tomato recipe.

The sound of the ATV's engine surprised her. She glued her nose right back to the window. Travis was driving back at a more sedate pace, hauling a trailer full of square hay bales behind the four-wheeler, but there was nothing sedate about his appearance, nor its effect on her. His shirt was unbuttoned all the way, flaring out behind him like a plaid cape.

Sophia bet it was no big deal for him. The day was hot, the drive was easy, why not unbutton his shirt and let the air cool his chest? But for her, it was a very big deal. The sexual turn-on was instant, a primitive response to the visual stimulation of a man's strong body. Six-pack abs in low-slung jeans were a big *yes* in her mind. Weeks ago, when Travis had come into the barn dripping wet, she'd felt that same instant, heavy wanting.

It was heavier now, because now she knew Travis, the man with the hands that handled kittens and controlled horses. The man with the voice that never tried to shout her down. The man who'd listened when she poured her heart out, then gifted her with those three little words she hadn't known she'd needed to hear: *I get it.*

And yeah, the man with six-pack abs. Hot damn, he looked good. Really good.

He was looking right at her.

She jerked away and dropped the curtain, as if he'd pointed a telephoto zoom lens at her.

That was a mistake. Now he was going to think she was embarrassed, as if he'd caught her spying on him.

He had.

Okay, so she'd been spying on him, but she should have played it cool, like she'd just happened to be looking out the window, checking the weather. It was probably too little, too late, but she did that now, using the back of her hand to lift the curtain oh-so-casually. *Hot and sunny, not a cloud in the sky. Same as always.*

Travis turned the ATV and started driving it straight toward the house.

Ohmigod, ohmigod, ohmigod. He was coming to say hello. She tried to fix her hair with her fingers. She wasn't wearing makeup, which wasn't ideal, but on the plus side, she was in her yoga clothes. He wouldn't look at her face if she exposed enough skin. She started to take off the loose green cover-up she'd thrown on over her black bra top. But wait—he'd already seen her in the window in the green. She couldn't open the door in a black sports bra now. Too obvious.

The engine went silent. Sophia peeked out the window and saw six feet of rugged male beauty striding toward her, buttoning his shirt as he came. He started high on his chest, bringing the shirt together with a single button. Then the next one lower. One button after the other, he narrowed the amount of exposed flesh until only one triangle of tanned skin flashed above his belt buckle, and then that was gone, too.

She steadied herself with a hand on the doorknob. If he took those clothes off with as much swagger as he put them on...

The knock on the door was firm. Suddenly, so was her resolve. She wasn't a giddy nineteen-year-old. She was twenty-nine, and she guessed Travis was around thirty. They were consenting adults, and after the sight she'd just witnessed, she couldn't think of a single reason why she shouldn't smile when she opened the door.

Her isolation had taken a turn for the better.

Travis was here. There was nowhere else she'd rather be.

"Howdy, stranger. Long time, no see."

Sophia Jackson purred the words as she opened the door.

Travis raised an eyebrow.

She draped herself against the door jamb as if she had all the time in the world. Her thin green top draped itself over her curves. She watched the effect that had on him with a knowing look in her eyes.

Yeah, she knew how good she looked. Travis put his hand on the door jamb above her head. He had no idea why the sex goddess was back, but it sure made ten in the morning on a Tuesday a lot more interesting.

"It's about time you came." She said it so suggestively, Travis knew she was teasing. Her eyes were crinkling in the corners with the smile she was holding back. "You told Grace and Alex you'd check on me. Are you here to hold up your part of the bargain?"

Her gaze roamed over him from head to toe, lingering somewhere around the vicinity of his belt before returning to his face. She'd done so before, after he'd hosed off at the barn. That time, she'd been serious and a little bit scared. This time, she was having fun, evaluating him as nothing more than a hunk of meat. Treating him as nothing more than eye candy.

He liked it.

But he didn't trust it. He waited for that moment of hesitation, her fear of this attraction they shared.

He didn't see it, so he played along, answering her question as seriously as she'd asked it. "A man's got to work sometimes. It's only been forty-eight hours since I talked to you."

She pouted prettily, picture-perfect. "But Grace and Alex were here for their little weekly visit at the same time. It doesn't count as checking on me when they're already checking on me."

"I'll keep that in mind." He shifted so that he leaned his forearm instead of his hand on the frame of the door. It brought him into her personal space. As they talked about nothing, he watched her the same way he'd watch a yearling when he approached her with bridle in hand for the first time.

Sophia didn't flinch from his nearness. "If you didn't come to check me out, then I have to warn you that this house is no longer accepting zucchini donations."

"I'm glad to hear it, because there aren't any left. Someone snuck into the barn and conspired with my horses to dispose of the rest."

She laughed and stood up straight, done with the exaggerated come-hither routine. She was still a sex goddess, whether she tried to be or not.

He stayed lounging against her door frame. "Samson incriminated you. I found zucchini in his stall. I'm surprised he ate any of it. Most horses aren't particularly fond of it, or else people around here would probably grow even more of it than they do now."

"I guess it all depends who's doing the feeding. Maybe some hands have just the right touch."

He didn't know why she was so lighthearted today, but she was irresistible in this mood.

It was a dangerous word, *irresistible*. He could imagine a future with an irresistible woman, but not with a celebrity. Sophia wouldn't be staying in his life, which was one reason he'd been staying away. He needed to enjoy this conversation for what it was and not think about what it might have led to in different circumstances.

"I'll see if Samson likes tomatoes tonight," she said. "They're going rotten because I can't cook them fast enough."

He got a little serious. "Don't do that. Tomato plants aren't good for horses."

She got a little serious, too. "Okay, I won't. I guess I would've figured it out when they spit them back out at me."

"They might have eaten them. Horses don't always have the sense to stay away from something that might hurt them."

And neither, he realized, did he.

"I didn't know," she said.

"Now you do."

"Déjà vu. Now I know fridges have casters and horses can't eat tomatoes."

He didn't have anything to say to that. If they were a couple, he would've dropped a sweet kiss on her lips and gone back to work. He would've anticipated having her alone tonight, a leisurely feast. Or hard and intense. Or emotional and gentle—any way they wanted it.

She bit the lip he was lusting after, but she looked

concerned, not carnal. "So, if you didn't come under orders to check on me, why are you here? I hope the two kittens are okay. I looked when I went to the barn last night, but I couldn't find them at all."

Kittens. Right. He forced his thoughts to change gear.

"The mother moves them every day. She's a skittish one, but the two kittens are doing fine."

Sophia wrinkled her nose, instantly repulsed. "She's a terrible mother. I lost a lot of sleep because of her. I'm glad your vet found a new mother for the one she abandoned."

It was interesting, the way she hadn't forgiven that poor cat for isolating one of her kittens. "In my business, any time offspring are thriving without my help, then the mother's all right. Some cats make one nest and stick to it for a month, some move their kittens around twice a day. The bottom line is that there are two kittens in that barn I don't have to worry about, so she's good enough in my book. Don't be so hard on her."

Sophia put a bright smile on her face, a fake one, putting her guard up. "So, are there any other cheerful topics you'd like to discuss?"

A cat seemed a strange reason to put up walls. Travis stopped lounging against her door. He'd gotten entirely too comfortable when he had work to do. "I wanted to let you know we're burning off some cedar today. If you look off your front porch and see smoke, you don't have to come check it out."

Now she was the one to raise an eyebrow. "You thought I'd come see what's on fire?"

"You should. It's what you do on a ranch. You look out for each other, remember? You go see why someone's laying on their car horn. If something's burning, you'd better know what it is."

"I'm hiding. I couldn't check it out even if I wanted to, *remember*?"

The hiding was of her own choosing, as far as he could tell. She could decide not give a damn about the paparazzi knowing where she was, and she could decide not to care if they did take her picture. Travis had asked Alex and Grace about the ex during their last visit, and they'd assured him that the DJ was too busy partying in LA to give Sophia a second thought.

Yet Travis had seen Sophia's scars, so he didn't feel free to criticize her. Maybe he'd choose to become a hermit, too, if he walked a mile in her shoes.

He simply nodded to let her know he remembered that she had her reasons. "Now you know that if you see smoke today, it's intentional, for what it's worth. I've got to get back to work."

"Hey, Travis?" she called after him. "Are all your cowboys going to be at the fire? If it's safe for me to go outside, I'd like to go see the horses."

"Even if they can't help you get rid of your tomatoes?"

"I need someone to talk to."

He wished it was a joke.

"Yes, you're safe."

Chapter 12

The horses were beautiful.

Sophia had only talked to them when they'd been standing patiently in their stalls at the end of the day. Of course, she'd seen them under saddle, working, but she hadn't seen them like this before.

She only came to the barn after sundown. She hadn't realized the horses spent their day in the pasture or the paddock or whatever this huge, fenced-in field was called. It ran from the barn at one end all the way to the stables at the other, a stretch of maybe a quarter mile. The horses were spread out the entire distance, swishing their tails and nibbling at grass. They looked happy and content, so much so that they paid her no attention as she stood on a fence rail in her sneakers and yoga clothes.

That was okay; she had Grace to talk to.

"This is so pretty. I'm glad I came out here on my day off."

Sophia was glad, too. The visit was a total surprise, which made it all the more special. Alex wasn't here, and Grace wasn't dutifully delivering groceries. This was just about them, two sisters who'd rarely been apart before this year.

Sophia jumped down from the fence and bent to scratch a black and gray dog behind the ears. When roundup had ended and all the horses and cowboys had come in, this dog had come, too, apparently part of the whole gang. Her name was Patch. Travis called her a cow dog, but she seemed keen to be with the horses.

"I brought you some of my neighbor's tomatoes," Grace said. "Don't let me forget to take them out of the trunk before I go. I probably shouldn't have left them in there. The whole car will smell like tomatoes in this heat."

The mere thought of the smell of tomatoes made Sophia want to gag.

Grace seemed extra talkative today, raving about her new job at the hospital where Alex worked. She was writing grant proposals and doing something with research studies, using all the organization skills she'd perfected as a personal assistant to a celebrity.

Sophia smiled and listened, but inside, she was hurting. Grace apparently had forgotten that her old job had been to work for Sophia. When she raved about how cool and great her new boss was, did she not realize that implied her old boss had been not so cool and not so great?

Sophia watched the horses and listened to how much better Grace's life was without her. She'd almost rather talk to the horses. She'd never done them wrong. They didn't care if she was famous or a loser or a famous loser.

"Do you know what I need?" Sophia asked.

Grace went quiet in the middle of her sentence. "What do you mean?"

"I need boots. Western ones, so I can learn how to ride. Get me four or five pair and bring them out next Sunday. I'll pick one. I need jeans, too. I've got those shredded Miami ones, but I need regular jeans, like Mom used to buy us. Something less than a thousand dollars. I'm not making any money right now."

"Sophie."

That was all Grace had to say. The warning note said the rest.

Sophia shut up, but Grace gave her the lecture, anyway. "I'm your sister, not your personal assistant. I'm not writing this down in a little notebook anymore, so you can stop dictating to me."

Grace seemed to know what kinds of thing sisters should do compared to what kinds of things personal assistants should do. Sophia didn't see this clear-cut distinction. Grace brought her groceries, for example, but when Sophia had handed her a pile of dirty laundry that first week, Grace had grown quite cool and informed Sophia that the house had a washer and dryer.

"I need a personal assistant. You promised to find me a replacement when you left me for Alex." Sophia didn't care that she sounded petulant. Sisters got petulant.

"I didn't leave you for Alex. I fell in love with Alex, and I still love you, too. I always will. Millions of people love their spouses and their siblings, both. I'm one of them."

She sounded so calm, so infuriatingly right. It reminded Sophia of the way Travis had talked to her, until she'd showed him her scars. "How do you suggest I do my own shopping for boots? You know I can't walk into a store. I could shop online, if I had any internet access. You're going to have to get me a laptop or a smartphone. Then I could be independent."

Grace bit her lower lip, a habit that Sophia knew she still did as well. She knew, because cameras caught everything.

"I don't think having internet access would be a good idea," Grace said.

"Why not?"

Grace couldn't quite look her in the eye. "Hackers will use it to find you."

"That's not the whole story, is it? What's on the internet that you don't want me to see?"

"It's just…things haven't really died down the way we'd hoped. Not yet. But they will. Um…when do you want to tell Deezee you're pregnant? Alex and I want to be—"

"I'm not pregnant." There. Those words felt much better out loud than rattling around in her head.

"What?" Grace's arm was suddenly around her shoulder. Her voice was all sympathy, shopping and laundry and every other offense forgotten. "Oh, Sophie. When did you miscarry? Why didn't you tell me?"

"I didn't. I was never pregnant in the first place. The tests can be wrong, you know. It says so in the instructions."

"So you got your period this month?"

That startled Sophia. She hadn't been paying attention, really, but she quickly counted the weeks up in her head. They couldn't be right.

She shrugged. "I don't feel pregnant. Look at me. Does this look like a pregnant woman's body?"

Grace looked at her, but not at her stomach. She smoothed Sophia's hair over her shoulder with an almost painful gentleness. The expression on Grace's face was unbearable. Concern, compassion, pity—just horrible.

Sophia turned back to the pasture and shaded her eyes with her hand. "Where's Samson? Do you see him? He's the big bay with black points." She forced a laugh. "Aren't you impressed with my cowgirl talk? That's just a horsey way to say brown with black trim. Travis left the ATV here. I bet he took Samson out for the day. Anyhow, Samson just loves Jean Paul's shampoo. When I get back to LA, I'm going to ship a gallon of it to the ranch."

"Sophia—"

"Just so he has it to remember me by."

"Sophia, you're pregnant."

She whirled to face her sister. "I am not. I wish I'd never done that test in the first place. It's just making everyone worry over nothing."

"You've missed two periods and had a positive pregnancy test."

Sophia kept her chin high. The fence rail was solid under her hands. She wasn't going to crack. She wasn't going to fall apart.

"I'm not, but it wouldn't matter if I was."

"It matters to me," Grace said.

"I had to get out of the spotlight for a little while, anyway, right? If I am pregnant, which I'm not, then I already told you the plan. I'll just have the baby and give it up for adoption."

"Why would you do that?"

"Why wouldn't I? Some couple is out there just dying to have a baby. I'd be a surrogate mother. That's a really noble thing to do, you know."

"But you're not a surrogate mother. This is actually your baby."

"I don't want to talk about it." She started walking toward the barn, done with the whole conversation, angry at her sister for bringing it up.

Patch stayed with the horses, but Grace dogged her heels. "Well, I do want to talk about it. It's the whole reason I came out here today."

Sophia nearly tripped on those words. She'd been suckered into thinking that Grace had sought her out because she wanted to be her sister and her friend, but it was just a betrayal. She didn't want Sophia's company. It had all been a trap to force Sophia to talk about something she didn't even want to think about.

Sophia broke into a run, sneakers pounding relentlessly into the ground until she reached the barn. Until she reached the office. Until she threw herself into Travis's chair.

"Sophie! Where are you?" Grace stopped in the office doorway, breathless. "Don't do this."

"Do what? Not talk about something I don't want to talk about? If I'm pregnant, it has no bearing on you."

"Yes, it does. I'm trying to plan a wedding. My wedding. And I came here today because I wanted to ask you to be my maid of honor."

Sophia closed her eyes. She'd hated herself plenty of times before, but this one was the worst.

"But we need to talk about your pregnancy." Grace had tears in her voice. "I tried to be flexible. I chose a bunch of different locations, but the soonest I could book any of them was September. You'll be showing in September."

"And you don't want a pregnant cow in your wedding." Sophia murmured the words more to herself than to Grace.

"No. That isn't it at all. If you were keeping your baby, then it wouldn't matter at all that you were showing. You'd have nothing to hide."

Grace took a deep breath, and Sophia knew she was about to hear something she didn't want to hear.

"But if you want to keep everything a secret, then I have to respect that. I tried guesstimating when you were due and how long it would take for your body to recover so that people wouldn't suspect you'd ever had a baby. If you're due in January, I think you probably wouldn't be comfortable trying to pull it off until April, even with the way you work out. I don't want to wait until next April to marry Alex. I want my big sister in my wedding, but it's not just about having a white gown and a party and some photos. It's about actually being married to Alex. I want to make him those promises now. I want to start our lives together now, not next year."

Sophia knew she was supposed to say something, but she had nothing to contribute. Grace had thought everything through while Sophia had refused to think of it at all.

"If you don't want to be seen, I thought about asking someone else to stand up with me. I've made some friends, and…well, I really like Kendry MacDowell. She's married to Alex's department chair, Jamie Mac-Dowell. When Alex was putting out feelers about finding a place off the beaten path, Jamie mentioned his mother's house was vacant, so that's how we found this place for you. His baby picture is on the wall in your house, isn't that funny? Anyway, his wife Kendry is my age, and—"

"I understand." Sophia didn't want to hear it. Neither she nor Grace had been able to make friends outside their two-sister world, not when deli clerks were bribed to expose them. She knew she should be happy for Grace, but she didn't want to hear how Kendry was going to hold Grace's bouquet while Alex put a gold band on Grace's finger and started a new life with her.

Her little Grace had lost the best mother. She'd gotten a skittish big sister as a poor substitute. But Grace wasn't letting anything get in her way now. She was doing so much better out of the nest on her own than she ever had when Sophia had dragged her around the world in pursuit of Hollywood dreams.

"I'm so sorry," Sophia said. She was. About everything.

"Don't be sorry. The wedding will be great. We're thinking about a ceremony earlier in the day. We found the cutest bridesmaid dresses, this lemon yellow that's short and swingy. It would be great for a daytime wedding. Kendry's expecting, too. She's further along than you are, so we were excited to find a dress that will work. Even though it's not a maternity dress, it will look cute on her."

Stop. Please, stop.

Sophia couldn't act her way out of this. *Kendry's expecting*, her sister said, like it was a good thing, something to look forward to. If it turned out that Sophia was really pregnant, there would be no excitement, only plans for damage control.

"It would look really cute on you, too. It's only June. You might change your mind by September. You could be in the wedding, too."

Sophia could only shake her head, a vehement denial, as her tears began falling.

She looked around the office, but there wasn't a tissue box in this male space. She already knew there were textbooks on crops and cows, a computer she couldn't access. There was a baseball on the shelf above the neat stack of T-shirts.

Sophia grabbed Travis's T-shirt and mopped up her face.

"Oh, don't cry, Sophie." Grace's voice was husky with her own tears, a sound Sophia remembered from those awful nights when they'd grieved together. "I just wanted… I wanted to talk to you in person. I've tried to ask you about it before, but you wouldn't…well, at some point, I just had to make the call, so we put the deposit down on this rooftop venue for September."

Sophia stood up, clutching Travis's shirt close in case she couldn't pull off the greatest acting job in her life. "September sounds like a good time of year for something outdoors on a rooftop. It won't be as hot as it is now."

Grace looked so concerned. Sophia was being as unselfish as she could. The least Grace could do was let herself be fooled by the act.

"This is just one day out of our whole lives," Grace said. "It doesn't change anything between us. We're sisters."

"Always." But Sophia felt a little frantic. She wanted to get out of the barn and go somewhere else. Be someone else.

Travis had a digital clock on the wall, the kind that gave barometric pressure and humidity and a lot of other stuff that wouldn't matter to Sophia once she gave up and went back to bed. "Look at the time. I have to go back to the house before anyone comes in from the range. Travis is the only one who knows I'm here. There are other guys working today, and one of them might come in any second."

It was a lie. Travis had told her she'd be safe, but she didn't feel safe. She needed to hide and lick her wounds.

Grace followed her out of the barn. "I've got a little bit of time before I have to go. I'm meeting Kendry at this florist that did her brother-in-law's wedding. Braden's. Do you remember Lana and Braden? They were at your table at the Texas Rescue ball…oh, never mind. Sorry."

"I met them. For about five seconds."

Before Deezee showed up and I made the dumbest decision of my life.

Grace did her best to keep talking as if that hadn't been an awkward reminder of a terrible event.

Sophia let Grace's voice wash over her as they walked side by side in the sunshine. The calm weather made a mockery of Sophia's inner turmoil. If she could just turn back time to the person she'd been before she met Deezee…

She'd thought the same thing after she'd tried to touch Travis's wet body and he'd turned her down cold. She'd been certain the pre-Deezee version of herself would've been more desirable. Yet this morning she'd flirted with Travis, and he'd dropped everything he was doing to stand a little too close to her under that kitchen door awning. He seemed to like the current version after all.

Grace had changed topics from her life to Sophia's. "I don't know how to keep you hidden at ob-gyn appointments, but there are midwives associated with the hospital who make house calls. That might work. They have patient confidentiality rules in place, but I'll look into a more comprehensive confidentiality contract, the kind we had for the housekeepers and staff back in LA."

Before meeting Deezee, Sophia had entrusted her day-to-day routine to her personal assistant, but she'd made all the big decisions herself. She'd set her long-term goals and planned out every strategic move to get there. Her reputation as a smart and savvy actor had been earned. Now, Grace was deciding Sophia's medical care for her.

"I'm worried about the press, though," Grace said. "If they wanted to know what you ate so badly, I can't imagine what lengths they'll go to for baby gossip."

Before Deezee, it had never been her assistant's job to decide what to do next. Sophia had never put that burden on her sister's shoulders.

"Hey, Gracie?"

They stopped by her sister's car.

"You've got enough on your plate without worrying about doctors and confidentiality and all the rest. I'm going to look into it."

"Are you sure? I was going to try making some anonymous calls to a few adoption agencies to see what's involved—"

"Stop, sweetie." Sophia took a deep breath. "You've been an absolute rock for me, but I've got this, okay? I can make the calls, if and when I need to. You, meanwhile, are the bride, and you've got an appointment in town with a florist and some friends. Go."

"Are you sure?"

Sophia nodded. This didn't feel like acting. This felt like being herself. Not her old self, not her new self, just herself.

She used the T-shirt to gesture toward Grace's car as she smiled at her beautiful baby sister. "Go be the bride. Order your flowers. No one will look at them when they can look at a bride like you, but get the prettiest ones you can, anyway."

"Oh, Sophie." But Grace's voice wasn't sad. She was excited. "Thanks for being so understanding. I can't tell you how nervous I was about this. You're the best."

The T-shirt in Sophia's fist couldn't crack. She wouldn't crack, either.

"Oh, I almost forgot." Grace popped her trunk with a press of the button on her key fob. "Look, a whole basket of tomatoes for you."

Chapter 13

We got a visitor.

The text message hit his phone when Travis walked away from the burning pile of cedar saplings. Cell phones were unreliable like that out here. One part of an empty field could get a cell signal and another part couldn't.

The text was from Clay, who was working at the pond near the edge of the property that bordered the road to Austin. The time stamp indicated the text was two hours old, just now reaching his phone.

His cell phone pinged again, receiving another text.

Same car as Sunday.

Grace or Alex had come to see Sophia, then.
Travis put the cell phone back in his pocket. He felt

like more of a forester than a rancher today, since he'd been swinging an ax instead of throwing a lasso. It had to be done, though. The cedar could destroy a pasture in a matter of years, multiplying and spreading roots that would hog all the water and kill the grass his cattle needed for forage.

Another ping sounded, rapidly followed by more, all the texts that had been lined up, waiting for a satellite to find his phone.

Got another visitor.

The time was ten minutes ago. The text had been sent to all the men working the River Mack today.

Blue 4-door sedan? Anyone know it?

No.

No.

When Travis's voice mail played its alert sound, he was already halfway to the shade tree where he'd left Samson.

He listened to Clay's message as he walked. "We got a visitor, boss. I'm too far away to get a good look, but I don't know the car. It doesn't look like it belongs here. I'm knee-deep at the pond. Might be faster if you could meet 'em at the next gate."

There were three sets of gates on the road that led to the house. The main gate was the one Clay had seen. The second set of gates were about a mile and a half farther into the ranch itself, and the third set of gates were a mile closer to the house from there.

This year's new ranch hand, always called the greenhorn, was standing with a shovel near the fire, his phone in his hand. Clearly, he'd just gotten the texts, too, and was reading.

"You want me to come with you?" he called to Travis, with all the excitement of a first-year cowboy in his voice.

"You can't leave a fire unattended," Travis reminded him as he untied Samson's reins.

"I'm gonna miss all the fun."

"Greenhorns aren't supposed to have fun."

He swung himself into the saddle. His horse's idea of fun was to be given his head so he could run, so Travis pointed Samson toward the ranch road and let him go with a sharply spoken *gid-yap*. They covered the mile or so to the second set of gates in a handful of minutes. The blue car had gone through the gate, but it was still there, waiting for its passenger to close the gate and get back in.

Travis reined in Samson, then walked him to the middle of the road and stopped a little distance away from the car. He didn't recognize it. More than that, he didn't like the look of the man that was closing the gate—or rather, he didn't like the camera that the man held in one hand. It had a two-foot-long lens that looked like it was compensating for some shortcomings in some other department. That, or the man was a professional photographer.

"What's your business here, gentlemen?"

The cameraman looked absolutely dumbfounded to

see a cowboy on a horse in the middle of the road. City folk. What did they expect to see on a ranch?

The driver stuck his head out the window. "You're in the way. Move."

Travis didn't bother answering that.

The driver threw up a hand. "What do you want?"

"I just asked you that."

"We're going to see a friend of ours."

That lie didn't really deserve an answer, but Travis supposed he needed to spell things out for them. "You can turn your car around and head back the way you came."

"We're not leaving," the cameraman said. "We're not doing anything wrong."

"That's not for you to decide. You're on private property."

"What's your name?" the cameraman demanded, as if he had the right to know.

That definitely didn't deserve an answer.

The cameraman lifted the huge lens and took a few photos of Travis. "We'll identify you."

It would be humorous if they showed the photos to the local sheriff to file a complaint against him. Travis knew the sheriff and most of the deputies, of course, but it was more than that. This was Texas cattle country. The rules had been in place here for well more than a century. If a cattleman didn't want you on his property, then you got off his property. The sheriff would laugh these men out of his office for complaining about a foreman doing his job.

The driver pulled his head back into his car. Stuck it out the window again. "C'mon, Peter. Get in the car."

Once the cameraman was in, the driver revved the

engine. He inched the vehicle forward, then revved the engine some more.

Pushy little bastards.

So these were paparazzi. Had to be. Travis imagined it would be a nuisance to have them following him and taking pictures while he walked down a public street. Coming onto someone else's land and sticking a camera in their face took nuisance to a different level. Trespassing was illegal. Trespassing and then taking photographs took a lot of gall.

Years of this would wear on a person. Travis had a better idea now of just how much it had worn on Sophia.

The car lurched forward a full car length, rushing his horse before slamming on its brakes. Samson threw his head up and gave it the side-eye, but he stayed under control. Travis gave him a solid pat on the neck, turned in his saddle, and pulled his hunting rifle out of its carrying case. He pulled a single bullet out of the cardboard box he kept in his saddlebag.

Carrying a rifle was part of Travis's job. Predators had to be dealt with; they'd found the remains of a calf that had been lost to a predator just yesterday. Travis would never kill a man over photographs, but he'd never let a car kill a horse, either. If he were to fire this weapon, every cowboy in hearing distance would come to check it out. If Travis happened to fire that signal shot in the direction of one of the car's tires, well, things like that happened.

One thing that wasn't going to happen? These men weren't getting any closer to Sophia.

Travis opened the rifle's chamber. Empty, as it should be unless he was about to use it. He slipped the bullet into place and locked the bolt into position. It made a

satisfying metallic sound for the benefit of the trespassers. Travis set the rifle across his thighs and waited.

The driver and the cameramen started making incredulous hand gestures. Then the driver laid on the
horn, nice and loud. Nice and long.

Travis smiled. Wouldn't be long now.

Clay had already been on his way, so he arrived
first. A few minutes later, Buck, a young hand working his second year on the River Mack, rode up. Buck
was as good-natured and laid-back as they came, but
between the text messages and the car horn, he arrived
looking serious. The men stayed on their horses, flank-
ing Travis.

"This road's getting mighty crowded," Travis said.

The driver laid on the horn again, longer and louder.

"Seems rude," Clay said.

"Doesn't he?"

The driver got out of the car. "This is very interesting. What are you guys hiding? Why don't you want
us to visit our friend?"

"We may be here awhile," Travis said to his men.
"He doesn't understand the concept of private property."

The driver addressed Travis's men, too. "Either of
you fellas know Sophia Jackson?"

Well, hell. Now it was like playing poker. Travis
had to act like he didn't know the cards he held in his
own hand.

"Her sister lives here in Austin. We spotted the sister coming out of a bridal shop, then she drove out here
to this ranch." The driver squinted at Clay. "Isn't that
interesting?"

"Not particularly."

Travis would have to call Alex this evening and let him know Grace was being followed.

"Rumor has it that Sophia Jackson's sister is planning a wedding on this ranch." He made a show of taking his wallet out of his back pocket. "We're just looking for a little confirmation."

"The movie star?" Buck was genuinely incredulous. "What in the hell is this man talkin' about?"

"I believe he thinks we run a catering service," Travis deadpanned. "You cater any weddings lately?"

Buck laughed, although Travis doubted he'd been that funny. Buck just liked to laugh.

The cameraman gestured to his grandiose lens. "Look, I'm just trying to do my job. To capture all the beauty of a wedding, I need to scope out the venue first. Is there a gazebo? Will there be a reception tent? Is Sophia Jackson going to be the maid of honor?"

Buck leaned around Travis to speak to Clay. "I thought you were digging an irrigation ditch today. Didn't know you built weddin' gazebos for movie stars." He cracked himself up with his own joke.

The driver, however, got impatient or insulted. It didn't matter which. What mattered was that he shoved his wallet back in his pants and got behind the wheel again. With his hand on the horn, he put his car in gear. It rolled toward the horses slowly but relentlessly.

Buck stopped laughing.

"Is he playing chicken with us?" Clay asked no one in particular.

Travis didn't believe in playing chicken. He didn't like trespassers, and he didn't like horses being threatened with a car that could kill them. He picked up the rifle, sighted down the barrel, and fired.

The front left tire deflated instantly.

"Never did like games," Travis said, using thigh and knee to keep Samson calm after the gunfire.

"It's about to get real," Clay murmured.

"Yep."

The driver started shouting, jumping out of his car and waving his arms like a caricature of a New York taxi driver. The cameraman got out and started photographing his flat tire.

"Make sure you get my gate in the background, so you can explain to the sheriff how far onto private property you were when your tire blew up." Travis turned to flip his saddlebag open and get another bullet out of the cardboard box. "I'll say this one more time: turn your car around and get off my ranch."

"But you shot out my tire. You *shot* it." The driver was more incredulous about that than Buck had been about movie stars.

"You got a spare, don't you?" Travis pulled back the bolt on the rifle and chambered another round. "How many spares you got?"

Clay nodded toward the west. "Company's coming."

Travis glanced at the two riders coming toward them with their horses at an easy trot. "Good. Haven't seen Waterson in a while." He looked back at the driver. "You get to changing that tire. We have some visiting to do."

It took the driver and cameraman longer to figure out how to get their spare out of the trunk and set up the jack than it did for Luke Waterson and one of his hands to reach the road. Luke was one of the owner-operators of the James Hill ranch, which bordered the River Mack.

He rode up to Travis and shook hands. "Happened

to be in the neighborhood when I heard someone's car horn get stuck. Then the gunshot made it interesting."

"Nice of you to stop by."

"What do we have here?"

Travis leaned his forearm on the pommel of his saddle, keeping the rifle in his other hand pointed away from men and horses. "I believe this here is what you'd call the paparazzi."

"Paparazzi? Which one of you is famous?"

As the men laughed, Travis spoke under his breath to Luke. "Mrs. MacDowell has a houseguest."

"I see." Luke *tched* to his horse and turned him in a circle, until he stood beside Travis. "Looks like we'll be staying until these paparazzi can get their tire changed and get on their way. How long do you think that'll take?"

"They're a little slow on the uptake," Travis said. "I'm gonna say twenty minutes."

"I'll take fifteen."

Clay was skeptical. "Ten bucks says thirty."

In the end, it took them the full thirty minutes, so Clay collected enough beer money to last him a month. Buck was sent to follow the car out to the county road. Waterson and his man headed back to the James Hill. Clay went back to clearing out pond weeds.

Travis turned his horse toward the house.

He had that impatient feeling again, that need to lay eyes on Sophia. *Need* was perhaps the wrong term. The photographers hadn't made it very far onto the ranch, so there was no need to think she was in any kind of distress. She was probably talking to the horses or taking a nap or even holding those yoga poses that had turned him into a voyeur. Travis *wanted* to see Sophia again.

Want and need were all twisted up inside him when it came to Sophia. If he just checked on her, then he'd be able to put his mind at ease and go back to his routine.

Travis told himself that lie for a mile, until the white pillars of Mrs. MacDowell's front porch came into view, and he saw Sophia standing there, hurling tomatoes at the sky.

Chapter 14

He might as well have been invisible.

He'd turned Samson out to the pasture and put on a fresh shirt. His hair still probably smelled like smoke, but Sophia noticed none of it when Travis walked up the front porch steps and joined her by the white pillars. She didn't acknowledge him at all.

It didn't matter. He leaned against a pillar and felt the tension inside him ease, anyway. She was here. He was here. It felt good.

She continued her little ritual as if she were in the middle of a meditation. She chose a tomato from a basket, examined it carefully, and then threw it with considerable skill.

"Had a bad day?" he asked.

"You could say that."

"I'm about to make it worse."

She paused, tomato cupped in her hand.

"I just met my first paparazzi."

"Oh." Her knuckles turned white on the tomato, but as he watched her, she loosened her grip. "I could crush this, but then I'd have to clean up the stupid mess myself."

"You could throw it."

She did.

"Nice arm," he said.

"My daddy taught me."

Right there, just like that, Travis felt something change. The hard squeeze on his heart was painful.

Standing on the porch less than an arm's length from Sophia, he saw her as a child, one who loved her daddy, a young girl determined to learn how to throw a baseball. She might have had pigtails, or she might have been a tomboy in a ball cap, but she'd been somebody's little girl.

Now she was a too-beautiful woman but a very real person, doing the best she could in the world, same as everyone else. She was mostly kind; she had her flaws.

She was irresistible. And the reason she was irresistible was because he was falling in love with her.

Strangers with cameras came to photograph her because that was a crazy side effect of her job. It had nothing to do with Travis and Sophia, two people standing on a porch, throwing tomatoes.His arm was already warmed up from a day spent chopping trees and handling horses and sighting down a hunting rifle for one easy tire shot. He picked up a tomato and threw it for distance, centerfield to home plate.

"Wow," she said.

"My dad taught me."

"Do you see your dad very often?"

Rather than answer, he picked up another tomato. Although he'd played shortstop, he took his time like a pitcher on the mound. Wound up. Threw.

"Now you're just showing off."

He winked at her, as if he were still a young college jock. "I can throw a baseball farther than a tomato."

She picked up another one. Studied it. Threw.

"Why are you killing tomatoes?" he asked.

"I'm sick of them." Her little hiss of anger ended in an embarrassed duck of her chin. "It's wasteful, though, isn't it? But I'm not a bad person. They were just rotting in place, anyway."

His heart hurt for her again, for the way she didn't want to be thought of as a bad person. The little girl had grown up to be defensive for a reason. She was judged all the time, not just for whom she dated, but for how her face looked, what she wore, what kind of sandwich she ate.

"I'll tell you a rancher's point of view. The tomatoes came from the land, and you're putting them back into the land. That's not wasteful. Birds are going to come out of nowhere tonight and have a feast, and I bet you'll see a few tomato plants popping up here next spring. In the catalog of possible sins a person could commit, I'd say throwing a tomato is pretty damn minor. You're not a bad person."

"I won't be here next spring." She sounded wistful. It was a gentle warning as well, whether for herself or for him, to not get too attached.

"I know." He threw another tomato, a sidearm hard to first base to beat the runner.

"So, do you see your dad or not?" she asked.

"Dad and I are on speaking terms again."

"What happened?"

"He slept with a married woman. It wasn't with my mother."

"I'm so sorry." Her voice, her posture, all of it softened toward him. For him. "That must have been awful."

"Tore up two families with one affair. But it's been fifteen years. We talk. Take in a game together when I'm in Dallas. Do you see your dad?"

"My dad passed away. The same instant as my mom, actually. Car crash."

He couldn't pick up another tomato.

"It's been ten years. I was nineteen. I became Grace's legal guardian. She was all I had left. She *is* all I have left. Now she's getting m-married."

The tiny stutter said it all.

"In September." She took a breath, and a little of the actress appeared. "Grace came out here today to tell me she'd set the date. She's planning everything without my help, since I'm kind of a liability in public, with the mob scenes and stuff. She's running her own life. She doesn't need me anymore, and I'm so proud of her for that. I really am. And she's happy and excited and everything a bride should be, and I'm so happy about that, too."

Travis waited.

Sophia traced the edge of the tomato basket with her fingertip. "But deep down, I wish she still needed me, and that, for certain, makes me a bad person."

"No, it doesn't."

It was shockingly easy to pull her into his arms. It was shockingly perfect, the way she fit against his chest. She burrowed into him, her cheek on his collarbone.

She brought her arms around his back, as if they'd always hugged away the hurt like this, as if they'd always fit together.

"Who is watching?" she asked. Not *Is anyone watching?* Just *who*.

"No one. It's only three o'clock. The men are working."

He set his cheek against her hair, the scent of her shampoo less dominant than the smell of sunshine. She'd spent the day outdoors, then, not in the dark and the air conditioning.

He savored the smell of her skin as he held her, but the embrace was not entirely about comfort. Hunger demanded attention. Travis felt her breasts soft against his chest, felt the heat of her palm on his shoulder blade, and told himself it was enough.

"The paparazzi aren't watching?"

"They won't be back unless they can afford a lot of new tires. They got a flat. It will happen again. Every time."

Tension spiked in her every muscle. "But they'll be back. They'll keep coming back."

He hushed her with a *shh* and another, the same way he soothed a filly being approached by a rider for the first time. "They think Grace might be scouting out the ranch as a place to have her wedding. When she gets married somewhere else in September, they'll stop wondering if her famous sister will show up out here."

"Oh. That's possible. You might be right."

"Don't sound so surprised."

She lifted her cheek. "Don't be so nice to me."

"It's very easy to be nice to you."

She set her hand on the side of his face, and he closed his eyes at the sweet shock of a feminine touch.

It had been a while since he'd been touched by a woman, but it was more than that. It mattered that it was Sophia's fingertips that smoothed their way over his cheek, Sophia's palm that cupped his jaw. Sophia, Sophia—he couldn't get her out of his head, not since the moment he'd first laid eyes on her.

When her thumb traced his lower lip, he opened his eyes just to see her again.

She looked sad. "This has no future."

"What doesn't?" He knew, but he wanted all the cards spread on the table.

"This thing between us. It has nowhere to go."

"I know." He bent his head, and he kissed her. Like the hug, it was as natural as if they'd always kissed. Of course he would press his lips to hers. Of course.

"I don't know where I'll be a year from now. I don't know where I'll be a month from now."

"I know where you are this moment." He placed a kiss carefully on her upper lip, to stop the tears that were threatening to start. "We have this moment."

She kissed him. Her mouth was soft but her kiss was strong. No hesitation. When he thought he'd like to taste her, she opened her mouth and tasted him. In contrast to her words of warning, she kissed him without any doubts.

He had no doubts, either. If this kiss on the porch was all they could ever have, he still wanted it. He needed one moment, just one moment, to stop denying this power between them. Want and need were the same thing: he needed to kiss her more than he wanted to breathe. He wanted to kiss her more than he needed to breathe.

The slide of her tongue was firm and perfect. It satisfied him deep inside, a moment of relief because that hunger had been answered. *Ah, finally, a kiss.* But then the hunger demanded more.

He wanted to know the shape of her, so he let his hands slide and explore. Her body was softer than it looked when she saluted the sun in those God-blessed yoga clothes. Her muscles were relaxed, languid. He shifted their embrace from one of comfort to one of desire. Her hips pressed against his hardness, a moment of bliss—but then he needed more.

Her hands tugged his hair harder than he'd expected. It was just what he wanted, just what he needed—for a moment. Then greed built like a fire, consuming them both. She rose up on her toes to get closer to him, so he cupped her backside and held her tightly in place.

Not tightly enough. She could still move, and she did, sliding up another inch along his hard body, straining for more as they stood on the porch, reaching for something clothing made impossible.

"I'm gonna lose my mind if you do that again." He was warning her, or he was begging her.

"I know. I know." Her words were panted out, raw with need, no purr, no seduction, nothing deliberate.

Still a sex goddess. *More* of a sex goddess.

She couldn't go higher on her toes, but she tried, hands in his hair, flexing her arms, seeking him. If they were only horizontal, she could slide up his body, and it would all work perfectly. They'd fit together, they'd find the release that was desperately needed now, right now, if only they were horizontal—

"Please." She panted the word against his mouth, and he knew exactly what the rest of the desperate plea was. *Please fix this. Please finish this. Please give me what I need.*

He kept one hand buried in her hair, cupping the back of her head, and watched her intently as he opened the door, waiting to see if that was what she really wanted.

It was; she told him what he needed to hear. "Yes."

She knew what she wanted, and she took the first step, bringing him with her, like a dancer leading with an arm around his waist. Two steps brought them inside, and he slammed the door.

Clothes were coming off. His hands slid under the loose green top to the black spandex underneath, the kind of sports bra that never came off easily, damn it, until he felt the hooks in back, thank God. She made short work of his belt with her sure hands while he unfastened her hooks. Her soft breasts spilled free. He filled his hand with one breast, a moment entirely of touch because he could not see her beneath the green top. Not yet.

He kissed her breast through the shirt. In response, she gasped and her hands on his fly shivered to a stop. She was his. She was perfect. This was all he wanted. Then the hunger roared again, and it wasn't enough.

He scooped her top up and over her head. She was so beautifully cooperative, raising her arms so he could draw the shirt completely off, shaking her wrist for him when the bra stuck there.

Together, they tossed away the barriers. She kicked off her sneakers and went to work on the button of his jeans. He dragged his shirt over his head while trying not to lose sight of her bare breasts, as beautiful as the rest of her, with one tiny, dark freckle on the curve of her left breast, just off center of her cleavage, a sexy imperfection he wanted to savor.

She unzipped his fly and slid her hands beneath the waistband to push his jeans to the floor.

Now she hesitated, but the look on her face was one of desire, not fear. After a pause to enjoy the anticipation, she closed the space between them and pressed her nude body against his.

Yes. Yes and absolutely yes, it felt absolutely right when she wrapped her arms around his shoulders and wrapped her legs around his waist. He lifted her higher, holding her thighs in his hands as she cried an inarticulate sound that meant *yes*, this was what she'd begged him for. They needed to get horizontal soon, needed to find a bed or a couch or hell, the floor would work—

But all Sophia did was take a breath, and it was enough to align their bodies at just the right angle, with just the right amount of pressure, and he was sheathed inside her.

He rocked backward, leaning against whatever piece of furniture was behind him, completely undone at the sensation. Nothing had ever felt so good, nothing in his life. He couldn't move, couldn't breathe. Sophia was hot and wet and all around him. All his.

Hot and wet, so wet…

He wasn't wearing any protection.

Her breath was in his ear. He rained kisses down her neck. "The pill," he managed to say. "Tell me you're on the pill."

"No. Don't you have a condom?"

He shook his head sharply. It wasn't something a

man needed to carry to work on the open range, damn it all to hell.

"Just—wait—don't—" He steeled himself—the coming sensation was going to be climax-worthy, but he couldn't, not without protection—then he cupped her bottom and slid her up and off his body. He was sweating from the effort to keep control, a desperate man. "Do you have a condom? In your suitcase? Anywhere?"

"No. I swore off men. Forever." She unwrapped her legs from his waist but stood on her toes before him, arms still around his neck, their bodies still pressed tightly together. "I didn't know there would be you. I never thought there could be you."

She kissed him again, loving his mouth the way their bodies wanted to be loving. He kissed her the way he couldn't have her, although God knew they were both willing.

Still, knowing she wanted him eased something in his chest, and her skin felt glorious against his skin, so when she ended the kiss, Travis found that he could smile, even tease her. "So when you said this wasn't going anywhere…"

She gasped-laughed and smacked his chest, but she was quick with the comeback. "You said we had one moment. It sounded kind of romantic at the time, but…" She made a little *shoo* motion with her hand. "There it was. Hope you enjoyed it."

"Oh, hell no. We're having another moment." There were a hundred ways to please a woman, and he was more than willing to try them all with Sophia.

He pushed her just a foot away, so he could finish stepping out of boots and jeans. She watched, then she touched, one finger trailing down his arm, then one finger trailing up the hard length of him.

He cursed softly, and she laughed, because she knew exactly what he meant by that curse.

She bit her lower lip. "The MacDowells lived here, right? Three guys. Don't you think they might have left something behind in a nightstand from their college days?"

Travis kicked the jeans out of his way and they held hands, jogging naked together through the house to the bedroom hallway. From one room to the next, he took the nightstand on the left side of each bed, she the right, but their search turned up nothing.

"They would've probably been expired, anyway," she said, hands on her hips, wrinkling her nose in disappointment while she talked to him, as if it were perfectly natural to chat with him in the nude. "Aren't you guys the same age?"

"Give or take a few years. I'm thirty-one, so yeah, we're looking for ten-year-old condoms."

They laughed at themselves, but the sound of an ATV brought them both to the window to steal a peek, side by side.

"The greenhorn's back from the cedar burn."

"Now what?" she asked.

"Now I hope he doesn't notice Samson's out in the paddock, so I won't have to explain where I've been later." Travis ran his hand lightly down her back, marveling again at the dip of her lower back and the curve of her thigh. "Much later, because I'm not leaving now. We've got some creative moments in the immediate future."

She kissed his cheek, such an absurdly innocent move. "You still smell like smoke."

"Had I known the best moment of my life was going to happen today, I would have showered before stopping by to throw tomatoes. And I would have brought a damned condom. Spontaneity isn't my strong suit."

She touched him, fingertips smoothing their way from his smoky hair down his chest. "You could take a shower here, and I could try to figure out just what your strong suit is."

"Is that shower big enough for two?"

"Let's find out."

Shampoo and slippery soap led to more laughter. Hands made discoveries, laughter faded into something more intense. Bodies were finally, shatteringly satisfied. As far as spontaneous moments went, although they'd been caught unprepared for basic necessities, Travis could have no complaints.

When he was dressed once more and walking the familiar path to his house, it wasn't the sex that occupied his thoughts; it was the moment that had come afterward. Under the steady, soothing stream of the shower, he'd cradled her against his body for a long, long time. Neither one of them had wanted to move. The water had run down their skin, and the silence between them had been as powerful as everything that had come before.

He was in love with her.

It could go nowhere. It was a fluke they'd found themselves on the same ranch. She was leaving, had been destined to leave since before she'd arrived.

They'd had their moment.

As he walked into his empty house, he already knew it would never be enough.

Chapter 15

"**I**'m getting married!"

Sophia smiled at her sister's excitement as she pulled groceries out of a brown paper bag. Eggs, flour, real sugar. Sophia had so much time on her hands and such a plethora of Mrs. MacDowell's old cookbooks, she'd decided to try her hand at baking a few things to supplement her frozen dinners. Besides, she could sneak the results of her successful attempts into the barn after dark. Not for the horses, but for Travis, her secret lover for the past two nights.

And tonight. She would definitely find him again tonight after sunset.

With a little thrill inside that she hoped wasn't obvious, she scooped up the five-pound bags of flour and sugar and headed for the pantry, laughing at her excited bride of a sister. "Yes, I know you're getting married.

September twenty-fourth. It will be here before you know it."

"No, I'm getting married in five days, and you're going to be my maid of honor."

Sophia stopped in the middle of the kitchen. "What?"

"Somebody had a big party planned at the place we booked for September, and they canceled it. It's Fourth of July weekend, which might not sound so romantic, but I think it will be special. The rooftop patio overlooks Sixth Street. You can see the Capitol all lit up for the night, and the city will have fireworks going off all around us."

"But that's less than a week away. A wedding in a week?" Sophia held the ten pounds of flour and sugar steadily as she stared at Grace. "Is that even possible?"

"The florist said she could do it. The corporation that canceled their party had already booked a bartender and music, so we're just scooping up the people they had reserved. Kendry and Jamie weren't going out of town for the holiday, anyway, so I have my bridesmaid and Alex has his best man. If you're in the wedding, then Alex wants to ask his friend Kent to be a groomsman, so we'll have two girls, two guys. Please say yes. It's perfect."

Alex came in the kitchen door. "I found Travis."

And then Travis was right there, hanging his hat on the hook, and Sophia wasn't sure how to act.

Travis had left her bed at dawn in order to get to the barn before his men, or so he hoped. She wondered if he'd made it there first. If he hadn't, then she wondered how he'd explained arriving from the direction of the MacDowells' house and not from his own. Had anyone arrived early from the bunkhouse?

She couldn't tell from Travis's face whether that had happened or not. He stood near the door with his usual impassive cowboy demeanor, but Sophia knew what he looked like when he laughed. She also knew what he looked like when he was at his most primitive, head thrown back, muscles straining, powerless to stop the climax she'd brought him to.

The flour slipped from her arm. She hitched it back up.

Alex looked like a very pleased Clark Kent. "So Grace told you the big news?"

"Just a second ago. I hardly know what to think."

Alex explained to Travis. "We're getting married this weekend."

"Congratulations." Travis stole a look at Sophia. He knew about September. She'd been throwing tomatoes, wishing her sister needed her in September. She hadn't wanted her sister to need her this badly, though. Not badly enough to ruin her own wedding.

"Are you sure this is what you want?" Sophia asked Grace. "There was nothing wrong with September. I'm afraid you're not going to have the wedding you want if you try to cram this in on short notice. What about your cake? What about your dress?"

"There was something definitely wrong with September. You weren't going to be there. You were so nice about it, but when I drove away, I didn't even make it halfway to Austin before I started crying."

"You seemed so happy when you left."

"Well, a hard conversation was over. You'd been so generous about it all, but I realized that I was settling for something I didn't want. I want you in my wedding. I started feeling kind of sorry for myself, that because of the paparazzi and all the pressure you're always under, I wouldn't get my wedding the way I want it. The bride is supposed to get what she wants, right? Well, this bride wants her sister. I sat down and called all the venues on our list one more time. It was my bridezilla moment."

Sophia couldn't help but laugh at Grace's pride in her supposed diva fit. "That's the sweetest bridezilla moment I've ever heard of."

"Seriously, Sophie, it's going to be one of the biggest days of my life, and I need you there. I just can't imagine getting married without my sister as my maid of honor."

"Oh, Grace." The tears were instant, blurring her vision. The sugar slipped from her arm, but somehow Travis caught it before it made a spectacular five-pound splatter on the tile. She smiled up at him through her tears. "Thank you."

"You're welcome." He took the flour from her.

Sophia wasn't sure why Alex had invited Travis in for this little family moment, but she was glad he was here. He'd been there for her when she was upset that her sister didn't seem to need her, so it seemed right that he got to share this happy moment, too.

Now that Travis had freed Sophia's arms, she could hug Grace, precious Grace, the sister who still needed her. "I can't believe you're doing all of this just so I can be in your wedding. Thank you." She turned to Alex. "And thank you. You're okay with this?"

The way his expression softened when he looked at her sister made Sophia feel mushy inside.

"I wanted to marry her yesterday," he said. "I wanted to marry her the day before that, and the day before that.

I'm very okay with this weekend instead of waiting for September. Very."

Sophia squeezed Grace's hands. "So you're doing this. What can I do? What about your dress? Do you want me to call in some favors? You look so good in Vuitton. I could ask them to overnight me some samples in white. I'll tell them it's for a big event. That's the truth, too. I'm sure we'll be photographed enough to make it worth their while."

Grace squeezed Sophia's hands in return. "I already had Mom's wedding gown taken out of storage and shipped here last month. It just needs cleaned and fluffed. The dress shop is going to detach the old crinoline and I'm going to wear a new one underneath, but they have that kind of thing in stock. It's not a problem at all."

"You're wearing Mom's wedding dress?"

Grace bit her lip. "I should have asked you. The crinoline is a minor alteration, I promise."

"You don't need my permission. I'm not your boss. It's as much your dress as mine."

"Yes, but is it okay with you?"

"You're going to be such a beautiful bride, you're going to make me cry, anyway, but this is really going to be unfair. I'm going to look like a blubbering mess in all your photos."

Because being with her sister felt like her old life, Sophia started brainstorming their usual plans. "We'll have to fly Tameka in to give me bulletproof makeup. If my nose turns red, I'll be in all the gossip rags as a coke addict or something. That's just what we need when I'm trying to let the controversy die down. We can fly in Jolin with Tameka. She does such great hair."

"No." Because this was not their old life, Grace interrupted. "I've already got a hairstylist here. Austin isn't exactly a backwater. My stylist is really good. The only person we're flying in from LA is you."

"Me?"

"It will look that way. We're going to sneak you off this ranch and fly you to the Dallas airport. You'll get a nice first-class seat from Dallas back to Austin. Everyone will text their friends that you're on their plane, and when you land here, the paparazzi will assume you flew in for the wedding. You, me and Kendry are going to set up base in a hotel suite, so that Alex doesn't see us before the big day."

Alex turned to Travis. "Which brings us to why I asked you to stop in. Texas Rescue, completely by coincidence, has decided to conduct a training exercise tomorrow. It involves extracting a practice patient by helicopter and transporting her to the Dallas airport's medevac facilities. We were wondering if we might be able to use this ranch as the starting point. It looks like you've got plenty of room for a helicopter to land around here somewhere."

As Travis and Alex worked out locations and timing for her escape, Sophia stood at the counter with Grace, pretending to be absorbed by their conversation. She really just wanted to look at Travis.

She reached into the brown paper grocery bag, and pulled out a random box. Instant oatmeal. That was fine.

But Travis, ah, Travis, he was more than fine, and he would be hers tonight.

Another box. Toothpaste. Fine.

She would have to make the memories of the coming night last for the next five days, though. The thought of not seeing Travis for nearly a week was hard. She'd just found him. Once she left for Austin—

"Sophia." Grace jerked Sophia out of her fantasy. She was shaking her head *no* as she pushed Sophia's hand back into the grocery bag.

"What is it?" Sophia looked into the bag. In her hand, she held the neat, rectangular box of a pregnancy test. She stared at it in horror; she'd almost taken it right out and set it on the counter.

"Why?" she whispered. "Why would you do this?"

Grace pulled her out of the kitchen with an artificial smile for Alex. "Girl stuff to talk about. Shoes for the dresses. Be back in a second."

Sophia yanked her arm free in the living room, the same room in which she'd stripped Travis just two short days ago, the room in which he'd stripped her. She wanted to stay that way, bared to him, unafraid to be her true self. He'd seen her tears and tantrums, her scars, her fears. When she'd thought she was being terrible, he'd stood beside her and thrown tomatoes at the world. Dear God, he'd said it was easy to be nice to her. He'd kissed every inch of her body.

Now Grace had brought a pregnancy test into her kitchen.

"Why?" Sophia pleaded.

"You need to know, Sophie. You can't keep telling yourself maybe it was a bad test, maybe you'll get your period. Once you know for certain, you can decide what you want to do."

No! The word was stuck in her head. She didn't dare say it out loud; it would come out as a scream that echoed off the rafters of this great big lonely house.

Grace had it so wrong. Sophia would *not* get to decide what she wanted to do. Once she knew for certain, then she would have no choice but to deal with adoption agencies and obstetricians. She'd have to deal with Deezee in the worst possible way.

What she wanted to do was spend more time with Travis. That would no longer be an option, because what she would have to do was tell him she was pregnant by another man, and her time with him would be over.

She'd always known her time with him would be short. This wasn't her house. This wasn't her career. She could not hide here forever and go broke. But dear God, when she'd stripped herself bare in this room, she'd thought she'd have more than two days. She needed more than two days.

"Sophie?"

"July seventh." The words sounded polite, if stiff. They should have sounded like they'd been ripped from her soul. "I should get my period on the sixth or seventh. If I don't, I'll do the test."

Sophia forced herself to relax her shoulders, and tilt her head just so, and let the tiniest bit of an encouraging smile reach her eyes. "So in the meantime, let's set that aside and focus on your wedding. I wouldn't want to have to tangle with Bridezilla Gracie. She sounds pretty fearsome."

Judging from the relieved hug Grace gave her, Sophia Jackson had just delivered another Oscar-worthy performance.

Chapter 16

Sunset finally came.

The men left for the day—the young bachelors to crash in the bunkhouse, Clay to his own place off the ranch—and Travis experienced the piercing anticipation of having Sophia all to himself.

At the first sound of the barn door sliding open, he left his office and headed for her, his boots loud on the concrete, and he knew he had the arrogant smile of a man who knew he was minutes away from getting exactly what he wanted with the only woman he wanted it from.

"Sophia."

Her sneakers were silent and so was she, tackling him so that he caught her and they turned 180 degrees, his arms around her body, her hands in his hair, their mouths meeting. It was like this every night now, this first moment of pent-up desire that had to be released in a crashing kiss.

He set her back on her feet, but she began kissing her way from just under his jaw down his neck.

He loved it, but he had to ask. "Are we celebrating a good day or blowing off steam after a frustrating day?"

She shook her hair back. "So many emotions."

"The scene with your sister? That had to be a good emotion." He didn't know why she couldn't have made the wedding in September, but clearly, the coming weekend had worked out for everyone.

Sophia locked her hands together behind his waist, as he did to her. Hips pressed together, focused on one another, they talked among the disinterested horses. Travis enjoyed the prelude; Sophia wasn't the only one who looked forward to having someone to talk to every day.

"I thought my role in Grace's life was kind of over. I can't believe she wants me in her wedding that badly. Just as badly as I wanted to be there."

"I can. If you were my sister, you'd be my hero, too."

"Hero." She wrinkled her nose.

"You stepped in when your parents died. You saved the day when her life could've easily fallen apart. You achieved your own success at the same time, and pretty damned spectacularly. I started downloading the line-up of movies that you star in. I didn't realize there were so many."

"I wouldn't say I starred in them all, if any. Except for *Pioneer Woman*, most were just small parts. Supporting actress or ensemble work, at best."

He gave her a tug, pressing her more tightly against the hardness that was inevitable when she was in his arms. "It's impressive. You're a hero, but I thank the heavens every day that you are not my sister."

She deflected his praise. "I hope I didn't show how

surprised I was when Alex came in the kitchen door with you. It was kind of fun to have to pretend we're just neighbors, or whatever we are. You were a very good actor, by the way."

"Poker face. I could hardly look at that blue tile countertop now that I know it is exactly the right height for—"

She stood on her toes and twined one leg around his. "For a midnight snack?"

He dropped that casual kiss on her lips, the one that a man could give a woman when he knew he had time with her. He took her hand to lead her to his office. "We need to talk about who knows you're here, though."

He sat in the desk chair, knowing she'd sit in his lap and drape an arm over his shoulder. She did, but she was frowning. "Who knows I'm here?"

"Just the MacDowells who signed the lease, and Grace and Alex. But someone else who is physically on the property should be aware, for days I'm not here. I want to let… I want…what are you doing?"

"I'm leaving tomorrow for five days. I want to stock up on my moments." She turned to straddle him.

He laughed a little until he realized she was serious. Her hand slipped in his back pocket for the protection he was now never without. She stood to wriggle out of her shorts. When she started to undo his jeans, he didn't object, not in the least, but there was an edginess about her tonight that wasn't familiar.

"There's a perfectly good bed about a hundred yards away from here," he said.

"I want you to think of me while I'm gone. Every time you sit in this chair, I want you to remember a special moment."

That didn't need an answer. It was obvious he'd never look at this chair the same way again. But there was that underlying edginess again, so he answered her anyway. "I'm never going to forget you, Sophia. Not one moment."

She looked at him, blue eyes filled with what he could only call longing, and he wondered for the millionth time if this thing between them was really destined to end.

She closed her eyes and kissed him as she tore open the foil wrapper. With her hands, she sheathed him. With her body, she sheathed him again, and he was lost to any kind of further analysis except *yes* and *more*.

He unbuttoned her cotton shirt, exposing the inner curves of breasts shaped by pink lace. He kissed the precious freckle first, then tasted as much softness as he could through the lace. She rode him, making him shudder almost immediately with the need to maintain some semblance of control. With his hands, he tilted her hips to make sure she was making the contact she needed for her own satisfaction.

She put two fingertips on his forehead and pushed his head back against the chair, then grabbed his wrist and moved his hand to the arm of the chair. Leaning forward, pink lace so close to his face, she spoke into his ear. "Hey, Travis? Sit back and relax. I've got this."

She did. She definitely did.

He tried to take in the moment, tried to comprehend that this dream was real, so unbelievably, incredibly real. When they reached their completion, Sophia collapsed against him, her head on his shoulder. As her soft breath warmed his neck, he wrapped her tightly in his arms and savored this moment, too.

The tenderness stayed with him, every time. Sophia seemed to want it as much as she needed the physical release. She was a sex goddess who cuddled afterward. He was the man who appreciated just how irresistible that combination was.

It might be impossible to live without it.

She wriggled closer yet, keeping him inside her. His body felt thick and full, but sated—for now. It was clear to him that the hunger for her would never be satisfied for long.

"I can't believe I have to leave you for five days," she said. "I don't want to. Not when we've just discovered each other."

He kissed the top of her head. Twirled a strand of silver and gold around his index finger.

She pouted. "It's kind of like the honeymoon phase, you know? That's a rotten time to be apart. It's not like we're some old married couple and we've been together ten years or whatever. Then five days wouldn't be such a big deal."

Was she trying to convince herself that the power between them was just a novelty, a new toy they'd lose interest in someday? Surely an old boyfriend hadn't lost interest in her and looked for greener pastures somewhere else.

"Sophia Jackson, if you push me into a desk chair and straddle my lap ten years from now, you will get exactly the same response from me. Ten years from now, twenty years from now, I will never have had enough of you."

The moment was suddenly charged with tension instead of tenderness. He'd crossed a line. He'd said something he shouldn't have, not when she'd told him from the first that this thing between them was going nowhere. It certainly wasn't going ten years into the future.

He wouldn't take it back. It was true: he would want her forever. He brushed the lock of her hair across his lips, and let it go.

She picked up her head and sat up a little straighter, then smiled as if she didn't have a care in the world. "I'm looking forward to making more moments. We've got to stock up five days in one night. I hope you ate a big lunch."

It was cute. She was overlooking his serious statement, offering to get them back on track. It was her olive branch.

He accepted it. "We may have to build in a dinner break. It will be more than five days. I spend a week with my family every Fourth of July."

Abruptly, the conversation was serious again. "You won't be here when I get back from the wedding?"

"Not for the rest of the week."

"No, you can't leave," she pleaded, startling him with her intensity.

He slid his hands up her ribs and gave her a reassuring squeeze. "I can't leave the ranch in May, but I do take time off. July is the slowest month for ranching. The calving's done, the weaning hasn't started. The cattle have plenty of natural grass to graze on. If I'm going to leave, this is the time to do it."

"You won't be here when I get back from the wedding? You'll be gone the rest of the week?"

"Right." He tried to soothe her with a smile. He offered his own olive branch, an easy way to keep things light. "But I'll make it up to you when I get back."

"Can you change your plans?"

The edginess was unmistakable, as if it were critical that he be available this week just so they could sneak into bed together after sunset. As if time were short, and this week in particular was all they had.

Something was so obviously wrong, dangerously wrong.

He held her more tightly. Her ribs expanded with each panicky breath between his palms.

"My family's expecting me. My mom, my grandparents, brothers, sisters. Most of us are in ranching one way or the other, so this is our big holiday get-together. Kind of like Christmas for the Chalmers family."

He shouldn't be able to speak so calmly. How could he explain the mundane routine of his life when the best thing to ever happen to him was literally about to slip from his grasp?

She put her hands on his shoulders, prepared to use him for leverage as she stood, but he stopped her, a reflexive grip to keep her from leaving.

Her fingers dug into his shoulders, as if she didn't want to leave, either. "When will you be back?"

"Sunday." He tried to make it sound as normal as it was.

"What date is that? July tenth? Eleventh? It's past the seventh, for sure."

"Something like that. I'd have to look at a calendar."

She said nothing, but misery was written all over her face.

"For God's sake, Sophia. Be up front with me. Is this your last week in Texas or something?"

"No, it's nothing. I hope. I don't know. I don't know

what I'll be dealing with next week. This thing between us..."

She kept stopping, running out of words. He couldn't tell if she was angry or frustrated, nor if it was directed at him or at herself.

"What about this thing between us?"

"I knew it couldn't last long," she said defensively. "I told you there was no future in it."

"This thing." He was disgusted with the term. "You mean this connection. We are connected in every way we can be at this moment. So at this moment, you owe me, Sophia. What are your plans? What's happening after this week? You can't just disappear without a word."

She looked away. "I don't think I will."

"You 'don't think'? What kind of answer is that?"

He deserved more. They deserved more.

"I don't even know how long your lease is for." He was angry that he should have to fight for basic information from her. He released her abruptly, but she clutched him as if he was her lifesaver.

What was going on?

She set her forehead against his, pinning him in place with such an intimate motion. Their noses touched as she whispered. "I have the house until January, the whole time Mrs. MacDowell's on her mission trip."

"But? Talk to me, Sophia."

"I swear I don't know what's next, Travis. The future is really up in the air, but believe me that I'm not ready for this to end. I want to be here when you come back. I do."

He wanted to take all these intense, bewildering emotions and push them into passion, make love to her until they were reduced to what they understood, communication of the most basic needs. His body was growing hard inside her. He couldn't talk like this, and hunger be damned, they needed to talk.

He set her aside, stood and turned his back to her. Got rid of the condom. Tucked his shirt in. Prayed for... God knew what. Just a prayer: *please.*

Please, let me keep her a little longer. She was everything to him.

What was he to her? Someone she might leave, someone she might not?

He turned around. She stood in his ranch office in her sneakers and short-shorts, with her million-dollar hair and lovely features. She didn't look like anything else in his world. She had no connection to his life.

And yet this *thing*, this power, this connection between them existed whether it should or not.

He'd known from the beginning she wasn't going to stay. Knowing it and facilitating a helicopter to take her away were two different things.

He forced himself to ask the question. "Are you going back to LA? Since the wedding forced you out of hiding, are you done here?"

"We'll make it look like I'm flying back to LA, just like we're making it look like I'm living there now. Grace is basically inviting the paparazzi to find her wedding by making sure I'm seen flying in. All I can do in return is try to appease the paparazzi so they don't get too aggressive and ruin her big day. I've got to stop and answer when they shout questions at me, smile while they take photos. They'll tell me to 'look this way' or 'twirl around and show us your outfit,' and I'll have to do it so they'll go away."

She trailed her fingers over the computer keyboard on his desk. "It will help. They love a cooperative star. But it won't be enough to bury all the negative publicity I already generated, so I'll come back here after the wedding. I need to continue staying off their radar."

She flicked a glance his way. He was sure his relief showed. He felt like he could breathe again.

She pushed the space bar on his keyboard, but nothing happened. He'd powered the machine down for the day.

"Have you never typed 'Sophia Jackson' in your search bar, just to see what horrible things I did?"

He shook his head.

"You weren't tempted, even a little bit?"

"Braden told me enough."

"Oh. The ball. I don't think all those Texas Rescue people are going to be too thrilled to see me at the wedding. Alex is one of their doctors, you know. Half of the guest list volunteers for them. Maybe they'll give me a second chance to make a first impression." Her gaze drifted from the keyboard to the floor as she shrugged one shoulder. "Just kidding—I know it doesn't work that way."

Perhaps Sophia had brought it on herself, but Travis feared she was going to be very uncomfortable for her sister's sake. She was going to appease the paparazzi. She was going to spend a night with people who had reason to think badly of her.

There wasn't a thing he could do to erase Sophia's past. Not one thing, but he tried to offer her some encouragement. "Braden had less to say about you than about the guy that jumped on your table."

She looked up quickly at that. "You know about Deezee?"

"Braden said he stepped on his wife's dinner and gave you a crappy apology."

"That's as good a summary as any, I suppose." She gave a halfhearted chuckle.

"Do you think he'll show up again?" Travis had that restless feeling again, that need to keep an eye on her— but Texas was a big state, and he'd be almost three hundred miles away with his family on the wedding day.

"That was all orchestrated by his publicist. Deezee is too lazy to set anything up himself, so I doubt it."

Travis couldn't leave without making sure she had some kind of plan in place. "If he does, don't try to appease him. Don't try to calm him down or take him aside. If he wants attention, you won't be able to save your sister's wedding from his type."

"The only reason he'd be there would be because of me. I think I'd owe it to everyone to try to stop him."

"Let Alex handle it. It's his wedding, not yours. Jamie MacDowell's the best man, right? You're the maid of honor, so you should be near Jamie. And you know Braden."

"He kind of hates me."

"He doesn't. You'll be safe with the MacDowells. Quinn will probably be there, too."

"I take it Quinn is the third one in all the family portraits at the house. I'll only recognize him if he still has braces and a bad middle school haircut."

"I'm serious, Sophia. I don't want you trying to deal with this Deezee jerk."

For once, he wished the paparazzi had been right. He wished Grace had been setting up a wedding tent

here on the ranch. He'd be here in September. He'd be
here if Sophia got harassed. Hell, she wouldn't get harassed on his ranch in the first place. That was the point
of her hiding here.

But now she was going to fly away, without him.

She acted like she didn't care, scoffing like she was
some kind of tough street kid. "Deezee's got no game. It
would just be a lot of noise. Same old, same old. While
you're gone, you can log on to your favorite celebrity
site and see if anything exciting happened. If it's really juicy, it might make TV. That would be a fun topic
around your family dinner table. 'Look what this crazy
chick who's staying on my ranch did.'"

He recognized the voice: she sounded like the woman
in the thigh-high black boots, the one who said she
didn't care when she cared so desperately. He knew
her, and he loved her. It made him sick to think that he
might have come home to find her gone to LA forever.

It would happen, sooner or later. In the meantime,
he wanted to cherish her while he could, yet they were
standing on opposite sides of a desk chair.

"I'm sorry, Sophia."

"For what? I'm the one who hooked up with a loser.
But hey, I've helped countless people make a living off
entertainment gossip as a result. It's all good."

That scoff. It was such an act. She couldn't hide her
pain from him.

He sent the chair rolling and hugged her. She held
herself stiffly, as if she didn't need affection. He held
her as if they'd just finished another round of amazing
sex instead of a round of bad feelings and painful sub-
jects, because she needed to skip right to the tenderness. So did he.

"I'm sorry you can't go anywhere without a camera in your face. I'm sorry you need a place to hide in the first place."

She made a small sound, a yip of pain like a hurt animal, and then she was hugging him back, burrowing into him in that way she had.

He realized she was physically hiding. He wrapped his arms around her more tightly, cupping the back of her head with his hand, letting her hide her face behind his forearm. He was grateful his life's work had given him the muscle she could literally hide behind.

"You've got a safe place here. Go do your wedding and get the paparazzi eating out of your hand. When you're done, come back here, and be safe."

She took a shivery breath. "But you won't be here."

It wasn't just the sex, then. It wasn't even the friendship and the camaraderie. She felt safer around him.

"I'll be back Sunday. Until then, Clay will know you're here. You won't be alone."

She shook her head against the idea. "Don't tell Clay. The more people who know about me, the less safe I am. Grace and I learned that the hard way. It's been just me and Grace for years."

"But now it's you and Grace and Alex and me, and you're still safe. You could depend on Clay, too." He stopped cupping her head and moved to lift her chin instead, wanting her to see that she had options. "You know Jamie and his wife, Kendry. Count on them. Braden MacDowell and his wife. She's a doctor. She knows how to keep someone's confidentiality. Quinn and his wife are trustworthy."

"I've never trusted that many people. Ever."

"But you could. The ranch that owns the Appaloosa

is just a few miles away, and the Waterson family is as solid as they come. When the paparazzi came calling, all I had to tell Luke was that the MacDowells had a houseguest, and he was there for me, no questions asked. You don't have to be so very alone, Sophia."

He let go of her chin to caress her face, not surprised his hand wasn't quite steady. He had too much emotion coursing through him. He loved her so damned much, and he wanted to give her this gift. "I'll build you a whole safety net here, baby. You can come here to stay."

She wanted it. He could see it in her expression as clear as day, but she didn't say yes. It hurt her not to say yes, but she didn't say it.

She raised her own unsteady hand to touch his face. "I love… I love that you care."

"I care."

"Did I ever tell you my secret fantasy about you?"

She was done with this moment of tenderness, then. It wasn't enough for Travis, but he was a patient man. He couldn't force Sophia to trust him any more than he could force a horse to trust him. Things took time. Things had to be earned.

For her, he would meet her on her terms. She wanted to talk fantasies.

"Does this fantasy have to do with more office furniture?" he asked.

But her smile was fleeting.

"In my fantasy, you take me on a date. We have a drink together at a place with a nice dance floor, and we talk while we have our first dance. By the second dance, maybe we stop talking, because it's so special to be moving in sync, and thinking this is a person you'd like to know better. You drive me home and say good-night, and you tell me you'd like to see me again. There are no cameras. No one calls me names on social media. No one runs a background check on you. No one cares at all, except the two of us, because we're the ones falling in love."

His heart squeezed so hard, he could only whisper her name.

"But it's a fantasy, you see, because that will never happen. This thing between us, it has no future, no matter how much I wish it did."

They had a future. He just didn't know what it looked like yet. But Sophia was afraid now, skittish and spooked, and he needed to be patient.

"We have this moment," she said.

He tried not to be spooked himself at the way she said the words, as if this could be their last moment.

"How would you like to spend it?" he asked.

"I want to make love to you all night and pretend that I don't have to leave for a wedding tomorrow."

"Then that's what we'll do."

He scooped her up as if she were the bride and carried her out of the barn.

Chapter 17

Sophia was the weird one.

She stuck out like a sore thumb at the reception, and nobody wanted to talk to her. She'd thought she was lonely at the ranch during that first month, but she'd forgotten how lonely she could be when surrounded by people. She just didn't fit in.

It had started at the airport. The flight attendants had been so deferential, but she'd told herself they treated all the first-class passengers that way. Then the passengers had started holding their cell phones at slightly odd angles, and she'd known she was being photographed. *OMG. Look who is on my plane!*

She couldn't even go to the bathroom like a normal person. She had to practically clean the bathroom before she left, careful to make sure she left no drops of liquid soap or a crumpled paper towel that would mark her as a slob. *OMG. Sophia Jackson left the lid down on the toilet. Does that mean she went number two?*

The only time she'd been able to forget she was different than everyone else had been in the hotel, when it had been only her, Grace and Kendry MacDowell. Kendry had overcome that invisible distance between celebrity and fan pretty quickly, and they'd had such fun as co-conspirators, trying to make Grace laugh through her bridal jitters. If only there were more Kendry MacDowells in the world...

I'll build you a whole safety net here, baby.

Travis. That man was something special. That man deserved a good life with a good woman, not with an outcast like her.

OMG. Sophia Jackson is at this wedding reception. She eats only shrimp and strawberries. What a freak.

Sophia stood in no-man's land, somewhere between the bar and the band. It was too embarrassing to sit at the head table, because Grace and Alex were on the dance floor, as were Kendry and Jamie. The other groomsman, Kent, was a bachelor who'd been pulled onto the dance floor by a group of single women who weren't letting him go any time soon. Sophia couldn't sit at the table alone.

OMG. Sophia Jackson is like a total bitch. She won't speak to anyone.

She kept a pleasant, neutral smile on her face and watched her sister glow with happiness.

The wedding ceremony had been gorgeous, a traditional service in a white church. At one point it struck her that Kendry was standing next to her with a tiny life growing in her belly. What if she, Sophia, were doing the same? In the hush of the church, surrounded

by flowers and lace, pregnant had seemed like an ul-
tra-feminine, almost divine thing to be. Even if Sophia
wasn't going to raise the baby herself, it was a miracle.

Would Travis see it that way?

It wasn't July seventh. She didn't have to worry about
that yet. With luck, she'd never have to worry about that.

She glanced at the roof of an adjacent building. She'd
been holding still too long. The cameraman had a clear
angle to her. She moved to the other side of the bandstand.

"May I have this dance?"

Travis. The man behind her sounded just like Travis,
and when she turned around, she saw that the handsome
man in the suit and tie was Travis.

"It's you. Oh, it's so good to see you. I'm dying to
hug you, but there are at least four telephoto lenses on
us right this second from a roof and two balconies."

"I missed you, too. Would you care to dance?"

"That would be lovely, thank you."

The band was playing a slower song, the kind where
the man and woman could hold each other in a civi-
lized ballroom pose and sway together, even if it was
their first dance. She really almost felt like crying, it
was so perfect.

"I didn't know you were here," she said. "I didn't see
you at the ceremony."

"I saw you. You looked radiant up there. Whatever
you were thinking, it looked good on your face."

This was their first dance, but they weren't strangers. Sophia lowered her voice. "I may have been thinking about you and a certain desk chair?"

"I don't think so."

"You and a kitchen counter?"

"Wrong again."

Oh, this was wonderful, to dance and flirt and feel like she belonged at the party. "How do you know what I was thinking?"

"Because I know the look on your face when you think of countertops and chairs, and that wasn't it. Probably a good thing when you're standing in a church."

It was wonderful to be with Travis, who knew her and didn't ask about filming *Space Maze* or whether she'd done her own stunts in *Pioneer Woman*.

"So what do you think I was thinking?"

"You were probably thinking about the child you helped raise, and how she's turned into a lovely woman. Grace is a beautiful bride. You must be very proud of her. I'm very proud of you."

Sophia felt her happiness dim. She had been thinking about a child, but it was one that, if it existed, would end this fantasy with Travis sooner rather than later.

"Grace was a teenager when I took over, not a child."

"You need to learn how to take a compliment. For example, you look very beautiful all dressed up. I've only ever seen you in yoga clothes and shorts. And one pair of thigh-high black boots. What did you do with those boots, by the way?"

She smiled. "I didn't know you owned a suit. It's kind of surreal to see you away from the ranch."

"Now that is exactly how not to return a compliment. I think you're very intriguing, though. Can I get you a drink?"

That's when it hit her. "Travis Chalmers. You're giving me my fantasy, aren't you?"

But he'd already turned to introduce her to a man he knew. Then a woman. He got the conversation onto a topic that everyone found interesting, and then he melted into the crowd. She hated to see him go, but she knew it would save anyone from guessing they were a couple.

She danced with some of the men she talked to. Then Travis returned for a second dance, as she'd known he would. A drink, two dances, an invitation to go out again: the fantasy she had said would never come true.

They swayed in silence this time, not just because that had been her fantasy, but because her heart was too full to speak for at least two verses and a chorus.

"This isn't just about my fantasy, is it? You came to make sure that the Texas Rescue people gave me a second chance."

"I think they like you. God knows the men are happy enough to dance with you. They just needed to see me do it first, so they'd know you were a mortal even though you look like a goddess. Beauty can intimidate people."

Tears stung her eyes. That hadn't felt like a compliment as much as a benediction. Travis believed in her. She didn't want to be the weird one, even if it meant she was the beautiful weird one, and he understood that.

"Clay is going to call you to tell you if I make it home safely, isn't he?"

"Yes, he knows you're living in the house now. I told you that I would do anything to help you whether you liked it or not. Telling Clay was one of those things. I couldn't leave you isolated in hiding. Anything could happen, even a house fire, and no one would have known you were there. It wasn't safe. Clay knows, and only Clay knows."

Subdued, humbled, she asked, "Where's Deezee?"

"He's working at a club in Las Vegas tonight. You won't be embarrassed by him, and your sister has already forgotten he exists."

I love you.

She wanted to say it, she was dying to say it, but Deezee did exist, and her sister wouldn't be the only one reminded of it if July seventh turned out the way Sophia feared.

"I'd like to see you again, Sophia. I'll be out of town for the rest of the week, but could I take you to dinner on Sunday? There's a place just outside of Austin that I think you'd enjoy."

She tried to play her role. "Really? Where?"

"My house. Genuine Texas cuisine."

She wrinkled her nose. "Zucchini and tomatoes?"

"Steak and a baked potato. Dress is casual. I'll pick you up at eight."

Her voice was thick with tears as the song and her fantasy ended. "I'll see you on Sunday. Have a nice visit with your family."

By Sunday, she would know one way or the other. Either she'd tell Travis she loved him, or she'd tell him she was pregnant with another man's child.

They had to part without a kiss.

Sophia wondered if she'd ever get a chance to kiss him again.

July sixth came and went without any hoopla. Sophia talked to Clay a bit and to Samson a lot.

The seventh came and went as well. Sophia tried throwing a few tomatoes, but it was too lonely without Travis leaning on a pillar, evaluating her technique. Instead, she breathed in the shimmering hot air as she poked around the front yard until she found the goose salt shaker, dirty but unbroken. She took it into the house and scrubbed it until there was no trace of evidence that Sophia had once pitched it into the night sky.

On the eighth, she had to do the pregnancy test. She'd promised. She intended to, but she felt that need to hibernate. She slept most of the day, and by the time evening fell, she thought it would be best to wait until morning. She'd gone back to Mrs. MacDowell's 1980s pregnancy handbook and flipped through the opening pages gingerly, with one finger. There seemed to be something magical about the first urine of the day. So really, she might as well go to bed and do the test first thing in the morning.

On the morning of the ninth, she took the test. She could no longer fool herself: she was pregnant.

She cried the entire day.

The movies had gotten it all wrong. The end of the world was not an isolated, brown landscape.

Sophia woke to summer sunshine pouring in her bedroom window, mixing with the bluebonnet paintings on the walls. It was beautiful.

But it was Sunday.

Travis was coming back, and at eight in the evening, he'd pick her up to take her back to his house for dinner. There, she was going to tell him that she was pregnant with another man's child, that she'd been pregnant all along but too stubborn and willful to admit it to herself, and because of that, she'd sucked him into a hopeless situation.

It was the end of the world.

Black seemed like the appropriate color. Sophia

dressed in black yoga clothes, tied on her sneakers, and went to visit the horses.

As always, Samson liked her best. She leaned on his great, warm neck and wished someone would yell *cut*.

The barn door slid open. After five days back in the public eye in Austin, that old reflex to keep her appearance together had returned. She stood properly, shoulders back and down, ankles together, hand on hip—but with her other hand, she tickled Samson under his chin. She hoped it was only Clay coming back for something he'd forgotten. No matter what Travis said, she didn't want more people knowing she was hiding on the ranch.

"Now, this is a fantasy."

"Travis." She drank in the sight of him as he stood just inside the barn door. He looked so achingly good, as if she hadn't seen him for a year instead of a week. Less than that, since he'd surprised her at her sister's wedding.

"To see a woman as beautiful as you are hanging out in cute shorts, talking to my horses, well, you just know that's some rancher's fantasy. Luckily, I'm a rancher."

She wanted to run and throw herself in his arms the way she always did, spinning him halfway around with the impact.

But she was pregnant. She held still.

Travis had no hesitation. He strode toward her, single-minded, confident. He scooped her up and spun her around, bringing enough momentum for the two of them.

His arms felt so strong. He smelled so good. Somehow, she'd been so focused on how they were going to be apart, it was startling to have him here—and still so happy with her.

Because he didn't know. Not yet.

"I didn't think I'd see you until dinner." How could her voice sound so normal when she was dying inside?

"I missed you," he said.

"I missed you, too." It was true. Surely she was allowed to say that.

He linked his arms around her waist, the way they did when they settled in to catch up on how their days had gone. Had he missed just talking to her? She thought her heart might burst.

"I watched a couple of your movies because I missed you so much."

She was grateful to talk about anything except what she needed to talk about. "Which ones?"

He named the crime drama, the one with the smoking-hot sex scene.

"Oh. That one." She felt her cheeks warm as she looked toward the tack room. She couldn't hold his gaze.

"I want credit for keeping my eyes on yours and not letting them drop lower, but if you don't look at me, how will you know how good I am at pretending I'm not thinking about your body?"

He sounded amused.

She looked at him then. "That scene doesn't bother you? I mean, knowing anyone could watch it?" She knew so many fellow actors whose significant others were bothered greatly by those kinds of scenes, even when carefully arranged bedsheets protected privacy. Her costar's girlfriend had been standing by as they filmed that one, anxious and jealous and making the role ten times harder to play. She'd been far more of a diva than any actress Sophia had worked with.

Travis kept his arms locked around her waist. "I've

seen rated R movies my entire adult life without thinking twice about it, but it is strange when you know one of the actors. It took a few scenes for me to adjust to hearing you speak with a Boston accent. If you're worried about the sex scene, don't be. I could tell it wasn't real."

"Oh, it's not. It's really not. There are a dozen people working, and you have to hold yourself in the most unnatural way, and there was this awful bubblegum smell, and I remember being thirsty and worried about how to deliver this line that I didn't think my character would really say, and they put makeup on everything. I mean everything."

"I know."

"You do?"

In the moment of silence that followed, she forgot they had no future. She could only think how lucky she'd be to have such an even-tempered man as her partner in life.

"How?" she asked, holding her breath.

"It didn't look real to me. Not the look on your face, which was sexy as hell, don't get me wrong, but it wasn't what you really look like with me."

"Oh."

He kissed her lightly. "You look sexier with me."

"Oh."

"I could guess about the makeup because your freckle was missing. The one that's right here." Without taking his eyes from hers, he placed his finger precisely on a spot just above the edge of her bra, on her left breast, exactly where she knew she had a little black dot.

"Oh. They hide that all the time, even if I'm just wearing a low cut gown or a bathing suit."

His grin slowly grew into a smile. "Good. I love it. I'll keep it to myself. The audience doesn't get the same you that I get."

She wanted to smile back, but she was dying inside. *We have no future. We have no future.*

"The movie I'll never watch again was the pioneer one," he said.

"That was my best. Everyone says so." The words came out by rote despite her frantic thoughts.

"You died. I don't ever want to know if that looked realistic. I can't watch that one again."

He kissed her as if he couldn't bear to lose her, and she kissed him back the same way. *No future, no future.*

She would lose him, soon, but she wasn't ready to say the words. She was supposed to have had until eight o'clock to prepare herself to say the words.

"Why are you here? I mean, why did you leave your family so early for me?"

"That was why—for you. I couldn't wait until tonight to see you. I just gave Clay the rest of the day off. I realize your fantasy includes a very traditional dinner that might end in a peck on the cheek, but I was going to try to persuade you to try a different fantasy now."

Her body was her traitor in every way. She knew she couldn't sleep with Travis again, but her body didn't care, pregnant or not. Just being near him was enough to make her come awake and alive once more.

Patch saved the day. With outstanding timing, she ran into the barn to greet Travis as if he'd been gone ten years.

Sophia stepped back to give the dog room. She pretended she didn't see the quizzical look Travis threw her.

"How're you doing, Patch?" He bent down to pet her

with both hands. There was something odd about the way he did it, almost like he was checking something, deliberately feeling his way from the dog's shoulders to her tail. "Still feeling good, girl?"

Sophia grasped at the distraction. "Is there something wrong with her?"

Travis stood again. "I wouldn't say it's wrong. She's going to have puppies. Judging from the amount of time she's been spending in Samson's stall, she's planning on having them there. I'll have to move Samson when she gets a little closer. They're best friends, but I wouldn't want him to step on a puppy."

Sophia felt her stomach tying itself into knots. "I can't take another abandoned animal crying from starvation. Is there replacer milk for puppies? Do you have any? We should get some right away. Right away."

She must have overreacted. Travis's quizzical look deepened into concern. "Patch is a good mother. This is her second litter, so I don't anticipate any problems, but sure, we'll keep some replacer milk here. I won't leave you with a starving newborn again, I promise."

He kissed her again, not on the lips, but on the forehead.

She told herself that was for the best. It was already starting, this transition from lovers to friends that she was going to rely on. She'd had time, too much time, to think about her options, and no matter what Grace had said, there weren't many.

Sophia had nowhere else to hide. She was going to have to stay on this ranch for the duration of her pregnancy, and that meant she was going to see Travis. Staying on good terms with him was essential, because frankly, she was scared to death to be without him.

She had a good speech she needed to be ready to deliver tonight that talked about how they'd be able to coexist quite nicely together despite their history. It left out the part about being scared.

Until tonight's dinner, she needed to not freak out. She smiled brightly at Travis. "First the cat, now the dog. Is everything on this ranch pregnant?"

Travis kept looking at her, but she told herself he was smiling indulgently. "We try to keep it that way."

She tossed her hair, praying for normalcy. "You know that sounds terrible, right?"

"That's the ranching business. We had a ninety-seven-percent pregnancy rate in the cattle last year. That's a very good year. But I don't breed cats. She did that on her own. And I suspect Patch here found herself a boyfriend over at the James Hill."

"If she'd been neutered, then you wouldn't have this problem." She couldn't quite keep her tone light. She'd said the same thing after the cat. She'd thought the same thing about herself.

"I wouldn't say Patch having puppies is a problem. She's the fourth or fifth generation of River Mack cow dogs. She's got real good instincts, passed down through her line. People in these parts are glad to have one of her puppies. This will be her second litter, though, so we'll have her fixed. I don't want her to get worn out. I need her working the herd this fall."

"What happens this fall?"

He was silent for a long time. Then he walked up close to her and, as if she were some kind of precious treasure, held her head gently in his hands and rested his forehead on hers.

"The last time we were together before the wedding

we talked just like this. You weren't sure if you'd still be on the ranch this week. You said you'd have a better idea of what the future holds when I came back. I'm back. Do you know? Are you going to be here this fall?"

It was hard, so hard, not to dive into the safety of his arms. He'd hold her close and she'd feel safe and everything would be all right.

Those days were over. Those days never should have been, so she stayed on her own two feet and answered him honestly. "Yes, I'll be here all the way until January."

As close as they were, she could feel the relief pass through his body, but she could see his frown of worry as well. She wasn't a good enough actor to fool him. He knew she was holding something back, but being Travis, he didn't push.

"Well, then," he said. "Would you like to see what the ranch looks like beyond the house and barn? It's a Sunday in July. There won't be a soul for miles around. I'll drive you around and tell you what you can expect from now until Christmas."

And tonight, I'll tell you what to expect.

But she was being offered a reprieve, a stay of execution, and she loved him too much to deny herself his company, just one more time.

Chapter 18

"I didn't realize there were so many flowers."

Sophia looked out the window of the white pickup truck. She was all buckled in, huddled by the door, and sad. The ranch had so much beauty, and she'd missed it all when she'd first arrived.

"What did you think it was if it wasn't flowers?"

"Brown. I just thought I was coming to live in exile on some ugly brown planet. But it's flowers. Yellow, purple and orange." She felt a little defensive. The old Sophia was just so pitiful. "You put those colors together, and you get brown."

"Until you take a closer look. Which you are."

She closed her eyes against his kindness. Of course she was in love with this man. How could she not be in love with this man? And he was going to hate her so very soon.

"Stop being so nice to me."

He drove in silence for another little while. "Why are you finding it so hard to be nice to yourself?"

She didn't answer him. Out the window, there were babies everywhere. Quite literally, every single cow had a calf suckling or sleeping underfoot. She could see the satisfaction and pride in Travis's expression—or she had seen it, before her misery had spilled into the pickup.

Travis slowed down the truck and squinted at a distant tree. "There she is. It's about time."

He parked the truck a little distance from the tree and got out. There was a cow under the tree, sleeping peacefully on her side. "You can come out if you want. Just be quiet about slamming the door."

Travis walked a little closer to the cow, not too close, and then crouched down. He checked his watch. And he waited.

And waited.

The minutes ticked by, until Sophia couldn't stand it anymore. She got out of the truck and practically tiptoed up to Travis before dropping down beside him.

"What's going on?"

"She's the last heifer of the season, and by season, I mean she's so far out of season, she's in a class by herself."

"I don't understand."

Travis checked his watch again as the cow huffed and made a halfhearted attempt to get up. The cow fell still again.

"We have our calving season in April and early May on the River Mack. That's when we want the herd giving birth."

"All at the same time?"

"More or less. You have to ride the herd several times

a day, looking for new babies to doctor, making sure the mamas are on their feet and nursing, and sometimes—" he stood up with a sigh "—you have to pull a calf."

He walked back to the truck, dug around the back, and returned with some blue nylon straps and a pair of long, skinny plastic bags. "This little lady tricked us pretty well. We thought she was pregnant during breeding, but turns out she wasn't. Then a bull jumped a fence, and here she is, totally out of sync with the rest of the herd. Accidents happen, though."

The cow moaned again. Travis shook his head.

"What's wrong?" Sophia stayed crouched on the ground, her fingertips on the grass for balance.

"She's a first-time mother. She isn't doing too well. She must have been at this awhile. See how tired she is?"

And then Travis walked right up to the laboring cow. Sophia stood to see better. There were two front legs poking out of the mother's…body. Legs with hooves and everything. Sophia cringed.

The mother seemed to get agitated as Travis stood there, but then the hooves poked out a little farther and the nose of a cow came out, too. Travis came back and crouched beside Sophia.

Nothing else happened for an eternity. He checked his watch and picked up the blue straps again, but then the cow made a pitiful sound of pain and the whole head of a tiny cow came out with its front legs.

"There you go," Travis said under his breath.

Sophia sat on her butt. "I'm gonna be sick."

He turned his head to look at her. "You've never seen anything being born?"

"No." She couldn't look. "What are the blue straps for?"

He seemed amused, which, given that he was in full cowboy mode, meant one corner of his mouth lifted in barely-a-grin. "You can wrap 'em around the calf's legs and help the mama out. It's called pulling a calf."

"You're kidding me. This is what you do all day? I thought you rode around on a horse and shot rattlesnakes or something."

He turned back to the laboring cow. "I do that, too. These mamas go to a lot of trouble to have their babies. It's the least I can do to make sure the babies don't get bit by something poisonous."

He would be the best father in the world.

The thought hit her hard, followed equally hard by sorrow at the memory of Deezee. She'd been so unwise, so very unwise.

But then the cow moaned and the entire calf came out in a rush of blood and liquid. It just lay there, covered with gunk, and Sophia's heart started to pound. The world got a little tilted. She grabbed Travis's arm, digging her fingers into his muscle to keep herself vertical.

"Come on, Mama," he said quietly.

The mother wasn't moving. The baby wasn't moving.

Then Travis was moving, on his feet and heading toward them as he pulled the plastic bags over his hands and arms—they were gloves. He grabbed the baby's nose, its lifeless head bobbing as he jerked some kind of membrane from around it. Then he grabbed the hooves in his hands and simply dragged the calf out of the puddle of grossness and across the grass to plop it right in front of the mother's face.

This was birth. This horrible, frightening death and

membranes and pain—*oh, my God*. Sophia rolled to her hands and knees and tried desperately not to vomit.

What had she been thinking? That she'd do yoga and eat well and sport a small baby bump? Maybe toward the end, around Christmas, she'd be a little bit roly-poly for a few weeks, but then the baby would be born and go off to some wonderful adoptive family and everything would be clean and neat and tidy. She'd move on with her life.

That wasn't how it was. She had to give birth, she had to *labor*, there was just no way out of it. There would be gushing yuck and pain and exhaustion. And if, at the end of it all, the poor little baby didn't move…

What if the poor little baby didn't move?

She dug her fingers into the dirt and panted.

"Sophia."

She was dimly aware that Travis had come back. She heard him cursing, saw bloody plastic gloves being dumped on the grass. His clean arm was strong around her waist as he picked her up and set her on her feet, but he kept her back to his chest, which was smart because she was about to throw up.

"Baby, it's okay. Look, the mama's taking care of her calf now. She was just too tired to get up and go do it, so I helped her out. It's okay."

"No, it is *not*!" She wrenched free from him and ran a few steps toward the truck, but there was really nowhere to go. "I don't want to do it. I don't want to."

"Do what?"

"You're a man." Her words were getting high-pitched, rushing together. "Would you want to go through that? It's awful. She could've died. That baby could've died. I don't want to do it."

"It's okay. You don't have to do anything." He captured her in his arms again and tried to soothe her, making little shushing noises like she was the baby.

She started to cry. "Yes, I do. I'm the woman."

She could feel him behind her, shaking his head like he was dumbfounded, but how could he be? He was the one who'd just gotten out straps and gloves. "Okay, you're a woman, but you're just spooking yourself. You're not going to give birth anytime soon."

She was crying so hard now, she was doubled over at the waist. She would have fallen if Travis didn't have his arm around her. "Yes, I am. I have to. I'm pregnant."

Travis was an ass for the next seven weeks.

For the first few minutes, he'd held Sophia as she'd choked and cried, although it was frankly a toss-up which one of them was more staggered.

Pregnant. They'd been careful, except for that very first time. He'd only been inside her for a minute, and he hadn't climaxed—but it was possible. That could be all it took, as they'd been warned in sex ed pamphlets given to them a hundred years ago at school. He'd assumed he was the father.

It would be nice to be able to claim that he'd felt some noble calling or had a divine moment of parenthood fall upon his shoulders at the news that Sophia was pregnant, but in fact he'd been trying to hold a woman who was about to vomit, and he'd been doing math. June plus nine months.

"March?" That had been his first brilliant contribution to her distress.

"January," Sophia had gasped, and his world had gone to hell.

His horse tossed his head. Travis was holding onto the reins too tightly. Again. He tried to relax in the saddle, but it was damned hard when he was getting closer to the house. He hadn't caught a glimpse of Sophia in seven weeks, but that didn't stop him from looking.

The rest of July had been a haze of hurt feelings. One of the reasons she'd come to the ranch in the first place was to hide her pregnancy once she got bigger. *She should have told me. Her sister should have told me. Her brother-in-law should have told me.*

He hadn't questioned that assumption in July, but it was the first week of September now, and he did. Why should they have told him? He was a stranger to them. How did he think that first day should have gone? Grace and Alex, standing by their open car doors, should have said what, exactly? *Are you the foreman? This is our sister, Sophia. She's pregnant.*

August had been hot and slow on the ranch. Travis had only ridden half days as he watched the cow-calf pairs thrive on summer grass. The indignation had changed to something else. *If only she'd told me at the beginning. If only her sister had told me. If only I'd known...*

But it was September now, and he realized he'd never finished the thought.

If only she'd told him at the beginning, *then what?*

DJ Deezee Kalm would still be the father. The week of the wedding, Travis had verified Deezee's schedule to make sure he'd keep away from Sophia and her sister. *If only I'd known...*

He still would have kept Deezee away from Sophia. The man was still a jerk. He'd still made life hard for Sophia in more ways than leaving her pregnant and alone. He'd hurt her career, her income, her self-confidence.

Sophia was planning on giving the baby up for adoption. Travis had been incredulous when she'd told him so on that awful day. His whole life was spent watching mothers rear their young. He couldn't imagine Sophia not wanting to rear hers, but now he wondered what kind of influence Deezee might have been on that decision.

Travis had that impatient feeling again. He needed to lay eyes on Sophia. Seven weeks was far too long.

He let his horse walk faster. The house wasn't far away now. He knew the terrain like the back of his hand. Down this slope, up the next rise, and he'd see the white pillars.

The old lie came to him as easily as it had so many times before. If he could just check on Sophia, then he'd be able to put his mind at rest and move on.

A gunshot rang out.

In an instant, Travis's thoughts crystallized: the only thing in his world that mattered was Sophia.

She was in danger.

Chapter 19

"Damn, girl. You look like a pregnant cow."

Sophia didn't bother to answer Deezee. She was twenty-one weeks along, halfway through her pregnancy, so of course she had a baby bump. She still wasn't wearing maternity clothes. Her stretchy yoga top covered her fine. Obviously, Deezee had never seen a pregnant cow if he thought she resembled one.

Deezee shut the door to his car, a black luxury sedan. He wasn't driving it, though. That privilege belonged to one of his ever-present buddies. Sophia didn't recognize this particular buddy. The back doors opened and two more men came out.

Afraid to be alone with your own thoughts, Deezee? Still?

But she wouldn't say anything out loud. She'd been expecting her lawyer, the one who was supposed to arrive first with the adoption papers for Deezee to sign with her. She'd texted Clay that a black sedan would be coming onto the property today, so it had come through all three gates unchallenged, she was sure. She'd never expected Deezee to arrive in such a traditional car.

Her little burner phone could only text and call, but it couldn't do either of those things right now, because it was in the house, and she was on the patio. If she made a run for the door, she had no doubt someone from Deezee's crew would get there before she had the door closed and locked behind herself. She didn't want to be locked in the house with these guys.

None of Travis's men would be coming to check on her. And Travis himself? He wasn't speaking to her. She'd never seen a man as shocked as he'd been when she'd told him the baby wasn't his.

Clay was her only point of contact at the ranch now, and she'd told him she wanted the black sedan to come to the house. Round and round, back to the beginning: Sophia was stuck for the next ninety minutes with Deezee and his posse.

A little shiver of fear went down her back.

"You're early," she said, then immediately wished she hadn't. They were almost three hours early. The lawyer had arranged it so that he'd be here long before they were, and Deezee was never early to anything, until today.

"No prob, girl. Let's check out the new place. What do you have to drink?"

She was an actor. She needed to pull this role off. "I don't have anything you like. I'm pregnant, so…no alcohol." She held up her hands and shrugged. "I think if you go back to the main road and head west, the very next road takes you to a local bar. That might be fun.

The lawyer won't be here with the paperwork for another hour, anyway. Might as well go do some shots."

One of the backseat buddies liked the idea. *Please, please, please talk your gang into going.* Of course, the next road to the west didn't lead to a bar. It led to the Watersons' ranch, but Deezee would probably drive a good half mile in before he realized it. Maybe the Watersons would detain them.

Travis trusted the Watersons. They would've been part of her safety net, if she'd been smart enough to accept it. She hoped the Watersons would forgive her for sending Deezee onto their property, but if they were friends of Travis, it was her best bet for safety.

"Let's go," the backseat buddy said, enthusiastic to find the bar.

Hope swelled in Sophia's chest.

"Nah-nah-no-no-no." Deezee waved off his buddy with a shake of his blinged-out fingers.

Hope burst like a bubble.

"I gotta check this place out. We are in the *sticks*. Damn, girl, whatchu do out here all alone?"

I cry.

She smiled. "Well, like you said, you've now checked the place out. This is all there is." She snapped her fingers. "You know where there might be some beer? In the bunkhouse. Just go past this barn and follow that fence. You can't miss it."

She knew exactly how the hands who had the day off would react to these four storming into the bunkhouse. *Please, Deezee, go get some beer from the bunkhouse.*

"Why are you so anxious to get rid of me?"

Sophia had not done her best acting. She was nervous. She'd never felt so vulnerable, and Deezee could see it.

"Don't you want to party anymore?" he asked. "Oh, yeah. You got a bun in the oven." He turned to his friends. "How about that, boys? I'm not shooting blanks. Who knocked up Sophia Jackson? This guy."

The gunshot took her completely by surprise. She jumped a mile. Even Deezee dropped the f-bomb on his friend for the deafening sound.

The man had pulled out a handgun and was aiming it at the barn. "Just testing out the 'you can't hit the broad side of a barn' thing." He fired again. "My father used to say that. I hated my father."

"Stop!" Sophia ran from the patio toward him. "There are horses in there. Dogs. Cats. You'll hurt something."

She grabbed his arm, but he shook her off and fired again.

"Please," she begged. "It's a real barn. You'll kill something."

"Give me that." Deezee held out his hand for the gun. He took more careful aim than his friend. "Calling the shot. Eight ball in the corner pocket."

"*Stop!*" Sophia yelled, lunging for his arm before the sound of pounding horse's hooves could register in her head.

Travis was there, off his horse while it was still galloping. He shoved Deezee's arm down. The gun fired into the dirt, then he twisted it from Deezee's grip. Travis ejected the magazine, cleared the chambered round, and then threw the empty gun as far as an outfielder to first base.

"Sophia, get in the house."

Deezee adopted all the arrogant posture he was capable of, but he backed up a step. "Who do you think you are, ordering my wife around?" He turned to the driver. "Show him the marriage license."

Sophia blinked as Travis decked her alleged husband. Deezee was out.

"What the eff, man?" the driver said to Travis. "You planning on taking on all three of us now?"

"Yes."

None of the three made a move against him.

"Sophia, get in the house." Travis repeated the order through gritted teeth.

She wanted to stay by Travis's side, but she felt the baby kick. This wasn't just about her safety, so she ran for the kitchen door as more men from the River Mack came thundering up the road.

"I want to go check on the puppies."

"Sophia, please, try to relax. Buck said the animals are all fine. Are you uncomfortable?"

She was lying on the couch with her upper body in Travis's lap and his arm supporting her neck and shoulders. His other hand hadn't stopped smoothing over her hair, her shoulder…her belly. She hadn't been this comfortable since the last time they'd made love.

"I'm fine. How are you? You're the one who had the fistfight."

"You're the one who's pregnant. My God, Sophia…" He cradled her closer for a moment, then put his head back and sighed.

"I'm okay, really." Her heart felt more and more okay each time he did that. "I never threw a punch."

"You didn't have to throw a punch to have all your muscles pumped full of adrenaline. I can feel that my muscles are worn-out from the tension, and yours are way more important than mine right now." His hand smoothed its way over her belly again.

"Thank you."

He was silent.

"Thank you for treating me right, and for coming to my rescue, and for being an all-around decent man."

"I've been an ass. You should be kicking mine instead of apologizing to me. I love you, Sophia. I have from the very first, and I could kick myself for wasting the entire month of August feeling sorry for myself."

"Well, it's kind of a big deal to find out your lover is carrying another man's child. Don't say it isn't."

His hand drifted over her hair again, petting her, soothing her. Loving her. "Okay, let's get this settled. It's a big deal, I agree. But I could have talked to you about it. I could have asked you my questions, instead of asking myself questions over and over that I couldn't possibly know the answer to."

"I know I should—"

"There's more."

He looked so fierce, Sophia's heart tripped a little.

"I apologize for taking so long to realize the obvious. I kept saying to myself, 'if only I'd known,' until I finally realized it wouldn't have mattered. What if I'd known you were pregnant when you first arrived here? I would have found you fascinating, anyway. What if you'd had this cute baby bump when you were throwing those tomatoes? We still would've ripped off our clothes in the living room."

"Travis—"

"What if you'd arrived here with a newborn baby? I still would have fallen in love with you. The key is you, Sophia. I will always love you."

"I'm—I'm—" She gave up and snuggled into his

chest, because he was big and strong and she could. "I'm going to live on that forever. That fills my heart up."

He kissed her, which was exactly what she wanted.

"Aren't you angry with me at all?" he whispered over her lips.

"No. I watch you through the window every day. You've looked so grim, and I've known it was because of me. I'm so sorry."

She didn't want him to think the worst of her. "I know this sounds hard to believe, but I really was in denial. I read that the pregnancy test could be false positive, and my brain just seized on that as the right explanation, because it was the only explanation I could handle. My career wouldn't be impacted. I wouldn't be tied to Deezee in any way. You came later, but once I met you, that was all the more reason to just ignore the possibility. I sound like an idiot, don't I?"

"There's nothing about you that sounds like an idiot." He kissed her sweetly, casually, like he had hours to kiss her whenever he pleased. "I'm sleeping here tonight. It's going to be a while before I can let you out of my sight. That's not too rational, either."

"I like that, though. You know you won't be sleeping with a married woman, right? I really want you to know I'm not in denial about that. Deezee is just trying to stir up gossip with that paperwork."

"I know. I'm glad the lawyer is releasing a statement for you."

The lawyer had shown up punctually, only to find himself being asked to clarify all kinds of points of law beyond adoption. A quick internet search had cleared up the alleged St. Barth's marriage certificate. Thirty days' notice was a minimum requirement to marry on that island, and they'd only flown in for the weekend.

More importantly in Sophia's mind, she'd never said *I do.* Deezee's antics at the altar had been her last straw. She'd thrown her bouquet at him when she was only half-way down the aisle, something that had made her look terrible in photos, but it had been her one justifiable tantrum.

She pulled far enough away from Travis to look at him directly. "I'm not married, and I've never been married."

He studied her for a moment. "Are you thinking of my dad?"

"Maybe. Yes. I know you don't admire what he did. I think you would never sleep with a married woman."

He brushed her hair back from her eyes. "If I had to wait for your divorce to be final, I would. After meeting Deezee, there's no way I would want you to stay married to him. Am I grateful that we don't need to wait for a divorce?" He laughed to lighten the moment. "That's like asking me if the sky's blue."

Sophia wished she could smile back. "You must question my judgment for even thinking about marrying him. I do. Grace hated him from the first, but he wasn't always quite so bad. He started using the drugs they sold at his raves. Then he started using even when there wasn't a party on. It got pretty out of control before I left him. It's magnified every flaw a hundred times."

"Sophia?"

"Yes?"

"I don't care about Deezee. You are an amazing woman no matter who you used to date."

Sophia placed her hand on her belly.

She cared. And she was scared.

Chapter 20

"I've got an early Christmas gift for you."

"Seriously?" Sophia asked. Travis thought she sounded equal parts excited and skeptical as she dumped the last scoop of oats into the trough in the mare's stall. "Wasn't a house enough?"

She'd fallen in love with the century-old foreman's house. She loved that it had a little parlor and a library and a dining room instead of one expansive space—so Travis had bought it for her. The MacDowells sold it to him along with a dozen acres or so, just enough land to make a nice little residential property along the edge of the River Mack. The renovations, including the baby's room, would be finished by the end of January, when Sophia's lease was up.

Until then, he would continue to live with her in the main house. Never again would he go seven weeks without seeing her. Sophia's next movie would begin shooting in July, and her new manager had added contract riders to keep the future Chalmers family together. Sophia's housing on location would accommodate the baby and a nanny, and Travis would arrive via the studio's private jet midway through the shooting schedule. Private jets and cowboys might seem an odd combination, but Travis figured he could handle the luxury. He'd go through hell to be with Sophia. If he had to adapt to luxury instead, well, there was no law that said life always had to be hard.

He walked up behind Sophia and slipped his arms around her, above her round belly, below her breasts, which had become even more lovely with her pregnancy. "I had a different kind of gift in mind."

"Here in the barn?" she asked, sounding like a sex goddess.

"Like that would be the first time."

Sophia pretended to droop her shoulders in disappointment. "I'm going to have to take a raincheck on that gift. I feel as big as a house this morning."

It was cool in the barn in December, so she wore a fluffy green sweater. Travis noticed that she rubbed her last-trimester belly in a different way today than usual, although the baby wasn't due for three weeks. Maybe the sweater was just extra soft and touchable to her.

Maybe not.

Sophia was adamant that a home birth was the only way to keep her birthing experience private. Her midwife could reach the ranch in a little less than an hour, but Travis didn't find that as comforting as Sophia did. He'd witnessed hundreds of animal births in his life, but Sophia was no animal, and he hoped when the contractions began, she'd change her mind and let him drive her to the hospital. She was no longer placing the baby up for adoption, so secrecy was no longer paramount. Her well-being was.

That was a discussion for next week's appointment with the midwife. Today was Christmas Eve, and he wanted to put a smile on Sophia's beautiful face.

"Close your eyes," he murmured. "Don't move."

He went into Samson's stall and scooped up the black-and-gray puppy he'd hidden there. The pup was four months old and probably fifteen pounds, but it was still a puppy with oversized paws and soft fur.

He placed the soft fur against Sophia's soft sweater. "Happy Christmas Eve."

"Oh! A puppy." Her smile was exactly what he'd hoped for.

For about five seconds.

Then it faded in confusion. "Wait. Is this one of Patch's puppies?"

"Yes. She was returned. I thought you might want to keep her."

"The poor thing. Poor, poor puppy." She buried her face in its fur and burst into tears.

Travis scratched the dog behind the ears. "Baby, the dog is happy. Why aren't you?"

"She was returned because she wasn't good enough, was she?"

"No, Roger just got a job offer in another state, and since he'd only had the pup for a few—"

"You don't have to keep pretending for me." Her tears fell as she kissed the puppy.

Having a fiancée in her final trimester had taught Travis that tears were possible over just about any topic.

He wouldn't dismiss every tear as hormones, however, not when he knew the unique challenges Sophia faced.

"Come into the office and sit. You and the puppy." He held the desk chair for Sophia, gave her a tissue from the box he'd learned to keep on his desk now that it wasn't just him in the barn, and then he waited to see if she would tell him what was really bothering her.

She did. "You said that everyone wanted Patch's puppies because she's a great cow dog, but for this litter, the father was a mystery. Now the dogs are being returned. It's the father, isn't it? Even with a great mother like Patch, people assume the puppies just aren't good enough. It's so unfair. The puppies didn't do anything wrong."

He crouched down in front of her. "This is the only puppy that's come back to the ranch, and it's because Roger got a job offer in another state. He'll be in an office building all day. That's it. I wouldn't lie to you, Sophia. That puppy is desirable, I guarantee it, whether we know who the father is or not."

"Maybe I should've stuck with my plan to place the baby up for adoption. No one would have known who the biological parents were. The baby would have started life with a clean slate."

That wasn't coming from as far out of left field as it seemed. "You saw the news today that Deezee was convicted of drug trafficking."

She placed one hand on her belly. "That's this poor baby's father. Everyone knows it. Deezee made sure of that, and now he's a felon. How can I make up for that? I'm not that great when it comes to motherhood material. Here's Patch, this legendary cow dog, and even she can't make up for the father. People think her sweet puppies aren't good enough because the f-father—"

"Sophia, listen to me."

Travis hated the son of a bitch who had just been convicted. He wasn't just a drug dealer who'd come to this ranch waving around a gun that could have injured Sophia, but he was the man who'd messed with Sophia's head, too. The fact that she'd once considered herself in love with Deezee still undermined her confidence in herself.

"You are going to be a great mother. I know this from the bottom of my soul. The fact that you are worried whether or not you'll be good enough for this baby proves that the baby is getting a mom who cares."

He'd tell her that as many times as it took. Deezee had told her crap for five months. Travis was going to tell her truths for the rest of her life. Travis was going to win.

She let go of the puppy with one hand and placed her palm on her belly in that same low place.

Travis covered her hand with his. "No one is ever going to look at this child and think he or she isn't good enough. Deezee chose to sell drugs for money. That's not DNA. That was a choice. Anyone from any parent could make the same choice, or not. Deezee's not going to be around to teach this baby about bad choices. I'm going to be."

He had to stop and clear his throat. Then he thought better of it. Let Sophia see how much he cared.

He looked up at her, and he knew she saw the unshed tears, because she looked a little bit blurry. "I cannot wait to hold this baby. This is the most exciting thing in my world. I may not have contributed any DNA, but I'm going to be part of this child, too. I'm going to teach 'em when to say 'gid-yap' and 'whoa' and not to let their horse step on their reins and to eat their zucchini and to love their mama. That's you."

Sophia's tears subsided. Her breathing was steady and the puppy in her arm was calm. Travis knew their future was bright. Just when Travis had relaxed, Sophia slayed him. "There are a million reasons I'm going to love this baby, Travis, but here's one of the biggest. If it hadn't been for this baby, I would never have come to your ranch. I would never have met you. For that, I will always owe the baby one."

Travis had to bow his head and clear his throat.

"Me, too, Sophia. Me, too."

Under their hands, he felt her stomach draw tight. She wasn't livestock, not at all, but Travis had felt that same kind of contraction in horses and cows. It could pass and not start again for another three weeks. It could be nothing.

"I don't like the look of the weather out there," he said. "Let's put this puppy back in her hay and head back to the house."

Sophia was suddenly keenly interested in rearranging all the ornaments on the Christmas tree.

Travis ran a ranch. He was a big believer that Mother Nature knew what she was doing, but as far as nesting instincts went, this one wasn't particularly useful.

"I'm gonna call the midwife," he said.

Sophia stopped in the middle of switching the locations of a sequined ball and a glass ball. "Why? I feel fine."

Travis nodded. "That's good, baby. Glad to hear it." He dialed the phone.

Outside, the rain turned to sleet.

The radio announced the highways were closed. Travis imagined that children all around Austin were afraid that Santa wasn't going to be able to get his sled through the bad weather tonight. He was afraid the midwife wouldn't.

He was right, damn it all to hell.

In the end, for all the times he'd insisted to Sophia that she wasn't a beast, he was grateful that there were similarities. It made the whole process a little less bewildering. They'd decided ahead of time which bed to use and had plastic coverings and extra sheets prepared. But as Sophia walked around the house rearranging Christmas decorations, he noticed she kept going into the master bathroom, a room he hadn't seen her use once in the four months since he'd begun living with her. It reminded him of a cow who'd kept returning to stand under a particular tree, or a mother cat who'd decided to leave her nice box for a treacherous rafter at the last minute.

He picked up the supplies the midwife had left last week and carried them into the master bathroom.

"I think I'll take a bath," Sophia said. "Then maybe we can watch a Christmas movie on TV."

She got undressed and sat in the tub, but she never turned the water on. She wasn't having any painful contractions for him to time, and the midwife kept telling him on the phone that a first labor could take twelve hours, easily, if Sophia really was in labor. By then, the roads would surely be open.

So Sophia sat in the dry bathtub and Travis pretended that was normal. Then the first painful contraction hit, and poor Sophia went from nothing to full-out labor in no time.

"I don't think this is right," she said, panting to catch her breath.

"Everything is working just like it should."

The pain was scaring her. "But it doesn't always work out. You lose calves every year. We almost lost that kitten—"

But another contraction hit her before the last one ended, and she started trying to do her *hee hee hee* breaths like the online course had taught them.

Another contraction. God, they were coming hard. Fast. His poor Sophia.

Travis kissed her temple, wet as it was from pain and the effort to handle the pain. He knelt next to the tub and kept his arm around her shoulders. He felt so utterly useless.

The contractions left her limp. He could only support her with his arm.

"That calf," she panted. "Mother Nature would have taken that calf and the mother with it if you hadn't been there to help."

"No, baby. You're remembering that wrong."

"You had those straps."

"I didn't have to use them, remember? I just watched and waited, and that baby was born just fine. Your baby is going to be born just fine. It hurts like hell—" and God, he wished he could do something about that "—but it's going just fine."

The contraction started building again, the pain rolling over her as she gripped his hand and tried to breathe.

"That heifer almost died. She couldn't move. She was so tired." Panic was in her voice. She was losing it, the pain was winning, and Travis thought his own heart was going to break a rib, it was beating so hard. She looked too much like her pioneer movie character, the one that had died onscreen.

Help wasn't coming, not until the sleet stopped. Travis couldn't control the weather. He couldn't control Sophia's labor. This was the most important event of his life, the one thing in his life he absolutely had to get right, and he was powerless.

Sophia lifted her head and started panting. *Hee hee hee.*

God bless her. She was still at it. She didn't have a choice. She couldn't quit.

He couldn't, either.

He shoved the fear and the images from that damned movie out of his head as he shifted his position a bit, leaning over the edge of the tub and adjusting his arm to hold Sophia even closer. Her fingers loosened on his as the wave receded.

She plopped her head back onto his arm. "I can't do it. This can't be Mother Nature."

"Listen to me. You are doing everything right."

But she wasted her precious energy to roll her head on his arm, *no, no, no.* "That calf would have died. You had to drag her over to that heifer."

Travis hadn't realized how heavily that still weighed on Sophia. They'd never talked about it before now. This was a heck of a time to talk about anything, but he didn't want her worrying about what could go wrong.

He kissed her temple again. "Everything is going to be okay. When you saw me drag that newborn calf over to the mama, I was just being helpful. She was tired, so I just brought that baby up close to her so she could take care of it. And you know what? When your little baby is born, if you're too tired to move, that'll be okay, too. I'm gonna scoop up that little baby and hold her right here for you." He brought his other arm across her breasts and completed a circle around her, keeping the woman he loved in his arms. "And it's gonna be you and me and that brand new baby, and the three of us are gonna be just fine."

"I'm sorry. This is…just…" She still looked a little unfocused, but not so panicky.

He could feel her body going under the contraction. "You're doing great."

"…just not how we planned it."

"I wouldn't miss this for the world."

"I love you."

He thought he'd never heard the words uttered in a better way. They pierced his soul. "I love you, too."

She let go of his hand and gripped the edge of the tub. The last of that dazed and confused expression lifted as she frowned fiercely. "I think—I feel like I should push. It hasn't been long enough, has it? What time is it? Ohmigod, I'm not kidding. I need to push. Am I supposed to push?"

Travis nodded. "If you think it's time to push, then you should push. I know you're right."

"Okay. Then I'm going to have a baby now."

He dropped one more kiss on her head. "You do that, Sophia. You do that."

And she did.

In record time, in a bathtub on the River Mack ranch on Christmas Eve, Noelle Jackson Chalmers was born, healthy and loved.

Travis wept. No one had ever been given a better Christmas gift.

* * * * *

Cathy Gillen Thacker is married and a mother of three. She and her husband spent eighteen years in Texas and now reside in North Carolina. Her mysteries, romantic comedies and heartwarming family stories have made numerous appearances on bestseller lists, but her best reward, she says, is knowing one of her books made someone's day a little brighter. A popular Harlequin author for many years, she loves telling passionate stories with happy endings and thinks nothing beats a good romance and a hot cup of tea! You can visit Cathy's website, cathygillenthacker.com, for more information on her upcoming and previously published books, recipes, and a list of her favorite things.

Books by Cathy Gillen Thacker

Harlequin Special Edition

Texas Legends: The McCabes

The Texas Cowboy's Quadruplets
His Baby Bargain

Harlequin Western Romance

Texas Legends: The McCabes

The Texas Cowboy's Triplets
The Texas Cowboy's Baby Rescue

Texas Legacies: The Lockharts

A Texas Soldier's Family
A Texas Cowboy's Christmas
The Texas Valentine Twins
Wanted: Texas Daddy
A Texas Soldier's Christmas

Visit the Author Profile page at Harlequin.com for more titles.

A TEXAS COWBOY'S CHRISTMAS

CATHY GILLEN THACKER

Chapter 1

"I blame *you* for this, Chance Lockhart!" Molly Griffith fumed the moment she came toe-to-toe with him just inside the open-air bucking-bull training facility of Bullhaven Ranch.

Chance set down the saddle and blanket he'd been carrying. With a wicked grin, he pushed the brim of his hat back and paused to take her in. No doubt about it—the twenty-seven-year-old general contractor/interior designer was never lovelier than when she was in a temper. With her amber eyes blazing, her pretty face flushed with indignant color and her auburn curls wildly out of place, she looked as if she were ripe for taming.

Luckily for both of them, he was too smart to succumb to the challenge.

His gaze drifted over her, taking in her designer jeans and peacock-blue boots, before moving upward to the white silk shirt and soft suede blazer that cloaked her curvy frame.

Damn, she was sexy, though. From the half-moon pendant that nestled in the hollow of her breasts to the voluptuous bounty of her bow-shaped lips.

Exhaling slowly, he tamped down his desire and prompted in a lazy drawl, "Blame me for what?"

Molly propped her hands on her hips. "For telling my son, Braden, he can have a live bull for Christmas!"

Somehow Chance managed not to wince at the huffy accusation. He set down the saddle and narrowed his eyes instead. "That's not *exactly* what I said."

Molly moved close enough he could inhale her flowery perfume, her breasts rising and falling with every deep, agitated breath. "Did you or did you not tell him that Santa could bring him a bull?"

Chance shrugged, glad for the brisk November breeze blowing over them. Still holding Molly's eyes, he rocked back on the heels of his worn leather work boots. "I said he could *ask* Santa for a bull."

Molly harrumphed and folded her arms beneath her breasts, the action plumping them up all the more. "Exactly!"

Working to slow his rising pulse, Chance lowered his face to hers and explained tautly, "That doesn't mean Santa is going to *bring* it."

Chance picked up the gear, slung it over one shoulder and stalked toward the ten-by-ten metal holding pen, where a two-year-old Black Angus bull named Peppermint was waiting.

One of the heirs to his retired national championship bucking bull, Mistletoe, he bore the same steady temperament, lively personality and exceptional athletic ability of his daddy.

After easing open the gate, Chance stepped inside.

Aware Molly was still watching his every move, he proceeded to pet the young bull in training. Once gentled, he set the saddle on Peppermint's back.

Swallowing nervously at the thousand-pound bull, Molly stepped back. With an indignant toss of her head, she continued her emotional tirade. "You really don't have a clue how all this works, do you?"

Chance sighed as he tightened the cinch and led Peppermint into the practice chute, closing the gate behind him. "I have a feeling you're about to tell me."

Molly watched him climb the side rails and secure a dummy on the saddle via electronically controlled buckles.

Feeling the unwelcome extra weight, Peppermint began to snort and paw the ground within the confines of the chute.

Even though she was in no danger, Molly retreated even farther. "A child writes a letter to Santa, asking for his most precious gift. Then Santa brings it."

Chance plucked the remote control out of his pocket. "That wasn't how it worked in my home." He signaled to his hired hand Billy to take his position at the exit gate on the other side of the practice ring. "I remember asking Santa for a rodeo for my backyard in Dallas. Guess what?" He shot her a provoking look that started at her face and moved languidly over her voluptuous body before returning to her eyes. "It didn't happen."

Molly rolled her eyes, still staying clear of the snorting, increasingly impatient Peppermint. Digging her boots into the ground, she fired back, "I cannot help it if your mother and father did not appropriately censure your wishes in advance."

Chance hit the control. Immediately, the sound of a rodeo crowd filled the practice arena. He released the gate, and Peppermint, tired of confinement, went barreling into the ring.

For the next few seconds, he bucked hard to the right and came down. Went up and down in the middle, then bucked to the left.

And still the crowd sounds filled the air.

Adding to the excitement, as Peppermint bucked higher and higher…and seeing the kind of athletic movement he wanted, Chance rewarded the bull with the release of the dummy.

It went flying. And landed facedown in the dirt.

Billy whistled.

Peppermint turned and followed the waving Billy out the exit gate and into another pen, where he would receive a treat for his performance.

Chance cut the crowd sounds on the intercom system. Silence fell in the arena once again, and Chance lifted a hand. "Thanks, Billy!"

"No problem, boss!" he replied before going off to see to the bucking bull.

Molly said, looking impressed despite herself, "Is that how you train them?"

"Yep."

"Too bad no one can train you."

"Really? That's juvenile, even for you, Molly."

He knew where it came from, though. She brought out the irascible teenager in him, too.

Chance went back into the barn, checking on his thirty bucking bulls, safely ensconced in their individual ten-by-ten metal pens, then took a visual of those in the pastures. Finished, he strode across the barnyard to a smaller facility, where his national champion was kept.

Mistletoe's private quarters, his ranch office, veterinary exam, lab and breeding chute, and equipment facility were all there. All were state-of-the-art and a testament to what he had built.

"Look, I'm sorry," Molly said, dogging his every step. "But I'm trying to help my son be realistic here."

Chance paused to pet Mistletoe. The big bucking bull had a little gray on his face these days, but he was still pleasant as ever to be around. "Is that what you're doing for Braden?" He gave his beloved Black Angus one last rub before turning back to Molly. "Helping him temper his expectations? Or censuring all his dreams?"

Molly muttered something he was just as glad not to be able to understand, then threw up her hands in exasperation.

"I want my little boy to grow up being practical!"

Chance spun around, and she followed him back down the center aisle. "Unlike certain idiot cowboys who shall remain nameless."

There she went with the insults again, but it was better than dealing with the smoldering attraction they felt whenever they were together.

Chance paused at the sink in the tack room to wash and dry his hands, then walked out to join her. Saw her shiver in the brisk, wintry air.

Aware the day looked a lot warmer than it actually was, he turned away from the evidence of her chill and drawled, "I think I *might* know who you're talking about." Rubbing his jaw in a parody of thoughtfulness, he stepped purposefully into her personal space.

Watching her amber eyes widen, he continued, "That rancher brother of mine, Wyatt, down the road. None too bright, is he?"

Molly made a strangled sound deep in her throat. Rather than step away, she put her hand on the center of his chest and gave him a small, equally purposeful shove. "I'm talking about you, you big lug."

Delighted by her unwillingness to give any ground to him, he captured her hand before she could snatch it away and held it over his heart. "Ah. Endearments." He sighed with comically exaggerated dreaminess.

Temper spiking even more, she tried, unsuccessfully, to extricate her fingers from his. "You're playing with fire here, cowboy."

So he was. But then he had to do something with all the aggravation she caused him. And had been causing, if truth be known, for quite some time.

He let his grin widen, surveying her indignant expression. Dropping his head, he taunted softly, "The kind of fire that leads to a kiss?"

"The kind that leads to me hauling off and kicking you right in the shin!"

It was good to know he could get to her this much. Because she sure got to him. The pressure building at the front of his jeans told him that.

He lowered his lips to hers. "Didn't your parents ever tell you that you can catch more flies with sugar than spite?"

Abruptly Molly's face paled.

Too late, he realized he should have bothered to find

out what kind of life she'd had as a kid before hurling that particular insult.

She drew a deep breath. Serious now. Subdued.

Aware he'd hurt her—without meaning to—he let her hand go.

She stepped back. Regaining her composure, she lifted her chin and said in a solemn tone, "I want you to talk to Braden. Tell him you were wrong. Santa doesn't bring little boys live bulls."

At that particular moment, he thought he would do just about anything for her. Probably would have, if she hadn't been so socially and monetarily ambitious and so out of touch regarding what really mattered in life, same as his ex.

But Molly was. So…

Exploring their attraction would lead only to misery.

For all their sakes, Chance put up the usual barbed wire around his heart. "Why can't you tell him?" he asked with an indifferent shrug. "You're Braden's momma, after all." And, from all he'd seen, misguided goals aside, a damn good one.

Molly's lower lip trembled, and she threw up her hands in frustration. "I have told him! He won't believe me. Braden says that you're the cowboy, and you know everything, and you said it was okay. And that's what he wants me to write in his letter to Santa, and I cannot let him ask Saint Nick for that, only to have his little heart broken."

She had a point about that, Chance realized guiltily. He'd hate to see the little tyke, who also happened to be the spitting image of his mother, disappointed.

Sobering, he asked, "What *do* you want Braden to have?"

Molly's features softened in relief. "The Leo and Lizzie World Adventure wooden train set." She pulled a magazine article out of her back pocket that listed the toy as the most wanted preschool-age present for the holiday that year. Featuring train characters from a popular animated kids' television show, the starter set was extremely elaborate. Which was no surprise. Since Molly Griffith was known for her big ambitions and even more expensive tastes.

It made sense she would want the same for her only child.

Even if Braden would be happier playing with a plastic toy bull. Or horse...

Sensing she wanted his approval, Chance shrugged. Wary of hurting her feelings—again—he mumbled, "Looks nice."

As if sensing his attitude was not quite genuine, she frowned. "It will bring Braden hours of fun."

Enough to justify the cost? he wondered, noting the small wooden pieces were ridiculously overpriced— even if they were in high demand. He squinted at her. "Are you sure you don't work for the toy company?"

She scowled at his joke but came persuasively closer, even more serious now. "Please, Chance. I'm begging you."

This is new, Chance thought, surprised.

He actually kind of liked her coming to him for help.

She spread her hands wide, turning on the full wattage of maternal charm. "Braden just turned three years old. It's the first Christmas holiday he's likely to ever remember. I really want it to be special." She paused and took a deep breath that lifted the lush softness of her breasts. "You have to help me talk sense into my son."

* * *

For a brief moment, Molly thought she had finally gotten through to the impossibly handsome cowboy.

Then he folded his brawny arms across his broad chest and let out a sigh that reverberated through his six-foot-three-inch frame. Intuitive hazel eyes lassoed hers. "I want to help you."

Pulse racing, Molly watched as he swept off his black Stetson and shoved a hand through the rumpled strands of his thick chestnut-colored hair. "But?"

Frowning, he settled his hat squarely on his head. "I can't do to your son what my parents did to me."

"And what was that?" she asked curiously.

"Try and censor and mold his dreams—to suit your wishes instead of Braden's."

Had Lucille and the late Frank Lockhart done that to Chance? The grim set of his lips seemed to say so. But that had nothing to do with her or Braden.

Molly stepped closer, invading his space. With a huff, she planted both hands on her waist and accused, "You just started this calamity to get under my skin."

His sexy grin widened. "I was already under your skin," he reminded her, tilting his head to one side.

True, unfortunately. Molly did her best to stifle a sigh while still stubbornly holding her ground. She wished he didn't radiate such endless masculine energy or look so ruggedly fit in his gray plaid flannel shirt and jeans. Never mind have such a sexy smile and firm, sensual lips...

She could barely look at him and not wonder what it would be like to kiss him.

Just as an experiment, of course.

"So you're really not going to help me?"

Chance's brow lifted. "Convince him he doesn't want to be a cowboy when he grows up? And have a ranch like mine that has all bulls on it? Or get a head start on it by getting his first livestock now?" His provoking grin widened. "No. I'm not going to do any of that. I will, however, try to talk him into getting a baby calf. Since females are a lot more docile than males."

"Ha-ha."

"I wasn't talking about you," he claimed with choir-boy innocence.

Yeah...right. When they were together like this, *everything* was about the two of them.

Molly shut her eyes briefly and rubbed at the tension in her temples. With effort, she forced her attention back to her child's fervent wish to be a rancher, just like "Cowboy Chance." Who was, admittedly, the most heroic-looking figure her son had ever had occasion to meet.

Trying not to think about what a dashing figure he cut, Molly turned her glance toward the storm clouds building on the horizon. It wasn't supposed to rain for another day or two, but it looked like it now. "I live in town, remember? I don't have any place to keep a baby calf."

Chance shrugged. "So ask my mother to pasture it at the Circle H Ranch. You're there enough anyway."

Molly wheeled around and headed back to the driveway next to the log-cabin-style Bullhaven ranch house, where she had parked her sporty red SUV. "Even if that were a plausible solution, which it's not, Braden and I aren't going to be here past the first week of January."

Squinting curiously, he matched his strides to hers. "How come?"

Trying not to notice how he towered over her, or how much she liked it, Molly fished her keys out of her jacket pocket. "Not that it's any of your business, but we're moving to Dallas."

Chance paused next to her vehicle. "To be closer to Braden's daddy?"

Her heart panged in her chest. If only her little boy had a father who wanted his child in his life. But he didn't, so...

There was no way she was talking to Chance Lockhart about the most humiliating mistake she'd ever made. Or the fact that her ill-conceived liaison had unexpectedly led to the best thing in her life, a family of her very own. Molly hit the button on the keypad and heard the click of the driver-side lock releasing. "No."

"No, that's not why you're moving?"

He came close enough she could smell the soap and sun and man fragrance of his skin.

Awareness shimmered inside her.

He watched her open the door. "Or no, that's not what you want—to be closer to your ex?"

Heavens, the man was annoying!

Figuring this was the time to go on record with her goals—and hence vanquish his mistaken notions about her once and for all—Molly lifted her gaze to his. "What I want is for my son to grow up with all the advantages I never had." Braden, unlike her, would want for nothing.

Except maybe a daddy in his life.

Not that she could fix that.

Chance's lip curled in contempt. "Ah, yes, back to social climbing."

He wasn't the only one who misinterpreted the reason behind her quest to get an in with every mover and shaker in the area. And beyond…

But for some reason, Chance Lockhart's contempt rankled.

Which was another reason to set him—and everyone else in Laramie County who misread her—straight. "Look, I don't expect you to understand. You having grown up with a silver spur in your mouth and all."

He grinned.

"But not all of us have had those advantages."

His hazel eyes sparkled, the way they always did when he got under her skin. "Like?"

"Private school, for one."

Chance remained implacable. "They have private schools in Laramie County."

"Not like the ones in Dallas."

He squinted in disapproval. "Which is where you want him to go."

Stubbornly, Molly held her ground. "If Braden attends the right preschool, he can get into the right elementary, then middle, then prep. From there, go on to an elite college."

Chance poked the brim of his hat up with one finger. "I'm guessing you aren't talking about anything in the University of Texas system."

Molly studied the frayed collar on Chance's flannel shirt, the snug worn jeans and run-of-the-mill leather belt. It was clear he didn't care about appearances. Coming from his background, he did not have to. "If Braden goes to an Ivy League school, the world is his oyster."

Chance rested his brawny forearm on the roof of her SUV. "I can see you've got it all mapped out."

Molly tried not to notice how well he filled out his

ranching clothes. "Yes, unlike you, Braden is going to take advantage of all the opportunities I plan to see come his way."

"How does Braden feel about all this?" Chance asked, not bothering to hide his frustration with her.

Had Molly not known better, she would have thought that the irascible cowboy did not want her to leave Laramie County. But that was ridiculous. The two of them couldn't get gas at the same filling station at the same time without getting into a heated argument. More likely, Chance would be delighted to see her depart. "My son is *three*."

"Meaning you haven't told him."

"He has no concept of time."

"So, in other words, no."

"I will, once Christmas is over," Molly maintained. She moved as if to get in her vehicle, but Chance remained where he was, his big, imposing body blocking the way.

"Has it occurred to you that you're getting ahead of yourself with all your plans to better educate and monetarily and socially provide for your son?"

Chance wasn't the first to tell her so.

She hadn't listened to anyone else.

And she wasn't about to listen to him, either.

Ducking beneath his outstretched arm, she slid behind the steering wheel. Bending her head, she put the key in the ignition. "What I think is that one day, my son will be very grateful to me for doing all that I can to ensure his dreams come true," she retorted defensively.

Chance leaned down so they were face-to-face. "Except, of course, ones that have to do with livestock."

What is it about this man? Molly fumed inwardly. He

not only provoked her constantly—he had the potential to derail her at every turn, just by existing!

Pretending his attempts to delay her so they could continue their argument were not bothering her in the least, Molly flashed a confident smile. "You're right," she admitted with a sugary-sweet attitude even he would have to find laudable. "I have gotten way, way off track."

He chuckled. "Back to train analogies?"

She gave him a quelling look.

He lifted an exaggeratedly apologetic hand. "I know. Even some of us big, dumb cowpokes who passed on Ivy League educations know a few big words."

She'd heard Chance had been just as much of a problem to his wealthy parents growing up as he was to her now. "How about 'aggravate'?" She looked him square in the eye. "Do you know what that means?"

He grinned. "I think that's what I do to you, on a daily, hourly, basis?"

So true. Molly drew a calming breath. She started the ignition, then motioned for him to step away. When he did, she put her window down. "I'm going to be at the Circle H this afternoon, meeting with your mother about the proposed kitchen renovation."

"Well, what do you know," he rumbled with a maddeningly affable shrug. "I will be, too."

She ignored the fact that their two contracting companies were competing for the renovation job. "Braden will be with me. It's your chance to make things right with my son. Please, Chance." She paused to let her words sink in. "Don't let us down."

If Molly hadn't framed it quite like that, maybe he could have bailed. But she had, so at five past three

Chance found himself driving up the lane to the Circle H ranch house.

Molly's SUV was already on-site. She and her son, Braden, were by the pasture, where a one-week-old Black Angus was pastured with his momma. Little arms on the middle rung of the fence, Braden was staring, mesmerized, at the sight of the nursing bull.

"Can I pet him?" Braden asked as Chance strolled up to join them.

Her pretty face pinched with tension, Molly shook her head.

Chance hunkered down beside Braden. The little tyke had the same curly red hair, cute-as-a-button features and amber eyes as his mother. "Petting the bull would scare it, buddy, and we don't want that, do we?"

Balking, Braden bartered, "I know gentle. Mommy showed me." Realizing Chance didn't quite understand what he was saying, Braden continued with a demonstration of easy petting. "Kitty cat—gentle. Puppy—gentle. Babies—gentle."

"Ah. You're very gentle with all of those things," Chance concluded.

Braden nodded importantly. "Mommy showed me."

"Well, listen, buckaroo," Chance continued, still hunkered down so he and Braden were eye to eye. "It's always good to be gentle," he said kindly. "And it's great to be able to see a real baby bull."

Braden beamed. "I like bulls!"

"The thing is, Santa doesn't really have any bulls to bring to little boys," Chance told him, quashing the kid's dreams against his better judgment.

"Uh-huh! At the North Pole," Braden said. "Santa has everything!"

"No." Chance shook his head sadly but firmly. He looked the little boy in the eye. "There aren't any bulls at the North Pole."

Mutinously, Braden folded his little arms across his chest. "Santa bring me one," he reiterated stubbornly.

Out of the corner of Chance's eye, he saw Molly's stricken expression. Yeah. She pretty much wanted to let him have it. Given the unforeseen way things were developing, he could hardly blame her.

"For Christmas," Braden added for good measure, in case either Molly or Chance didn't understand him. He pointed to the pasture. "Want mommy bull. And baby bull."

Okay, this was not going according to plan, Chance thought uncomfortably.

"Baby needs mommy," Braden added plaintively, just in case they still weren't getting it.

Molly lifted a brow and sent Chance an even more withering glare.

Fortunately, at that moment, his mother walked out of the recently renovated Circle H bunkhouse, where she was currently living, her part-time cook and house-keeper, Maria Gonzales, at her side. The young woman often brought her own three-year-old daughter, Tessie, to work with her. The little lass peeked at Braden from behind her mother's skirt.

"Braden, Maria and Tessie were just about to make some Thanksgiving tarts. Would you like to help them?" Lucille asked.

He looked at his mother for permission.

Molly gave it with a nod, then pointed to the ranch house on the other side of the barns. "Miss Lucille,

Chance and I are going to walk over there and have a meeting. Then I'll come back to get you. Okay?"

Braden took Maria's outstretched hand. "'Kay, Mommy."

Maria and her two young charges set off.

In the past, the sixty-eight-year-old Lucille had ignored interpersonal tensions for the sake of peace. However, a recent series of life-changing events had caused Chance's mother to rethink the idea of sugarcoating anything. And now, to everyone's surprise, it turned out she could be as blunt as Chance's older brother, Garrett.

"What's going on between you two?" Lucille demanded as she looked from Molly to Chance and back again. "And don't tell me nothing, because I can feel the mutual aggravation simmering between you a mile away!"

Chance would have preferred to keep their tiff private. Unfortunately, Molly had other ideas. "Chance told Braden that he could ask Santa to bring him a real live baby bull for Christmas!" she sputtered.

Lucille turned to him, formidable as always in an ultrasuede sheath, cashmere cardigan and heels.

"I was trying not to quash his dreams," Chance insisted hotly.

"So, instead, you lit fire to impossible ones, and now he wants not just a baby bull but a bovine mama to go with it, too," Molly accused him, looking furious enough to burst into tears.

"Look, I—" Even as the words came out of his mouth, Chance had to wonder how Molly had managed to put him on the defensive.

She stomped closer and waved a finger beneath his nose. "If you hadn't brought that baby bull over with his momma to pasture at the Circle H—"

"If you hadn't brought your son with you to discuss making a bid," he volleyed right back.

Molly planted both her hands on her slender hips. "I had no choice!"

He mocked her by doing the same. "Well, neither did I!"

Completely exasperated, Lucille stopped worrying the pearls around her neck and stepped in between them. "Enough, you two!" she chastised. "You are acting like ornery children. It's five weeks until Christmas…we will figure out a way to work this out."

Chance and Molly separated once again.

Satisfied things were calmer, at least for the moment, Lucille walked up the steps to the rambling, homestead-style ranch house and across the spacious front porch. "In the meantime, I have a job big enough for the two of you," she said over her shoulder, leading the way into the house.

Chance and his crew had spent the fall getting the two bedrooms and bathroom upstairs remodeled, the staircase rebuilt and all new energy-efficient windows installed. A new roof and fiber-cement siding had been put on, and the exterior had been painted a dazzling white with pine-green shutters. They'd also followed the plans of the structural engineer and gutted the downstairs into an open living-kitchen-dining area, a laundry room and mudroom, and what would one day be a spacious master suite with luxury bath for Lucille.

For the moment, however, only the framework of the redesigned first-floor rooms and the original wood floors—which were in need of refinishing—stood.

In the center of the space, in front of the original

limestone fireplace, were two big easels. One held Molly's proposed design, the other Chance's.

Lucille turned to her son. "Although I love the rustic nature of your plans, honey, I am going to go with Molly's vision for the first floor."

There wasn't a lot of difference in the plan for the master suite, since Lucille had been very specific in what kind of fixtures and the size closet she wanted. As for the rest...

"You know that's going to cost you twice what mine would," Chance pointed out.

Lucille nodded. "True. But your vision for the space is so...utilitarian."

Exactly! It was what made it so great.

Chance pointed to the samples of his proposed maple cabinets and black granite countertops, the top-of-the-line stainless steel appliances and plentiful pantry shelving. "It'll get the job done, Mom."

Where he had been trying to be economical, his competition had gone all out. Dual dishwashers, two prep areas, double ovens and countless other features. Everywhere you looked there was some sort of up-charge.

Lucille smiled. "Molly captured what I was looking for. Unfortunately, I don't think she and her crew can manage to finish the entire downstairs in the next five weeks."

Molly's triumph faded. "Did you say five...weeks?"

Lucille nodded. "I want to reserve December 19 for delivery of the furniture from my previous house in Dallas that's currently in storage, the twentieth and the twenty-first for decorating and the twenty-second for my planned fund-raiser for the Lockhart Foundation and West Texas Warrior Assistance program. And of course Christmas Eve and Day for my family celebration."

Chance frowned. "Which means all the wiring, plumbing, drywall and paint, as well as kitchen and master suite bath, will have to go in by then."

His mother remained undaunted. "You have six people on your crew, Chance. Molly has seven. If you have all thirteen people working, it's easily feasible. I'll pay overtime if necessary."

All business, Molly nodded. "How are we going to divide the work?"

Matter-of-factly, Lucille explained, "Molly will be in charge of the design and the materials, and Chance will supervise the construction and installation. Then, of course, Molly, I'd like you to do the yuletide decorating." She flashed a smile her way. "I'll give you a free hand with that since part of the reason for the rush is to help you showcase your skills during the fund-raising open house, and make the connections with my Dallas friends that will help you drum up business there."

Chance turned to his mother and gave her a warning look. He would have expected Lucille, who, better than anyone, knew the downside of leaving the warm, supportive utopia of Laramie County behind, to be urging caution. Not cheerleading. "You're really supporting Molly in this lunacy?" he blurted before he could stop himself.

Molly had a growing business. A home. Dozens of people who looked out for her. A young son who was thriving in the small-town environment. Why she would want to leave all that for the coldness of the big city he had grown up in was beyond him.

"I wouldn't call it that." Lucille regarded him sternly.

"And, yes, I fully understand Molly's desire to be all that she can be."

Resolved to inject a little common sense into the conversation, Chance scoffed, "In terms of what? Money? Social position?"

Molly glared at him. "Don't forget dazzling professional success! And all the accoutrements that come with it."

Chance looked heavenward. "I don't expect you to understand," Molly said stiffly, her emotions suddenly as fired up as his.

"Good," Chance snapped back, running his hand through his hair in exasperation. Then, pinning her with a glare of his own, he said exactly what was on his mind. "Because I don't."

Chapter 2

"Avoiding me?" a husky voice taunted.

Molly thought work had wrapped up for the day. Which was, as it turned out, the only reason she was at the Circle H ranch house this late.

Turning in the direction of the familiar baritone, Molly took in the sight of the indomitable cowboy. Clad in a knit thermal tee, plaid flannel shirt and jeans, a tool belt circling his waist, Chance Lockhart strode toward her purposefully.

Working to still her racing heart, Molly held her clipboard and pen close to her chest. She lifted her chin. "Why would you think that?"

Chance stopped just short of her and gave her a slow, thorough once-over. "We've both had crews working here ten days straight, and you and I haven't run into each other once."

Thank God.

Aware the last thing she wanted was to give Chance another opportunity to tell her what he thought of her plan to improve her and her son's lives, Molly shrugged. "I guess we have different schedules."

His, she had deduced, kept him at his ranch, taking care of his bucking bulls early mornings and evenings. Hence, it was usually safe to arrive at the remodeling site during those hours.

Except today, he'd varied his routine. Why? To try to catch her in person, rather than communicate through endless emails and texts?

What she knew for certain was that it would be dark in another fifteen minutes, and all she had for light was a 220-volt camping lantern.

As seemingly unaffected by their quiet, intimate surroundings as the cell phone that kept going off with a sound that usually signaled an incoming text message—checked, then unanswered—in the holster at his waist, he glanced around. "What do you think thus far?"

That even with rumpled hair and a couple of days' growth of beard on your face, you are without a doubt the sexiest man I've ever seen. Which was too bad. Molly sighed inwardly, since Chance wasn't at all her type. But if he were…she could definitely lose herself in those gorgeous hazel eyes, big hunky body and wickedly sensual lips. Luckily he didn't know that.

With effort, she switched on her camping lantern, set it on the floor and got out her tape measure. She measured the front windows and door for window treatments and wreaths. The fireplace and staircase for garlands. Jotting down the numbers in her leather notebook, she said, "I think our combined crews have made amazing progress."

Under Chance's direction, new rooms had been framed out and a first-floor powder room for guests added last minute. Plumbing and electrical wiring had been installed, new drywall put up and taped, crown molding and trim work done.

Chance moved to the fireplace. He ran his big, calloused hand along the new wooden mantel. It was cut out of the same rustic oak as the support beams overhead. "The floors will be repaired where needed and sanded tomorrow."

Which took them all the way up to Thanksgiving, she knew. The one day every one of them would have a break from the demanding schedule.

"You got the tile for the kitchen and the bathrooms, and the paint colors picked out?"

Trying not to think what he would be doing for the holidays, Molly replied, "Still waiting on final approval from your mom. She wants to see samples in the light here before she decides. But we've narrowed it down to a couple of shades for each space."

Chance ambled over and switched on several of the portable construction lamps. "The new appliances and light fixtures?"

Instantly the downstairs became much brighter. "On order."

He walked around, inspecting some of the work that had been done. Finding a tiny flaw, he stuck a piece of blue painter's tape on it. "Kitchen and bath cabinets and countertops?"

"Will all be delivered in time to meet our schedule."

He nodded, as aware as she that one major glitch

could throw everything off. Fortunately, thus far anyway, luck had been completely on their side.

He came toward her.

Her heartbeat picked up for no reason she could figure. Molly cleared her throat. "Speaking of the holiday... I wanted to talk to you about Thanksgiving." She moved around restlessly. "I've given my crew the day off."

Joining her at the hearth, Chance took a foil-wrapped candy from his shirt pocket. "Same here."

There was no way, she thought, he could know that was her very favorite. Trying not to salivate over the treat, Molly continued, "But they've all agreed to work on Friday."

He nodded, ripping open one end. Immediately the smell of dark chocolate and peppermint filled the small space between them.

"Mine, too."

Chance's cell phone buzzed again, this time with the ringtone "I Saw Mommy Kissing Santa Claus."

Telling herself that particular choice in no way involved her, either, Molly watched as, once again, he checked the screen and ignored it.

He held out the partially unwrapped confection. "Want one?" he asked.

Now she knew he was flirting.

"I've got another..." he teased.

Hell, yes, she wanted some of his dark chocolate peppermint. But if she started taking candy from him on a whim, who knew what might be next?

She returned his assessing look and said as innocently as possible, "Thanks, but no."

His eyes gleamed.

"I don't really like those."

His sexy grin widened all the more.

Then his phone buzzed yet again. With the maddeningly suggestive holiday song…

Thinking maybe he really should answer that, and would if she weren't standing right there, Molly picked up her lantern before she ended up doing something really stupid—like kissing the smug look off his face—and headed for the staircase.

Able to feel the heat of his masculine gaze drifting over her, she tossed the words over her shoulder. "I've got to measure the upstairs windows before I go."

"Want help?"

"No!"

He chuckled, as she had known he would.

Molly fought back a flush. This was exactly why she had been avoiding him. Luckily she had work to keep her busy. Chance might even be gone before she left.

She had just finished measuring the first window when she heard a door open, then close. Lucille Lockhart's lyrical voice echoed through the first floor. "Chance? Why aren't you picking up? I just got another call from Babs Holcombe. She said she's been trying to reach you for days!"

Who the heck is Babs? Not that she should be listening…

"Been a little busy, Mom," Chance growled.

Lucille's high heels tapped across the wood floors. "You owe her the courtesy of a return call. Or at the very least an email!"

"After the way things ended with Delia?" Chance scoffed.

Delia? Molly perked up, edging a little closer despite herself.

"I admit that wasn't one of their finer moments," Lucille conceded reluctantly, "but they've both done a lot to support the Lockhart Foundation in the three years since."

"Okay," Chance countered gruffly.

"Okay you'll call her," Lucille pressed, sounding beside herself with irritation, "or okay you won't?"

Silence reigned once again.

Molly could imagine the bullheaded look on Chance's face. The disapproving moue of his mother. There was a brief murmur of disgruntled talk she couldn't decipher, then the sound of Lucille leaving. The front door shut. Chance's heavy footsteps crossed to the center of the house. "You can come down now!" he called cheerfully up the stairs.

Aghast that he knew she had been eavesdropping, heat flooded her cheeks. Measurements taken, she walked back down, pocketing her pen. "Sorry. Didn't mean to intrude."

He gave her a look that said, "I'll bet."

Falling into step beside her, he accompanied her out onto the front porch. The air had the distinct damp chill of late November. Dark clouds gathered along the horizon, where the sun was setting in streaks of purple and gray.

"How is Braden doing? Were you able to steer him toward the Leo and Lizzie World Adventure train set?"

Surprised that Chance recalled the name of the toy, Molly grimaced. "Ah, no. Not yet."

Concern etched his ruggedly handsome face. "Meaning you haven't really tried yet?"

Molly only wished that were the case. Taking her first real break of the day, she perched on the railing edging the front porch. "Meaning, like with most men, subtlety doesn't work on Braden. Nor does direct conversation."

Chance took a seat opposite her, mesmerizing her with the blatant interest in his eyes. "So he still wants a live baby bull and a momma."

"As well as a daddy bull."

"Wow."

She sighed, relieved to be able to talk about what had been bothering her all day. "Wow is right."

His expression grew thoughtful. "What are you going to do?"

With effort, she forced herself to meet his probing gaze. "Honestly? I don't have a clue."

"I had a few ideas."

Molly pushed to her feet. Feeling her pulse skitter, she turned her head to the side. "I think you've done enough," she quipped, using sarcasm to hide her worry.

He accompanied her down the steps to her SUV. "Seriously. I think I might be able to dissuade him, given another opportunity. And since you have Thanksgiving Day off and so do I, and my mother is hosting her annual dinner at the bunkhouse, I was thinking you and Braden might want to come as my plus two."

Aware the mood between them was quickly becoming highly charged and way too intimate, Molly unlocked her vehicle. "You're asking me for a date?"

To her consternation, he didn't exactly deny it.

"There will be a lot of people there. Three of my siblings and their significant others and or friends. And a few other family friends."

Molly tossed her bag into the front passenger seat. "First of all, your mother and I get along so well because I know my place."

His brow lifted.

"Furthermore, Braden and I have our own holiday tradition."

He rested a muscular forearm on the open driver-side door. "You cook?"

Molly lifted her chin. "I take him to the buffet at the cafeteria in San Angelo."

Sympathy lit his gaze. "Sounds…lonely."

Lonely, Molly thought, was being a fifth wheel at the big family gatherings of friends. Knowing, you'd never enjoy the same.

She shrugged. "Crowded is more like it. But it's not too bad if we get there at eleven, when it opens, and then Braden and I have the rest of the day to do whatever we want." Which usually involved a family activity of their own.

Chance stepped back. "Well, if you change your mind, the invitation stands."

Molly slid behind the wheel. "Thanks, but I won't." She looked up at him.

Whether Chance admitted it or not, she was out of his league socially, too. "And don't worry about Braden. I'll figure out a way to handle his misconceptions about what is possible for Christmas. And what is not."

Except she wasn't handling it, Molly thought the following day when they entered the popular San Angelo cafeteria. At least not as well as she or her son would like.

"I'm hungry, Mommy," Braden complained as the line of customers inched forward.

Although she had been hoping to make this Thanksgiving really special for him, he'd been grumpy since waking that morning. "I know." Molly inched up slightly, clear of the entrance. "It will be our turn soon. See?" She pointed to the lighted display cases up ahead.

Braden stamped his cowboy boot. "Don't want to wait," he fumed.

"I know." Thinking he might be overheated, Molly knelt down in front of him and unzipped his fleece hoodie. She figured he would be fine once they sat down. Avoiding a meltdown before that concerned her.

"Can we go home now?" Braden persisted.

"Oh, you don't want to do that," a familiar low voice said from behind them. "I hear the holiday buffet here is not to be missed."

Braden lit up like a Christmas tree. "Cowboy Chance!"

"Hi, buddy!" Chance held out his palm. Braden high-fived him.

Slowly, Molly straightened to her full height. To her dismay, she was ridiculously glad to see him. Especially looking so fine.

Like her, he had upped his game a notch. Slacks, a starched shirt, tie and tweed Western-cut blazer, instead of his usual flannel shirt and jeans. "Aren't you supposed to be at your mom's today?"

"Already made my appearance."

Which accounted for his neatly combed chestnut hair and freshly shaven jaw.

"I'm tired," Braden complained.

Molly inhaled the sandalwood and leather fragrance

of Chance's cologne, mixing with the usual soap and fresh air scent of his skin.

"Probably a little bored, too." Chance winked. He reached into his jacket pockets. "Which is why I brought you these." He pulled out a toy reindeer with a big red nose and a coordinating winter sleigh.

Braden beamed. "Rudolph!"

Molly gave Chance a look her delighted son could not see. "What are you doing?" she demanded sweetly.

Grooves deepened on either side of his mouth. "Working on that solution."

Aware how easy it would be to fall for this sexy cowboy's charms, Molly stiffened. "I fail to see how—"

He clapped a hand on her shoulder. "All in good time, my darlin'. All in good time. And—" he nodded at the space behind her "—you're going to want to move on up."

The line was indeed pushing forward.

Molly inched ahead. "I don't remember inviting you," she murmured so only he could hear, while her son energetically played with the reindeer and sleigh.

Chance leaned down to whisper in her ear. "That's the good thing about having Thanksgiving here. You don't need an invite." He looked around, impressed. "Although given how crowded the establishment is quickly getting, it would probably be considerate of the three of us to share a table, rather than unnecessarily take up more chairs than we need."

"You're impossible." Despite herself, she was glad to see him.

Braden tugged on Chance's blazer. He tilted his head back so he could see his idol's face. "Thank you for toys."

Chance ruffled her son's hair. "You're welcome, buddy. It was my pleasure."

To Molly's surprise, it was hers, too.

"So what next?" Chance asked as the three of them finished their turkey dinners.

Molly looked out the cafeteria windows. The rain that had been threatening since the previous evening had started midmeal. It was now coming down in sheets. She sighed. "No playground, unfortunately…"

Braden stopped playing with the toys Chance had brought him long enough to scowl. "Promised!"

Molly used a napkin to wipe some cranberry sauce off her son's chin. "I know, honey, but everything will be all wet, so we'll have to do something indoors."

"Bouncy house?"

"Afraid not. It's closed because today is a holiday."

"Cowboy Chance play. My house."

She did have activities planned there, two they had already started, in fact, in addition to Braden's usual time set aside to do whatever he wanted. "I'm sure Mr. Chance has other things to do, honey."

He met her eyes. "Not really." Chance turned back to Braden, his cordial tone as reassuring as his presence. "What kind of toys do you have?"

"Trucks and cars."

"Trains?"

Braden shook his head.

Abruptly Molly saw where Chance was going with this.

If he did have an idea how to convince her son to yearn for the holiday gift she had chosen for Braden…

could she afford to turn Chance down? Especially if the end result was Braden's happiness?

Braden tugged on her sleeve. "Go now, Mommy!" He stood on his chair and held out his arms to their lunch companion. "Cowboy Chance, too!"

Chance caught Braden in his big arms.

Trying not to think how natural the two looked together, Molly said, "We won't expect you to stay long."

Chance stood, Braden still in his arms. "I won't wear out my welcome. On the other hand…" He winked and shrugged in a way that opened up a ton of possibilities. A shiver of awareness swept through her. He probably would be a good time, Molly thought despite herself. Too good a time.

She shook off the awareness. Stacking their dishes and trays, she asked, "You know where I live?"

He nodded, looking as unexpectedly content in that moment as she felt. "Spring Street in Laramie."

Molly led the way. The drive back to Laramie took thirty-five minutes. It was still raining when Chance parked behind Molly's SUV and got out of his pickup truck.

Her home, a former carriage house, sported a three-foot-high white picket fence and was sandwiched between two large Victorians. The one-story abode, while much smaller and set back a ways from the sidewalk, was just as attractive—if not more so—than every other home on the prestigious street. A front porch with white wicker furniture spanned the width of the thousand-square-foot house, which featured gray clapboard sides, white trim and black shutters.

The scent of fresh-cut pine hit Chance the moment he walked in the door.

A Christmas tree stood in the corner of the comfortably outfitted living area, boxes of lights and decorations beside it.

The state-of-the-art kitchen, situated at the back of the main living area, was banked by a wall of floor-to-ceiling windows that flooded the small, cozy space with light. Plentiful cabinets, painted a dark slate, and an island that also served as a dining area were a nice counterpoint to the white quartz countertops, bleached wood floors and stainless steel appliances.

Standing there, noting how beautiful her home was, he couldn't imagine why she would ever want to leave it.

Her son, however, had other things on his mind.

Barely standing still long enough for his mother to wrestle him out of his damp rain jacket, he set his Rudolph and sleigh on the coffee table, next to a soft blue blanket, then headed importantly for the kitchen, where a delicious fresh dough and orange smell emanated. "Come on, Mr. Chance. We cook!"

Braden grabbed a tyke-size navy chef's apron off the hook, and then handed Chance one, as well—frilly and floral. "Put on!" he demanded.

Molly's amused expression dared Chance to do so.

Clearly, he noted, she did not think he would. Which just showed how much she knew. "Sure thing, buddy," Chance agreed drily, pulling the garment over his head. The cloth barely covered his broad chest, and the waist hit him at mid-sternum. Tying it seemed impossible, given the fact he couldn't find the strings.

Grinning, Molly stepped behind him. "Allow me." Her hands brushed his spine as she secured it in place. His body reacted as if they'd kissed. Fortunately, she was too on task to notice. She opened a drawer and pulled out a plain white chef's apron, that was, as it happened, much more his size.

She tilted her head, her gaze moving over him humorously. "Want to trade?"

Aware this was the first time he'd seen her eyes sparkle so mischievously, he motioned for her to turn so he could tie her apron strings, too. She needed to goof around like this more often. Not be so serious all the time. "Nah, I'm good."

The three of them took turns washing their hands; then Braden climbed onto the step stool next to the island. "Ready, Mommy?" the tyke asked eagerly.

"Let's see." Molly pulled a linen towel away from the top of a large bowl. Inside was a billowy cloud of dough. "I think so."

She positioned the bowl in front of her son. "Ready to punch it down?"

With a gleeful shout, Braden went to town, pummeling the buttery dough until all the air was released. "What are we making?" Chance asked. It sure smelled good, even at this early stage.

Molly moved close enough he could catch a whiff of her perfume. It was every bit as feminine and enticing and delectable as she was.

"Christmas *stollen*." She tilted her head curiously. "Ever had it?"

"I don't think so."

"Well, you're in for a treat." She turned the dough onto a floured wooden board and divided it into three sections—which she quickly rolled out into long loaves. Wordlessly, she retrieved a bowl of dried cherries, cranberries and almonds, soaking in what appeared to be orange juice, and drained the excess. "Time to sprinkle on the extras."

Braden—no novice at baking—positioned his fruit and nuts very seriously, dropping them one by one onto the dough. "You, too, Cowboy Chance."

"Yes, sir," Chance said, soberly following Braden's lead. Molly joined in.

When they'd finished, Braden clapped his hands. "I done now, Mommy?"

"Yes. You did a very good job." She wiped his hands with a clean cloth. "You can go play while I get this ready for the second rise."

He hurried off to retrieve his Rudolph and sleigh. Then he brought out his toy dump truck to give them a ride.

With Braden playing happily, Chance settled on a stool at the island. "Where did you learn to do this?"

"My mother taught me." Molly showed him how to knead the dough until it was soft and elastic, and then shape it into loaves. Carefully, he followed her lead. "Her grandparents emigrated here from Germany. Baking was an important part of their holiday tradition, and she passed it on to me, as her mother had to her."

Remembering his earlier faux pas, he trod carefully. "Where is your mom now?"

Sorrow pinched Molly's face. "She died of meningitis when I was fourteen. My dad never really got over the loss, and he died in a car accident just before I graduated from high school."

He wished he had been around to comfort her, but that had been years before he'd moved to Laramie. "That must have been rough."

"It was." Molly carefully transferred the loaves onto baking sheets and covered them with linen cloths, the actions of her hands delicate and sure. "But I had a lot of help from the people in the community. The local bank gave me a second mortgage on this house, so I'd have somewhere to live, and enough funds to get by on while I studied construction and interior design at the local community college and did what was necessary to obtain my general contractor's license."

His gaze drifted over her. She wore a long-sleeved emerald dress that made the most of her stunning curves, black tights and flats. Her auburn hair was curlier than usual—he supposed it was the rain. "What made you want to pursue that?"

Molly lounged against the counter, her hands braced on either side of her. "Tradition, I guess. My mom taught classes in nutrition and cooking at Laramie High, and she did interior design work on the side, and my dad was a general contractor who did mostly handyman work."

She paused to rub a spot of flour from her hip. "Following in their footsteps made me feel closer to them. Plus, both my parents had substantial client lists that I initially utilized to get work. So I was able to get on my feet financially a lot faster than I would have otherwise."

Braden walked into the kitchen. He stepped between them merrily. "Puddles, Mommy?"

Grinning, Molly looked out the window. The rain that had been landing in torrents was now coming down gently. "You want to go outside?"

Braden nodded.

"Then let's get you suited up." Molly walked into the mudroom off the garage, then returned with a pair of yellow rain boots, matching slicker and wide-brimmed hat. Braden brimmed with anticipation. "You come, too, Cowboy Chance?"

"We'll both watch you from the front porch," Molly promised. "Unless…" She paused to look at Chance. "You have somewhere else you need to be?"

Chapter 3

This was Chance's opportunity to make a graceful exit.

To his surprise, he wasn't in a hurry to leave. In fact, he was sort of lamenting the fact that the time would eventually come. "Actually," Chance admitted good-naturedly, "I was hoping I'd be able to see what the Christmas *stollen* looks like when it's finished."

"Yummy!" Braden declared, rubbing his tummy.

Chance chuckled. The little buckaroo's enthusiasm was infectious. "You think so?"

Braden nodded magnanimously. "We share. Mommy. Me. You."

Chance turned to Molly. "Is that okay?" he asked casually, wanting to give her the option of throwing him out—if that was what she wanted.

"You probably should see what you've been missing," she said drily.

He had an inkling. And he wasn't just thinking about baked goods.

"Outside?" Braden asked again, impatiently.

"Let's go." She grabbed a rain jacket for herself, then opened the door. A blast of unexpectedly warm air hit them. No doubt brought in by the front. "I was going to offer you a cup of coffee," Molly said, looping the jacket over a wicker chair, "but maybe it should be iced tea."

"Coffee's fine." Chance smiled. "Thanks."

Molly watched her son march down the front steps and out into the light rain. They both grinned as Braden lifted his face to the sky and stuck out his tongue to catch a few raindrops. Fondly, Molly shook her head, then turned back to Chance. "Can you keep an eye on Braden for a minute? He knows not to go outside of the picket fence."

"No problem." Chance took the seat she indicated on the front porch. For the next few minutes, he watched Braden investigate everything from the water running out of the gutters to the drops pearling on the leafy green shrubs.

He'd forgotten what it felt like to look at the world with such unvarnished appreciation.

Maybe it was time he remembered...

"Sure you wouldn't rather be at your mom's watching football with your brothers?" Molly teased, returning with a tray containing a carafe, two mugs, sugar and cream. She set it on the table between them.

Chance grinned at her son, who was now hopscotching his way through a series of puddles on the front walk.

He turned his attention back to Molly. Her cheeks flushed with happiness, her auburn hair slightly mussed, a smudge of flour across one cheek, she had never looked more beautiful. Or content.

He liked seeing her this way.

"Oh, there's no football at my mom's on Thanksgiving."

Her delicate brow pleated. "Seriously?"

As she neared, he caught the fragrance of her lavender hand soap mingling with the sweet, sexy scent of her hair and skin. Pushing the electric awareness away, Chance sat back in his chair. "She says that's why DVRs were invented. Social events require socializing properly with each other, not tuning everyone out watching TV."

Molly handed him a mug of steaming coffee. She wrinkled her nose at him. "Sounds like Lucille."

Chance watched as she settled in the chair beside his. The hem of her knit dress rode up a little. She crossed her legs at the knee and tugged it down discreetly, but not before he had seen enough of her long slender thighs to make his heart race.

Chance worked to keep his mind on the conversation. "No doubt about it. My mother's big on etiquette, always has been."

Molly waved at her son, who was now marching around the perimeter of the inside of the fence. Braden stopped to lift his arms high and turn his face to the slowly clearing sky overhead. "Still, the menu would probably have been better…"

Chance couldn't recall when he had enjoyed a holiday meal more. "I thought we had a fine meal at the cafeteria. Turkey. All the trimmings. Not to mention choice of dessert."

She chuckled, holding her mug against the softness of her full lips. "You did have two pieces of pie."

He watched her blow lightly on her coffee, then take a dainty sip. Shrugged. "Couldn't make up my mind."

He was certain about one thing, though.

He wanted to ravish Molly Griffith.

And would…

"Look, Mommy!" Braden shouted. "Rainbow!"

They both turned in the direction he was pointing. Sure enough, there was one arcing across the sky.

"Come here, Mommy! Come see!"

"Just when I wish I had my camera out," she murmured with a rueful grin, rising to join her son.

Not wanting to intrude, Chance stayed behind to make her wish come true.

Chance Lockhart was full of surprises, Molly thought minutes later, looking at the series of action photos he had taken on his cell phone while she and Braden had admired the burst of colors streaking across the late afternoon sky.

"Thank you for capturing that moment," Molly said softly when they walked back inside a few minutes later to put the *stollen* in the oven. Chance had not only gotten several nice shots of her and Braden together—something that rarely happened on the spur of the moment since she had no other family member to do the honor—but he'd also managed to capture a close-up of the wonder on her little boy's face.

Priceless.

"I thought you would want to remember it. Not every day you see a rainbow on Thanksgiving."

Not every day she spent a holiday with such a sweet,

handsome man. Not that this was a date. Even if it had started to feel like a date.

Molly finished getting Braden out of his rain gear, then showed her little boy the photos Chance had taken on his phone and emailed to her.

"That's me," Braden said gleefully. "And Mommy!" He pushed the phone away. "Can we dec'rate tree?"

That had been her original plan.

Chance shrugged his broad shoulders affably. "I'm up for it if you are," he said.

"You're really into Christmas, aren't you?" She hadn't met many single guys who were.

Or were this kind to her son.

"Hey." Chance aimed a thumb at the center of his chest. "When the opportunity to be chivalrous presents itself…"

He was on board, Molly thought. Which just went to show how badly she had misjudged the gorgeous cowboy.

By the time the oven timer went off half an hour later, they had the lights strung and on. Half a dozen ornaments later, the fruit-and-nut-studded pastry was cool enough to finish.

Aprons went back on. Although this time Molly made sure that Chance had the larger garment. Together, they all brushed on melted butter, then sprinkled the tops of their masterpieces with granulated sugar.

"And now for the pièce de résistance!" Molly declared triumphantly, showing her son how to use the sifter to cover the pastry with a final snowy-white cover of confectioner's sugar. She handed the sifter to Chance, watched as he did the same to his and then followed suit.

The three pastries made a lovely, Christmassy sight.

"Eat now?" Braden asked.

Molly grinned. "Let's taste it." She cut off a two-inch slice for Braden, a larger one for Chance and a slightly smaller one for herself.

They all bit down on the soft, citrus-flavored nut-and-fruit bread with the sweet and slightly crunchy exterior. "Wow." Chance's hazel eyes lit up. "That's... amazing."

"Yummy," Braden agreed.

Molly had to admit, between the three of them they had done a good job. Before she could think, she offered, "Want to take a loaf home with you?"

Luckily he didn't read any extra meaning into her impulsive gesture. An affable grin deepened the crinkles around his eyes. "Sure you don't mind?"

Remembering what her late mother had told her—that the way to a man's heart was through his stomach—Molly shrugged off the importance. "I'll be baking all month long."

His gaze skimmed her appreciatively. "In that case—" he winked "—I'll have to remember to come around more often."

Molly caught her breath at the implication.

Was he truly interested in her?

She knew she desired him. Always had. Even though they were clearly all wrong for each other. Still...

"All done, Mommy!"

Switching quickly back to parenting mode, Molly gently wiped the sugar from her son's hands and face. Braden reclaimed the Rudolph and sleigh, along with his favorite blue blankie. Yawning, he snuggled on the sofa.

Chance arched an inquisitive brow. "Nap time?"

"Two hours ago," Molly confirmed softly, watching Braden struggle to keep his eyes open.

"Oh." A wealth of emotion—and understanding—in a single word.

"Yeah. I was hoping—" Molly moved closer to Chance, whispering even more quietly "—he'd be able to get through the day without one. Especially since it's so late."

Chance shook his head fondly. Putting an easy hand on Molly's shoulder, he nodded in the direction of the couch. "Looks like he's already asleep."

Molly took in the sight of her child, blissfully cuddled up, auburn lashes fanning across his cheek. She sighed. "Indeed, he is."

Chance caressed her shoulder lightly. "That's a problem?"

Molly's heart raced at the casual contact. "He'll be grouchy when I do wake him up before dinner and may have trouble falling asleep tonight."

"Anything I can do?"

If you were here, sure. You won't be. Molly looked up at Chance. Time seemed to suspend. Suddenly there was just the two of them. "Cross your fingers for me?"

His eyes darkened. He brushed his thumb across her lower lip and continued to regard her steadily. "How about something even better?" he said huskily, lifting her hand to his lips. He pressed a kiss across her knuckles. She caught her breath. And then she was in his arms. Wrapping both his hands around her small waist, he caught her against him, so they were length to length.

Molly's breath hitched again.

"Chance," she whispered.

His head lowered. Slowly. Purposefully. "Just one,

darlin'…" He tunneled his hands through her hair and his eyes shuttered. "That's all I'm asking."

Molly saw the kiss coming, and she knew she should do something to stop it. She was attracted to Chance enough already. If his lips were to actually touch hers…

With a small, sharp intake of breath, she lifted both hands and spread them across the muscular warmth of his broad chest. His heart was beating, strong and steady. His head lowered even more. And then there was no stopping it. Their lips connected, and a shiver of pure delight went through her. Her usual caution gone, she opened her mouth to the seductive pressure of his. He tasted like rich black coffee and freshly baked *stollen*. And man. And she could no more deny him than she could deny herself. It was Thanksgiving, after all. A day to count blessings. Be happy. Thankful. At ease. And she'd never felt more at ease than she did at that very moment.

Chance knew he was taking advantage, that Molly deserved a lot better than the overture he was making. He also knew opportunities like this did not come along all that often.

Molly had a wall around her heart, strong enough to keep the entire male species at bay. She was driven by fierce ambition. And a robust little chaperone that kept her on the straight and narrow.

Had he spent time with her before now, he would have realized what a beautiful, complicated and magnificent woman she was.

He would have known there was a lot more to her than her need for tremendous financial security, and the social status that came with it. But he hadn't, so he had squandered the two years he had resided in Laramie County. Two years in which he could have pursued her like she was meant to be pursued.

Fortunately, he still had a month left.

He wasn't going to waste it.

Or make any more mistakes.

So he kissed her passionately until she kissed him back and curled against him. And it was only then, when they started to make the kind of connection that rocked both their worlds, that she suddenly gasped and wrenched her lips from his.

"Is this the point where you haul off and slap me across the face?" Chance joked.

It was definitely the point where she gave herself a good hard shake, Molly thought. What in all Texas had gotten into her? She couldn't start getting involved with someone! Or even have a fling. Not when she was getting ready to leave rural Laramie County and build a life in the city.

Reluctantly, she stepped out of the warm cocoon of Chance's strong arms. She went to a drawer on the opposite side of the kitchen and pulled out a roll of plastic wrap.

Her lips and body still throbbing from the thrilling contact, she lifted a staying hand and admitted softly, "That was my fault every bit as much as it was yours."

"Fault?" With displeasure, he zeroed in on her low, censoring tone.

"Holidays can be really lonely."

He gave her a considering look. "They don't have to be."

Irritated he saw so much of her feelings when she wanted him to see so little, Molly admitted, "It's easy to find yourself reaching out in ways you normally wouldn't."

His eyes filled with a mixture of curiosity and compassion. "Is that what happened with Braden's daddy?"

"No," Molly said, trying hard not to succumb to the unexpected tenderness in Chance's expression.

He leaned against the counter, arms folded in front of him, and continued to study her. "Then?"

Maybe if Chance knew the worst about her, he would forget the sizzling physical attraction between them and realize their backgrounds were too diverse for them to ever be more than casual friends.

Molly drew a deep breath. "I don't want to go down the wrong path again."

"With me."

It upset her to bring this up, but she knew for both their sakes, it had to be said. Chance had to start facing the fact they were and always would be all wrong for each other. "With anyone who was born outside my social standing."

His brow furrowed. "You really think I'm that much of a snob?"

She flushed and dropped her gaze to his muscular chest. "I think, in this respect, you might be as naive as I once was."

"I'm listening," he said.

Molly grabbed the spray cleaner and paper towels, then began scrubbing down the counters. "I never really dated much after my dad died. I was too busy trying to put myself through school and get my business going."

He moved so she could reach behind him. But not quite enough. As she reached, her shoulder lightly brushed his bicep. "Sounds like you had to grow up pretty fast."

Molly straightened. "All that changed when Aaron Powell III came to Laramie to look for lakeside property that could be flipped." She grimaced at the memory. "I was asked to give a bid. I did and won the work on several houses that he and his family purchased." She removed her apron and hung it back on the hook. Recalling her first taste of unfettered luxury, she admitted reluctantly, "I'd never been friends with anyone that ostentatiously wealthy, and Aaron swept me off my feet."

Chance's expression relaxed in understanding. "How long were you together?"

"About three months."

Taking her by the hand, he guided her onto the stool. Sat down beside her. "You didn't expect it to end?"

Molly shrugged, still wishing she hadn't been quite so naive. Shifting so the two of them faced each other, she said, "I knew Aaron's life was in Houston, that his shuttling back and forth continuously would stop when my work was done and the lake properties were listed. But I was okay with that. I was perfectly willing to move where he was."

Chance's expression darkened. "He didn't want that."

Humiliation clogged Molly's throat. "He didn't think that would go over so well with his fiancée."

An awkward silence fell.

"You had no idea," Chance guessed in a low, even tone.

"None," Molly was forced to admit. Restless, she got up and began to pace the confines of the kitchen. "Unfortunately, I was pregnant by then. And I'd already told him."

Giving Chance no more opportunity to ask questions, Molly rushed on. "The next thing I know the Powell family lawyer is at my door with a contract for me to sign. All I have to do is agree—in writing—not to ever publicly acknowledge paternity and a nice six-figure check is mine."

Jaw taut, Chance stood. "I'm pretty sure that's not legal."

Molly nodded as he circled the counter and strode closer.

"I could have forced the issue in court. I also knew if I did that, Aaron and his attorneys would use my modest financial circumstances to allege I was a gold digger and make our lives a living hell. My only priority was to protect my child from hurt."

The compassion in Chance's hazel eyes spurred her to go on.

"So I hired a lawyer and countered with an offer of my own. I would never pursue any claims of paternity, or child support, if Aaron would promise to do the same and allow me to raise Braden completely on my own." She drew a breath. "Aaron was more than happy with that, since he didn't really want children, never mind a bastard son from a woman from a lower social echelon." Molly wrung her hands and lifted her chin defiantly. "So we signed an agreement…and that was that."

Chance searched her face. "Did you ever regret it?"

Wasn't that the million-dollar question!

Molly shrugged, the barriers coming up to protect her heart once again. Steadily, she held Chance's gaze. "I regret mistaking big, expensive romantic gestures for love. And the fact that Braden doesn't have the devoted daddy he deserves."

His gaze drifted over her, igniting wildfires wherever it landed. "The latter could be fixed," he pointed out matter-of-factly.

Maybe someday. For the first time, she was beginning to see that.

In the meantime, she had the next phase of her life plan to execute. Molly handed Chance the wrapped, freshly baked *stollen* and escorted him to the door. Wary of her still-sleeping son, she eased it open, then stepped with him all the way out onto the porch. It was unseasonably warm, and the sun sparkled down on them.

"The point is, even if fate works against us and Braden never gets the loving daddy he deserves, I still have to support my son to the very best of my ability."

"Which means?" Chance prodded, suddenly looking a lot less pleased.

Molly said determinedly, "I've got to move to a place where I can make a lot more money than I am now. And give Braden the kind of boundless future that he deserves."

And that meant no more getting too friendly with Chance.

And definitely no more kissing him!

Chapter 4

"How was your Thanksgiving?" Chance asked the two newest members of the Bullhaven family, now temporarily quartered in a private pasture at the Circle H.

"Mine was the best I've ever had." He set out premium feed. "You think I'm exaggerating, but I'm not."

Even though Molly had sort of kicked him out at the end, he'd left with a warm feeling in his chest that had continued through the night and had still lingered there when he woke up, maybe because he was going to see her again soon.

"Yeah, yeah, you're right. I've got it bad…" But there were worse things than knowing what you wanted. And what he wanted right now was a Christmas holiday spent with Molly. And her adorable son.

The momma Black Angus came toward the bucket, her bull calf, Mistletoe Jr., at her side. While she ate, the calf searched for a teat. Momma mooed gently in approval and then licked at her calf as it started to nurse.

Satisfied all was well, Chance went to his pickup truck. The morning was slightly cool, and rain had left the air smelling clean and brisk. He got out the rest of his breakfast—a thick wedge of Christmas bread—and a thermos of hot black coffee.

Leaning against the fender, he enjoyed the early morning quiet. Until his brother Wyatt drove up and parked beside him. An ornery look on his face, he nodded at the confection in Chance's hand. "What's that?"

Chance savored another bite. *"Stollen."*

Wyatt blinked. "A—what?"

Chance let the citrus-flavored bread melt on his tongue. "It's a German Christmas bread made with fruit and nuts."

Wyatt nodded, practically salivating now. "Looks good," he said.

It was more than simply good, Chance thought. It was the most amazing thing he had ever eaten. Better yet was the fact he had helped Molly and Braden make it.

"Can I have some?" Ready to help himself, Wyatt ambled closer.

Chance held it out of reach. "Sorry."

Wyatt blinked in surprise. It wasn't like his brother to be greedy. "What do you mean no?" he demanded.

Chance moved farther away. "I'm not sharing."

His brother stared at him as if he'd grown two heads. "Why the devil not?"

Chance shrugged as Molly's car turned into the lane and parked in front of the Circle H ranch house, too. "Just not."

She emerged from the driver's side, looking as stunning as usual in a pair of faded jeans, a long-sleeved white T-shirt and a cropped denim jacket. She had a pair of fancy burgundy engineer boots on, a tape measure attached to her belt and a pen stuck behind one ear. Clearly she was ready to work.

Wyatt angled a thumb at him as she approached. "Can you believe this?" Wyatt grumbled. "Chance is eating *stollen* and refusing to share."

Mischief lit her pretty amber eyes when her gaze fell to the treat in his hand. Chance gave her a look, imploring her not to give his brother information to dissect. What he and Molly had experienced was too special, too fragile, to risk or share.

The corners of her lips turning up all the more, she sipped coffee from the travel mug in hand. Then shrugging, she gave Chance a barely tolerant look before turning back to Wyatt. "Can't say I'm surprised." She sighed loudly. Exactly the way she would have before they'd started working together on this job. "Your brother has never had particularly *good* manners."

That had been true, up to now, when it came to Molly. That was going to change. Because now they'd stopped quarreling long enough to kiss, he couldn't imagine being anything but a complete Texas gentleman around her.

Wyatt exhaled in frustration. "Fine." He swung back around to Chance, growling as Chance popped what was left of his breakfast into his mouth. "Where did you get it then? 'Cause I don't remember Sage making German bread at her coffee shop in town."

Quickly, Chance shut down that line of inquiry. His

only sister was worse than his mother when it came to interfering in his love life.

"Wasn't there," he confirmed.

"Then where was it?" Wyatt persisted hungrily.

Molly stepped between the two brothers. She interjected, "Maybe he made it?"

Wyatt shook his head. "Nah. I don't think so." He squinted, about to deliver another round of questions.

Figuring Molly'd had enough amusement at his expense for one morning, Chance lifted a hand. "If you must know, it was a holiday gift from someone I do business with. Okay? Happy now?" Ignoring Wyatt, he turned to Molly. "You ready to go over the project financials…make sure we're still on budget?"

Her reply was cut off by the loud *thump-thump-thump-thump* of a helicopter approaching overhead.

This wasn't an uncommon sight. A lot of wealthy people had homes in or around Laramie. They often flew in and out of the local airstrip either via private jet or chopper. The hospital used air ambulances, too. But this chopper was flying incredibly low. And coming right toward the Circle H.

While the momma cow and her baby bull hurried for cover in a strand of faraway trees, the chopper hovered over a large pasture, currently empty of livestock, and slowly, noisily set down. The motor slowed, then cut, the gusts of air fading.

"What the…?" Chance and Wyatt murmured in unison. The door to the chopper opened. And just like that, Chance was taken back to a time and place he had never wanted to revisit.

Feeling every bit as stunned as the two men beside her, Molly watched as a fiftysomething woman in a long white fur coat and ostrich boots stepped out. The silvery blonde was followed by a tall, lanky man in chinos, a sweater, a black leather biker jacket and sneakers. He had a decidedly unathletic air and appeared to be in his early forties. Last out was a thin, sophisticated blonde about Molly's age who looked like a younger version of the first woman. She had chic sunglasses over her eyes that matched her all-black clothing and body language that screamed indifference.

"Do you know them?" Molly asked, aware that the normally unflappable Chance seemed more perturbed than the unexpected landing should have made him.

Nodding at the approaching trio, Wyatt leaned over and quipped in Molly's ear, "The lady in fur is Babs Holcombe, Chance's would-have-been-mother-in-law-from-hell."

Oh, dear.

"And his ex, Delia Holcombe."

Who was, Molly noted, quite beautiful in that dissolutely wealthy way.

"No clue who the other dude is," Wyatt continued helpfully.

An unwelcoming look on his handsome face, Chance looked past them to where Mistletoe Jr. was cowering next to his momma. Sharing the concern, Wyatt touched his brother's arm. "I'll see to them. You take care of this."

Stopping just short of them, Babs looked at Molly. "You can leave, too."

Before Molly could react, Chance had an arm around her shoulders. "She stays," he said gruffly.

Molly hadn't been planning to. But…okay…if Chance felt in need of some kind of backup, she would provide it.

Watching as Chance dropped his arm, Babs said drolly, "Hello, Chance."

His scowl deepened. "Did you have permission to land that chopper here?"

Babs waved off any difficulty. "I'm sure your mother won't mind."

"What do you want?" he demanded.

Molly hitched in a surprised breath. In all their time together, she had never heard Chance be that rude.

"To introduce you to Mr. X—the founder of the X search engine."

No wonder the tall, sort of geeky guy looked familiar, Molly thought. She'd seen him being interviewed on TV. He'd also starred in commercials featuring the product that was on par with Google and Yahoo. One of the most famous new faces on the tech front, he stood to make much more than the billions he already had.

"Mr. X would like to purchase your bucking-bull business and Bullhaven Ranch."

Chance snorted as if that were the most ridiculous thing he had ever heard. And with good reason. Molly couldn't imagine the tech mogul running a rodeo enterprise. Even through proxy.

Chance's ex, who was lingering in the foreground, still appeared as if she wanted to be anywhere but there. Molly could hardly blame Delia. Coming here unannounced was a bad idea all around.

But Mr. X did not appear to know it. Grinning enthusiastically, he told Chance, "I've already purchased an alligator farm in Louisiana, a minor league hockey team in Minnesota and a salmon fishery in Washington State."

Babs explained, "He's aggressively adding to and

diversifying his business portfolio. And he's willing to pay top dollar."

Chance folded his arms, biceps bulging beneath his denim work jacket. "How nice for him."

Molly winced at Chance's biting sarcasm. Glaring, he continued flatly, "My bucking-bull enterprise is not for sale."

Undaunted, Babs handed over a piece of paper. "You haven't seen his offer yet."

Not surprisingly, Chance refused to accept or even look at it.

"At any price," he reiterated flatly.

Delia took off her sunglasses and rubbed at her temples as if she had a migraine. She gave her mother a sanctioning look, then stepped forward slightly. "Just look at it, Chance. Please."

"You'll be pleasantly surprised," Mr. X predicted happily.

Chance turned to his ex. Something painfully intimate passed between them. Exhaling, he took the paper. Read the number, shook his head. "Not for a thousand times that."

Before anything else could be offered, a powder-blue Cadillac drove up behind them and parked in the drive. Chance's mother emerged, looking coiffed and pulled together, as always. "Isn't this a surprise!" Lucille Lockhart said.

More introductions of Mr. X followed. Babs explained why they were there. Lucille Lockhart nodded agreeably. "Let's all go down to the bunkhouse, where I'm living now," she said.

Mr. X consulted his watch. "Actually, I'm not sure we have time. I have to get back to Silicon Valley for a board meeting this evening, and I really want to tour Bullhaven Ranch before I go." The billionaire frowned, impatient. "We could only see so much from the air."

Delia gauged Chance with the wisdom of an old friend. "I don't think it's going to happen."

Her mother sent Delia a swift, censoring glance, which seemed to deflate the young woman's spirit, before flashing a triumphant smile Chance's way. "Never say never!" Babs murmured, linking arms with Lucille. "But you're right. We do have some catching up to do first…"

Or in other words, Molly thought, Babs was planning to use Lucille to pressure her son into cooperating.

At Lucille's cheerful urging, the trio climbed into her Cadillac while the chopper pilot appeared to get comfortable in the aircraft. In the distance, Wyatt could be seen herding the momma cow and her calf toward the safety of the barn.

Chance was already bolting for his pickup, which made Molly wonder if he and Delia were really over or not. Every feminine instinct she had told her there was definitely some fragile connection remaining. What, precisely, she didn't know. Nor did she understand why it mattered so much to her what that connection was based on. Anger? Lust? Regret? It wasn't as if she were jealous or anything…

"I have to go check on Bullhaven," Chance called to her. "Make sure their flyover inspection didn't cause any ruckus there."

Molly hurried to catch up with him. "What about going over the financials on the project as we planned?"

He made an offhand gesture. "I'm not doing it here with Babs and crew still in the vicinity."

She could hardly blame him for that. She resisted the urge to compassionately squeeze his arm. Stepping away, she asked, "Where then?"

His gaze skimmed her face. "My place. Unless you want to wait until later today or tomorrow?"

"No. It really needs to be done ASAP." She headed for her vehicle. "I'll follow you over."

By the time Molly got out of her SUV, Chance was already talking to his hired hands.

"Everything okay?" she asked when he joined her in the parking area adjacent to the garage.

"Yeah. Luckily, none of the bulls had been put out to pasture yet. So they were all in the barns when the helicopter flew over."

"That's good."

"No kidding." Chance compressed his lips and ran a hand through his thick chestnut hair. "If any of them had been spooked..."

Molly wouldn't want to be around to see the fallout from that. "So where did you want to go over the project statistics to date?" she asked. She'd seen a small office in the barn.

"Ranch house."

Molly nodded. That was her choice, too. It'd be more comfortable, and they were less likely to have interruptions from his hired hands.

Although she had viewed his home the day she'd driven over to talk to him about Braden, she had never been inside the sprawling log-cabin ranch house.

It was just as she would have expected. Big, open living area with a cathedral ceiling and massive field-stone fireplace. Finished interior walls that were light enough to soak in the sun pouring in from the plentiful windows. Dark trim and wide-plank floors that matched the arching beams overhead. Leather furniture.

Chance strode to the kitchen, which bore a remarkable resemblance to the one he'd wanted to install for his mother in the Circle H.

He shrugged off his denim jacket and went to the sink. Rolled up his sleeves and lathered up to his elbows with gusto. "Can I get you something?" He rinsed his powerful forearms one at a time. "Coffee? *Stollen?*"

How about you? she thought, then pushed the forbidden notion away. Just because they'd spent a pleasurable afternoon together and kissed did not mean they needed to pursue the attraction.

A little flirtatious banter, however, wouldn't harm anything. "Really?" she teased, splaying a hand playfully across her chest. "You'd share with me?" 'Cause he sure hadn't been willing to share with his rancher brother.

He gave her an audacious wink. "You're cuter than Wyatt. Have better manners, too."

Her heartbeat picking up, Molly circled around to the other side of the island. Maybe banter wasn't such a good idea.

"Good to know."

He opened the well-stocked fridge, peered inside. "Juice?"

Since he was already pouring some for himself, she said, "Sure." Her throat was feeling a little dry. Their fingers brushed as he handed her the drink. Molly ignored the tingling sensation. "So…" She cleared her throat. "About you and Delia."

He cocked a brow. Turned, let his glance drift over

her lazily. "I was wondering how long it would take you to get around to that."

Promising herself that her interest was purely that of a friend, and in no way meant to protect her heart, Molly savored the sweet-tart apple juice. She tilted her head, and their glances clashed once again. He hadn't shaved that morning, and the stubble lining his jaw gave him a ruggedly handsome look. "How long ago were the two of you an item?"

More to the point, is there any chance the two of you will ever reunite? Because if there was one thing Molly did not want, it was to be involved in a love triangle again. He quaffed his juice in a single gulp, then poured some more.

"We ended our relationship three and a half years ago."

Molly took her laptop computer out of her bag and set in on the counter. "Delia's mother seems bitter about it."

Chance sent her a bemused look, retrieved his laptop and set it on the counter. Then he sat down next to her. "Babs is all about accruing more money."

"So?"

"She didn't like the fact that my parents decided too much money would be the ruin of their children, and instead bequeathed us each property in Laramie County, where my parents had both grown up."

Trying not to think how cozy it felt, being with him like this, Molly forced herself to recollect the facts she knew about the Lockharts. "Sage got a bakery and an apartment in town. Garrett was gifted a Victorian and an office building in Laramie that now houses the Lockhart Foundation headquarters and West Texas Warrior

Assistance. You and your other two brothers received ranches. And your parents bought the Circle H, your mom's childhood home, for the two of them."

"Right. The rest of the wealth my parents had amassed over the years—and there was a lot of it since my dad started and ran a very successful hedge fund—went into the Lockhart Foundation."

"Which originally operated out of Dallas."

Proudly, Chance said, "The charity helped over one hundred nonprofits until roughly half of the funds were embezzled."

Molly let out a slow breath. "I remember that," she said sympathetically. "It was all over the news last summer."

The family had been trashed for weeks before eventually being vindicated by the embezzler's daughter, Adelaide Smythe.

Chance shifted in his seat, the hardness of his knee briefly brushing hers in the process. "Since then, it's become a much smaller organization, with my brother Garrett as CEO. Although my mother is building it up again with constant fund-raising, the upcoming Open House being her largest effort yet."

Molly nodded. The two of them got up simultaneously to move their stools a little farther apart, so crowding wouldn't be an issue. She climbed back on her stool. "That's all very meaningful and noble. Why didn't Babs understand that?" Weren't the truly wealthy supposed to be into philanthropy, too?

For a moment, she thought Chance wouldn't answer. Then something shifted in his expression. As if there was a chink in his armor. Exhaling roughly, he finally explained, "Delia and I grew up together. We dated on and off for over ten years."

That was a very long time, Molly thought with a pang.

"And were about ready to get engaged when my parents made their decision and it became clear that I was not going to be the multimillionaire son-in-law Babs had expected."

"Still, it was Frank and Lucille's decision to make."

"Not in Babs Holcombe's view. She wanted me to convince my parents they were making a mistake. And if I couldn't do that, then fight the terms of my father's will in court."

"You refused."

His jaw tautened. "Damn straight."

"Why?"

His broad shoulders flexing beneath the soft cotton chamois of his shirt, Chance sighed. "Because my dad was right. Too much money is more of a burden than a blessing."

Not in my book, Molly thought uncomfortably. *There could never be enough in the bank to make me feel safe.*

"And I wanted to be my own man and make my own fortune," Chance continued. "However much it turned out to be."

Their eyes met and held.

Noting the charcoal color of his shirt made his hazel eyes look more gray than green, Molly nodded. She valued her independence, too. Unable to help herself, she touched his arm gently. "I can understand and respect that."

Chance caught her hand before she could draw it away and turned it over. Tracing the lines on her palm with his fingertip, he exhaled, admitting, "Initially, Delia did, too. Until her mother convinced her that she would never be able to be happy with a struggling cowboy on what was then a broken-down ranch." He dropped her hand and sat back. "So Delia ended it, and that was that."

Molly felt bereft from the absence of his touch. She kept her eyes on Chance. "Except now Delia and Babs are back."

He got to his feet and walked over to the coffee-maker. "Only because Delia is part of the business sales and acquisitions company her mom owns. And Mr. X is a pretty big fish."

And recently single, if the gossip mags were correct about him getting dumped by a famous Hollywood actress who wanted a "less nerdy" beau.

Molly watched Chance put a paper liner in the filter. "Do you think Babs is trying to matchmake Mr. X and Delia?" Otherwise, what reason could there have been to have the recalcitrant Delia along? She certainly hadn't been actively trying to sell anything.

"A billionaire and her only child?" Chance opened a bag of dark roast coffee. "Oh yeah."

Restless, Molly got up and walked over to the windows overlooking his backyard. Neatly fenced pastures as far as the eye could see. "Then why bring Mr. X here, if that was Babs's goal? Surely there are other ranches they could have shown Mr. X." *Without running into you*, Molly thought a little jealously.

"True. But..." Chance added cold water to the machine. "Bullhaven is the best bucking-bull outfit in Texas."

Molly folded her arms in front of her, recalling the

way Chance and Delia had looked at each other at the end of the meeting. There'd been a lot of residual emotion between them. Not attraction, but something she couldn't quite put her finger on. "It seems like there's more to it than that," she insisted stubbornly. Wishing, once again, that he would be more forthcoming.

Chance squinted. "Like what?"

Molly shrugged as the tantalizing fragrance of fresh-brewed coffee filled the room. "Maybe Babs wants to use your studly presence."

The rich sound of Chance's laughter filled the room. "Studly?"

Molly flushed. "You know what I mean."

"Yeah." He waggled his brows suggestively, ambling closer. Cupping her shoulders lightly, he gazed down at her. "And I'd like to know more."

The last thing Molly wanted was to find herself in the midst of a resurrected love affair. She'd made enough of a mess of things falling for Braden's daddy without first making damn certain Aaron wasn't romantically entangled with anyone else. No way was she doing that again.

She drew a breath. "Is it possible that Babs is trying to use your past relationship with Delia to make Mr. X jealous and realize if he doesn't act—and soon—in pursuing her gorgeous single daughter that someone else, like you, will?" And if that were the case, was it possible something could be reignited between Chance and Delia? Even if only for a short time?

Chance cut off her speculating with a resolute shake of his head. "Not going to happen."

Molly propped her hands on her hips, trying not to notice how masculine and undeniably sexy Chance looked in the sunlight pouring in through the abundant windows.

Unexpected emotion simmering inside her, she pressed the issue. "You're saying there is no reason for Mr. X to be worried about you and Delia? You don't feel anything for her?"

Chance's gaze sifted leisurely over her face, lingering on her lips, before returning slowly to her eyes. "I feel pity."

Now they were getting somewhere, Molly thought, still feeling as if she were pulling oil out of shale. Tingling all over, for no reason she could figure, she demanded, "Why?"

"She's never been able to stand up to her overbearing mother."

And there it was, the trademark chivalry of the Lockhart men. The same chivalry that had brought Chance to her and Braden's rescue at the cafeteria on Thanksgiving Day.

"You wanted to help Delia do that when you were together?" she guessed.

"Initially, yes." Looking as if he wouldn't want to be anywhere else, he lounged against the kitchen island, watching as Molly went back to their "temporary work area" and powered up her computer. "But eventually I realized Delia had to do that on her own."

Too restless to sit down again just yet, Molly curved her hands around the back of the counter stool, and asked, "What does Delia feel for you?"

Lifting one broad shoulder in an indolent shrug, he came toward her. "No clue."

"You don't want to know?"

She caught her breath as he neared. He shook his

head, serious now; whatever initial irritation he'd had at seeing his ex again had faded completely. Now he was focused solely on Molly. And that focus was causing all sorts of chaos deep inside her. "What Delia and I had is over," he informed her, his voice a sexy rumble.

Molly wanted to believe that, just like she wanted to be rich. In money and family and love. "But if…"

"Molly." His impatience mounting, Chance gave her a look of pure masculine need. "There's only one woman I'm interested in," he told her, taking her in his arms and pulling her flush against him. "And that woman is you."

Chapter 5

Chance could see Molly didn't believe him. So he did the only thing he could to convince her. He lowered his head and, ignoring her soft gasp, covered her lips with his.

She resisted at first, splaying her hands across his chest, but his instinct was to deepen the kiss.

Claim her as his. The need to protect her triumphed. He lifted his head enough to look into her eyes. The mixture of desire and need told him all he wanted to know.

The two of them had been destined for this moment, from the first time they'd laid eyes on each other two years before. All the quarrelling and mistrust had been nothing but a prelude to what was turning out to be a magical Christmas season.

"Let me love you," he whispered, kissing her cheek,

her temple, the sensitive spot just beneath her ear. His body hardened as he felt her quiver.

She lifted her face to his, then looked at him with all the yearning he had imagined she felt and knew he experienced. Then kissed him back with a sensuality that further rocked his world. Her hands slid around his waist, and she pressed intimately against him. Her moan of compliance was as blissful as her touch. "Only if you promise it'll be a no-strings-attached kind of thing."

Was she that kind of woman? He didn't think so, even as her soft, pliant body surrendered against his. But if she needed to believe so… "Whatever you want, darlin'," he promised, heartbeat quickening. "Starting now."

He swept her up into his arms and carried her down the hall to his bedroom. He laid her gently on the rumpled sheets, then followed her down. The kissing resumed, deep and evocative, every fantasy he'd had fulfilled. Molly moaned low in her throat. His body hardened all the more.

He pushed the edges of her sweater up, drew it over her head and reached behind her to unfasten her bra. Her nipples peaked into rosy buds of arousal. Cupping the silky globes with both hands, he drew first one, then the other into his mouth. She put her hands in his hair, holding him close, and arched against him as if she never wanted to let him go.

Loving her response, he lifted his head. Unbuttoned the clasp of her belt. Feeling intoxicated by her nearness, by the fact she was finally…*finally*…about to be his, he asked, "More?"

Cheeks and eyes flushed with excitement, she smiled. "Even better, cowboy. Free rein."

"Exactly what I wanted to hear." Pure male satisfaction pouring through him, he paused to tug off her boots, then drew the zipper down and eased her jeans down her long, lissome legs.

Her bikini panties were made of silk. "Nice…" He slid his fingers beneath, finding the soft, damp nest. "But not as nice as this," he said, kissing her through the cloth until her back arched off the bed.

"Nice doesn't begin to cover this." Molly whimpered, uttering a strangled sigh that drove him wild.

The truth was, she thought, tangling her hands in his hair and hauling him close, she had never felt so cherished and adored. So completely overpowered by what was happening between them. And they had barely gotten started.

"But we're getting ahead of ourselves here," she warned, wiggling free. If they were doing this, it was as equals. "I haven't done my part yet." Sitting up, clad only in her panties, she swung one leg over him. Once fully astride him, she shimmied down the hard, masculine length of him, kissing everywhere she passed, admiring his broad shoulders and muscular chest.

He was so strong and virile. And willing to let her take them wherever she wanted, however she wanted. Grinning, she paused to kiss the burgeoning arousal beneath his jeans, through the cloth, then moved lower still. Taking off his boots. Moving back up to unbutton his shirt. He lay quietly, a complicit smile on his handsome face. Catching her hand, he kissed the back of it. "I could get used to this."

So could she.

Not sure she should tell him that—at least not yet anyway—she opened the buttons on his shirt, drew it, and the T-shirt beneath, off. His chest was as sleek and powerfully muscled as she had imagined, with a sexy mat of chestnut hair that spread across his nipples before arrowing down past his navel to the waistband of his jeans. Her fingers followed the path, eliciting a few groans from him and a bigger thrill for her. Wow, did she ever desire him. Every inch of her was throbbing, pounding with the need to be touched, loved, held. But first…

"I've got to see where this leads." Sating her curiosity, she unbuttoned his belt. Undid his fly.

"Trouble," he muttered.

"Then it's my kind of trouble," she purred, slipping her hands inside his pants and finding the hot, hard length of him.

Their reaction was simultaneous. He groaned. She trembled with pleasure.

Eager to explore him more fully, she divested him of his jeans and boxer briefs. Her hands moved across his abdomen. Down his thighs. Upward. Caught up in something too primal to fight, she cupped him again, with both hands, and then bent to kiss the hot, satiny length of him.

He groaned again, on the verge of losing control.

"I think it's time you found a little trouble of your own," he murmured, shifting her onto her back. The next thing she knew, he had taken complete control and whisked her panties off. Hands spreading her thighs wide, he found her with lips and mouth and hands. Exploring. Adoring. Sensation spiraled through her, unlike anything she had ever known. She gripped his shoulders, urging him upward. "Now," she gasped. "Before I…"

"Patience…" he said roughly, sweeping past the last of her barriers. She arched again as he found the most sensitive part of her and brought her to the very edge.

She quivered as his hands took on an even more intimate quest. She was close. Too close. Fisting her hands in his hair, she panted. "I want you inside me when…" *Oh heavens!* "…we…"

"You'll have that, too," he promised as a wave of sensation started deep inside her. With a growl of satisfaction, he pulled her toward him. And just that suddenly, her release came, her entire body melting in boneless pleasure.

He kissed her navel, still stroking the insides of her thighs. "Worth it?"

No fibbing about that when she was still shuddering with the aftershocks of a 6.0 quake. "Yes." She gasped as he palmed her breasts and took her taut, aching nipple into her mouth. "Heck, yes…"

Grinning, he slid upward and once again captured her mouth with his. "I aim to please."

No kidding, she thought, opening her mouth to the commanding pressure of his.

They kissed as he stretched out over top of her and brought his whole body into contact with hers. She could feel his erection pressing against her, hot and urgent. Desire welled inside her. "Now?" he rasped, pausing only long enough to roll on a condom, then kissing her in a way that was so wild and reckless it stole her heart.

"Now," she gasped, knowing she would hold on to this moment forever.

Hands beneath her hips, he spread her thighs and slid inside, penetrating deep. She couldn't get enough of the taste and feel of him, the confident and soulful way he merged his body with hers, the seductive, indomitable manner in which he possessed her.

To her delight, he seemed just as hungry for her. Intent on taking his time. Drawing out the unimaginable pleasure. He kissed her with the same insistent, tantalizing rhythm, letting her know how much she deserved, how much he wanted her to have. And then she was wrapping her legs around his waist, drawing him deeper, exploding with emotion, awash in sensation. With a low groan of pleasure, he followed. And together, at last, they found blissful release.

Chance rolled onto his back, taking Molly with him. A mixture of fierce physical satisfaction and raw emotion washed over him as he savored their closeness. He pressed his face into her hair, drawing in her scent, her softness, while Molly snuggled closer. Still wrapped in his arms, Molly tucked her face against his neck, her eyes closed, body still shuddering, her breath slowing.

Finally, she drew a deep breath, her body still pliant and molded tentatively against his. Lifting her head, she smiled and opened her eyes. "Well. Christmas sure came early," she drawled.

He laughed, relieved that the regret he had half feared he would see was nowhere in sight. "It sure did," he returned softly. He couldn't wait for the next round.

The picture of sated elegance, Molly rose, wrapping the sheet around her midriff. She ran a hand through the mussed layers of her hair, then bent to gather up her clothes, giving him a fine view of her curvaceous backside in the process. "It's too bad it can't happen again."

Whoa. He had definitely missed something here. "What do you mean?"

Looking as if she suddenly found his bedroom too intimate for comfort, she disappeared into the adjacent bath to dress. When she walked back out, she had a too-serene-to-be-believed expression on her face. "Once is a fling." She sat down on the edge of the bed to put on her socks and boots. "Any more than that is complicated." She paused to give him a meaningful glance as he got dressed, too. "And my life is complicated enough right now."

He could see that she wanted him to argue with her. Persuade her otherwise.

Only she wasn't about to let him convince her. At least not in this moment. "You're right," he fibbed, putting on his boots, too.

She stood. "I am?" Skepticism rang in her sweetly pitched voice.

Aware two could play at this game—and that's all it was, a game—he shrugged. "You're moving to Dallas." *Unless I can work a holiday miracle.*

She brushed by him in a drift of the lavender perfume she favored. "Exactly."

He fell into step behind her. "It's a phenomenally busy time of year."

She shot him a look over her shoulder as she glided down the hall with womanly ease. "And the holidays are always ridiculously sentimental."

Which makes Christmastime all the more perfect for finding someone, he thought. Aware she likely did not want to hear that, either, he watched her rummage through her shoulder bag. "And you have a son to care for."

Molly plucked out a lip balm and smoothed some over her kiss-swollen lips. Finished, she pressed her lips together to set the soft gloss. Dropping it back into her purse, she brought out a brush and began running it through her soft auburn curls. Although she looked much neater now, she still glowed from the inside out. Anyone who knew her, seeing her, would know she had just made love.

With him.

And though Chance liked his privacy, he wouldn't mind anyone knowing that Molly was spoken for.

"Not to mention," Molly continued, oblivious to the serious nature of his thoughts, "a problem regarding Santa and a trio of bulls to solve."

He studied the color in her high, sculpted cheeks. Had she ever looked more beautiful than she did at this moment? "I have that covered."

"You think you do," she said skeptically.

Grinning, he closed the distance between them. It was all he could do not to take her in his arms again. "I know I do," he corrected her arrogantly.

Molly danced away. "We'll see about that."

Determined to make this the best Christmas she and Braden had ever had, he chuckled. "You bet we will."

Molly took a calculator out of her bag. "In the meantime, we still have to reconcile the projected numbers on the Circle H renovation project with the actual costs thus far."

Another thing they had in common. They both took the success of their businesses very seriously.

Chance nodded. "Let's get to it."

An hour and a few cups of coffee later, Molly sat back in her chair and looked at Chance with amazement. "We've not only managed to stay exactly on schedule, we're fifteen percent under where we figured we would be in terms of projected labor costs."

He shared her pride in a well-managed project.

Something that only happened when everyone came together as a team. "We work well together."

They did, indeed.

But apparently wary of reading too much into it, she said, "If this holds through the rest of the project, how would you feel about passing the extra revenue on to members of the crew in terms of an additional year-end bonus?"

Once again, the two of them were completely in synch. A miracle in itself, considering how much they had argued about literally everything a few short weeks before.

Chance smiled his approval. "I think it would make for a merry Christmas for everyone. And let's face it— as diligently as our crews have worked, they deserve it."

Molly smiled back and continued surveying him curiously. She moved her counter stool ninety degrees so she faced him. "Can I ask you something?"

He pivoted his seat, too. "Sure."

"How come you're still wearing two hats professionally?"

He nudged her knee with his. "You do the same thing."

She wrinkled her nose and took another sip of coffee. "Interior design and general contracting sort of go hand in hand. Bucking bulls and remodeling do not."

He reached for the thermal carafe. She covered the top of her mug, signaling she'd had enough caffeine, so he emptied what little was left into his. "Actually, they do. If I hadn't had the skills, I wouldn't have been able to remodel my ranch house or build the barns at anywhere near the cost I paid."

Molly powered off her laptop. Seeming as reluctant to leave as he was to see her go, she raked her teeth over her lush lower lip. "How did you get into both businesses anyway?"

"Construction was my first job out of high school," he replied, shutting down the accounting program on his computer.

Molly smiled at his screen saver—a photo of the retired Mistletoe being inducted into the Bucking Bull Hall of Fame. Their gazes met. "You didn't go to college at all?"

"My parents made me apply, and I was accepted, but I knew it wasn't going to work. I'm just not the kind of guy who's happy sitting at a desk."

Her eyes softened with compassion. "I'm guessing Lucille wasn't happy about that."

Talk about an understatement. "She and my dad both went through the roof. They also cut off my allowance and took away my car, thinking that would shake some sense into me."

"It didn't."

"I got a construction job and learned the trade that way for a couple of years. When I tired of doing that in the Texas heat, I went to Wyoming for a while. Lived in the high country and got a job on a ranch as a hired hand."

Her intense interest made it easy to confide in her. "That's where I learned cattle management and the rodeo stock business. And started saving up for my own ranch. But I also knew—" he stood and carried his coffee mug to the sink "—that goal wasn't going to be achieved in this lifetime unless I upped my income."

She grinned and joined him at the dishwasher. "Sounds familiar." She slid her cup in next to his.

They straightened, bumping shoulders in the process.

Aware all over again just how much he had enjoyed holding her in his arms, he let his gaze rove her face. "We do have ambitious natures in common."

"Sorry. I derailed you."

He tugged on an errant lock of her silky auburn hair. "You constantly derail me." *In a good way.*

It was her turn to laugh. "Go on."

He suspected he had better if they didn't want to end up in bed again.

"I want to hear how you came to be so good at ranching and building."

With effort, he turned his attention back to the conversation at hand. "Mostly by working both jobs simultaneously. I worked out a deal with my employer to help him with some home renovations, in addition to my usual duties as hired hand. I started saving every penny I could, took some business courses online and got my general contracting license." He cleared his throat. "I was about to buy a place in Wyoming and open my own general contracting firm when my dad got sick. So I came back to Texas, and my parents gifted me with Bullhaven. Then I moved to Laramie, and the rest, as they say, is history."

"Are you ever going to give up being a general contractor?"

"No. I like doing both. Plus, it gives me the cash flow to keep expanding my bucking-bull business without going into debt or taking on partners there."

He paused, happy to see she didn't think it odd—or unnecessary—to want to keep honing both skills. "What about you? Would you ever give up being your own general contractor on jobs just to concentrate on design?"

Her lips twisted thoughtfully. "In a perfect world, maybe. But I probably won't because having my own crew ensures the quality I want on every project."

"And control is important to you," Chance guessed.

Molly nodded. Returning to the island, she packed up her computer and then grabbed her shoulder bag. "Very."

"Cowboy Chance coming? See me?" Braden asked hours later.

Seeing her son's excitement, Molly couldn't help but wonder if she was doing the right thing. He had no father in his life; Chance could easily fill the bill. If things were different...but they weren't.

She was moving.

Chance was staying here.

Hence, it was best to keep them in the strictly friends category, even if Braden—and the most womanly part of her—clamored for more.

"Doorbell, Mommy!" her son shouted, racing toward the door. Molly expected her heart to give a little leap when she saw the man on the other side of the portal. It seemed to do that a lot these days regarding Chance. However, she didn't expect the sexy cowboy to be carrying a rectangular folding table and three chairs. "Are we playing bridge?"

"Cute. Want to hold the door for me?"

"Whatcha doing, Cowboy Chance?" Braden planted both hands on his little hips.

Chance sidled past, being careful not to bump his cargo into anything or anyone. "I'm bringing in a present for you and your mommy."

"I like presents!" Braden declared.

Chance winked. "I thought that might be the case, buddy."

Unsure how this was related to their baby bull problem, Molly gave their guest a quizzical look.

"Patience," Chance said, setting up the table in a corner of the living room, well away from the tree.

He'd said the same thing when making love to her earlier that day. She flushed at the memory, all her girlie parts tingling.

His gaze raked her lazily from head to toe. With a tip of his hat, he said, "I'll be right back."

Molly and Braden stood at the door, watching, while he went to his truck. He returned, this time with a piece of plywood covered in sturdy white fabric, with cotton balls glued along the edges, and a shopping bag.

"Now I'm really curious," Molly admitted.

"Me, too!" Braden jumped up and down.

Carefully, Chance set the piece of cardboard onto the portable table. Molly wasn't surprised to see it fit precisely. He reached into the bag and pulled out a small colorful building. "Guess what this is," he asked Braden.

Molly read the letters on the front. "Santa's Workshop?"

"Right!"

"And some elves." Chance handed her son several figurines.

Braden set them down on the "snow"-covered board next to the building. Then ran off. "I get Rudolph and sleigh!"

The rest of the bag was empty.

Molly blinked in surprise. "No Santa?"

"Patience…"

Her body reacted. Again.

Flushing, she whispered, "You have to stop saying that."

"How come?"

She admonished him with a lift of her brow. "You know why," she breathed.

Mischief radiated from every fiber of his being.

Braden returned, the two toys Chance had already given him clutched in his hands. He climbed on the chair and set the sleigh and Rudolph next to Santa's Workshop. "I like this!"

Chance patted her son on the shoulder. "I'm glad you do, buckaroo."

Molly propped her hands on her hips while her son began to play with the four toys on the snow board. "I take it there is a method to this madness?"

Chance folded his arms across his chest. "There is. But for the next phase, it will require the two of you coming out to Bullhaven tomorrow morning."

Being alone with him, even with a small chaperone along, always seemed like a dangerous proposition to her way too vulnerable heart. She cleared her throat and lifted her chin. "Really?"

The corners of his eyes crinkled. "Really," he said just as firmly.

She stared into the hazel depths. "To do what?"

"See where and how real bulls live."

But was that all, Molly wondered, studying the sparkling invitation in Chance's smile, that he wanted her to see?

Chapter 6

Chance wasn't sure Molly would take him up on his invitation, even before she gave him a halfhearted, "We'll have to see how things go tomorrow morning... Braden can be pretty tired by the end of the week."

He knew that they'd made love too soon. And because of that she was every bit as determined to keep him at arm's length as he was to get her back in his arms. He also knew that she and her son were a package deal.

Convincing her that condition was more than okay with him, however, was going to be tough. Fortunately, he knew, even if Molly didn't yet, that he was more than up to the task. And he was ready to prove to her they could have something more than dissension between them. She'd finally accepted his offer. Late Saturday morning, she drove up the lane.

He walked out to greet them. "Glad you both could make it."

"Braden really wanted to come and see all of your bulls." She emerged from the SUV and sent him a meaningful glance as she opened the rear passenger door. "And I got to thinking, maybe you're right, that it's a good idea for Braden to learn where and how real live bulls live."

He was glad she understood at least this much of his plan. "That they're only babies, pastured with their momma for a very short time."

She nodded.

"Hey there, pardner," Chance said, after Molly got Braden out of his safety seat. He held up his palm for a high five.

Grinning, Braden fit his small palm to Chance's.

"You're just in time to see some bucking bulls get loaded onto a truck."

Behind them, an 18-wheeler headed up the lane.

Molly lifted her son into her arms.

The three of them watched as the truck parked just outside the barn. The driver—a husky, dark-haired cowboy in his early fifties—got out. "Three of our bulls are going to compete in a rodeo in Arizona next weekend," Chance explained.

Molly blinked. "They're leaving now?"

Noticing Braden was a little heavy for Molly, Chance put out his hands. Grinning, Braden slid into his grip. Amazed at how right it felt to hold the little tyke in his arms, Chance explained, "Bucking bulls can only travel ten hours in one day before needing to be pastured at night at one of the rest ranches along the way. And then they need an equivalent time to recover from the rigors of travel once they do arrive at the rodeo site."

Chance's hired hand Billy walked the first bull out

of the barn. The sleek Black Angus had a name tag on his ear and, as always, was perfectly content to be led into the divided compartment readied just for him on the truck. "That's Kringle," Chance explained.

A second bull was walked out by Pete with equal calm.

"And Saint Nick," Chance said, grinning as the third bull was walked out.

"And last but not least, Dasher," Chance concluded as Braden waved merrily at the bulls.

Amused, Billy and Pete both waved back at Molly's son.

She turned toward him in a drift of orchid perfume. Was that new? If it was, he had to admit he really liked it.

"Are all your bulls named in response to the Christmas holiday?" Molly asked wryly.

His gaze trailed over the hollow of her throat, past her lips, to her pretty amber eyes. "You might say we have a theme going."

She shook her head, clearly not sure what to make of that.

Before she could say anything more, a ruckus sounded in the pasture. Noticing what was going on at the semi-trailer, Mistletoe had crossed the grassy terrain and come to the fence. Looking straight at the truck, he lifted his head and let out another loud bellow.

Molly moved in closer to Chance and put a hand up to protect her son. "What's going on?" she whispered nervously.

Chance laughed. Holding Braden in one arm, he wrapped his other around Molly's shoulders. "Mistletoe may be retired, but he's still a prime athlete and he still wants to compete. He understands getting on a semi-truck means riding to a rodeo, and he wants to go, too."

Braden looked at Chance, listened to Mistletoe and then let out a loud bellow of his own. "Mist'toe," the little boy repeated, then again imitated the loud bellowing sound.

Chance and Molly both laughed.

Mistletoe looked in their direction and bellowed again.

Chance shook his head. "What can I say?" he joked as Molly, understanding they were in no danger, relaxed beside him. "Once a competitor, always a competitor."

The driver came over. Last-minute instructions were given. Papers signed. They all waved as the truck headed back down the lane. Mistletoe remained against the fence in disappointment.

"You want to know what might make Mistletoe Jr.'s daddy feel better?" Chance murmured.

"What?" Braden asked eagerly.

"A bath."

Molly stared at Chance. This morning was turning out to be quite a surprise. She had worried a little he had just invited them out to try to hit on her. However, she could see, given how much was going on at the ranch, she needn't have worried.

There was a lot more to him than an ability to make mind-blowing love and seduce her into tearing down boundaries and spending time with him. He was good with kids. Especially Braden. Kind. And fun to be around.

Had she not been moving 150 miles away, he might have been the perfect man.

If he hadn't also grown up wealthy, that was.

Aware Chance was grinning at her, as if wondering where her thoughts had drifted, she blinked herself back to ranching activity. "Bulls take baths?"

"Well, more like a shower, but yeah, they do."

Braden clapped his hands in excitement. "Hurrah!"

"This we've got to see," Molly agreed.

While she took charge of her son again, Chance grabbed a halter from the barn and went to get Mistletoe. As he brought his prize bucking bull back across the yard, he pointed toward a building on the other side of the complex of barns and training facilities.

At the end of the big bull barn was a cement-floored paddock that was the size of a drive-through car wash. The sides were open, but there was a stop gate along the back. The big black bull stepped calmly up to it. Whistling merrily, Chance tied Mistletoe to the steel gate, then went to get two folding chairs for Molly and Braden and a box full of grooming gear.

He got them situated on the other side of the stop gate, far enough away so there appeared to be no risk of them getting wet, then walked around to grab the long hose hanging on the wall.

"Do all bulls get washed?" Molly asked.

Chance put down the hose long enough to remove his denim jacket. He tossed it on the grass next to Molly, then pushed up the sleeves on his light gray thermal-knit T-shirt. "All of mine do."

Molly's mouth went dry as she watched the powerful muscles of his arms and back flex beneath the clinging cloth. Remembering how all that satiny skin and sinew had felt the day before, beneath her eagerly questing hands, she asked, "How often?"

"Once or twice a month."

"Do you always do it yourself?" she asked.

"Pete and Billy help out." He turned on the water. "But I usually wash Mistletoe myself," he admitted.

It was clear, Molly thought, from the way Chance looked at the bucking bull that Mistletoe was as much a beloved family pet as impressive revenue source. Which went to show yet again how loving and gentle a man Chance was, deep down.

He wet the bull from end to end, then turned a dial on the handle of the hose and directed a sudsy stream into the hide. It seemed to work on the massive animal like a massage.

"Mis'toe likes it!" Braden exclaimed, clapping his hands again.

Chance chuckled and followed the soaping with a thorough rinse. "You're right. He does."

Molly leaned back in her chair as the fragrant smell of the soap filled the air. "When and where did you get him?"

Smiling fondly, Chance turned off the water and plucked a big brush from the bag of grooming tools. "My first Christmas in Wyoming. I was working at a cattle ranch, and one of the pregnant cows went missing. She'd gone off to give birth, got caught in a blizzard that killed her." Chance stopped brushing long enough to pat Mistletoe's head. "This fella was barely breathing when I found him."

Molly could only imagine how horrifying that had to have been. "But you revived him."

Chance sobered. His low tone took on a sentimental rasp. "Against all odds. Even the vet said he'd never make it, but if he did, my boss said, I could have him."

And Chance loved a challenge.

"So…" He got out the clippers and trimmed some of the stray hairs around the bull's face and tail. "I spent the next few months bottle-feeding Mistletoe in the barn, seeing he stayed warm and healthy, and the rest, as they say, is history."

Finished, Chance dried off his hands with a towel. Pride radiating in his handsome face, he retrieved his phone and showed them more photos of the two of them in the barn. Apparently, Mistletoe wasn't the only one who'd been young and cute, Molly noted with an appreciative smile.

Chance turned on a blower to move the air through Mistletoe's sleek black coat.

"So now," Molly gathered, holding on to Chance's phone for him, "Mistletoe is the oldest of your bucking bulls."

"As well as a national champion and the sire to every other bucking bull I own." Chance patted Mistletoe fondly. The bull let out a low sound that seemed like the cattle version of a purr of pleasure.

Molly flushed, recalling when she had done the same beneath the caress of those large, talented hands.

"Mis'toe likes baths!" Braden noted yet again.

"Do you think he would fit in the bathtub at your house?" Chance asked Braden with exaggerated curiosity.

Molly saw where the handsome cowboy was going with this. It was all she could do not to applaud his subtlety.

Braden shook his head defiantly. "Mis'toe too big!" he declared.

"I guess you're right." Chance pretended to consider the matter. "I guess he'll have to continue taking his baths here with all the other bulls."

Braden spread his arms wide as inspiration hit. "Mommy build big tub!" He aimed a thumb at his small chest. "My house."

Molly had to hand it to her son. He had a talent for solving problems.

Chance squinted at Molly. "The perks of having a contractor for a parent?"

"Or a too-bright-and-imaginative-for-his-own-good offspring?"

In any case, they had yet to solve the quandary of how to convince Braden he couldn't possibly have a real live bull for Christmas.

Pete suddenly appeared. "Boss? There's someone here who wants a word with you."

Chance responded to the interruption with a lift of his palm. "Tell them I'll call them back later."

The hired hand winced. "Ah. I don't think she's going to…"

She? Molly wondered.

Please tell me I haven't made the same dumb mistake I made with Aaron, that Chance is not involved with someone else, too.

"Chance?" Delia rounded the side of the bull wash. She whipped off her sunglasses. "We have to talk!"

Of all the people Molly had expected to see that morning, Chance's ex was not one of them. She started to rise.

Chance waved Molly back down. Then he informed Delia curtly, "Tell Babs the answer is no."

Delia put her sunglasses on top of her long silvery-blond hair. Once again, she was dressed all in black. "You don't even know what my mother said."

He nodded at the folder in her hand. "Is that an offer?"

Delia straightened, indignant. "Yes."

He handed the grooming box off to Pete. "Then we've got nothing to discuss."

The hired hand exited quickly.

Ignoring Molly and Braden, Delia moved imploringly toward Chance. She looked her former lover right in the eye. "Look, I'm not into chasing lost causes any more than you are, Chance. You know that better than anyone! But Mr. X authorized our firm to purchase your bucking-bull business for *well over* the assessed value."

Her words fell on deaf ears.

Chance unhooked the lead and began steering Mistletoe out of the washing area. "Maybe you and Babs should try showing him some ranches and rodeo operations that *are* for sale?"

Delia stomped closer to Chance, staying well clear of the bull. "He wants *yours*."

His jaw set. "Then Mr. X is going to be disappointed," he predicted grimly.

"At least think it over." Delia pushed the folder at him. When he refused to take it, she shoved it into Molly's hands before turning and sauntering back to the waiting limo.

"What do you want me to do with this?" Molly asked Chance when the newly tranquil Mistletoe had been put back out to pasture and they'd retreated to the house for the casual lunch Chance had promised.

She couldn't help but notice that although there had been no yuletide decorations of any sort the day before, now he had a tree up and a wreath on the front door.

Had he done all that for her and Braden?

Or just simply because it was time?

There was no clue in the impassive set of his features.

Chance looked at the sleek black-and-white Holcombe Business Sales & Acquisitions folder and nodded in the direction of his desk. "There's a shredder over there."

Molly's jaw dropped. "Seriously?"

Nodding, Chance brought out what looked to be a brand-new box of plastic building blocks for Braden and set them in the middle of the living room floor. Together, they opened it and dumped them out. He patted her son's shoulder. "Have at it, buddy."

Braden settled in the midst of the toys, beaming up at their host. "Thanks, Cowboy Chance!"

"No problem." He rose to his feet.

Folder still in hand, Molly followed him over to his workstation. Keeping her voice low and tranquil, she looked him in the eye. "You're not even going to look at it?"

"No need." Handsome jaw set, he took it from her, walked over and fed it to the shredder, cover and all. He closed the distance between them and took her hands in his. "Why does this surprise you?"

Her pulse raced. "I don't know. I figured you'd at least be curious." She would have been in his place.

He dropped his grip on her and walked into the kitchen. "I know what Bullhaven means to me."

As always, his ultramasculine presence made her feel intensely aware of him. "There's no price for it?" she guessed, wishing he hadn't been quite so quick to let her go.

"No." He went to the fridge and brought out a package of hot dogs, buns and all the fixings. "I gather you don't feel the same way about your own home and business?"

Molly sat at the island, watching as he turned the

flame on under the stove-top grill. "I love the home I grew up in. I'm going to do everything I can to keep it as a retreat. My work will go with me."

Something flickered in his expression, then disappeared. "Any of your employees planning to move to Dallas with you?" he asked her casually.

Molly cast a look at her son, who was now happily stacking blocks. "No. But I've made calls on everyone's behalf. They'll all have jobs in the area after I leave."

He turned, his expression deliberately closed and uncommunicative. "You didn't call me."

She flushed under his continued scrutiny. "We weren't on friendly terms last fall."

"Ah." He moved toward her, throwing her off guard once again. He stopped just short of her. "Are we now?"

"More so…"

The wicked gleam in his eyes said if they were alone, he would have kissed her. And she would have let him. Luckily for them both, a faint chime sounded. Averting her gaze from his, she pulled out her phone.

"Expecting something?"

Molly drew a deep breath, glad to have someone to confide in about this. "A couple of things, actually. You know that special T-R-A-I-N set I had my eye on? It's all sold out. I can't find it anywhere online. And I've set up alerts."

He picked up a pair of tongs. "A knockoff maybe?"

"The reviews on those aren't nearly as good." Molly sighed.

The hot dogs sizzled as they hit the grill, quickly filling the room with the delicious smell of roasting meat.

He wrapped the buns in foil and set them in the oven to warm. "What else?"

This was a little harder to talk about. But she did need to vent. Molly rested her hand on her chin. "I was supposed to hear from Elspeth Pyle, the headmistress at Worthington Academy regarding an appointment for Braden. They're interviewing and testing prospective students and their parents next week. But so far there's nothing on my phone, or email, although something could still come via the postman this afternoon."

"You thought he was going to get one?" Chance asked sympathetically.

Molly sighed again. She knew she was reaching for the stars on her son's behalf, but she had really hoped. "Alumni recommendations are supposed to carry weight in the admission process, so the letter Sage wrote on his behalf should have helped."

His gaze narrowed. "Is that really what you want for him?"

Why wouldn't she? Molly ignored his clear disapproval. "The school is one of the very best in Dallas."

"Mommy?" Braden joined them and tugged on the hem of her fleece. "Hungry."

"Well, that's a good thing." Chance winked. "Because lunch is ready!"

Half an hour later, replete with hot dogs, chips, clementine slices and ice cream, Braden could not stop yawning. "I better get him home for an N-A-P," Molly said, leery of wearing out their welcome. Though, to his credit, Chance had been a very good sport about keeping up a nonstop conversation with her loquacious three-year-old son.

"No. Nap." Braden yawned again.

Molly figured he'd last maybe five minutes on the

drive home before conking out. "You can look out the window then and wave at all the cows and horses."

Braden cheered. "'Kay!"

Molly found her son's jacket. "Can you say thank you to Cowboy Chance?"

Braden hugged Chance's knees. "Thank you."

Chance ruffled the auburn hair on the top of his head. Then he picked him up in his arms for a face-to-face goodbye. "You're welcome, buddy."

Molly accepted Chance's offer to carry her son out to her SUV. Though she knew it was past time, she really hated to leave.

She paused, her hand on the driver-side door. Then she said, "Seeing the bulls was fun, even if it didn't yet have the desired effect."

He looked down at her, his chestnut hair glinting in the sunshine. "It's early," he told her with his usual confidence. "Speaking of which," his eyes softened even more, "would it be too much for me to bring by another installment of the 'solution' this evening?"

Molly's heart leapt at the thought of seeing Chance again so soon. She also knew the faster they were able to adjust her son's expectations regarding the bulls, the better. Besides, it was Saturday. "Not at all. But come ready to work," she cautioned with a smile, soaking in his charismatic presence.

As long as they kept it casual and had a little chaperone, their relationship would stay safely in the just-friends zone. Wouldn't it?

Molly smiled. "We're baking Christmas cookies this evening, too."

Chapter 7

Braden answered the door at seven that evening, Molly by his side. Chance looked at the smiling penguin wearing a Santa hat on the front of Braden's knit shirt and the red-and-white stripes on his pants. "Nice pajamas."

Braden took in the second plywood board, covered in white, and folding table Chance carried in his right hand, the shopping bag of goodies in his left. His eyes widened in delight. "Mommy, look!" he shouted happily.

Molly wrinkled her brow. "You're going to spoil us," she said.

Chance winked. "Then mission accomplished. And by the way—" he let his glance drift over her cream-colored V-neck sweater and formfitting black yoga pants "—you're looking mighty fine, too."

"Then that makes three of us," she said, nodding

at his green corduroy shirt and jeans. Grinning, she opened the door wide. A front had blown in since they had seen each other earlier, bringing gusting winds and taking the temperature down to freezing. Worse, it was the kind of damp cold that went right through your clothes. Molly reached past him to hold the door. "Come in out of the cold."

With a nod of his head, Chance obliged.

"What's that?" Braden asked as Molly shut the door behind them, once again sealing them into the cozy warmth of her home.

Chance winked at the little boy. "Let's see." After handing Molly the bag, he took the folding table over and set it up flush against the matching one he'd brought over the previous night. The white fabric-covered board went on top.

"We've got a North Pole over here, with Rudolph and the sleigh, and what is going to be a Christmas ranch over on this side."

"I like ranches!" Braden jumped up and down.

"Then let's build one, shall we?"

Together, the three of them set up a corral, a barn and a snow-covered ranch house decorated for the holidays. Three horses, a dog and a cat completed the menagerie. Last but not least were a number of snow-covered trees that could be placed on either side of the increasingly elaborate Christmas village.

Yet there was plenty of room for more.

"I play?" Braden asked.

"What do you say first?" Molly prompted.

Braden encompassed Chance in the biggest hug he could manage. "Love you, Chance!"

A lump the size of a walnut formed in Chance's throat at the unexpected declaration.

There was no doubt the earnest little boy meant it.

Chance knelt down, aware this was a first. "Love you, too, buddy," he said thickly, accepting Braden's joyous hug. In the foreground, he saw Molly, tears shining in her eyes. She needed a moment as much as he did.

Braden went back to playing.

Molly returned to the kitchen. She plucked an apron off the hook. When she had a little trouble tying it, he stepped behind her and did it for her.

He caught the scent of orchids before he stepped away. She was wearing that perfume again.

But then maybe she wore it a lot.

Maybe he had just never noticed.

"I guess this is what they mean when they say Christmas is for kids."

She nodded, her head bent over the handwritten cookie recipe on the counter. "Thank you for helping us with our dilemma, although I'm still not sure I see how that's going to convince him that it's not likely he will get a L-I-V-E trio of B-U-L-L-S."

"Patience," he teased. He saw her blush, just the way she had when they'd made love.

His body reacted in kind.

Aware this was no time to be going down that path, however, not with her son in the next room, he took an apron off the hook for himself and put it on. "We'll work it out."

Brightening, Molly put six eggs into the mixing bowl of her stand mixer and turned it on high speed. "Speaking of things working out unexpectedly...guess what I got shortly before you arrived?"

Chance watched her pour milk and baking powder into another bowl.

"A call from Elspeth Pyle, the headmistress at Worthington Academy! Braden has an interview on Monday afternoon. They'll give us a tour of the school at that time and also talk to me privately. Which means I need to take another adult along."

Maybe more than she knew if things went the way they usually did at the Academy. Casually, he volunteered, "I wouldn't mind going." For starters, it would give him more time with both of them. There were other things in Dallas that could be accomplished, as well.

As Molly zested the skin of a lemon, the bright flavor of citrus filled the room. She paused to look up at him. "I didn't think you were gung ho about this."

He shrugged, not about to enter that particular minefield and chance spoiling the evening.

A furrow formed along the bridge of her nose. She added softened butter to the whirring mixer, then sugar. "Not going to confirm or deny?"

He fought the urge to take her in his arms. "If you need someone, I'll be there. It'll give us a chance to take care of another matter while we're in the city."

She peered at him through a fringe of thick auburn lashes. "Like what?"

"I got a call from our tile guys this afternoon. They said some of the tile for the kitchen backsplash was damaged or is not as perfect as you want it to be."

She frowned, already taking the matter in stride. "That's a special-order material."

"I know. I found some at a warehouse in Dallas, but I think we should probably take a look at it before we buy it, make sure the same flaws don't exist in that batch."

Molly nodded. "Absolutely." She paused, thinking. Then ran a hand across her brow. "This is going to put us behind, isn't it?"

He stepped closer. "A little bit."

Their eyes met, and he felt the connection between them deepen. "How come no one called me?"

"I told them I'd talk to you about it. Just in case you wanted to—" conscious of her little boy playing a short distance away, he mimed an arrow to the heart "—the messenger."

"Smart-ass." They all knew neither of them ever took any of their frustrations out on the crew. Mix-ups and snafus were par for the course of any building project. Molly took them in stride, just as he did.

The customer was not always as understanding. "Did you tell your mom?" Molly added lemon zest, anise extract and salt to the mixer.

Chance shook his head. He really enjoyed watching her move about the kitchen and work her magic. "I thought you might want to do that."

"I do, since it really falls on the design side. I'll see if I can get her to pick out something else as backup, just in case we don't have time to get her first choice and still make the Open House deadline."

"Sounds good."

She turned the speed down on the machine and handed him a bowl of flour. "Can you put this in, a cup at a time, while the mixer is still going?"

"Without making a mess?"

Her amber eyes glittering jovially, she patted his biceps. "I have faith in you."

He was glad someone did. He was competent in the kitchen but not a pro like her.

Still, it was nice to be included, he thought, carefully adding the first of what looked like half a dozen or so cups of flour.

He watched her retreating backside as she went off to get out the baking sheets. She looked good in jeans and skirts, but this was the first time he had seen her in something as formfitting as the black yoga pants. They hugged her slender but curvy frame with disturbing accuracy.

Whirling back around, she came toward him once again. Standing next to him, she watched him add the last of flour. As soon as it was mixed, she turned.

He cleared his throat. "So what are we making here?" he asked. When all he wanted to make with her was love…hot, wild love.

She smiled, oblivious to the effect she had on his libido. "*Springerle.* It's a German shortbread cookie with a design stamped on top."

Feeling the pressure building at the front of his jeans, he noted with mock gravity, "Fancy."

She laughed, bending forward to remove the latch holding the mixing bowl in place. The V of her sweater gaped slightly as she moved, giving him an unexpected view of the delectable uppermost curves of her breasts and the satin edge of her bra.

His body hardening, he resisted the urge to take her in his arms, and instead, contented himself, watching her move gracefully about her task.

"It's one of those things that looks harder than it actually is." She picked up a wooden rolling pin with pictures carved into it. "Thanks to this."

"*Really* fancy."

She laughed again. Nodded at the other room. "Want to tell Braden that it's time for him to come and help?"

Chance gestured toward the sofa. "Ah, I think it might be too late for that." Braden was curled up, his favorite blanket beneath his cheek, the Rudolph Chance had brought him in one hand, a horse from his Christmas village in the other. "Long day?"

"Very." Molly unlooped the apron from around her neck, then set it aside. "I'm going to have to carry him to bed."

Aware he had flour all over the front of his apron, Chance took his off. "Want me to do the honors?"

Suddenly looking as if it had been a very long day for her, too, Molly sighed. "If you think you can without waking him."

"What's that saying?" He tilted his head. "Anything you can do I can do better?"

She elbowed him in the ribs, taking the joke in the spirit it was intended. "Just don't disappoint me, okay, cowboy?"

It was a casual request.

Yet one he wanted to take seriously.

"Never." He leaned down and lightly kissed the top of her head. Then after carefully picking her son up in his arms, blankie, toys and all, Chance followed Molly up the stairs.

Molly tried not to react to the sight of Chance gently laying Braden in his toddler bed. But it was impossible. The sight of the big, strong man tenderly cradling her son, and setting him down on the pillows, created an ache in her heart that was so fierce it nearly brought tears to her eyes.

Up until now, she had convinced herself that Braden was better off with one parent who loved him with all her being. Now, with Chance in their lives, even temporarily, she could no longer deny the truth. Her son needed a daddy.

He deserved one.

Had circumstances been different, had she and Chance been more compatible in all the ways that really counted when it came to long-term relationships, their future might have been different.

But they weren't the same.

He was the kind of man who could reject financial offers without even looking at them.

She was a woman who would upend her entire life to better financially provide for her son.

And money, she knew, was on the top three list of things couples fought about.

"Tell me you're going to let me stay around long enough to at least taste the *springerle*," he said when they were back downstairs again.

What harm could there be in a little more time with him? Molly wondered. Especially when the two of them were becoming such good friends. "Sure." Molly drew a bolstering breath and handed him his apron. "But be warned," she said with a playful look. "I plan to put you to work."

And work they did.

After rolling out the dough and then using the special pin to leave an imprint, they carefully cut and transferred the stamped cookie dough onto parchment-lined cookies sheets. Finally, it was time to put the first two pans in the preheated oven. "What about the rest of the dough?" Chance asked.

Molly smiled at the way he was really getting into the holiday baking. "I'm going to save that for Braden to do, first thing tomorrow morning." She covered the bowl and set it in the fridge.

"So now we wait," he said.

"We wait," she confirmed, her stomach suddenly clenching with excitement for no reason she could figure.

She liked cookies.

But she wouldn't empty the bank for them.

On the other hand, to be held in his arms again and or have another one of his kisses…

Hazel eyes glittering with a wealth of emotions she wasn't so sure she should decipher, he brushed aside a lock of her hair. "Have I told you how much I appreciate you having me here, with you and Braden?"

She laughed off the significance of her actions and tried to harden her heart. "No choice really, given the ongoing live-bull situation."

Looking confident they would solve that dilemma, Chance wrapped his arms around her, pulled her close. "Oh, there's always a choice, Molly," he murmured huskily.

And the first one she had to make was whether she was going to let him kiss her again.

Chance saw the indecision in her eyes. Luckily for both of them, there was no indecision in him. He knew exactly where he wanted this liaison of theirs to go. Giving her no room to protest, he lowered his mouth over hers. She smelled like an intoxicating mix of orchid, cookies and delectable woman. And she tasted just as sweet, her lips as heavenly soft and supple as he recalled. Her body just as warm and although not quite yielding, not pulling away, either.

He slid a hand down her spine and back up again. Worked to erotically deepen and further the kiss. The move was rewarded with a soft, sultry moan and a surge against his body that had him hard as granite, and hungering for more. "Chance…"

Sensing she was a woman who had never been valued the way she should be, he wove his hands through her hair. "Just a kiss or two, Molly," he rasped, kissing his way up the nape of her neck, the sensitive place behind her ear. "That's all I'm asking."

And all, he was certain, she meant to give. She uttered another soft sigh. Wrapped her arms around his neck, rose on tiptoe and pressed her breasts to his chest. "Two kisses, then," she whispered, her eyes a dreamy amber as she looked up at him. "That's all."

Two kisses that would mean everything, Chance determined, savoring the way her heart pounded against his.

Resolving to make her realize how much they could have if she just gave them the opportunity, Chance resumed kissing her. Soft and sweet, slow and deep, and all the ways in between. He let her know with every stroke of his lips and tongue how much he wanted to be there for her, to let her know he cared. Enough to be as patient and gentle as she required, while cherishing and honoring her as she never had been before.

He kissed her until she was as caught up in the all-consuming passion as he was. And it was only then that he realized the kitchen smelled of burning sugar.

Molly noticed at the same time he did.

She broke away. Stared in dismay at the smoke coming out of her oven vents. Then jumped into action, as did he. She swiftly hit the power-off button on her oven and covered the vents with two oven mitts, stifling the smoke and cutting off the flow of oxygen before anything could burst into flames. Chance grabbed a chair, stepped up and undid the plastic covering on the smoke alarm just as the first earsplitting warning screech sounded for half a second, then abruptly stopped when he managed to disconnect it.

Chance and Molly tensed, waiting to hear if Braden cried out. Thankfully, only silence reigned.

Her face pale, she opened the oven door. The cookies inside were indeed burned black, but not on fire. With a grimace, she pulled out both sheets, carried the horribly smelling cookies outside and set the pans on the concrete patio behind the house.

He went in the opposite direction and opened a couple of windows at the front of the house for cross ventilation. Almost instantly bitter-cold air swept into the living area and wafted through the kitchen, easing the smoky smell.

Molly jerked in another breath, still distressed. "I'm going upstairs to check on Braden." She dashed off while he stayed behind. And as soon as the residual smoke was cleared out by the winter wind now gusting through the downstairs, he reassembled the alarm.

Eventually Molly returned. She still looked a little shaken but was composing herself quickly.

Aware how quickly the temperature had dropped inside her home, as well as between the two of them, he moved to shut the windows. "'Everything okay up there?"

She nodded, her face flushed blotchy pink with embarrassment. "Braden's still asleep. No smoke made it up there."

He gave her the physical space she seemed to need. "Sorry about the cookies."

She scoffed and ran a hand through her hair. "I'm not."

How was that possible, he wondered, given how much work they'd put in?

Molly retrieved her baking pans and shut the door behind her. Back stiff, she carried the remains to the sink and dumped the contents. Whirling to face him, she lifted her chin. "I needed a reminder to stay focused. And not get distracted by this…attraction between us." She swallowed, amending half-apologetically, "Nice as it is."

At least she admitted that.

As for the rest…

She held up a hand before he could interrupt. "I'm not going to lie to you, Chance. I enjoyed making love with you." She squared her shoulders defiantly. "But I meant what I said. It's not going to happen again. And this disaster here—" she indicated the burned-black cookies now filling her kitchen sink "—is evidence why."

Chance could have argued the culinary disaster was not a harbinger of events to come, but the look on Molly's face told him their relationship—and it *was* a relationship whether she wanted to admit it or not—would be better served by giving her some time alone to sort out her feelings. So he called on every bit of gentlemanly reserve he had, bid her good-night and left.

On Sunday, Molly was "too busy" to see him.

He had a lot to do before he left Laramie, too. Including making hotel reservations for the three of them Monday night and an appointment with the tile vendor first thing Tuesday morning. He also arranged a surprise for Molly and Braden that he hoped would go a long way toward solving their "live bull" problem.

Unfortunately, when he went to pick them up first thing Monday morning, Molly looked more stressed out than he had ever seen her. Her son was in a foul mood, too.

"Something wrong, buddy?" Chance asked gently, figuring it would be best to talk to the little fella first. He and Molly could discuss whatever was on her mind while he was driving.

Braden crossed his arms over his chest, looking every inch as stubborn as his mommy. "Want my friends," he said.

Chance looked at Molly. She compressed her lips. "He knows today is Monday, and that's a school day."

Braden stomped his foot. "Go school *now*!"

Molly sighed. "I've explained we're going to visit another school this morning, one that's a little far away."

Braden dug in further. "No 'nother school."

Molly turned her glance skyward. "Let's just say he is not in a cooperative frame of mind," she said under her breath. "On this of all days."

No kidding, Chance thought. He turned back to Braden. "Some people like playing hooky."

Braden made a recalcitrant face at Chance.

"He doesn't know what that is," she explained, wringing her hands.

And there was obviously no time to go into it.

"Right." Realizing that Molly was probably nervous enough about how things were going to go at Worthington Academy for all of them, and further delaying their departure would not help that, he glanced at his watch. "Maybe we should just hit the road."

Molly relaxed enough to send him a grateful glance that made him glad he had decided to tag along and provide the much-needed moral support. "We really don't want to be late," she agreed.

At her request, they took her SUV. He drove.

Braden fell asleep in his car seat soon after they started out. And they arrived in the city with just enough time to eat a quick lunch. Molly changed Braden—who'd gotten ketchup on his clothes—in her vehicle. A wash of his face and hands and a quick brush of his hair and they were ready to head for the Worthington Academy campus.

As they approached the glitzy private school, Chance shot Molly a reassuring glance, even as he wondered whether she would feel instantly at home there or completely out of her depth. And what either of those options would mean for Braden, or for the two of them.

Given how much research she had done on private schools in the upper echelon of Dallas society, Molly thought she would be prepared for her first glimpse of Worthington Academy. She wasn't even close. And hence, she could only stare as Chance drove through the manicured grounds at the Colonial-style ivy-covered brick buildings and numerous athletic fields, all with individual bleachers.

With the familiarity of an alumni, Chance pointed out the PE building that housed the indoor swimming pool and basketball and volleyball courts. Braden gaped at the students in uniform, walking in orderly lines across the quad. "It's even lovelier than the brochure photos," Molly murmured, impressed.

Chance nodded, his face an inscrutable mask.

"And you and all your siblings went here?"

Chance nodded as he stopped and waited for the cross-country team to run en masse across the street in front of them.

"Did you like it?"

Chance drove on. "Wyatt and I had a tough time with all the rules."

Not exactly a ringing endorsement.

"Zane, Garrett and Sage thrived." He parked in the visitor lot, outside the administration building. Paused long enough to put on his tie and jacket, and then they were off.

Elspeth Pyle, the headmistress, greeted them cordially. The slender fortysomething brunette was as elegant as Molly had imagined she would be.

She introduced them to the sophisticated silver-haired woman at her side. "This is Dr. Mitchard. She's our school psychologist for the pre-K division. She'll be administering the cognitive evaluation for Braden while you tour the facilities and observe an actual classroom environment. And this is Julianne." She pointed to a young woman who looked fresh out of college herself. "One of our tour guides."

"Mommy. You stay," Braden said when Dr. Mitchard attempted to usher him into the testing center.

Molly knelt down. "Chance and I'll be right back, honey. You just go with Dr. Mitchard and answer her questions. Okay?"

Braden's lower lip trembled.

For a second, Molly thought her little boy was going to have a complete meltdown.

But something in the confident, encouraging way Chance was looking at her son bucked him up. Braden squared his little shoulders and took Dr. Mitchard's hand. They disappeared into a room filled with toys and puzzles. Moments later, Molly could hear him chatting happily.

The testing under way, Molly and Chance were led down a hall, to the wing that held the pre-K classes. The doors had glass insets. A press of the intercom button next to the door, and they could hear what was going on inside.

In one, A. A. Milne was being read and animatedly discussed.

In another, the teacher was holding up large prints. The children were confidently and correctly calling out the name of the artists—Monet, Rembrandt, Picasso.

Molly was unable to help but be enthralled. Her son would thrive here. She was certain of it. And she would be able to rest easy, knowing she had made sure he started out life with every advantage.

To her relief, Braden certainly looked happy when she had finished her own interview with the admission counselor and headmistress.

She joined him and Chance in the preschool lobby, where they were seated in armchairs, side by side, engaged in some sort of nonsensical game that had her son quietly giggling.

Unable to recall when he had enjoyed another adult's company so very much, Molly smiled at them.

Chance smiled back.

Braden, Molly noted, wasn't the only guy really enjoying himself here.

"We go, Mommy?" Braden ran over and embraced her fiercely.

Hugging him back, Molly nodded.

Braden moved between them, taking her hand and Chance's. Together, they followed the brick path through the elegantly landscaped quad to the visitor parking lot.

"Good meeting, I guess?" Chance said.

Molly nodded. All her questions had been answered. "The staff was surprisingly thorough."

"When will you find out whether he's admitted or not?"

Molly jerked in a breath, suddenly feeling anxious again. Aware Chance was waiting for her answer, she replied, "The decisions will be made by the end of next week, and all midyear applicants will receive a letter via regular mail the week after that."

Which meant she would know before Christmas. Would her wish for her son be granted? Molly could only hope. Meantime, they had what was left of the afternoon ahead of them. Work on the Circle H ranch house that still needed to be completed. And to do that, they needed all the supplies.

"Do you think it's too late to go to the tile warehouse?" Molly asked after getting into her SUV.

Chance glanced at his watch. "They close at six. With traffic, probably. But there's a place nearby that I'd like to show you."

Braden piped up from his safety seat in the back. "Want to play!"

Chance shot him an affectionate look in the rearview mirror. "I think that can be arranged."

* * *

"Wow," Braden breathed when they walked into the Highland Village Toy Emporium.

Wow was right, Molly thought, taking her son by the hand. The exclusive store was decorated for Christmas and filled to the brim with all the latest playthings.

A well-heeled older woman approached them, a huge smile on her face. "Mr. Lockhart!" she said, introducing herself to Molly and Braden as the store owner, Rochelle Lewis. "A little early."

Chance flashed a winning grin. "Not too early, I hope?"

"Definitely not!" Rochelle beamed. "We can take you upstairs now, if you like."

"What's upstairs?" Molly asked curiously.

Chance reached out and took her and Braden's hands. "You'll see."

They followed Rochelle through an employees-only door, up a set of cement stairs, through another big door.

Inside, the large area had been divided into three sections. Elaborate dollhouses with thousand-dollar price tags and play kitchen sets on the left, very fancy riding toys in the middle. On the left was the elaborate Leo and Lizzie World Adventure train set and all the accoutrements, which was sold out everywhere.

Braden, who couldn't have been less interested when Molly showed him the brochure, had an entirely different view when confronted with the reality of the fancy wooden tracks, windmills, stations, bridges and locomotive engines and sidecars. "Wow," he said again.

In addition to the basic components—which could have been located anywhere—there was a mini-set featuring the Golden Gate Bridge in San Francisco. Another that traveled through the Grand Canyon. One with Big Ben and Buckingham Palace and the Thames in London. The Eiffel Tower in France. The pyramids in Egypt. Even one with the River Walk and the Alamo in San Antonio, Texas—a place where Braden had actually visited. Twenty in all, thus far. With new adventure sets coming out twice yearly.

"Take as long as you like," Rochelle said.

"I'm not sure showing him this is a good idea," Molly whispered to Chance while Braden moved a train along the wooden track, looking thoroughly entranced. "Given that we—I mean I—can no longer get even the basic components."

Chance shrugged with the ease of a man who had grown up with an unlimited bank account. "True, but the emporium has two remaining deluxe collector's sets left that include every item made to date. One of which is yours, if you want to buy the whole thing."

"They won't break it up?"

"Manufacturer won't allow it. Already asked."

Rochelle was back, price list in hand.

Molly took it.

And when confronted with the total, nearly fainted.

She had barely recovered when her son turned to her plaintively. "Want Leo and Lizzie trains, Mommy."

"I know, honey." She forced herself to smile, as the store owner trailed off to give them some privacy. "Aren't they wonderful?" And when the basic set did come back in stock, probably at some point after the holidays...

"Santa bring?" Braden inquired hopefully.

"Santa Claus has all kinds of trains," Chance soothed

him. He was obviously more prepared to handle the situation than she was.

Braden got the mutinous look back on his face. "Want these," he stated, then turned and again began to play.

Chance stepped back. When she joined him, he whispered in her ear, "They have locomotive sets at the superstores, in a much less costly version."

But it wasn't the one she had wanted and now Braden yearned to have, Molly thought in disappointment.

"I checked. The other brands are in stock, too, so if you want me to go out tonight, while you know who is asleep, and take care of it for you…" Chance continued.

Molly drew a deep breath.

The store owner returned "I hate to rush you, Mr. Lockhart. Especially given how much your family has patronized our emporium over the years, but there are two other customers, standing by, ready to…"

Molly looked at the train set again.

Then the price.

With the kind of tuition she was going to have to pay at Worthington Academy, she just couldn't do it. "I'm sorry," she said reluctantly. "The deluxe collector's set is a little much for him right now."

Oblivious to the whispered negotiations going on behind him, Braden continued moving the train along the tracks.

"I understand."

Rochelle looked at Chance.

"I'd still like the stuffed giraffe we talked about for my nephew, Max," he said.

"Certainly."

Chance turned to Molly. "Mind if I go down and take care of it?"

Molly forced a smile. "No, of course not."

It would give Braden a little more time to play.

Which sadly, as it happened, was going to be as close as he got to owning a Leo and Lizzie World Adventure train set this holiday season.

"Sorry. I didn't mean to upset you," Chance said when they were leaving the upscale toy emporium.

She knew his heart had been in the right place. It always was where she and her son were concerned. She reached over and squeezed his hand. "It's good to have reminders why I need to work harder, bring in more salary, so that next year at this time, cash reserves won't be an issue." *A few of those jobs for Lucille's über-wealthy friends,* she encouraged herself silently, *and...*"I'll be able to do whatever I want, whenever I want."

Chance studied her, his emotions as veiled as his eyes. Once again, they seemed at odds.

Finally he said, "You really think Braden would know the difference between the high-priced versus the low-priced locomotive sets?"

"Before he'd actually seen and played with them? Probably not, but I would," Molly admitted honestly.

She could see she had disappointed Chance with her frankness. She couldn't help that, either, she thought on a troubled sigh.

He'd always had money. She'd never had enough. And like it or not, that created a divide between them that was not liable to go away.

Chapter 8

Noting it had been quiet for a good twenty minutes now, Chance crossed the hall. Rapped quietly on Molly's hotel room door. There was a pause; then she opened it just enough so they could talk, without inviting him in.

"Everything okay?" he asked her quietly.

"You heard the meltdown?" she whispered back.

Chance doubted anyone on their end of the hall hadn't heard it. But figuring she didn't need to be reminded of that, he complimented facetiously instead. "Your son's got quite a set of lungs on him."

She cracked a faint smile at the joke. "Tell me about it."

"But he's asleep now?"

Nodding, she moved so she was no longer blocking his view, and Chance could see inside the room. Braden was curled up in the middle of the king-size bed, his favorite blue blankie tucked beneath his chin. His cherubic face still bore the evidence of his earlier tears, but he seemed to be resting peacefully now. Molly shook her head. "He finally exhausted himself."

Chance commiserated with the little tyke. "And no wonder. Given the trip from Laramie to Dallas this morning, the afternoon spent being tested at the Worthington Academy—"

"Followed by the trip to the emporium to see the toy trains, and the dinner out he really did not want to sit through."

Even though they had tried to make it simple and fast.

Molly leaned against the door frame, still keeping her voice low as she confided, almost as one parent to another, "Usually his bubble bath relaxes him, but tonight not even that did the trick. He just went into full temper tantrum. It was all I could do to get him into his jammies, never mind read him his usual bedtime story."

Chance wished she had called on him to help. "Tomorrow will be better," he soothed.

She looked doubtful.

Wishing he could take her in his arms and make love to her until her tension eased, he said, "Can I get you anything? Bucket of ice? I don't mind hitting the gift shop if you want juice or milk."

"That's really sweet of you."

Sweet was not exactly the way he wanted to be perceived.

"But I think I'm going to take a cue from my son and try to get as much sleep as I can tonight."

"Okay. Just so you know, though. My room may be a few doors down, but I'm just a text away."

"Thank you. For everything today." Without warning, Molly rose on tiptoe and pressed her lips to his cheek. She drew back and looked him in the eye. He caught her against him and kissed her back. At first on the cheek, gently, reverently, and then as she turned her face to his, on the mouth. Not in the way he had when the cookies were burning, but in a way that encouraged her to give him—them—a second chance.

Again, Molly drew back.

The yearning was in her amber eyes, even if she remained conflicted.

Yearning, Chance thought, was good.

Down the hall, the elevator dinged. Heavy metal doors could be heard opening. Voices, as other guests stepped off.

Aware he really did not want to push it, Chance reluctantly let Molly go. "Tomorrow then?"

"Bright and early," she promised.

To Molly's relief, by midmorning the next day, Braden's mood was much improved. He handled their visit to the tile warehouse with his usual good cheer, and was still smiling and chattering exuberantly, as they all headed home.

"I like trains!" He lifted his hands high in the air, despite the constraints of his car seat safety harness.

Glad her son was so excited about Christmas, even if she had yet to exactly work out a solution regarding his gift, Molly countered cheerfully, "I know you do."

Braden kicked his feet energetically. "I like bulls!" he shouted.

As usual, Chance showed no worry over that issue. Which made Molly wonder what he knew that she didn't. "Mistletoe and Mistletoe Jr. like you, too," Chance reassured him.

Braden let out a joyous whoop. "Santa bring me trains *and* bulls!"

Again, Chance seemed confident it would all work out.

Again, Molly was not sure how.

Deciding, however, not to worry about it at this moment, when she had so much else on her agenda, she clapped her hands together and shifted toward her son, as much as her seat belt would allow. "Who wants to sing Christmas carols?"

Braden grinned. "Me do! Me school!"

Chance sent Molly a glance. "You're going to have to translate…"

Trying not to notice how handsome he was in profile, or how closely he had shaved that morning, she explained, "He's talking about the Christmas program his preschool is having. They've been working on the music for weeks now."

Chance looked interested. "When is it?"

Molly's heartbeat picked up. "December 18th,"

"What time?"

"Seven p.m."

"Can anyone go?"

Meaning you? "Yes," Molly said cautiously, her excitement rising.

"But?" he prodded, when she said nothing more.

She took a deep breath. Aware her son never missed a beat in a situation like this, she parsed her words carefully. "I'm just not sure."

He flashed her a sexy sidelong grin. "I'd be interested?"

Clearly he was.

In lots and lots of things.

Her.

Braden.

Kissing her again.

Maybe more than kissing…if the strength of his arousal during the cookie-burning incident was any indication.

Heavens, Molly brought herself up short when she realized the silence had gone on too long and Chance was clearly wondering why. What was wrong with her? Why was she such a welter of feeling and desire whenever he was around? She'd certainly never reacted like this before!

Not with Braden's daddy.

Not with anyone!

Except Chance.

"Because," the object of all her wildest fantasies continued persuasively, "I am interested, Molly. Very much so."

Swallowing around the knot of emotion in her throat, she tried again. "I know. I can see that."

"Then?"

She gestured inanely, wishing she were driving because then she'd have something else to concentrate on other than how ruggedly masculine Chance looked, even in a navy flannel shirt and jeans, or how good he smelled, like soap and sandalwood and man.

With effort, she babbled on. "Those programs are a lot to handle. Overeager parents. Way too excited kids." *And me, making a sentimental fool of myself, getting all misty over the slightest thing.*

Did she really want Chance to see her like that?

"Chance watch me sing!" Braden called from the backseat.

Chance smiled as if the matter was settled. "Sounds good, buddy!"

Braden clapped his hands. "Hurrah! Chance see me!"

They really had to get out of this loop before Braden invited Chance to anything else.

"Speaking of singing," Molly said brightly. "Here we go, now! 'We wish you a merry Christmas…'"

Chance joined in, along with Braden, their voices blending in if not perfect harmony, at least perfect good cheer. The sound of that and the other holiday tunes that followed was enough to warm her heart. For the first time, she wished she could stay in Laramie, and see where this was all going with Chance and still give her son everything he should have. But she couldn't. The visit to Worthington Academy had shown her that.

To do that, she was going to have to be all in—in Dallas. Not leaving her heart behind with Chance.

"Does Braden always fall asleep like that?" Chance asked twenty minutes later. The child had dropped off midsong. A check in the rearview mirror had showed him snoozing away.

Molly shot him the kind of affectionately rueful look he imagined mothers gave their babies' daddies. The one that said, "We're in this together."

And they were…

"Pretty much. Especially in the car. It's good though." As their eyes briefly met, he felt warmed through and through. "We have to drop him at preschool when we get to Laramie."

We. He liked the sound of that.

Molly thumbed through the calendar on her smartphone. "And he has a playdate with his best friends, Will and Justin, right after school, so I can meet your mother at the ranch house to look at the new tile we picked out this morning. Make sure she likes the way it looks in the light there before we take what's already up of the current backsplash down."

"I'm sure she will."

"I hope so," she said, her soft lips tightening anxiously. "A lot is riding on this job."

A lot was riding on a lot of things, Chance thought. He continued driving while Molly got on the phone with the crew working at the remodeling site.

He'd never considered himself that much of a family guy.

But then he'd never traveled with anyone like Molly, or anyone as cute as Braden, either.

He'd been cast in the daddy role and found he liked it. A lot. But then this holiday season was full of surprises, he realized, as he hit the town limits and parked in front of Braden's preschool.

Molly woke her son and walked him in, then Chance drove Molly home, so she could change clothes before driving out to the ranch to meet him and his mother and the rest of their work crews.

He walked her as far as her front door.

She rummaged for her key. "You don't have to stay."

"Don't want me to come in?"

She paused and looked at him in a way that said she did. "We're already running late."

And he knew if he did go in, they might very well be even later.

Putting his disappointment aside—this was something that could be picked up later—when they weren't rushed—he turned and headed for his own truck, which had been left parked at the curb. "I'll see you at the Circle H."

Smiling, she waved goodbye. "I won't be long."

He grinned back, aware he was counting on that. And much more.

"You look happy," Lucille observed, when he walked in to the renovation in progress, at the Circle H ranch house.

He felt happy. Not wanting to discuss his feelings, he shrugged, and turned his glance to the work that had been done in their absence. "Time of year, I guess."

"Mmm-hmm."

"Don't read more into this, Mom," Chance warned.

"Hey." Lucille lifted her well-manicured hands in surrender. "I'm just happy you're happy."

"Who's happy?" Molly asked cheerfully, strolling in, too.

"Everyone, it seems." Lucille smiled.

Especially Molly, Chance thought. She had never looked better in a pair of designer jeans, cranberry cashmere turtleneck and a black down field jacket. Sexy. Competent. Warm. Kind. Feisty. Pretty much everything that was on his list for the perfect woman.

Oblivious to the direction of his thoughts, Molly asked his mom, "What do you think of the substitute tile we picked out, now that you can see it in person?"

Lucille viewed it from all angles. "I actually like it better than the original."

"Good." Molly's body relaxed in relief. "Then we'll get started on taking down what we put up, so we can go forward."

"Wonderful!" Lucille said.

Tank, one of the construction guys on Chance's crew, entered. "Express delivery service van from Dallas out here for you. Somebody want to sign?"

Chance bit down on an oath. *Not good.*

"I'll get it," Molly volunteered.

"That's okay." He moved around her, motioning for her to stay put. "I'll get the tile."

Molly shot him an odd look and dug in. "I want to check it out before he leaves." They'd taken the samples in her SUV. The rest had needed to be delivered via courier. "You can do that in here," Chance said gallantly. "The guys and I will carry the boxes in."

Molly gave him another odd look. "I can carry some."

"You really don't need to do this," Chance dissented.

Molly looked mutinous, but then Lucille stepped in. "Goodness, let's all go then."

They'd barely made it through the door when the delivery driver said from the back of the van, "Are the boxes from the Toy Emporium going here, too?"

Molly looked at Chance. He wasn't about to get into this here and now. "Those should go to the bunkhouse," he decreed quickly. "Mom, would you mind showing the driver?"

An old pro at social maneuvering, Lucille covered her confusion. "Not at all."

Molly peeked into the back of the van. "Are *all* those for here?"

The uniformed driver nodded. "Somebody's going to have a *very good* Christmas from the looks of it."

Except it wasn't a good surprise for Molly, Chance noted, judging by the aggrieved look on her lovely face as she turned around, got in her car and left the ranch. It was more like her worst nightmare.

Lucille patted him on the arm. "Looks like you have some explaining to do, son."

And then some, Chance thought, wincing.

It would be better done without an audience.

Molly had no sooner gotten home than her doorbell rang.

Chance stood on her porch. "We need to talk."

She glared at him, not sure when she had felt so hurt and simultaneously left out. "Do we?" She didn't think so.

He brushed past anyway. Waited for her to shut the door behind them. Then shrugged out of his coat, his tall body seeming to fill up the space of her foyer the way the rest of him filled up her heart. Grimly, he surmised, "You're mad at me because I bought a train set for Braden."

Knowing she had to do something with her hands or she would probably throw something at his handsome head, Molly went back to what she had neglected to do earlier—unpack her overnight bag.

Grabbing the handful of dirty clothing from the day before, she carried it to the back of the house to the laundry room.

"It's not just any train set, Chance. It's the deluxe collector's edition. The one with every Leo and Lizzie component ever made thus far. The one that costs more than some small cars!"

Brawny arms folded in front of him, he watched as she sprayed the ketchup stains on Braden's clothing with prewash, then tossed them into the washing machine.

"As you once pointed out to me, it's quality stuff that will last for years. And could even be passed down to the *next* generation."

She threw up her hands in exasperation. "Please don't tell me you actually believe that!"

"Okay, how about this?" he countered, reaching for several pieces of laundry she had dropped.

Unfortunately, it was her red satin bra and bikini set.

He crumpled them in his hand, much as he had the first time he'd undressed her. "I wanted him to have it."

Snatching the lingerie from his fingers, Molly tossed them in the wicker basket she kept for unmentionables. Trying not to put momentary pleasure ahead of long-range goals, she tried again to talk sense into Chance. "I'd *like* Braden to have a lot of things, but this is way too much."

He lounged in the portal, gaze moving over her lingeringly, as if he were already mentally ending this argument by making love to her. "So let me give him some of it now, and then some more on his birthday and so on. Kind of like I've been doing with the Christmas villages, which, by the way, aren't finished yet."

Molly put two shirts in the washer, then realized they were navy and black and everything in the tub was white. She plucked them back out again, lest she get further sidetracked, start the darn machine and then have everything she washed turn an ugly blue-grey.

Deciding to leave starting the machine for later, she marched past him. "This is different, Chance."

He followed. "How?"

She removed Braden's blanket and Rudolph from the suitcase and set them on the sofa for him to find when he returned home.

Aware Chance was truly trying to understand now, she drew a deep breath. "It was one thing for you to buy a brand-new set of building blocks for Braden to play with at your place when you invited us to lunch. It made sense for you to have something for him to do," she told him kindly. "And you can use those for your nephew Max when he comes over to play." So it wasn't all for Braden.

"But?"

Molly could tell from the sardonic curve of his lip he still thought she was in the wrong. "This excess on your part just highlights the difference between us when it comes to money. To you, this is nothing. To me, it's a year of mortgage payments!"

He came closer. "If you are so concerned about excess, then why apply to Worthington Academy, where the tuition is more than some colleges?"

"A place like that will bring him boundless life opportunities."

"It will still cost an arm and a leg."

Ducking her head, she zipped the suitcase and reluctantly admitted, "He's applying as a scholarship student." Embarrassed to have to say that, because it made her feel like a failure, as a parent, to have to rely on charity to meet her son's needs, she rushed on, "The stipend Worthington Academy offers doesn't pay everything, of course. But it's *enough* that, if Braden does get in, I could afford it and then, hopefully, after a couple of years at a much higher income for me, he wouldn't even need that financial assistance to go there."

Chance spread his hands wide. "Look, if he gets in, I can help you with that—if it's what you really want for him. You don't *have* to rely on scholarship."

Molly carried the suitcase to the garage and stuck it on a shelf. She spun back around and marched into the house. Once again, he was using money—his money—to solve everything. "You're missing the point, Chance," she said angrily.

"No. You're missing the point!" Chance returned gruffly. "I did what I did because I care enough about you and your son to want to see you *happy*."

Tears of frustration blurred her vision. With trembling fingers, Molly wiped them away. "Buying us extravagant stuff won't achieve that!"

"Then what will?" he demanded, taking her by the shoulders.

Love, Molly thought.

Shocked by the notion, she shook her head. Too late, he had seen the raw need reflected in her eyes. He caught her hand and pulled her to him. The next thing she knew he was sliding his fingers through her hair, kissing her lips, her cheek, her hair and then, ever so wantonly, her lips again. It was almost as if he were on a mission, not just to make her his but to give her every Christmas wish she had ever wanted.

A man in her life who would give her everything.

A man who adored her son as much as she did.

A hot affair.

Someone to share life's up and downs with.

He cradled her cheek in his hand. "Tell me you forgive me for overstepping," he whispered, kissing her hotly, thoroughly again. "Tell me you'll give me a second chance."

"To be friends?"

"To be a hell of a lot more than just friends." He slid a hand beneath her knees. Lifting her into his arms, he carried her up the stairs, down the hall to her bedroom. He had never been in there before. And she wouldn't have wanted him to see it now, with clothes draped everywhere. "Burglary?" he joked.

"Wardrobe crisis," she murmured in a strangled voice. *For the trip to Dallas. Because I wanted to look good for you.* Somehow she managed not to hide her eyes. "Don't ask."

"Okay if we clear a space?" He set her down gently on the floor.

"I'll help." Her sense of humor returning as quickly as her smile, Molly picked up an armload of garments and tossed them onto a nearby reading chair. He laughed and carried the rest over and set it on top.

The sheets were already rumpled. She hadn't had time the previous morning to make her bed.

"Now, where were we?" he asked her, easing his hands beneath the hem of her sweater.

"Kissing and making up?" At least that was where she wanted them to be. She hated fighting with him. Hated the thought that they might go back to what they had been, irritants who did nothing more than get each other's goat.

He grinned. "I think I can pick up there..." He gathered her close and lifted her face to his. Their mouths met, and she savored the feeling of his lips moving over hers. He kissed her like there was nothing standing between them, nothing but this moment in time. And it wasn't hard to stay in the moment, not when his hands were sifting through her hair, his tongue was playing with hers, even as the powerful muscles of his chest abraded the softness of her breasts and, lower still, his hardness pressed against her belly.

Something was happening between them, something that thus far had surpassed her wildest expectations. And she could no more deny it than the desire welling up inside her. Her knees weakening, her whole body swaying, she threw herself into the kiss. She ran her hands over his chest, unbuttoning his shirt, tugging the thermal tee from the waistband of his jeans. She smoothed her hands over the warm, satiny muscles of his pecs, finding out his nipples were as hard as hers. She kissed his neck, savoring the salty taste of his skin.

He did the same, easing his palms beneath her sweater, unfastening her bra, then smoothing his palms over her breasts. Quivering as he found the taut, aching buds, Molly lifted her mouth to his. And still they kissed. Caresses pouring out of them, one after another. Feelings built and desire exploded in liquid, melting heat. Unable to stand it any longer, they undressed. Quickly. Then joined each other in the mussed sheets of her bed.

He found protection, and she strained against him. Wanting. Needing. Pleasing. She lifted her hips. The hard length of him pressed into her. She had time to draw one breath and then they were kissing again, as if the world, their world, was going to end. Her inhibitions fled, and she arched against him, drawing him in.

He held her arms above her head. Timing his movements, increasing her pleasure, then his. Building, probing, taking her to the very depths. Until she was clenched around him, gasping his name, and he was saying hers. They were racing toward the edge, spinning over, drifting ever so slowly back to consciousness. Then holding each other, kissing ravenously, they started all over again.

* * *

"I'm going to work late tonight. Want to join me?" Chance asked an hour later.

Molly shook her head. "I have to pick up Braden from his playdate."

"I could come by later. We could all have dinner together."

Silence.

"Or not," he said.

Molly swallowed. Clad only in her bra and panties, she sat on the edge of her bed. Now that the lovemaking was over, and it was back to the normal routine, whatever that was, she seemed confused and on edge. And that gave rise to an unexpected insecurity in him, as well.

Molly paid an inordinate amount of attention to the act of putting on her wild purple socks. "Even with the nap he had in the car this morning, en route back from Dallas, it's been a really long day for him."

Chance resisted the urge to take her in his arms and make love to her all over again. Until she finally believed, as did he, everything was eventually going to be okay. "You want to put the little tyke to bed early?" he presumed.

Turning, Molly nodded.

"You want to put yourself to bed early, too?"

She trembled with exhaustion and something else. "I think so, yes." She flashed a weak grin.

He wished he were invited, but he could see it wasn't going to happen. Not tonight anyway. He rose and began to dress, aware there was one thing they hadn't finished. "About the Leo and Lizzie toys…"

Her eyes lifted to his. The turbulent sheen was back.

"I know you went to a lot of trouble, but I'm going to have to think about that. Let you know."

Another harbinger of trouble to come? Or just a necessary time-out? Chance couldn't tell. And he still didn't know when he got back to the Circle H. The guys were preparing to work late to finish the removal of the last of the backsplash tile that had already gone up. Chance told them to go on. "I'll finish it," he said.

"Sure, boss?"

He nodded. Truth was, he needed some time alone. Needed to be busy. Needed not to think about what would happen if Molly did what she was promising all along, and left for Dallas in January.

"Things went badly with Molly, hmm?" Sage observed, walking in, covered dinner plate in hand.

Chance looked up from his hammer and chisel.

The lovemaking between he and Molly had been spectacular. To the point he was still replaying it in his mind, and would be, he figured, all night. Molly's reaction afterward, the way she had pulled away emotionally yet again, had not been so great. But none of this was something he wanted to discuss with his sister, even if he could see she was trying to help.

"What makes you think that?" he asked casually.

"Duh. Mom told me how upset she was about the Toy Emporium boxes." Sage set his dinner plate down. "Sounds like you really blew it."

Chance kept right on chiseling off tile. "You wouldn't think that if you could have seen Braden's face when he was playing with those trains, the way he lit up. Plus, it'd be a great way to get him off the subject of expecting Santa to bring him a live bull for Christmas, if he had to make a choice." In fact, Chance was pretty sure it would solve the problem entirely. And hadn't that been the goal from the outset?

Sage settled on the sawhorse. "Look, there's no denying your heart was in the right place, even if it was your stubborn attitude that got you into this mess in the first place. But you have to understand. To do all that on top of what you did to get Molly and Braden interviewed at Worthington Academy—"

A piece of tile fell out of his hand and shattered as it hit the floor.

Grimacing, Chance hunkered down to sweep up the shards. "Molly doesn't know I had anything to do with that. She thinks it was your alumni letter of recommendation that opened the door."

Sage paled. "If she finds out."

"She won't. I talked to Elspeth Pyle, the headmistress."

Sage paused. "Is Braden's acceptance a sure thing?"

Chance shook his head. "No. The decision, whatever it is, will be merit based. I made sure of that."

Another heavy silence fell. Finally, his sister got up to hold the dustpan for him. "What I don't understand is why you got involved with any of this elite private school stuff at all, Chance. Given the way you felt about your education there."

He took the pan and emptied it into the trash barrel with the rest of the broken tile.

Aware Sage was still waiting, he explained, "I did it because it was what Molly wanted." And he wanted her to have everything she wanted and more.

Sage settled on the sawhorse once again.

Figuring if he ever wanted his little sister to vamoose, he was going to have to eat, Chance picked up the plate and removed the foil. "And because up to now it's been more idealistic than real for Molly." He shoveled up a bite of tamale pie that was, he admitted, as delicious as everything else his chef sister made.

"In what sense?" Sage asked.

"Molly's a small-town girl from a protected environment. She hasn't had a clue what she would really be getting into, moving among those kind of people." He paused to eat a little more and let his words sink in. "I wanted her and Braden to see and experience it firsthand."

Sage went to the cooler they kept for the workers and fished out bottles of flavored water for them both. She uncapped and handed him his. "Did the tour of the academy discourage Molly the way you hoped?"

That was the hell of it. "No."

"So she may still be leaving Laramie County after all," Sage surmised, as unhappy for him as he felt.

"She's still got time to reconsider," Chance said.

Sage studied him, empathy in her eyes. "But you want them here with you."

He did. More than he wanted to admit. Even to himself.

Chapter 9

"You've got company," Billy said.

Chance turned in the direction his hired hand indicated. Sure enough, a red SUV had parked in the drive beside the ranch house. His pulse picked up as he saw the driver-side door open. Molly stepped out.

It had been nearly seventy-two hours since they'd spoken. Although it had been hard as hell, he'd given her the space she requested. Hoping that once she thought more about it, she would see that his heart had been in the right place, even if his actions regarding Braden's gift had been—in her view, anyway—completely misguided.

"Want me to take over for you?"

"Yeah." Chance opened up one last gate. Jingle All the Way lifted his head and eagerly moved out of his stall into the bull exerciser. With all four slots filled, Chance turned toward his visitor.

Molly came toward him, a vision in a red wool coat, snowy white blouse, jeans and boots. That quickly his heartbeat sped up.

She inclined her head toward the circular slow-moving metal fence that connected to a long chute from the barn. "That looks like an open-air revolving door."

Chance closed the distance between them. Just as he had hoped, she was wearing that orchid perfume he liked. "Bucking bulls are athletes. They need to stay in shape." He pointed out the four individual sections that kept the animals apart. "The competition of following the bull in front of them keeps them interested."

Molly smiled and stepped even closer to Chance. "Pretty cool way to keep them in shape." She tilted her face up to his. "How long do they stay in there?"

"Thirty minutes daily."

"Impressive."

He quirked a brow. "That why you're here?"

"Nope. I need to talk to you. In private, if possible."

He wanted to be alone with her, too. As they headed away from the bull barns, and the attention of his hired hands, her soft lips twisted ruefully.

"I want to apologize for not being more appreciative the last time we saw each other." She paused to get a pretty glass container with a ribbon wrapped around the top from her vehicle. She had to lean across the driver seat to reach it. The hem of her coat rode up, revealing her nicely rounded derriere and slender, shapely thighs.

She inhaled deeply, as she straightened and faced him once again. Solemnly, she continued, "In retrospect, I see you were trying to help me achieve my goal of gifting Braden the Leo and Lizzie toys in a way that was impossible for me. So, if you will accept my peace offering of *Vanillekipferl*, or almond crescent cookies, I'd like to make a deal with you."

He accompanied her up the steps to the ranch house. Aware he was happier than he'd been in three days, he paused to hold the door for her. "I'm listening."

She scooted past. Allowing him to take her coat, she waited for him to remove his, then handed him the cookie jar. "I'd like to purchase the Leo and Lizzie World Adventure train table from you. The basic starter track set. And one of the destination kits from you. Preferably the San Antonio River Walk setup, since Braden's actually been there."

Tenderness spiraled through him. "The rest?"

"You can do whatever you like."

Then that was easy, Chance thought. He'd keep them for the future, to give to Braden, one at a time, on the holidays and birthdays to come.

Oblivious to his thoughts, Molly suggested, "You can sell the other components to parents who are still looking for them or gift them to your nephew Max."

Chance worked the lid off the jar and ate one of the cookies. *Delicious.* "He just took his first steps so he's a little young yet for the train."

Molly paused. "Right. Well, anyway, does that sound good to you?"

What was right was having her here again, in his home, meeting him halfway on an issue that was very important to both of them. He couldn't help but think that was a sign of more good things to come.

"I took all the boxes and put them in the spare room I use for storage. They're still in the shipping cartons, so you may want to open them so you can get a better look at what you'd be buying." There were colorful pictures on every box.

Molly's amber eyes gleamed. "Sounds good."

He went into the kitchen and got a pair of scissors for her.

Figuring he'd give her more of the space she had requested, then join her when she was ready for his company, he pointed down the hall that led to the bedrooms. "First room on your left."

"Thanks." With another grateful look, Molly disappeared down the hall.

Outside, a purring car engine halted. Doors slammed.

Chance went to the window and swore at what he saw.

Molly had just cut open the first box when she heard the feminine voice coming from the living area. "Stop being so stubborn, Chance Lockhart!" Babs's distinctive drawl echoed through the home. "This is a fantastic offer!"

"I told you," Chance growled back. "I'm not selling to Mr. X, and I'm certainly not going to become partners with him!"

"Think of the capital he's ready to infuse!"

"Rather not, Babs."

Silence.

"If you do things Mr. X's way, you'd finally be able to make it up to Delia—"

"Mom! Our commission on this deal is not Chance's responsibility!"

No kidding, Molly thought.

"Wouldn't it be nice to finally be able to give Delia what she deserves?" Babs persisted. "Since you wasted nearly ten years of her eligibility, stringing her along, *pretending* to be interested in something long term, like marriage?"

Ouch, Molly thought. Although she could hardly imagine Chance pretending anything. He was usually as straightforward as possible.

"First of all, *Mom*," Delia cut in again. "Those weren't wasted years! Chance and I learned a lot from each other."

Chance's heavy footsteps moved across the wood floor. "Ladies, thanks for stopping by. Next time—" the front door opened "—save yourself the trip."

Molly surreptitiously looked out the window blinds into the yard. A miserable-looking Delia was already getting into the sleek black limo. Her fur-clad mother was unable to resist one last insult lobbed Chance's way.

"And here I was hoping you would have gotten at least a little wiser when it comes to what is important in life." Babs sniffed, glaring at Chance. "Apparently not!"

Molly moved away from the window as the limo drove off.

She walked back to the main living area in time to see Chance feeding another set of papers to the shredder.

"You heard."

"Impossible not to. You okay?"

"Just frustrated."

"Why do they keep coming back when you've already told them no?" Molly thought about the lingering emotional connection she'd heard briefly in Delia's voice. Babs had to be aware of it, too. "Is Babs trying to reunite you and Delia via reverse psychology?"

Chance laughed mirthlessly. "I would hardly think so."

But there was something devious going on with the older woman. Molly felt it in her bones.

"The last thing Babs wants is her daughter on a ranch in the middle of nowhere. Even if the proposal she just hammered out would likely quadruple my income in the next year."

She did a double take. Unable to suppress her shock, she echoed, "Quadruple it? *Really*?"

He lifted his broad shoulders in a derisive shrug. "Sure, if I wanted to sell half interest in all thirty of my bulls and start aggressively marketing bull semen."

They were standing so close she could feel the heat emanating from his powerful body. "Why don't you want to do that?"

He walked over to plug in the Christmas tree. The lights added a cheerful glow to the glittering silver-and-gold ornaments. Noticing the star at the top was listing slightly to one side, he reached up to straighten it, then turned back to her. "If you partner with someone on a rodeo bull, the partner gets an equal say in how often, when and where, you let the bull compete."

"And that's a problem because...?"

He opened up a tin of the dark chocolate peppermint patties he favored and offered her one. This time she took it.

"Partners can get greedy and think more about the bottom line than the health and welfare of the animal."

Eyes still on his, she ripped open the foil covering. "What about stud services?"

"Again, I prefer to pick and choose. Keeping the offspring genetically admirable keeps the price high."

He opened the fireplace screen. "Letting just anyone breed off your bulls can affect the quality of calves, and that in turn can affect reputation. And lowered reputations mean lowered prices." He added a few more logs to the grate, adjusting them just so. "Plus, I like the size of the ranch and stable I have now." He added tinder and lit a match. "I don't want any more."

Molly moved close enough to admire the leaping flames. "I can understand that. Sometimes independence is more important than more money in the bank." She stepped back as he closed the screen again and stood, too. "What I don't understand is why Babs is so fixated on arranging the sale of Bullhaven to Mr. X. I mean, I know that Mistletoe is a national champion, and you have an incredible reputation within the business, but it's not like she couldn't find another bull operation in Texas for Mr. X to invest in." She furrowed her brow in confusion. "And since he wants to add venture capital, too, and become a half-interest partner, he could easily find people with the skills to vastly improve whatever bucking-bull operation he does end up purchasing."

The brooding expression on Chance's face indicated this was bothering him, too.

Molly paused. "Is she trying to wreak some sort of revenge on you for not giving her daughter the kind of pampered lifestyle Babs feels Delia deserves? By either taking away or disrupting what she knows means the most to you? Your ranch?"

He grinned, his ardent gaze roving her upturned face. "You sound protective."

Molly flushed. She *felt* protective. Even though, technically, she really had no right to be that involved in his life. Given that they were simply friends—and temporary lovers—Molly squared her shoulders and drew a bolstering breath. "I just don't want to see you used by someone who definitely does not seem to have your best interests at heart. No matter what Babs tells her daughter. It's not right."

"Right or not, that's the way Delia's mother operates."

Molly squinted, her need to protect Chance and everything he held near and dear increasing tenfold. "What do you mean?"

"Babs always has an agenda. Right now, my guess is that it has more to do with Mr. X than me, since it's his billions she wants for her daughter."

Molly took a moment to think about what he was saying. "So Babs is using you and your past with Delia—" *and Delia's residual feelings for you, whatever they are* "—to make Mr. X jealous."

"Maybe." Chance shrugged, not seeming to care either way. He walked toward her and took her in his arms. Molly gasped as he ran a hand down her spine, flattening her against him.

"What are you doing?"

He scored his thumb across her lip before continuing in a voice that melted her resistance, "Giving you that make-up kiss I owe you."

Chance wasn't sure that Molly was going to let him make love to her. At least not then. It was, after all, the middle of the workday.

Yet the moment he took her in his arms, he felt her cuddle against him. As if she had been waiting for and wanting this moment, too.

Grinning, he reached into his pocket. Found the little branch of leaves and berries he had been carrying around in his pocket. "I also want to get at least one kiss in under the mistletoe this holiday season," he teased, holding it above her head.

She rose up on tiptoe, the scent of her inundating his senses. "I think," she whispered, her yearning for him clear as day, "this is the place where I get a kiss in under the mistletoe, too." Her mouth opened beneath his, and their tongues mated in an erotic dance. Pleasure swept through him as he stepped between her legs. Anchoring an arm beneath her softly curving derriere, he lifted her up and situated her so her weight was against his middle. She wrapped her legs snugly around his waist, and his blood heated even more.

He carried her down the hall to his bedroom, loving the way she felt against him, so warm and womanly. Their eyes locked as he set her down next to the bed. Undressing her felt extraordinarily intimate, pleasurable.

She eased off his shirt, kissing him, her lips softening beneath his. She clung to him, her fingers dipping into his shoulders, back and hips. Savoring everything about this moment, he delighted in the sweet taste of her. Of the way she continued undressing him, just as he had unwrapped her.

They drank in the sight of each other. She moaned as he rained kisses across her cheek, behind her ear, down the slope of her neck, before zeroing in on her mouth again.

She surged up against him, wrapping her arms around him, then tumbled him onto the bed.

He laughed in surprise. Tempestuous need glittered in her eyes as she followed him down and playfully straddled his middle. She threaded her fingers through his hair and stretched her body out languidly over the length of his, her heat cradling his pulsing hardness. He knew she thought this was just about sex. But it wasn't, he thought, as he let her deepen their kisses and rock against him. It was so much more.

Determined to make this lovemaking more memorable than either of them had ever had, he rolled so she was beneath him. He parted her knees and lay between her thighs. She came up off the bed as his lips lowered, suckling gently. Her thighs fell even farther apart as Chance kissed and stroked. And still it wasn't enough for either of them.

Molly teetered on the edge as he found a way to touch her that made her feel pleasured and desired, wanted and protected. Although she had promised herself she would wait for him, there was no delaying. She shuddered and fell apart in his arms. He held her tenderly until the aftershocks passed, then took her mouth again in a long, hot, tempestuous kiss. She shivered as the hardness of his chest teased the sensitive buds of her breasts, and lower still, the velvety hardness of his arousal nestled against her sex. She was so wet and so ready. And still he kissed her, until she throbbed and whimpered low in her throat. And only then, when she could stand it no longer, did he slide inside in one smooth, languid stroke. She clenched around him as he filled her completely. Taking her and making her his. Letting her possess him in response. Until her wildest Christmas wish was every dream fulfilled.

Afterward, Molly snuggled against him. He stroked a hand through her hair. Then she asked, "Would you ever consider moving to Dallas?"

His hand stilled. He continued to study her as if trying to figure something out. "I grew up there, Molly."

She focused on the unmistakable warning in his voice. "And never want to go back?"

His eyes darkened. "I don't mind visiting."

You'll never get what you want if you don't try. She drew on all the courage she possessed. "Would you ever consider visiting Braden and me, when we move there next month?"

He sat up against the headboard, the sheet draped low across his hips. "As...?"

Molly drew her gaze away from the flat plane of his abdomen. A distracting shiver tore through her. "What we are now. Friends."

He ran a hand down her arm. "Lovers?"

She wished he didn't look so damn good, even in his disheveled state. "If we can work it out." It would mean babysitters. Rendezvousing. Arranging things in a way that wouldn't leave Braden—or her—confused.

Molly understood that Chance wanted more than that.Yet he also had to know what a big step this was for her.

He watched her tug the sheet a little more snugly beneath her arms. "Does this mean we're exclusive?"

Heat gathered in her chest, and spread, from the tops of her breasts into her face. She worried her bottom teeth with her lip. "Does it?"

"I already feel that way about you, darlin'."

Molly relaxed. Her body nestled against his. "I don't want you seeing anyone else, either," she admitted softly.

"Then that settles it." He pulled her against him for

a long, thorough kiss that quickly had her tingling from head to toe. "We're officially a couple."

She splayed a hand over his broad chest, aware they still had a few hurdles left. "We will be," she stipulated firmly. "After the Open House your mother is hosting."

He paused. "What are you talking about?"

Molly swallowed and sat up against the headboard. She had to be completely honest with him or this would never work. "Lucille has invited me to attend as her protégé. She wants to give my design business a big boost."

"I knew that."

She wet her lips. "If it were known that I was also seeing you romantically, it might look like I was only with you to get ahead, or she was just helping me as a favor to you."

He sobered understandingly. "You'd be called a gold digger."

She nodded. Embarrassed, but determined. "I don't want to complicate my business future like that." She jerked in a breath, rushed on. "Because if Braden does get accepted at Worthington Academy, I'm really going to need more than just the two small jobs I already have lined up to make a real go of it."

She studied him, a wry smile tugging at the corners of her lips. "So, can you keep our relationship under the covers for just a little while longer?"

It was Chance's turn to look pained. "Are we talking weeks?"

"I'd rather not say anything until much later in the spring."

So months, he realized unhappily. He pushed a little higher against the headboard, too. "You don't think people are going to catch on to us spending so much time together?"

Molly took his hand. "If I were still living in Laramie, yes, of course. If I'm in Dallas…it's a lot easier to keep things on the down low there if we stay out of the high-profile places." She squeezed his hand lightly. "What are you thinking?"

Chance frowned. "I've never been asked to stay in the shadows before. Usually people are all too eager to claim a relationship with me, whether one really exists or not."

"Exactly." Molly laid her head on his shoulder. "You're the son of Lucille and Frank Lockhart. You come from one of the most socially prominent families in the state. People want to make use of that connection." She lifted his hand to her lips, kissed the back of it.

"Only you don't," he said, threading his fingers through her hair, lifting her face to his. He slanted his mouth over hers, kissed her again, softly, appreciatively.

Her worry, that they wouldn't be able to make this work long-term, fading, Molly swung her body lithely over top of his. Her heart swelling with all she felt for him, she confided, "I don't want anything from you. Except friendship." She nipped playfully at his lips. "And this…" To show him how deeply she cared, she made love with him all over again.

Chapter 10

"What you got me, Cowboy Chance?" Braden asked early one evening, a week and a half later when Chance came through the door, another yuletide shopping bag in hand.

"Whoa now. You don't know that's for you," Molly told her son. Although for most of the last ten nights, Chance had been there with her and her little boy, baking cookies, and working on their Christmas village in progress.

But prior to this, he had shown up with only one new item at a time.

Molly had appreciated his restraint.

Tonight, however, appeared to be different, Molly noticed as she and Chance exchanged looks.

"That's true." Chance backed up her efforts to instill manners in her little boy. He hung his jacket up and walked over to the sofa. "But as it happens—" he winked at Braden as they drew all three folding chairs up to the folding tables "—what's in here is for you and your mommy."

"Can I see?" Braden asked eagerly. "Please?"

Chance motioned for Molly to sit down on the other side of her son. He opened up the bag and lifted out a rectangular figurine. "Let's start with this."

Braden's eyes widened in appreciation. "That looks like our house," Molly said of the bungalow with the white picket fence.

Her son set them up carefully between the ranch and the North Pole.

Chance opened the bag. Braden pulled out more. "Mrs. Santa Claus!" her son exclaimed. "And more reindeer!"

"To go with Rudolph and the sleigh."

Braden hopped up and down and put them in the North Pole section of their Christmas village.

"Maybe we should let Mommy open the next one," Chance said.

Braden clapped. "Yes. Mommy do it!"

Not sure what this was all about since Chance wouldn't tell her much except that he had decided he needed to vastly accelerate his "plan," to allow for more focus on the Leo and Lizzie train set as they got closer to Christmas, Molly opened it up. Inside were two figurines to add to the ones Chance had already brought. One of a modern Western woman with auburn hair similar to Molly's, and one of a redheaded little boy— also in Western gear. Beneath the figurines, Chance had written the identifying information.

"Gosh," he said, leading the conversation. "That sure

looks like you, Mommy. And this one looks like you, Braden."

"I think it is us!" Touched, Molly laid her hand across her heart.

Braden admired both, then reverently put them by the bungalow with the white picket fence. He studied the scene for a long, thoughtful moment.

To Molly and Chance's mutual dismay, his happiness turned to confusion. Plaintively, he walked over to Chance and looped his arms around their visitor's neck. "Where you, Cowboy Chance?"

"Sorry about that," Molly said after Braden had finally gone to sleep. She moved around the kitchen, baking that evening's batch of cookies—*hausfreunde*. "When Braden gets stuck on a question, sometimes he can't get off of it."

Chance understood the little boy's need to make them a family. He felt it, too. He sampled the buttery almond-apricot sandwich cookie dipped in bittersweet chocolate that Molly handed him. "Do you want me to get a likeness of myself?"

Molly dipped another cookie, then set it on waxed paper to dry. "I don't know. I mean...you might not even be with us next year." She paused to send him a hesitant glance—the kind that only came up when they were discussing their relationship.

She swallowed, her soft lips compressing, and turned her glance away. "If the long-distance thing doesn't work..."

He caught her around the waist and tugged her close. Bending his head, he kissed her lips lightly. Tasting chocolate. "It'll work, Molly. And I'll be here."

He studied her as they drew apart. "So what else is going on?"

Molly bent her head over her baking, a clear sign she was evading. "What do you mean?"

He gave her the room she seemed to need. "I could tell something was bothering you the minute I walked in the door."

This time, Molly did look up. Her eyes glittered with disappointment. "I received a letter in the mail today. Braden was wait-listed at Worthington Academy."

Chance didn't know whether to celebrate the fact that Molly's reasons for leaving Laramie in January had just diminished or share in her deep disappointment. "I'm sorry, darlin'." He took a seat on the other side of the island. *Tread cautiously.* "Did they say why?"

"No." Molly's lips twisted into a troubled line. "But I was offered a Skype conference with the headmistress and admissions counselor, so I plan to see what kept him from getting in, and what his chances are of getting off the wait list. And if they aren't good, if there is a chance he will be admitted in the fall semester."

Chance couldn't help but be disappointed that Molly had yet to change her mind about enrolling Braden there. He sent her a brief commiserating glance. Then, speaking from his own heart, he encouraged firmly, "Braden's a great kid, Molly. He will thrive no matter where he is."

"I know." Her eyes still glimmered with tears, but she shook off the rising emotion. "I just really wanted him to have this opportunity. But if he doesn't get it this year, I've already got a deposit down at a safety preschool in the area where I intend to rent a house."

Now it was Chance who felt like he'd received a

major blow. Not that he hadn't been warned. He had. "Have you put a deposit down on a home, too?" He kept his attitude casual.

"No." Molly relaxed, as well. "That's the good thing about Dallas. It's so big there are plenty of places that would fit my needs in the short term."

If he couldn't dissuade her, he could sure as hell join her.

"You'll let me know if there is anything I can do to help?"

She smiled at him sweetly. "Of course. But I think I've got everything covered...

Meaning what? Chance wondered.

She didn't need him?

Or didn't want to need him?

How was he going to change that? He wondered, perplexed. Because he sure as hell was beginning to need them.

"Is there something wrong?" Molly asked Lucille several long, productive days later, when she arrived at the site to find her client upset.

She exchanged puzzled looks with Chance. He seemed as out of the loop as she felt.

"Is there something you don't like, Mom?" he asked in a low tone.

Heaven knew they didn't want Chance's mother to be unhappy with the renovation. This was their first joint project. The reputation of both their contracting firms was at stake.

Lucille glanced around at the finished backsplash, gleaming new appliances, countertops. Although the tile was newly sealed, there were smudges on the windows and stickers on the appliances. The newly finished wood floors bore the occasional dusty footprint. But all that was to be expected.

"We'll get a cleaning crew in here as soon as the touch-up painting is finished. The whole house will sparkle before we bring a speck of furniture in next week."

Lucille waved off the concern. "The renovation looks even better than I imagined. It's the Open House."

Sage walked in. Chance's eldest brother, Garrett, and his wife, Hope—a crisis manager and public relations expert—were at her side. "We got your message," Garrett said, cradling their nine-month-old son, Max, in his arms. The former army doc was now Lockhart Foundation CEO and medical director of West Texas Warrior Assistance.

Hope kissed her mother-in-law's cheek. "I'm not sure we understand the message you left."

Lucille fretted, "You all know I sent out a ton of invitations."

"Because you want to raise as much money as possible for the military vets we're helping," Garrett said.

"Most of the people I invited live in Dallas or Fort Worth. Since it's the holidays, I didn't think we would have that many acceptances."

"Let me guess," Sage said. "You were pleasantly surprised."

Lucille threw up her hands in distress. "We have four *hundred* people coming—so far. I don't know where we're going to put everyone!"

Hope already had her phone out. "It's not a problem. I can get some tents and tables and chairs. Heaters, too, if that cold front continues our way."

"I'll just make a lot more food," Sage said, with a former caterer's aplomb.

Lucille paced. "We're talking five days from now."

"It will work out, Mom." Chance wrapped his arm around Lucille's shoulders.

"The ranch house will not just be done—it will be letter perfect," Molly promised. "It will be decorated beautifully inside and out, too."

Lucille frowned. "What about entertainment? If it was a much smaller gathering, I was just going to have holiday music playing unobtrusively in the house, but now…"

"Some of the military vets have a band," Garrett said, shifting his son a little higher in his arms. "They've played at some of our parties."

"They're really good," Hope put in. She grinned as Max reached over and tangled his fingers in her hair. Pulling her close, he gave his mommy a kiss.

Molly envied the sight of Garrett, Hope and Max. They made such a cute little family. The kind she could have if only she stayed.

"I'll see if I can get the band to play," Garrett offered.

The meeting went on for another twenty minutes. Finally, everyone left. Molly walked out with Chance to get the lights and garlands that she planned to go ahead and string on the front porch. She sent him a companionable glance. Strange as it was, just now she'd felt a little like family. Maybe because the Lockharts had gone out of their way to include her.

"I've never seen your mom that rattled."

Frowning, Chance carried the stepladder onto the porch. "It's because she hasn't seen a lot of those folks since she left Dallas."

Molly took the lights out of the packaging. "Sage said some of them had turned their backs on Lucille when the scandal regarding the Lockhart Foundation came to light."

The brackets on either side of Chance's mouth deepened. "Actually," he reported grimly, snapping his tool belt around his waist, "it was most of the people Mom knew."

"That must have been hard."

Chance propped the ladder against the roof of the porch and began to climb. "The amazing thing is Mom doesn't blame them. She says if she had been guilty of withholding funds from the nonprofits the foundation claimed it was helping, they'd be right to dismiss her. Anyway, she's all about the fresh start, concentrating on what really matters."

Molly handed him the end of the strand. "And for her, that's helping people."

He secured it to the newly painted facing. "And taking care of her family." Having put up as much as he could reach from that vantage point, he climbed back down the ladder.

Molly tilted her face to his. "What's important to you?"

He grabbed her around the waist, tugging her close. "Right now?" He waggled his brows teasingly. "You."

Before she could stop him, he had delivered a slow, deep kiss that had her knees ready to buckle, her toes tingling.

Molly planted her hands on the center of his chest. "Chance," she reprimanded. "Someone might see."

The pleasure they'd experienced faded. His expression became inscrutable once again. "Right." He nodded, compliant but clearly unhappy, too. "We're still on the down low…"

Molly swallowed. She didn't want to hurt him, but she had to be honest about her needs. "It's just until I get my business efforts in Dallas off the ground," she said.

Chance stepped back, something even more indecipherable in his hazel eyes. "Does that mean I'm uninvited to the preschool program this evening?"

"No. Braden really wants you there. But I think it might be better if we drove separately, and then met up at my house later for a little after-school program gala for Braden." She paused. "Does that sound okay?"

A muscle ticked in his jaw. And for a moment, Molly thought he was going to say, *No, it isn't okay at all*. Then the moment passed. He climbed right back up the ladder again. She handed him the next section of the light strand. "What time should I be there?" Chance asked quietly.

Molly relaxed. "The program starts at seven," she informed him with a relieved smile. "I'll save you a seat." It was going to make Braden so happy, having Chance there. Her, too.

"Chance Lockhart, what are you doing at a preschool program?" Mary Beth Simmons, the local PTA president and resident busybody, demanded.

Practicing my down low, Chance thought grumpily, then shrugged and mimed total innocence. "I heard it was an event not to be missed."

Mary Beth squinted. "Who told you that?"

First rule of hiding something? Not that he'd had a lot of experience. *Be as honest as possible.* "Braden Griffith," he said and watched Mary Beth's gaze turned speculative. "Molly Griffith and I combined forces on a rush job for my mom, so we've been seeing a lot of each other. I've gotten to know her son. Cute kid."

Mary Beth tilted her head. "There are a lot of cute kids in Laramie, Chance."

True enough. He flashed an indulgent smile. "Most of them have a ton of family. Braden doesn't." He leaned toward her in a gossipy manner, meant to satisfy her need to be in the know. "And I think, times like this, the little tyke is beginning to notice the difference between his life, and—" Chance nodded at little Ava Monroe, who had her own fan club of McCabes and Monroes in attendance.

Chastened, Mary Beth straightened. "I see what you mean."

"Anyway, since I was invited, I volunteered to make his lack of extended cheerleaders not so obvious for little Braden."

Mary Beth laid a hand across her heart. "What a giving thing for you to do," she said, impressed.

Chance flashed a humble grin. "'Tis the season…"

"What was that about?" Molly asked, discreetly texting him as soon as he sat down next to her.

Aware she smelled like orchids…which meant she was wearing that perfume he liked. And that this was the closest thing to a date—albeit a clandestine one— that they'd ever had, Chance pulled out his phone and texted her back. I was pretending I was dragged here as a Good Samaritan.

"Oh." Molly formed the words with her soft lips.

He leaned down and whispered in her ear, longing for the day when they would have actual dates. And more. "We both know that's not the case." He hadn't been dragged. He'd been elated to be invited.

Around them, other phones and video cameras were being readied. He lifted a curious brow. Molly explained. "Everyone's going to record it."

"How about I record, and you just watch? I'll email it to you later. That way you can just enjoy."

"Thank you."

He stifled a smile and kept looking straight ahead at the stage. "My pleasure."

They stopped talking at that point. Nevertheless, they got a lot of curious looks despite their efforts to be casual. Soon the kids marched up onstage, proud as could be, and the program started.

Chance was glad he was focused on recording. Otherwise someone might have seen the tear that came to his eyes as Braden puffed out his little chest, and belted out "We Wish You a Merry Christmas" and a half-dozen other holiday tunes at the top of his little lungs. That was, when Braden wasn't grinning and waving at Molly and him.

When the program came to an end, Chance was on his feet, clapping and whistling and hooting, as proud as any parent there. Everyone else was so caught up in the proud moment that his enthusiasm went unnoticed.

By all but Molly—and Braden.

"Cowboy Chance!" Braden cried, hustling down from the stage. "Hey, everybody!" He turned and waved vigorously at his two frequently mentioned best friends. "Come see—Cowboy Chance!"

Will and Justin got permission from their parents and hightailed it to Braden's side. "He's got bulls!" Braden declared loudly.

Molly realized her son's vowel sounded more like an *a* than a *u*.

Several horrified adults turned in their direction.

"Black Angus bucking bulls of the national championship variety," Molly explained cheerfully to one and all.

A few parents, apparently not familiar with rodeo terms, looked even more confused.

"And barns!" Braden yelled blithely, as everyone around them chuckled at his earlier mispronunciation.

"And lots of other things, as well," Chance added. "Like bull barns."

"And fences!" Braden shouted.

"And training facilities."

"And *baby* bulls!" Braden repeated his earlier mispronunciation while slinging an index finger in Chance's direction. A gesture that, thanks to the discrepancy in their heights, ended up pointing a foot below Chance's waist.

More chuckles.

A few of the guys sent sympathetic, dad-to-dad glances Chance's way.

Which would have been funny, Chance thought, as the merry double entendres flying right above the toddler's heads increased, if not for Molly's increased embarrassment. Determined to spare them all any more unnecessary attention from the crowd, Chance knelt down so he and the little boy he adored were at eye level. He put his hand on Braden's shoulder. "Proud of you, buddy," he said fiercely, meaning it with all his heart. "That was a *great* job, singing."

Chance expected Braden to grin the way he always did when he was praised. He didn't expect him to look at Chance with equal affection and lift his hands, wordlessly asking to be picked up the way a lot of the other three-year-olds were being picked up for hugs by their dads.

A lump in his throat, Chance complied.

Braden hooked his hands around Chance's neck and hugged him like he never wanted to let go. For the first time in his life, Chance had an inkling, a real inkling of what it would be like to be a father. And not just any father. Braden's daddy.

He liked it.

Almost as much as he liked the idea of one day being Molly's husband. Wasn't that a Christmas surprise?

Chapter 11

"There is no doubt Braden is a very bright little boy," Worthington Academy's psychologist, Dr. Mitchard, said when the Skype conference Molly had requested began. "He had no trouble conversing on any subject that interested him. Like bulls."

Oh, dear.

"And Cowboy Chance."

Somehow Molly managed to keep a poker face. Even as her heart skipped a beat just hearing Chance's name.

"However, when we attempted to get him to focus on the word or number problems presented to him, he refused to speak," the headmistress told Molly.

"At all?" Molly could hardly believe it. Yes, her son's sentences were rudimentary, but Braden always had something to say. In fact, the hardest thing to do was get him to stop talking.

The psychologist, who had supervised the testing, nodded. "Even when he seemed to know the answer to our inquiries, which I'm sorry to relate, wasn't all that often, he refused to divulge it to us."

"Additionally, he does not have the background of second language, early reading and math, music and art instruction that our accepted students have. Hence, it's our considered opinion that he's not ready for such a rigorous academic pre-K curriculum," Elspeth Pyle said.

"If you know all that," Molly said, feeling hurt and confused, "why did you invite us to come all the way to Dallas for an in-depth admissions interview?" *Why did you have me drop everything to be there on such short notice?*

The two women exchanged glances.

The headmistress said, "Because we are always looking to diversify as much as we can, without lowering our high standards, and we don't currently have anyone in the three-year-old class who has come from a rural environment."

"Actually," Molly said, recognizing an evasion when she heard one, "we live in town."

"Well, he talked like he spent an inordinate time on a bull ranch!" the psychologist said.

"We were confused as to whether he might be living there, instead of the address on the application," Elspeth Pyle reiterated.

Chagrined, Molly admitted, "No. We've never stayed there." *Much as I might have wished.* "Braden's just visited a few times. He loves all animals, though." She spun it as best she could. "And he'd never seen any kind of cattle operation in person. So I guess it made a bigger impression on him than I realized."

"Perhaps so." The two administrators exchanged tense smiles. "Do you have any more questions?" Elspeth asked.

"Just one." Molly asked with a determined smile. "What are my son's chances of getting off the wait list?"

"At this point, not good. Not good at all."

"What you got, Cowboy Chance?" Braden asked several hours later when Chance stopped by just before bedtime, gift bag in hand, and scooped him up in his strong arms.

"A Christmas cowboy?" Braden hoped. He wrapped his arms around Chance's neck, giving him a happy hug. "Just like you?"

"I think we might get a couple more people for the village," Molly said in an effort not to put Chance on the spot. Not that the rugged rancher seemed to mind the request. "They have them at Monroe's Western Wear in town."

Chance set Braden in the middle of the sofa and sat down on one side of him. Molly took the other, watching as Chance opened up the by-now-familiar gift bag. "Let's see." Chance pulled out the first rotund figurine.

"Santa!" Braden clapped his hands.

"And look." He plucked out three Black Angus cattle figures.

"Mommy, daddy and baby bull!" Braden shouted excitedly.

"Hmm." Molly played along with the thoughtful gambit as her son kissed his new figures and hugged them to his chest. "Looks like the toy Santa Claus brought you the toy bull family that you wanted."

"And—" Chance plucked out a small square of Astroturf, surrounded by fence "—a pasture for them to stay in."

Braden turned to her. He seemed to understand in the brief silence that fell that this was a very elaborate consolation prize. So much for the school officials who had deemed him not able to understand enough, Molly thought in vindication.

"Real...want real...for me," Braden said emphatically, looking frustrated they still didn't understand what he was trying to communicate.

Except they did, Molly thought wistfully, withholding a sigh.

Solemnly, Chance interjected, "I talked to Santa on the phone about that."

Oh, boy, they were in dangerous territory now. Territory they probably should have discussed beforehand. On the other hand, Braden was far more willing to accept what Chance said as gospel than anything his mere mother stated. Probably because Chance cut such a heroic figure. Which was definitely an anomaly around their house...

Braden stared, wide-eyed. "You call Santa?"

Chance shifted Braden onto his lap with the ease of a natural daddy. "He was very upset that he couldn't do this for you, because Santa Claus knows what a very good boy you have been this year, but he said a real bull family would not fit on his sleigh. He only has room to bring you a very special toy present. And you know what I said?"

Braden considered. Finally, he screwed up his little face into a hopeful expression.

"I said, that you know that all the toys that Santa

brings are so very special, that you will be happy with whatever Santa brings you."

"Well, do you think we handled it?" Chance asked Molly after they tucked Braden into bed.

A sentimental look on her pretty face, Molly paused to admire the Christmas village they had put together over the course of the last weeks. It had a ranch like Chance's, a bull family, a house that looked like hers, figures that represented her and Braden, and a North Pole with Santa, sleigh and reindeer. The only thing it didn't have was Chance. As Braden had once again noted. The thing that sucked was that Chance wanted to be represented in the panorama that had come to mean so much to Braden, too.

What Molly wanted, however, was a lot more tenuous.

She wanted temporary. He wanted much more. But opinions could change. And he knew how to build on small successes, turn them into more.

"I think so." Molly turned and went into the kitchen, where she was preparing *Lebkuchen*. "I mean, you saw the way his face lit up at the Toy Emporium."

The tantalizing smell of fresh-baked German gingerbread cookies filled the space. Chance settled opposite her, predicting softly, "It'll be a big moment."

Molly bent to pipe white icing on each confection. "It will." She handed him a finished treat to taste. It was, as he had expected, completely delicious. As was everything she made.

Molly eyed him closely. A pulse was suddenly throbbing in her throat. "You know, you were such a big part of it, I think we should invite you. But—" she lifted a wary hand "—only if you want to see him when he first lays eyes on it."

He circled the counter and took her in his arms, aware how frequent moments like these could be if they joined forces and lived not just in the same county but under the same roof. "Is that an invitation to stay the night?"

She relaxed into the curve of his body, looking deep into his eyes. "Ah, no. I'm not doing that until I get married. And who knows if that will ever be."

But she was talking about it. Mulling over the possibility. A month ago she wouldn't have even done that.

He smiled, willing to be patient a little while longer. "Then how will this work?"

She looked up at him, as if in awe how good it felt to simply hang out this way. "Um…well, we could set the time for your arrival on Christmas morning at 5:00 a.m." An affectionate twinkle lit her amber gaze. "If he's not awake yet, we could have *stollen* and coffee while we wait. Then open presents and have a proper man-size breakfast later."

Her excitement was contagious. He kissed her temple. "It's a date."

Smiling, Molly went back to icing cookies.

Chance lounged against the counter. "By the way, how did the Skype meeting with the Worthington Academy staff go this afternoon?" He wanted to hear that Elspeth Pyle, Dr. Mitchard and the others had been as considerate of Molly's feelings as they would have been to any of the wealthy parents they dealt with.

Unfortunately, that did not appear to have been the case. Her expression troubled, Molly briefly related what had been said to her. He couldn't have disagreed more.

"They're wrong about Braden being ready for a more rigorous program," Chance said fiercely. "I've spent time with him. I know he could more than handle whatever they threw at him."

Molly grinned. "Watch it. You're sounding like a proud papa." As soon as the words were out, she blushed. Averting her glance, she amended hastily, "You know what I mean."

Chance curved a comforting hand around her shoulder. "I do," he admitted solemnly. "And you're right. I am very protective of him." *And you, too*, Chance added silently. *Much more than you know.*

Looking as if the Skype meeting had brought out all her worst insecurities, Molly nodded, admitting, "It's hard not to be protective with little kids. They're so vulnerable."

"True." Sensing she needed him more than she would admit, he turned to her and pulled her all the way into his arms. "But there's something very special about Braden." He stroked a gentle hand through her hair and lifted her face to his. "I felt a connection to him the first time we met."

"And he, you," Molly said, her shoulders tense in a way they hadn't been before they'd begun talking about Worthington Academy.

"Did they say anything else?" Chance pressed, wanting to know the whole story.

"No." Her casual, self-effacing tone hinted at the vulnerability she felt inside. "It was more a feeling I had."

He waited. Guilt that she might have found out what he had done to put her in this position, despite the precautions he had taken to prevent just such a revelation, roiled in his gut.

Molly shook her head, moving on to the next tray. "Like…" She struggled to put her intuition into words. "They'd been *forced* to interview him or something."

Maybe because they sort of had been.

He studied her, maintaining a poker face. "They said that?" His temper rose.

"No. It just…" She put more icing into the piping bag. "What they did say about needing to interview him for the diversity in backgrounds of their student body. I didn't buy it."

"How so?" he asked carefully.

"Well… I mean, you saw the children in the classes we observed. Even in identical uniforms, you could see they were all privileged kids from wealthy backgrounds. Their haircuts, their perfect body mass indexes, their posture, their demeanor…" She sighed heavily. "These were all kids who were used to being pampered, revered, adored."

The same could easily be said about her son, except for coming from money. "Braden has confidence, too," he pointed out.

Molly's face took on the fierce, maternal line he knew so well. "Not the confidence that comes from never having to want for or worry about anything."

Money in the bank only went so far. Chance disagreed. "Confidence is confidence."

Molly huffed and went to the sink to rinse the icing off her fingers. "You say that because you come from the other side," she accused him over her shoulder. "The side that had all the advantages. I didn't."

Chance waited until she turned around, then put a hand on either side of her, not touching her but effectively trapping her against the counter just the same.

"Do you ever think that's part of what makes you who and what you are?"

His challenging tone had her lifting her chin. "And what am I?" she sassed.

Plenty. "Strong, independent, resilient, savvy, talented, gorgeous…" Watching the color come into her cheeks, he teased, "Shall I go on?"

She folded one arm against her waist, not touching him, either, and tapped her finger against her lips. "I like that you put my beauty at the end of the list." She wrinkled her nose playfully. "Such as it is."

Enough of her downgrading herself. He pulled her all the way into his arms, pressing her softness against his hardness. "What it is," he growled, "is amazing. Heart poundingly—" he paused to kiss her deeply "—wonderful."

She shook her head at him in silent remonstration. "You can stop now," she chided, even as her eyes filled with affection. "Compliments are not necessary."

Chance sobered. His heart ached for all that was still missing in her life. That could be so easily corrected. "They're not compliments, darlin'." He stroked his hand down her cheek and bent to kiss her again, tenderly this time. "They are heartfelt observations." And what he felt when he looked at her was all heart.

Chapter 12

"I can't believe we're doing this," Molly murmured the next afternoon. She stepped out of his shower and wrapped a towel around her.

Chance shut off the spigot, his body still humming from their last incredible bout of lovemaking. Blotting the dampness from his hair and skin, he hung up his towel and joined her at the mirror. Coming up behind her, he aligned his naked body against hers and planted a kiss on the back of her neck. "Taking a long lunch hour?"

Molly turned to give him a mischievous glance that swept over him hungrily from head to toe, then ran a brush through her hair, restoring order to her still-damp curls.

She pivoted to face him. As she pressed against him, he could feel how much she wanted him. If only they had the time…"I can't believe—" she sent him an alluring glance from beneath her lashes, her nipples pearling beneath the towel "—we're taking a long lunch hour in your bed."

"And shower," he teased, following her into the bedroom. "I can." His body humming with resurging need, he watched her bend to pick up her clothes. Not ready to see her leave just yet, he tugged her against him for a sweet, leisurely kiss. "I think that was the best pre-Christmas present I ever had."

"Me, too," Molly murmured, kissing him back even more languidly.

He threaded his hands through her hair, wishing he didn't have to worry about rushing her into the next step. "Besides—" he kissed his way down her throat "—with the Circle H ranch house finished…"

Molly flitted out of his arms with a reluctant sigh, then slipped on her satin burgundy panties and matching bra. Shifting into the business mode he knew so well, she reminded him, "We still have to help decorate the interior for the Open House at the Circle H tomorrow morning. Make sure Sage and her catering staff have everything they need for the evening's festivities."

Noting the pleat of new worry between her brows, he shifted into work gear, too. Pulling on his boxer briefs, then his jeans, he reassured her confidently. "It's all going to go smoothly. We have Garrett's wife, Hope, in charge, remember? There's no crisis my sister-in-law can't handle. So even if there are problems, and I'm not expecting any, Hope will find solutions for them."

"I know." Molly eased a black turtleneck sweater over her head.

Chance's mouth went dry as she shimmied into her jeans. Dressed or undressed, she made him go hard with need. "Garrett and Wyatt have also volunteered to help. In fact, the only family member who won't be around to support Mom's entry back into the fund-raising non-profit world will be Zane."

Molly sat down on the edge of his bed to tug on her favorite peacock-blue cowgirl boots. She extended one showgirl-quality leg, then the other. "Your mom mentioned Zane was going to try and get home for Christmas this year."

Chance nodded, his worry over his Special Forces brother briefly coming to the fore. "Even if he does make it, and there's no guarantee of that, it would likely be just in the nick of time, not for the Open House."

Molly sobered. "One of the disadvantages of serving in the military, I guess." Her frown deepened.

"I don't think Zane minds. In fact, I'm pretty sure he thrives on all the uncertainty and danger."

Molly nodded, her mood becoming even more distant.

Chance wrapped his hands around her waist and tugged her close. He bent his head to nuzzle the softness of her hair, inhale the sexy fragrance that was uniquely her. "My question is, what's really bugging you today?" Loving the way she felt in his arms, he kissed his way across her temple. She'd been moody all morning. Which was why he'd suggested their noontime rendezvous rather than try to get an actual date with her that evening. "The only time I've had your full attention is when we were making love."

She blushed in a way that made her look prettier, more womanly than ever, then admitted wryly, "Listen, cowboy, it's a little hard to think of anything else when you're…um…"

He chuckled, a deep rumbling low in his throat. "I know." He caressed the slender curve of her hip. "And don't think you're going to distract me asking me to show you what other extraordinary skills I have."

For a second, she looked just as tempted as he felt.

"Seriously." He brushed the pad of his thumb across her lower lip, wanting to help her out if he could. He looked deep into her eyes. "What's bothering you?"

Molly balled her hands into fists and blew out a frustrated breath. "If you must know, I don't have anything appropriate to wear to the Open House."

Chance squinted. "I've seen your closet, Molly. You're a clotheshorse."

She walked out of his bedroom and down the stairs, leaving him to follow. "Yes, but my clothes aren't designer duds. Which is why your lovely sister, Sage, volunteered to act as my stylist for the evening and lent me an absolutely gorgeous cocktail dress and the accessories that went with it."

He caught up with her in the kitchen. "That was nice of her."

Figuring she had to be as hungry as he was, he pulled out the cold cuts and cheeses. Handed her a plate and a loaf of multigrain bread.

With a sigh, she began assembling a sandwich. "Yes, well, we lamented our wardrobe crises together."

He got a plate and did the same. "What has Sage got to worry about?"

Molly looked in his fridge and brought out the mayo, spicy mustard and leaf lettuce. "Promise you won't mention it to her?"

Chance made an X over the center of his chest.

With a commiserating moue, Molly told him, "She

had to have the dress she planned to wear to the gala let out at the seams. Apparently she's gained a little weight since coming back to Texas and opening her café bakery."

Chance shook his head in consternation. If he lived to be a hundred he would never understand why women worried about the shift of a few pounds in either direction.

He cut his sandwich in half, then went to find the chips. "Hard to see how, since she's had the stomach flu twice in the past six weeks."

Molly took a seat beside him at the island. "I heard she had been under the weather a couple of times." She picked up a sandwich that was as thin as his was thick. "Anyway, I have to get over there in forty-five minutes to pick up the dress, so as soon as I finish this, I've got to run."

He poured a couple of glasses of iced tea, not about to let her go before he'd nailed down their next time together. "Will I see you tonight?"

If she was free, maybe he could talk her into an official date. Even if they had to go all the way to San Angelo to have it, to avoid her fear of being seen together socially.

"Tomorrow morning. I have to spend the evening completing the pre-enrollment paperwork for Braden's new preschool in Dallas. They need it before Christmas if he's going to start there in January."

Chance was happy Molly had selected a place other than the high-stress Worthington Academy to put her son. Not so happy it was a good 150 miles away. He forced himself to be supportive anyway. "How does he feel about the move?" Chance asked cheerfully.

Molly broke a potato chip in two. "I haven't told him."

Chance narrowed his gaze. Molly was usually very up front with her son about what was going to happen next. And what was expected of him.

Her cheeks turning pink, she explained, "Once I have a rental home picked out to go see and the school set up, we'll take another trip there. I'll explain it all then, when I can show him where we are going to live and so on."

Disappointment knotted his gut. "So you're really doing this?"

She wasn't surprised he didn't want to see her go. However, his feelings did not change her mind. "I really am," she confirmed.

Except, Molly knew, as she left Chance and drove away from Bullhaven, she wasn't nearly as brave as she sounded.

The truth was the closer she got to actually making the big change, the more she did not really want to do it after all.

Yet the more rational part of her knew that she couldn't let last-minute jitters affect putting what had been a years-long plan for her and Braden's future into action.

Her son deserved the very best. She wanted him to have everything he could possibly have. The kind of opportunity and vast choices she had never been afforded.

She wanted the kind of financial security Chance and his siblings had grown up with, so that if, heaven forbid, anything ever happened to her, or Braden, she would have the money and resources to deal with it.

Right now she didn't.

And wouldn't if she stayed in the moderate-income range she currently enjoyed.

So like it or not, she was headed to the big city come January.

And she and Chance would have a casual, long-distance romance, or perhaps just fade out entirely.

Either way, she had to be a grown-up about it. She couldn't do what she did before with Aaron and be ready to base her whole life, all her plans for the future, on a man.

Because if her growing relationship with Chance didn't work out—as the affair with Braden's daddy hadn't—she would be devastated. Professionally and personally. The setbacks and fallout might be impossible to overcome.

She couldn't do that to herself. She couldn't do it to her son. So she would enjoy this Christmas the way she had never enjoyed a holiday before, she reassured herself fiercely, and move on from there.

"Sure you don't want me to pick you up?" Chance asked the following evening. Why was just the sound of his deep, gravelly voice so sexy? Why was his rock-solid presence so comforting and enticing? A lump rose to her throat as unbidden tears sprang to her eyes. Shaking off the unwelcome emotion, Molly finished slipping on the shoes that matched her borrowed dress.

Feeling part imposter, part Cinderella, she cradled the phone to her ear. "No, I have to drop off Braden. He's having a sleepover with Will and Justin tonight, at Justin's house."

"Ah." Chance chuckled softly. "Can we have a sleepover, too?"

Why not? Given how precious little time they had

left to spend with each other. Plus, if the evening went as well as Lucille had predicted it would go for Molly, she'd likely have a lot to celebrate.

"Possibly," she murmured coyly, moving a small distance away from her son, who was busy playing with his Christmas village. "If you're a good boy and we're discreet."

"Oh, that can certainly be arranged, darlin'," he reassured her playfully. "So." His husky baritone was rife with promises. "My place?"

"Yes." She could leave very early tomorrow morning, before his hired hands arrived to take care of the bulls.

"See you soon then." His enthusiasm engendered her own. "And, Molly?"

Heavens, she was going to miss this man. So much. "Yes?"

"I want you to know." The warmth of his emotions kindled hers. "You and Braden have made this the best yuletide season of my life."

Molly smiled, knowing deep down she could not want for more. "Right back at you, cowboy."

Several hours later, Chance stood at the fringes of the crowd milling through the Open House at the newly renovated Circle H ranch house, making good on his promise not to be seen with Molly. It wasn't easy keeping his distance. She looked gorgeous as hell in a shimmering emerald-green cocktail dress, black velvet evening blazer and stiletto heels.

As previously arranged, his mother had her arm looped through Molly's and was taking her around, introducing her as the hottest up-and-coming interior designer.

From what he could see, a lot of interest was being generated. Which meant Molly would soon be as successful and financially secure as she dreamed of being.

In Dallas…

While he was here. Right where he wanted to be. Or had, until she and her young son had sauntered into his life.

"A million bucks for your thoughts," Chance's younger brother Wyatt gibed, joining him.

They clinked glasses. "Very funny." Chance sipped his Bourbon & Branch.

"Actually, it's appropriate."

Chance lifted a brow at the most cynical of his siblings.

With a knowing smirk, Wyatt informed him, "Mr. X is here, with Babs and Delia, and they're coming for you."

Chance promptly changed the subject to something his horse-ranching brother would *not* want to discuss. "As long as we're talking about affairs that are long over," he said smugly, "I saw Adelaide Smythe." She was Wyatt's very single, very pregnant with twins ex-girlfriend from way back, who Wyatt had never really gotten over.

Wyatt remained unflappable. Which meant, Chance intuited, the two had already crossed swords.

"As the new CFO of Lockhart Foundation, Adelaide would be expected to be here. The piranhas on the lookout for you, however, would not."

So true, he admitted reluctantly. "Mom invited them?"

"Apparently, Garrett and Hope found out that Mr. X has a reputation for supporting nonprofits geared to helping our military and their families, so they suggested to Mom that she invite the very deep-pocketed Mr. X. I don't think they expected him to show up personally. But then, they hadn't heard about how he'd been attempting to buy you out." Wyatt lifted his glass to Chance. He nodded toward the trio emerging from one of the tents. "And here they come…"

Wyatt stepped aside to make room, but he stayed to watch the show. The woman who would have been his mother-in-law closed in. "Last opportunity," Babs told Chance.

Mr. X looked at Chance, too. "I'll even go down to only a forty-nine percent stake in the business, if that will turn the tide in my favor."

Chance shook his head.

Delia rolled her eyes. "Chance is. Just. Not. Interested."

Babs sent an irritated look at her daughter. "Chance doesn't need you to defend him, sweetheart."

Wordlessly, Delia spun away and headed into the crowd. Mr. X followed.

Babs glared at Chance. "I'm going to get Delia to forget you once and for all, if it is the last thing I do, Chance Lockhart!"

Chance was pretty sure that was already the case. He relaxed as Babs stormed off.

"Is Delia still carrying a torch for you?" Wyatt asked curiously.

Chance shook his head. "No."

But Mr. X sure seemed to be intent on pursuing Delia. The slightly geeky billionaire caught up with Babs's daughter at the fringes and put his hand on her waist. Leaning down, he said something into her ear.

Delia shrugged free. Took off. Mr. X was right behind her, looking more determined than ever.

Thirty seconds later, Chance got a text from Delia.

Molly saw Chance winding through the crowd, walking past the bandstand toward the barns. She was about to follow him, hoping to surreptitiously get a moment alone with him, when Babs stepped out in front of her.

For once, the aggressive sales and acquisitions exec was not with her daughter or Mr. X, who, to Molly's surprise, had both also appeared there that evening. "Hello, dear," Babs said cheerfully. "I'd like to speak to you about doing a decorating job for me."

Molly was not at the point she could turn down any business in her new city. Though if she could have, this would have been the job she passed on. Determined to be professional, she plucked her phone from her blazer pocket and brought up her calendar. "Absolutely."

Babs wrote the address on the back of her business card. "The job is here in Laramie County. A house on the lake that I'm considering buying as rental property. Can you be there at 9:00 a.m.? The Realtor is going to open up the house. Then we can talk about what is possible in terms of renovation."

Out of the corner of her eye, Molly saw Mr. X come out from behind the barn. He was alone, and he looked ticked off.

Wondering what that was about, Molly turned her attention back to Babs. "I'll see you then."

Babs pivoted to see what Molly had been looking at, then headed off in the direction of Mr. X. Molly continued threading her way through the dwindling crowds, toward the barn.

As she neared it, she saw Delia standing in the shadows just behind it, arms folded in front of her. Chance was standing opposite his ex. They were talking. Seriously, it seemed. Delia did not seem to like what she was hearing from her ex. She threw up her arms in frustration and walked away, head bowed.

What was going on here? Molly wondered, stalled in her tracks.

Was there still something left between Chance and Delia?

Had Mr. X discovered the two of them together? Or had the three of them been talking in private—about the bucking-bull business yet again?

She had no more chance to ponder because Chance was striding toward her. He stopped just short of her. He waited until they were well out of earshot of other partygoers passing by, then grinned casually and quipped, "Am I allowed to talk to you yet?"

"Yes," Molly said, ready to bolt this fund-raiser once and for all. Right or wrong, she wanted the safety of Chance's arms. "Just not here," she said.

Chapter 13

As soon as they got back to Bullhaven, Molly filled Chance in on her conversation with Delia's mother. Chance didn't even have to think about what his recommendation would be. "Turn her down," he said.

Molly slipped off her heels. Her lips slid out in the adorable pout he knew so well. And could never stop wanting to kiss. "I can't."

He lit the fire, then went into the kitchen and brought them back a couple of bottles of water. Molly sank onto his big leather sofa and bent over to rub her arches. "Babs is not just one of your mother's longtime friends—"

"I'm not sure I'd call them that exactly," Chance interrupted. "They're more like acquaintances who once frequented the same social scene."

Practically trembling with the exhaustion and adrenaline accumulated after such a long evening, Molly waved off his pointed objection. "Regardless, Babs is very well connected. Doing a job for her, and doing it well, could bring me a lot of future business."

Already wanting her so bad he ached, Chance shifted Molly into the corner of the leather sofa and drew her legs across his lap. Adjusting his posture to ease the pressure building at the front of his slacks, he massaged her left foot gently, from toes to heel. Felt her start to blissfully relax, even as his desire built. "She could also blackball you," he pointed out quietly.

Molly drew her legs away from his lap and swung them back onto the floor. Sitting up, she looked him straight in the eye. Beneath their evening clothes, their thighs touched. "Believe me, I am very well aware of that, too," she snapped. "That's why I'm treading carefully."

Yes, but you shouldn't have to, he thought, as a tense silence fell.

They stared at each other.

She sighed and ran her hands through her hair.

Finally, he tried again. "I talked to Delia tonight."

Molly's lips tightened. Briefly she turned her glance away, clearly angry now. "I know. I saw the two of you come out from behind the barn."

That sounded a lot worse than it had been. Knowing how lame it sounded, he explained, "She wanted to talk to me without her mother seeing."

Molly's delicate brow lifted, and the pink in her cheeks deepened. She folded her arms in front of her and glared at him. "Sounds cozy."

She wanted to believe him. He could see that. She just wasn't sure she should.

He tore his eyes from the lush fullness of her lips. "Delia's worried her mother and Mr. X are up to something."

Her expressive brows lowered over her long-lashed

eyes. Molly uncapped her water bottle and took a long, thirsty drink. "That's hardly old news." She shrugged. "The two of them have been scheming ways to somehow buy out or takeover your bucking-bull business for weeks now."

"Something besides that," Chance clarified with concern.

"Like what?" Molly asked impatiently.

"Delia doesn't know. But Bab's sudden interest in hiring you indicates you're involved in her devious plans, too."

Molly flinched. He'd never seen her so overwrought or incredibly, passionately beautiful, and he edged closer.

"Babs couldn't just want me on board because I'm talented?"

Chance saw he'd hurt her feelings. But there was too much at stake—most importantly, their relationship—to sugarcoat the situation. "No."

Molly's lips tightened. Slowly but surely the walls around her heart began to go back up. "Thanks a lot."

Wanting to protect her more than ever, he covered her hand with his. "Listen to me, Molly. Mr. X told Delia he's prepared to pull out all the stops to get her to go out with him. And Babs is a manipulative shrew who never forgets a slight."

"So?" Molly shook her head as if that would clear it. "How is any of that our problem?"

"Babs blames me for the fact her only daughter has never married or brought a new influx of major money into their family coffers. She's particularly unhappy about the fact that Delia has been rejecting all of Mr. X's advances thus far. And she's told Delia repeatedly that she would like nothing better than to see me as unhappy as Delia has been. Worse, Babs apparently realized correctly the best way to get her long-awaited revenge on me is through you, Molly." Chance paused to let his words sink in. "I don't want you getting hurt via collateral damage," Chance finished tersely. *I don't want Babs ruining what we have.*

And it was so fragile, Babs just might.

Molly huffed out a breath. "I think you're overreacting."

Chance only wished he was.

Extricating her hand from his, she stood and moved gracefully to the fireplace. She stood with her back to the flames. "Babs doesn't know we're dating. Nor does anyone else. Everyone thinks we've just buried the hatchet long enough to become temporary co-contractors on your mother's renovation and casual friends."

Chance wasn't so sure about that. Molly wore her heart on her sleeve, whether she realized it or not.

He was equally bad at hiding his feelings where she was concerned. Whether she liked it or not, the two of them had been getting a lot of curious looks. People, like his siblings and their crews, were starting to put two and two together. Heck, even three-year-old Braden realized they'd forged a heck of a lot more than a casual connection. And could have a lot more, if Molly would only give them a shot.

Unwilling to see what was right in front of her, Molly continued blithely, defiantly keeping her blinders on. "So there's no reason for Babs to come after me."

Okay. So Molly didn't want to believe him. Maybe because she had yet to see the dark side of the world he had grown up in. She'd been raised in Laramie County, where neighbor took care of neighbor, and a man or woman's word was worth more than any gold.

He would have to accept her naive outlook in this matter, and for now, at least, try another tact. "Why risk it, in any case?" he said with a reassuring smile. He rose and joined her at the hearth. "There will be other jobs."

"It doesn't matter if there are, or aren't." Molly angled her chin at him, fury glittering in her amber eyes. "I'm not like you, Chance. I don't have the luxury of turning down work or money!" Her slender body quivered with emotion. "I can't just throw lucrative offers into the shredder without even looking at them."

He returned her pointed look. "You did it once— with Braden's daddy."

"Yes." Sadness turned the corners of her mouth down. "And I've regretted it ever since."

Molly didn't know where the words had come from. She could barely fathom thinking them, never mind saying them aloud. To Chance, of all people.

He clasped her elbow lightly and drew her toward him. "You don't mean that," he said quietly.

The truth hit her with the force of the north wind, chilling her from head to toe. Ignoring the shocked and disillusioned expression on Chance's face, she lifted her face to his and went on with gut-wrenching clarity. "I'm not saying it would have been the right thing to do." She knew, deep down, that morally and ethically it would not have been.

Chance's wish to understand her helped her go on. "Given how Braden's daddy felt about having a child at all, never mind with me, it would have been disastrous to bring Aaron into the equation. Because all Braden would have been to Aaron was a problem to be managed." Her voice cracked a little. "And Braden would have been devastated to realize he wasn't loved or wanted the way he should be."

Chance twined his hands with hers. Squeezed. "I agree."

Molly was determined to let Chance see the differences between them as clearly as she did. She looked him in the eye. "But that doesn't mean I don't wish—on some level, anyway—that I could have figured out a way back then to provide for and protect Braden. Even if it injured my pride."

She paused to let her words sink in.

"Because if I had accepted the money to just go away, then I would be able to afford to put Braden in any elite school I chose without asking for scholarships, and be at least a little more selective about which jobs I took on. I wouldn't have to worry about what might happen to us if I ever got sick or injured or couldn't work."

Chance dropped his grip on her, stepped back. "But you would have been selling your soul had you done that."

"I make compromises all the time."

"Not like that, you don't."

The truth was, Chance thought irritably, Molly had no idea how cold and ruthless some of the truly wealthy could be, and he didn't want her to ever know. Not first-hand, anyway. She'd come close enough to finding out in her dealings with the vaulted Worthington Academy.

"I'm asking you not to be naive," he said again.

Molly angled her thumb at the center of her chest. "And I'm asking you to consider my position." The soft swell of her breasts rose and fell. "To imagine what it is like to not have that fallback of security that comes from family money and connection."

She rushed on, giving him no chance to interrupt, "Because if I did have that, Chance, I wouldn't have to work so hard to build my business."

Her lips pinched together stubbornly. "Or meet Babs tomorrow. Never mind leave everything and everyone I know behind and move to Dallas. But I don't have that luxury, Chance, and odds are, I never will. The most I can do is earn as much money as possible as quickly as possible and provide for my son."

She had a point, he acknowledged silently. For a lot of reasons she wasn't as secure financially as she wanted to be at this point in her life, and given how hard she worked, she should be.

She was also his woman—whether she admitted it yet or not. He was her man. Yes, he had acted on her son's behalf, but he hadn't done nearly enough to protect *her* feelings or keep *her* safe. That would change. Effective immediately. "Let me go with you tomorrow," he said.

She moved away from the mantel. "I don't need your protection."

Except she did. He caught up with her as she retrieved her shoes. Tried again. "Molly…"

She perched on the edge of his sofa and slipped on her heels, then stood. "If you understand nothing else, understand this. I have to move forward and do this the way I always have. On my own."

Molly had plenty of time to regret the abrupt way she'd left Chance's ranch the evening before and returned to her home in town. The truth was she hadn't been nearly as irritated with him as she was with herself.

The womanly side of her kept telling her she was making a mistake in not allowing Chance to stand by her side or run interference for her. Whereas the independent single mom told her it would be a mistake to rely on anyone other than herself, lest she upend the life she had already built for herself and her son.

As for the romantic part of her?

Well, she knew what that required.

A long-term future with Chance.

But was that even realistic, knowing how he felt about everything that mattered to her? The first of which was earning enough money to obtain real financial security.

Molly had no answer. What she did know was the meeting with Babs could be the key to a lot of things. Hence she had to go. Even if it meant disappointing Chance.

So Molly dressed in her most elegant business suit, the one she reserved for premiere networking events, grabbed her briefcase and headed out to Lake Laramie.

Two cars were already in the drive. A sleek white Mercedes and a minivan with a Realtor sign on the side. She walked up to the fixer-upper, one of many year-round rentals at the lake. It had an artificial wreath on the door and a sparsely decorated small Christmas tree inside. The Realtor, whose daughter attended Braden's preschool, said hello to Molly, then turned back to Babs. "I'll wait to hear from you."

"You'll have an answer on the property by noon," Babs promised.

The Realtor left them to discuss possible renovations. Molly turned to Babs, her attitude professional. "How much were you thinking of doing?"

Babs laid a silk scarf over the worn sofa, then perched on it. "Actually, I'd like to sit and talk first."

Getting better acquainted might help break the ice,

but something felt off. Ignoring her growing sense of unease, Molly sat opposite her.

Babs smiled. "I understand you have a son, Braden, and that he was recently wait-listed at Worthington Academy."

Molly's alarm deepened, but she kept her outward cool. "How do you know that?"

"I do background checks on all prospective business associates. As it turns out, Worthington Academy recently did one on you."

Molly had agreed to a credit check as part of the application process. It was standard at most businesses requiring a long-term payment commitment.

She hadn't expected such information to become available to anyone but school officials.

But if Babs had had her investigated, it would have shown up. The same way all the details of her life had shown up when Aaron's family had her life scrutinized by a PI.

Molly felt as punched in the gut now as she had then.

Seeming to realize she'd caught Molly off guard, Babs continued haughtily, "The school wants to know who the parents of their prospective students are. Delia attended WA, and I've maintained my connections there, to help business associates, so I made a few calls to see how the process was going."

Without my knowledge or consent? That was unacceptable.

But wary of insulting a person she still hoped to get work from at the end of the day, Molly merely smiled. "I don't understand what my son's education has to do with this job."

"I still have pull at Worthington. I can get him off the wait list before Christmas."

That would be nice. Had it been merit—not connection—based. Doing her best to appear as if this sort of thing happened to her every day, Molly asked calmly, "Why would you want to do that?"

"Oh, honey." Babs shook her head at Molly. "It wouldn't be without quid pro quo. You'd do a favor for me. I want you to help me shake some sense into my daughter once and for all."

Molly's insides twisted with anxiety. Chance had said she had blinders on...

Babs frowned. "She's been mooning after that ne'er-do-well cowboy for years now. Lamenting their breakup to the point she won't date respectable beaux more than once or twice. And then only if forced."

Molly could see why that would not make for a happy situation. For anyone. "Again..." A hint of steel entered her tone. "What does this have to do with me?"

Babs waved a dissolute hand. "Delia, as you know, does not like to chase lost causes. She needs to see that Chance has indisputably moved on. With you. And the most dramatic, lasting impression way for that to happen is for her to catch you with him, in flagrante."

This was getting surreal. Molly felt the room sway. "You're...joking."

Babs opened her handbag. "I assure you I am not. Now, Chance will be here in about ten minutes. If not sooner, given the message I left for him just shortly before you arrived. Delia will be here ten minutes after that."

Babs fished her keys from her bag. "All you have to do is seduce Chance in plain view, right here in the living room, and you will not only have more work than you can handle in Dallas but your son will be admitted to Worthington Academy, his tuition for the next five years fully paid in advance."

The proposition was so outrageous it took her a moment to recover. "I don't know why you think I would even consider something so preposterous."

"Let's not play games, Molly."

"I'm not," Molly gritted out.

Babs's expression turned ugly. "You had no qualms asking Chance Lockhart to pay for Braden's interview at Worthington Academy."

Sure she hadn't heard right, Molly blinked. "What are you talking about?"

Babs smirked, as if she still held the high card. "You didn't know? How sweet." She leaned closer, telling Molly snidely, "The problem is, as usual, Chance was a little too cheap. It would have taken a much larger donation to secure a spot for Braden at semester. Fortunately, I am prepared to spare no expense, if it means getting my daughter to start taking advantage of her own good fortune with Mr. X." Babs stood and shrugged on her mink coat. "So you see, Molly, you and I have that in common. We're both willing to do whatever it takes to safeguard our children."

Shock reverberated through her. "But I'm nothing like you!" Molly insisted.

Babs flashed a manipulative smile. "Aren't you? We will see. You have approximately six minutes to decide…"

Chance passed Babs on the road leading to the lake house. She was driving with her usual cool confidence. Which made him wonder what had happened with Molly.

Molly's red SUV was in the driveway.

He walked in. She was on the sofa, her head in her hands. "Molly?"

She looked up, her complexion ashen.

Damning himself for ever letting her make this venture alone, he crossed quickly to her side. He knelt in front of her, consoling her the best he could under the circumstances. "What happened here?"

Molly stared at him, a thousand emotions shimmering in her eyes. Anger, hurt, resentment. Disbelief…

"What in hell did Babs say to you?" Clasping Molly's hands, he pulled her to her feet. She moved woodenly into his embrace.

He wrapped his arms around her. Instead of melting against him the way she usually did, she pulled away.

"Chance, no!" she said in a strangled voice, looking all the more upset and betrayed. "I don't want—" She choked up, shaking her head. "We can't…"

Aware he'd never seen her more devastated, he threaded his hands through her hair and lifted her face to his.

Beneath her confusion, a glimmer of need shone in her eyes. "Molly," he said again as his head lowered to hers. Desperate to comfort her in any way he could, he touched his lips to hers just as the front door opened behind them.

"Really," Delia's low voice rang out in the chilly room. "You don't have to put on a show just for me. I already know what Mother's scheme is."

That was good, Chance thought. Because he sure as hell didn't.

Chapter 14

Molly could see why Delia was upset. She lifted her hands. "I didn't agree to help your mother with her sleazy machinations."

Delia took off her sunglasses, her demeanor as world-weary as her tone.

"And yet here you are in Chance's arms," the heiress observed, as if she couldn't bear yet another disappointment.

Chance frowned. "I initiated that. Molly wasn't cooperating." Looking irritated to find himself being a third wheel in whatever was going on, he turned his level glance back to Molly. "Is this why?"

Figuring he was going to find out eventually, Molly folded her arms in front of her. Chance had been right. She never should have come here today, no matter how lucrative the job or how coveted the connection. Sometimes a job just wasn't worth it. "Babs offered to get

Braden accepted at Worthington Academy, his tuition paid for the next five years, if I would be caught in flagrante with you!"

Chance did a double take. "What the *hell*?"

Delia nodded, her shoulders hunched in defeat. "Mother's determined to show me that Chance and I are still all wrong for each other. What she refuses to accept is that we've been over for years now."

Molly wanted to believe that. Just as she wanted to believe that the difference between her background and Chance's would not keep them apart. "Babs thinks you still have feelings for him."

Delia scoffed, "Of course I do! I'll always care about you, Chance. Even though things ended badly. We knew each other too long and too well for me *not* to care for you."

Chance exhaled wearily. "Seeing you again has shown me the same thing."

Delia slid her sunglasses on top of her head. She loosened the belt on her black trench and perched on the edge of the sofa. "But coming all the way out here, going through the offer process with you, finding out how you still feel about monetary success, has also shown me that Mother was right to break us up. I never would have been happy living on a ranch named Bullhaven out in the middle of nowhere, with all those big, smelly Black Angus. Never mind going through the hassle of simultaneously building up two relatively small-time businesses from scratch!"

Molly took umbrage with that. "First of all, Chance's bulls don't smell. I've been around them."

Delia waved off the details. "Maybe not to you. To me, everything out on that ranch is yucky and disgusting. I'm a city girl through and through."

That Molly could see.

The question was…was she?

Was Braden—who loved their small town and Chance's ranch so much—a potential city boy?

Or would her son wish for his roots, the way she was beginning to, and they hadn't even left Laramie County yet!

Her expression sober, Delia continued, "Being dragged out here—repeatedly—on what was clearly a lost cause, also made me realize I don't want to work in the family business anymore, even as second in command. I really hate my mother's maneuverings and all the drama."

"What do you want to do?" Chance asked his ex kindly.

Delia gestured haphazardly, her elitist attitude coming to the fore once again. "Honestly? No clue. Thanks to the trust fund my daddy left me, however, I don't have to be in any hurry to find out."

Molly had always wanted to have that particular option. Now, studying Delia's self-indulgent expression, she wasn't so sure that was such a good thing.

"So maybe you should just tell your mother all that," Molly proposed.

"So she'll leave Molly and Braden alone," Chance added protectively.

"And you." Molly turned back to him.

Once again, just like that, they were a team. At least for the moment.

Delia scoffed. "First of all, talking to my mother, telling her what's in your heart never works. She thinks the world revolves around cold hard cash." Delia paused to let her words sink in. "And Mother's right, for people like us, who have grown up with the world as their oyster, it really does. Which is why I've decided to take Mr. X up on his offer to rescue me from all this and fly back to San Francisco with him."

Suddenly Molly realized why Chance was so concerned about Delia. She'd obviously been sheltered to a fault. And hence, she'd remained incredibly naive despite her overall sophistication. "Are you sure you want to do that?" Molly asked gently. *Be used like that? Like I once was? By a rich man who, at the end of the day, only cares about his own happiness?*

Delia paused to look at Chance, who remained stone-faced, then turned back to Molly. "Mr. X and I have been straight with each other. He wants a beautiful woman on his arm, one who's very good at playing hard to get, to enhance the reputation he wants to build as a ladies' man. So he can up his game."

Game, Molly thought. *How appropriate.*

"And I need a break from my mother's constant haranguing—which Mr. X has agreed to give—by hinting he wants to marry me. Mother won't do anything to interfere with possible billions coming my way," Delia continued.

They all knew that to be true.

"Anyway," Delia finished with an airy shrug as Chance moved closer to Molly and slipped his arm around her waist. "If you want me to tell Mother you carried through on your end of the bargain and got caught in a passionate clinch with Chance so you'll go ahead and get what you need regarding your son's school, I'm happy to do so."

The knowledge Delia felt Molly could be part of any scheme, never mind one that low-down, rankled. His grasp on her tightening, Chance looked equally ticked off by the intimation.

Her fury rising yet again, Molly reminded Delia, "Except I didn't set you up deliberately." She had been trying to do just the opposite.

"Who cares?" Delia moved gracefully to her feet, suddenly looking very much like her mother. "Mother deserves to get scammed the way she was trying to scam me!"

Molly knew revenge was a dish best *not ever* served. "Thanks," she said tightly. "But Braden and I are fine." In fact, this whole episode gave her second thoughts about trying to enroll her son with other children of the very elite. "I'd just as soon not have your mother's involvement."

Delia sighed. "I hear you. Comes with way too many strings." She said her goodbyes. The door closed behind her.

Chance turned to Molly. "I'm sorry you got dragged into the middle of all this."

Molly thought of all that had gone on behind her back.

All she and Chance still had left to discuss.

She stepped away from his warm, comforting embrace, then said, with a deep soul-wrenching bitterness that surprised even her, "You know what, Chance Lockhart? You really should be."

Chance could tell by the quietly seething way Molly was looking at him that she was accusing him of something. And just when he thought, especially now that Babs and Delia and Mr. X were out of the way, that he and Molly were ready to take that next big step. "Did I do something?"

"Maybe you should tell me." When he said nothing

immediately, her brow arched. "Unless there's *more* than one thing?"

There was only one mistake, and he saw now it had been a big one. He swore fiercely to himself, aware he should have leveled with her way before now. "You found out I intervened on Braden's behalf at Worthington Academy to see he at least got an interview."

"Well, you must not have given enough, because he didn't get accepted."

He resisted the urge to haul her into his arms and kiss some sense into her only because he didn't want hot sex being the only thing keeping them together. "Is that what this is about? You wanted me to buy his way in, the way Babs bartered? Instead of just asking that he be tested and interviewed and given a fair shot?" He studied Molly in confusion. "Because I could still do that," he said carefully.

She tossed her head, her silky auburn curls swirling around her pretty face. Edging closer, she glared at him as if it were taking every ounce of self-control she had for her not to slug him on the chin. "No, you moron! It's about the fact that you found it necessary to buy his preadmission interview and consideration at all, never mind behind my back!"

He set his jaw. "How do you think my four siblings and I all got in there? How do you think the academy got such an over-the-top campus and facilities without charging six-figure tuition for each and every student? Parents make *huge* donations to pave the way for their kids and if necessary keep them there. It's just the way things are done at that echelon, Molly."

She inhaled deeply, her luscious breasts lifting beneath the sophisticated evergreen business suit. "I see that now." She raked her teeth across the plumpness of her lower lip. "What I don't see is why you didn't explain all that to me a whole lot earlier."

That part, at least, was easy, Chance thought. He returned her frustrated glare. "Because if I had told you that you needed more than just a letter from Sage, another alumni, to boost consideration chances, that you needed a big fat check of at least five figures just to get an interview there, you wouldn't have allowed me to help. And I knew if you were ever going to understand what you were truly asking, in attempting to move to Dallas so Braden could enroll at Worthington Academy or another place just like it, was if you and he experienced it firsthand."

Hurt shimmered in her pretty amber eyes. "You figured I would think it wasn't for him."

Another trap.

"I didn't know how you'd react, frankly. Because, yes, there are a lot of good things about the school, if you subtract the greased wheels and social hierarchy and all that."

"But you didn't think Braden would belong."

Chance stood, legs braced apart, shoulders back, hands on his waist. "He loves bulls, Molly. Loves his cowboy boots. And his hat. And his friends here. Which isn't to say he wouldn't love a uniform, too. But, yeah, I hoped when the decision finally had to be made that you would want to stay in Laramie and leave him in the school he is in right now." Exhaling roughly, he raked a hand through his hair. "Not because it's going to in any way further enhance or detract from his opportunities, academically or any other way, but because he is *happy* there, and if you ask me, *that*'s what school should be about, making a kid feel happy and confident!" Damned if he didn't suddenly sound like a parent. And an incredibly caring and overprotective one at that.

"I agree."

Chance blinked. Almost afraid to think they might be on the same page once again.

Molly shook her head, her mouth taking on a troubled tilt. "I've been reconsidering my education goals for Braden for days now. Ever since I Skyped with the academy administrators and had that uncomfortable meeting about why he didn't get accepted. And then came back here and saw his Christmas program at the preschool."

Chance moved closer. He cupped her shoulders gently. "If you were having second thoughts, why didn't you tell me?" So they could have talked about it. So he could have confessed what he had already done, and why, and had her understand.

She whirled, sending a drift of perfume heading his way. "Because I hadn't made up my mind entirely! And I didn't want to say anything before I had."

He felt like he were facing off with a bear with his paw caught in a trap. "And now?"

"I've decided to stay in Laramie through the rest of the school year."

That didn't have the permanence he yearned for. Yet, wary of pushing her too hard too fast again and ending up pushing her away, he asked quietly, "What about the two jobs you already have set up in Dallas?"

Regret glimmered briefly in her gaze. She seemed to think she had failed on some level.

He wanted to tell her she hadn't.

He didn't think she would want to hear that, either.

So he remained silent.

With a sigh, she pointed out, her dejectedness more chilling than her earlier anger, "As you said, they are small tasks. And if we put our crews together, we could easily get them done in a couple of weeks. I just wouldn't take on any more out of Laramie County for the time being."

"Well, that's great news," he said, beginning to think she was holding out for the same long-term future he was. In fact, the best Christmas present ever. "To have us working together again."

She didn't seem to think so.

She squared her slender shoulders. "But that doesn't eliminate my need to build up a heck of a lot more of a financial safety net." She looked all the more conflicted. "So I'm still going to eventually have to—"

He held up a hand before she could continue. Grasped her hand before she could move even farther away. "I don't want you and Braden to ever have to want for anything, either," he told her huskily, tightening his fingers on hers. He paused to look deep into her eyes. "And you were right, merging our businesses into one would only bring you in another ten or fifteen percent annual revenue. Nothing close to what you're trying to do moving to Dallas and entering that much more lucrative market."

Her eyes were steady, but her lower lip trembled. "I'm glad you understand that," she said quietly.

"I do. And that," he said with a burst of excitement, "brings me to your Christmas gift." Ignoring the skeptical expression on her face, he led her to the sofa. Sure everything was finally going to work out, he sat down next to her. Reaching into his jacket pocket, he pulled out a red envelope with her name on it. Handed it to her with a flourish. "Open it!"

She reacted as if he had given her a time bomb instead of a gift. Lips tightening in distress, she protested, "But…it's not Christmas yet. I haven't even gotten you your gift."

Like he cared what she gave him, if she let him fully into her and her son's life, the way he desperately wanted to be. He regarded her steadily. "I want you to have this now," he told her solemnly, giving her hands another gentle squeeze. "So you'll feel better right away."

Still holding his gaze, Molly drew a deep breath, some of her usual good cheer returning. "Well, now I'm curious…"

She eased open the seal. Unfolded the contract. Read quietly. Blinked once and then again. She stared at him uncomprehendingly. "You're gifting me half ownership of Mistletoe?" She narrowed her eyes as if it couldn't possibly be true.

Heart filling with all he felt for her, he confirmed, "And Braden will get half ownership in Mistletoe Jr." Imagining the little tyke's reaction, Chance grinned. "So he actually will have all his wishes come true and get a Leo and Lizzie train set and a real live bull for Christmas. Which, of course, will be kept at Bullhaven Ranch."

The pages detailing the gift fluttered to her lap. One hand splayed across her heart. "This is crazy," she gasped.

"It's what you and Braden deserve," he said. And so much more!

Molly thrust the papers back at him. Pushing him aside with one arm, she shot to her feet. "Chance, you can't do this on a whim!"

"I'm not." It hurt that she would even think that.

Her delicate brow arched.

"I've been thinking about it for days," he rushed to confess. "Wanting to do it." Just not sure how...

She stared at him, clearly not believing a word he said. "You never share interest in your bulls or co-own them with anybody!"

"Until now," he admitted. "You're right. I haven't."

Expression grim, she snatched up the gift notification and waved it in front of his face. "This is worth—"

"Millions, yes." If that didn't prove his devotion to her and to Braden, what would?

Molly swallowed, tears filling her eyes. "And it's completely one-sided," she said as if he had just plotted to utterly destroy her, heart and soul. Instead of make her feel as safe and secure as she had always wanted to be. "You're giving me a ton of revenue."

Including stud fees and endorsements for the retired Mistletoe? Potential winnings for Mistletoe Jr.? He nodded. "Six figures annually, easy." Enough to make relocating herself and her son completely unnecessary. Starting now.

Molly's chin quivered. "And I'm giving you nothing in return."

Okay, maybe he should have considered how the ultra-independent and self-reliant Molly would feel about any one-sided arrangement.

He could still fix this.

"I wouldn't say that." He attempted a joke to lighten the mood. "I wouldn't mind, say, a lifetime supply of breakfast *stollen* or homemade German pastries and cookies."

She shook her head. "Chance, this is too much. It's

way too much. It's—" Her voice caught on a small sob. She gulped, unable to go on.

Oh, God, he'd hurt her. Which was the last thing he wanted. He pulled her into his arms. Abruptly feeling like his whole life was on the line, he buried his face in the softness of her hair. "The best Christmas gift I could think of to give you."

Her slender body hunched in defeat. "Just like with the Leo and Lizzie train set," she recollected sadly.

He knew he'd gone way overboard there. Maybe here, too. But they had fixed that. And they could fix this, too, if she gave him half a chance. "I care about you and Braden." He let her go long enough to get down on one knee, take both her hands in his. "And if this is what it takes to persuade you to stay in Laramie County, then…" His voice got rusty.

"Wow." Molly shook her head, still looking completely shell-shocked, and something else he couldn't identify. Something really treacherous. Her low voice was taut as a string on a violin. "I don't know what to say." She disengaged their hands.

Trying not to read too much into her stiff posture, he rose. Leaning down, he massaged the tense muscles of her shoulders and whispered in her ear, "How about yes?"

"Braden's daddy wanted to pay us to go away." Her voice rich with irony, she placed both her hands on his chest and shoved him away. "Now you're trying to pay us to stay!"

She shook her head, tears flowing from her eyes. "What's that saying?" she asked as if something inside her had been broken irrevocably. Staring at him, she lifted her chin. "The rich really are different?"

Her words stung. He was not the one here with a cash register for a heart. "You act like I'm trying to insult you," he fired back just as angrily.

Amber eyes narrowed. "Aren't you?"

Gut tightening, he stepped back. Aware that the thought of a life without her and Braden was more than he could bear, he reminded her, "You're the one who's always said what you really want is that big financial safety net so you'll never have to worry." He paused to let the weight of his words, the sheer enormity of his gift, sink in. He spoke slowly and deliberately, so if she thought about it long and hard enough, she would understand this was a gift from the heart, pure and simple. *"I'm giving you that."* He was offering to extend his family and merge it with hers. There was no greater gift.

She nodded, her expression maddeningly inscrutable. "Because, as you've said before, money means nothing to you."

"Well, you can't take it with you." Once again, his attempt to lighten the mood with a joke fell flat. He tried again. "You know money doesn't mean anything to me."

"Except it does mean something to you, Chance, just in a very different way." Her low voice trembled with emotion. "For you, it's the freedom to do what you want, when you want, how you want. Without ever having to worry about it."

He shrugged, not about to argue that. "I agree. It's a means to an end."

"Something that allows you to buy whatever you want and or need? Like, say, me?"

He would never be that coarse and manipulative. And if she thought that…did she really know him at all? Did they know *each other*? His frustration rising, he bit out, "I'm not asking you to be my mistress, Molly."

To his surprise, she looked even more betrayed. "Don't you get it, Chance?" Her voice was as flat and final as the look in her eyes. "I wouldn't accept a gift like this from you even if I were your wife!"

Clearly, Chance noted, that was something not about to happen, either. Unless he miraculously managed to fix things.

He spread his hands wide. Tried again. "You're taking this all wrong—"

This time it was she who cut him off with an imperious lift of her hand.

"No, Chance," she reiterated. "I'm not. In fact, I understand *exactly* what you're trying to do here. And that's fix something that can't be fixed by throwing money at it."

He was getting a little tired of being accused of being mercenary when she was the one all about cold hard cash! He glared right back. "There are worse things than searching for a solution, Molly."

"Not like that, not in my view." She steamrolled past, gorgeous ice princess on parade. Her lips pursed. "Which is why this affair has to end."

Another sucker punch to the gut. What little holiday cheer he had in him evaporated completely.

"You're breaking up with me?" he asked, staring at her in disbelief. "Because you didn't like my gift?"

She grabbed her coat and bag and rushed out the door as if her heart were breaking, pausing only to send him one last glance. "You're damn right I am."

Chapter 15

Early on December 24th, Molly put her personal devastation aside, and set out, as per tradition, to deliver her holiday gifts while Braden played with friends. First stop? The beloved Circle H Ranch.

A warm and welcoming look on her face, Lucille ushered Molly into the bunkhouse where the matriarch planned to continue to live until after the holidays. At which point she'd relocate to the recently renovated main ranch house. She accepted the festive platter of German holiday cookies. "Did you bake all these?"

With Chance's help.

But that had been when he'd been at her home almost nightly. Now that seemed unlikely to ever happen again.

A fact Braden was lamenting, too.

Her son hadn't stopped asking for Cowboy Chance.

And Chance was keeping his distance. Going so far as secreting the Leo and Lizzie train set over to Molly's house via his little sister, Sage. So it would be there for her to wrap and Braden to receive "from Santa" Christmas morning, as planned.

Had things turned out otherwise, had Chance not shown her how different they were and always would be, he would have been there, too.

Sharing in the joy. Making the three of them feel like family.

Pushing away the dreams of what might have been, Molly smiled at his mother. "I wanted to say thank you for all you've done for me and for Braden over the last year," she said sincerely.

Lucille responded with a warm hug. "It was my pleasure. And now I have something for you!" She brought something from her desk. "Here is the list of people who've contacted me since the Open House about you doing some work for them."

Molly looked at the printout containing twenty names. She forced a wry smile. "Who says Christmas can't come early?"

Lucille beamed as proudly as if she had been Molly's mother. "Women in my circle like to redecorate yearly, and thanks to the work you did at the ranch house, they all want you."

Molly was pleased with the results. She could not, however, take full credit. "It wasn't just me and my contractors. Chance and his craftsmen put in a lot of effort, too."

Lucille poured Molly a cup of coffee and gestured for her to have a seat at the long plank table. "The two of you make a really good team."

A lump rose in Molly's throat. "We did."

Lucille brought cream and sugar to the table. She sat down. "So it's over?"

So over. Yet even as she thought it, it sounded so final. Too final…

Her heart aching, Molly wiped at a tear spilling down her cheek. Had he only understood her. But he hadn't. "He tried to bribe me into staying here in Laramie."

Lucille frowned. "That was wrong. What you do with your future should be your decision. Period."

The irony was Molly had just about decided to stay in Laramie, not just until summer but permanently. Would have, had Chance not shown her what he really thought of her. Although she supposed at least some of that was her fault, since up to now she had based all her life goals on the premise of one day earning more money and securing a very healthy nest egg to fall back on.

"You have to do what is right for you and your son," Lucille continued, patting the back of Molly's hand. She drew back and looked in her eyes, advising gently, "Just don't let your pride stand in the way."

Pride? Could that be all it was? Molly hesitated. Ready to partake of the older woman's wisdom, she asked, "What do you mean?"

Lucille ran her hand over the rim of her coffee cup. "When my late husband and I dreamed up the Lockhart Foundation, I am ashamed to admit, it was as much about increasing the stellar reputation of our family as the good works we planned to do with all our accumulated wealth."

Molly paused. "That doesn't sound like you."

Lucille exhaled in regret. "Maybe not now, but I've learned some hard lessons along the way."

Molly guessed Lucille was referring to the financial scandal with the foundation the previous summer that had since been resolved.

Lucille fingered the pearls at her neck. "Although I'd sat on many boards, I'd never actually run a nonprofit."

Molly sipped her coffee. "And that was a problem?"

Grimly, Lucille recollected, "From the very beginning, I realized I was in over my head, but I'd made such a big deal about being the CEO, and I knew it was what Frank had envisioned for my future before he died, so I stayed on the wrong path for much longer than I should have. Because I didn't want to admit I'd made the wrong decision."

Like she was making a mistake now? Molly wondered uneasily.

"Don't let your understandable anger with Chance now rob you of the long-term security that you crave."

Aware Lucille was the closest thing she'd had to a mother in a very long time, Molly fought back the tears clogging her throat. "You think I should stay in Laramie?" *In the community where I grew up, with all my friends? And, like it or not, the man who still turns my heart inside out with just a glance?*

Tenderly, Lucille shook her head. "Only you can intuit what is right for you and Braden, Molly. Just know that if you find yourself headed in the wrong direction, like I once was, that U-turns are not just allowed—they're recommended."

On the morning of Christmas Eve, Chance sat in his kitchen, looking at the set of legal papers he had tried to give Molly before she had shown him the door.

Slowly, he unwrapped the last tiny bit of Christmas *stollen* he'd stored in his fridge and took a bite. Once fragrant, soft and delicious, it was now hard, dry and… still delicious. Like a yuletide biscotti.

He sighed, swallowing the last bite he'd been—up till now—unable to part with. Maybe because he had known in his heart that he and Molly would never work out the way he wanted.

Would it have made a difference if he'd told her how he felt about her and Braden, before he'd shown her the legal papers he had hoped would create their family and cement their future?

He didn't know.

Now, would never know…

Outside, he heard the sound of multiple vehicles. Doors slamming. Footsteps coming across his porch.

Grimacing—because he had an idea who this was—he rose and went to answer the insistent knock on his door.

All four of his siblings stood on the porch. Including Zane, his youngest brother, a Special Ops soldier who was usually deployed to parts unknown.

"What happened to you?" Chance gave Zane a hug. Glad to see he was all in one piece, even if Zane did sport a fading bruise across his jaw, and a thick bandage encompassed his left hand.

"The usual," Zane replied cheerfully, looking happy to be home in time for Christmas—something that had almost never happened since he had enlisted.

"You could tell me, but then you'd have to…" Chance mimed a knockout, finishing the age-old combat joke.

"Sounds like I might need to do that anyway," Zane said, hugging him fiercely, before striding in. "What were you thinking? Giving your woman two live bulls for Christmas!"

"They weren't her only Christmas gift!" Chance retorted. He'd had something even better and more romantic planned for that. Not that he'd ever gotten an opportunity to give that present to her.

Wyatt followed, still in ranch clothes. "Just an enticement?"

Chance threw up his hands. "I was trying to give her a reason to stay here in Laramie County, where she belongs."

Garrett strolled in, too. Now happily married himself, he seemed to be the resident expert on domestic bliss. He prodded, "Just not the right reason?"

Chance exhaled in exasperation. "Molly's never made any secret of the fact she wants real financial security for herself and her son. Big-time connections. She could have had all that with me." Even if social climbing was definitely not his thing.

"Just not what every woman wants most of all," Sage murmured, shutting the door behind them.

"And what is that?" Chance asked in frustration. What was everyone seeing that he was missing?

"If you don't know the answer," she scoffed, "you're more clueless than any of us thought!"

Silence fell all around.

Still on the hot seat, Chance eventually asked Sage, "I'm guessing you organized this?"

His little sister nodded, appearing as ridiculously romantic as ever. "I figured you might not listen to me."

True, Chance thought.

"But with all of us here," she insisted stubbornly, "we might have a chance of getting through to you."

He appreciated the sentiment behind their support, if not their actual interference. Chance folded his arms across his chest. "Thanks, but I don't need help with my love life."

Garrett squinted. "The facts say you do."

Wyatt made himself at home. "Look, Chance, we can all see that Molly is the one for you."

Still favoring his injured hand, Zane eased onto a stool, too. "From what I've heard from Mom, the only one."

Glad his Special Forces brother had made it through whatever calamitous event caused his injuries, Chance asked, "Why isn't Mom here, if this is a family meeting?"

"Because," Garrett said triumphantly, "she's at the Circle H, talking to Molly."

Hope rose within Chance. He knew how much Molly loved and respected his mother. If anyone could get his woman—and he admitted he still considered Molly to be his woman—to reconsider their breakup, it was bound to be the matchmaking Lucille.

He studied the faces of his siblings. "Is Mom having any success?"

Shrugs all around. "No clue. You'll have to meet up with Molly to find that out," Wyatt advised.

"The point is," Sage added, "you have an opportunity to make this Christmas the most memorable one you've ever had, Chance, if you can find it in your heart to stop trying to steer the situation to your advantage. Ignore the shield Molly is hiding behind. And give her what she really wants and needs, most of all."

Just after eight o'clock Christmas Eve, Molly kissed her sleeping son and eased from his bedroom. She wasn't surprised they'd only been able to get halfway through "Twas the Night before Christmas." Her son was deliriously excited.

Whereas she knew she still had so much to do to make amends before the holiday ended.

She reached for her phone just as a knock sounded on her front door.

Molly looked through the glass.

Chance?

Heart pounding, she opened the door.

He stood on her doorstep in a sport coat, snowy-white shirt, Santa Claus and Rudolph tie, and jeans. He'd recently showered and shaven. His hair had that mussed, sexy look she loved. But it was the hopeful sparkle in his eyes that got to her the most.

She nodded at his tie. "Glad to see you haven't lost your sense of humor."

The crinkles around his eyes deepened. "I thought you might like it."

She liked more than that.

She liked everything about him.

Especially this. The fact that he knew just when she needed him most and showed up.

Because it was the showing up, it was the being there, that was most important of all.

"Seriously." Chance's voice dropped a sexy notch, his gaze devouring her from head to toe. "I hope it's not too late."

Flushing beneath his tender scrutiny, Molly swung the door open wide and motioned him in. "Actually, your timing is perfect," she whispered, ushering him back to the kitchen, where their voices were least likely to carry. "I just got Braden to sleep." Knowing now was the time to give him a gift from the heart, too, she ignored the shaking of her knees and hurried on. "I've been wanting to talk to you. I don't like the ways things ended the last time we—"

He put a finger to her lips. Hazel eyes serious, he

interrupted sternly, "If anyone is going to apologize, it's got to be me."

This she hadn't expected.

Shaking his head ruefully, he took her all the way into his arms. Threaded one hand through her hair, wrapped the other reverently around her waist. "I'm sorry, Molly. For trying to maneuver you into making the decisions I wanted regarding your future." He hauled in a rough breath, admitting, "My only responsibility as the man in your life is to do everything I can to support you in whatever you want."

Molly splayed her hands across his chest; the rapid beat of his heart matched hers. Tears of happiness misted her eyes as the relief inside her built. "You mean that?"

"I do." He nodded soberly. Then bent to tenderly kiss her brow. "I don't care where we live, Molly, as long as we're together."

She knew what it took for him to concede that. "But Bullhaven…" Her voice broke.

"Can be run with or without me on the premises every day."

"But there's Mistletoe and all the other bulls, not to mention Mistletoe Jr."

He promised gruffly, "I'll work that out, too."

She saw he meant it. With all his heart and soul. Still…"It's your life work."

He nodded. His eyes held hers. "And only part of what I want," he said thickly.

Her heart pounded like a wild thing in her chest. She moved in closer, taking in all the heat and strength he had to give. "What's the rest?" She let her eyes rove his handsome face. Memorizing this Christmas for all time.

He lifted her hand, kissed the back of it and then held

it against his chest. Their gazes still locked, he told her, "I want you. And Braden. And a life together." His voice caught as the tears she'd been holding back spilled over her lashes and flooded her cheeks.

"Which is why you tried to give us part ownership in Mistletoe and Mistletoe Jr. Because they are the most precious gifts you have to offer."

He tightened his grip on her. "So you do understand that I only gifted them to you to secure your financial future, and show you how much I wanted us to be family?"

She nodded. "I know how much you love your prize bulls. And that you giving us half ownership in them was a very big deal."

"Then why did you take it as an insult?"

"Because the enormity of the gift—the long-lasting deeply personal nature of it—scared me, Chance." She tipped her head back to better see into his eyes. "For years now, I've been telling myself I didn't need anyone, so long as I had enough money to keep Braden and I safe. I thought my duty as his parent was to provide all the material things and opportunity denied me as a child. I couldn't see—didn't want to see—that we already had everything we needed, here in Laramie. A great home. A caring community of friends and neighbors."

Chance drew her close. "A school that fits him and his exuberant, engaging personality."

She leaned into him. "I wanted more for him."

He stroked a hand through her hair. "More for you?"

Molly nodded. "All of it, based on the things that I've since realized matter the least." His strength and tenderness gave her the courage to go on. "And then you came into my life. Challenging everything. Showing me whether I wanted to acknowledge it or not that the grass wasn't always greener and the luxe life was no guarantee of happiness."

She wreathed her arms around his broad shoulders. "And while financial security will always be important, it's not nearly as crucial as having someone to love who will love you back." Her voice trembled with emotion as she took the biggest leap of faith of all. "And I do love you, Chance." Letting him see and feel just how much, she kissed him deeply, sweetly.

"Damn, Molly," Chance kissed her back with all the yearning she had ever wished for. "I love you too," he whispered, kissing her again. "So much…"

Chance released her and got down on one knee. He reached into his pocket. "Which is why I got this…"

Inside the box was a diamond engagement ring. He lifted his face to hers, an endless supply of hope and faith shining in his eyes.

Mirrored in her heart.

He clasped her hand tightly, looking as if this were the most important moment in his life. "Marry me, Molly."

The joyful tears overflowed again. She tugged him to his feet and drew him back into her arms. "On one condition," she promised, holding him so close their hearts pounded in unison. "We stay in Laramie."

Surprise warred with the pleasure and relief on his handsome face. "You're not moving to Dallas?"

She shook her head, kissing him again, tenderly and persuasively. "This is where I want to be, for Christmas and forevermore." She gazed into his eyes. "Right here with you."

Epilogue

One year later...

"Is it time to go yet?" Braden asked. "Can we give the bulls their Christmas presents?"

Molly looked at Chance. It was still half an hour before the appointed feeding time on Christmas Eve, but if they didn't spring into action soon, their little guy was going to burst with excitement. A fact the love of her life seemed to know very well.

Chance grinned. "I think we can go now, buddy."

The three of them donned their hats, coats and gloves and headed out to the barn, a little red wagon full of specialty grain sacks, emblazoned with each bucking bull's name, behind them. One by one, Braden called out a jubilant "Merry Christmas!" to each and every animal. Then, with Chance and Molly's help, he carefully poured the yuletide gifts into the buckets of regular feed before Chance set them in the stalls.

Finally, they made their way to the barn that held the trio of prize-winning cattle.

Seeing them walk in, Mistletoe let out a low bellow. Jr. and Momma followed suit. Both bulls came over to the edge of their pens. Chance hoisted Braden in his arms. As had become custom, Braden gently petted their heads under Chance's supervision, while Molly went over to check on the only female of the bunch. Eventually, Chance and Braden came over, too, their twin sets of cowboy boots echoing on the cement barn floor.

Braden peered through the opening in the metal pen rails. "How come Momma Cow is getting so fat?" He frowned at her sagging, barrel-shaped tummy.

Molly had been wondering when Braden would notice the unmistakable weight gain. "She's going to have another baby bull in the spring."

Braden perked up. "I like babies!" he said.

Molly took a deep breath. "That's good." She and Chance had been waiting for the right time. Maybe this was it. "Because Daddy and I like them, too. So we were thinking," she continued as casually as she could, "that the three of us should have a baby, too." Smiling, Chance telegraphed his support and reached over and squeezed her hand. "Then you'd have a little brother or sister."

Braden tipped his cowboy hat back and thought that over. "Is the baby going to be born in the barn?"

Molly and Chance choked back laughter. Soberly, Chance knelt down. "Probably the hospital," he said.

"Okay." Braden happily considered that, then moved on. "Can we put out the treats for Santa?"

It was a little early yet for that.

On the other hand, they had a Lockhart family party to go to in a little bit, so maybe it was good to do as much as possible now. "Sure," Molly and Chance said, as in tune about this as everything else.

They went inside and washed up. Molly poured a small glass of milk while Braden arranged a selection of treats on a plate, then went to play with his Christmas village and ranch.

As delighted about their expanding family as she, Chance ran his hand possessively over Molly's tummy. Briefly he inclined his head at Braden, murmuring, "That went better than expected."

They hadn't been sure how Braden would take the news. Although they had *hoped*…

The thought of the new life growing inside her filled Molly with warmth. "I think so, too."

She turned to Chance, aware how much had changed in the months since they'd first become involved.

They'd married in July. She'd converted her home in town to an interior design studio and office for their joint general contracting firm. Chance was teaching her and Braden the bucking-bull and ranching business. Best of all, not only was Braden thriving in the school he had always gone to but he was relishing his new "cowboy" life on an actual ranch. And he had the doting daddy she'd always wanted for him, too.

She paused to kiss her ruggedly sexy husband. "Have I told you lately that thanks to you, all my dreams have come true this year?"

All the love she had ever wanted shone in his eyes. "Mine, too," he rasped contentedly.

She hugged him close, aware she had never felt so joyous. "Merry Christmas, cowboy."

Chance stroked a hand through her hair and tenderly kissed the top of her head. "Merry Christmas to you, too, darlin'."

* * * * *

Despite lying on her résumé, Amanda Lowery still manages to land a job designing Halcyon House for Blake Randall—and a place to stay over Christmas. Neither of them have had much to celebrate, but with Blake's grieving nephew staying at Halcyon, too, they're all hoping for some Christmas magic.

Read on for a sneak preview of Jo McNally's It Started at Christmas…, a prequel in the Gallant Lake Stories miniseries.

"Amanda, I didn't mean to upset you. I don't ever want to do anything that scares you."

She sucked in a deep, ragged breath, looking so terribly lost and sad. Her eyelids fluttered open. She stared straight ahead, talking to his chest.

"You don't understand, Blake. There are days when… when everything scares me." Her voice was barely above a whisper. His heart jumped. He thought of that first day, when she ended up unconscious in his arms.

Everything scares me.

She'd kicked her shoes off earlier, and in her bare feet the top of her head barely reached his shoulders. He put his fingers under her chin and gently tipped her head back.

He wanted to kiss this woman.

Wait. What?

No. That would be wild. He couldn't kiss her. Shouldn't. But how could he not?

Her hair tumbled off her shoulders and down her back in golden curls. Before he knew it, his free hand was slowly twisting into those curls. She didn't pull away. Didn't look away. He lowered his head until his face was just above hers. He felt her breath on his skin. She smelled like citrus and spice and blueberries and red wine. Her lips parted and she stared at him with her enormous eyes.

"I swear I don't want to scare you, Amanda. But… may I kiss you?" His voice was a raw whisper. "Please let me kiss you."

His words came out as a plea. He'd never begged for anything before in his life. But here he was, begging this sweet woman for a kiss. Ready to drop to his knees if that was what it took. He heard his father's voice in his head, mocking his weakness. That was when he started to straighten, started to come to his senses. Then he heard her whispered answer.

"Yes."

Was there any sweeter word in the world? Adrenaline surged through his body, and his hand tightened in her hair. His eyes opened to meet those two oceans of blue. Dangerous blue. Deep enough to drown in.

She was frightened, but she was trusting him. And that realization scared him to death.

Don't miss It Started at Christmas… *by Jo McNally, available December 2019 wherever Harlequin® Special Edition books and ebooks are sold.*

Harlequin.com

HSEEXP1119

Looking for more satisfying love stories
with community and family at their core?

Check out **Harlequin® Special Edition**
and **Love Inspired®** books!

New books available every month!

CONNECT WITH US AT:

Facebook.com/groups/HarlequinConnection

 Facebook.com/HarlequinBooks

Twitter.com/HarlequinBooks

Instagram.com/HarlequinBooks

Pinterest.com/HarlequinBooks

ReaderService.com

**ROMANCE WHEN
YOU NEED IT**

Don't miss *Stealing Kisses in the Snow*,
the heart-tugging romance in

JO McNALLY's

Rendezvous Falls series centered around
a matchmaking book club in
Rendezvous Falls, New York.

As Christmas draws ever closer, so do Piper and
Logan. Could these two opposites discover that all
they want this Christmas is each other?

Order your copy today!

www.HQNBooks.com   PHJMSKIS1119

Looking for inspiration in tales
of hope, faith and heartfelt romance?

Check out **Love Inspired**® and
Love Inspired® **Suspense** books!

New books available every month!

CONNECT WITH US AT:

Facebook.com/groups/HarlequinConnection

 Facebook.com/HarlequinBooks

 Twitter.com/HarlequinBooks

 Instagram.com/HarlequinBooks

Pinterest.com/HarlequinBooks

ReaderService.com

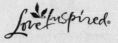

LIGENRE2018R2